W9-DEW-140

A SAKURA STEAM SERIES NOVEL

⊕

Stephanie R. Sorensen

PALANTIR PRESS
Leadville, Colorado

PUBLISHED BY PALANTIR PRESS

www.palantirpress.com
Leadville, Colorado

Cover design by Marko Stankovic

Publisher's Cataloging-in-Publication
(Provided by Quality Books, Inc.)
Sorensen, Stephanie R., author.

Toru : wayfarer returns / Stephanie R. Sorensen. --
First edition.
    pages cm -- (A sakura steam series novel)
    LCCN 2015917682
    ISBN 978-0-9969323-0-1
    ISBN 978-0-9969323-1-8
    ISBN 978-0-9969323-2-5
    ISBN 978-0-9969323-3-2

    1. Japan--History--Tokugawa period, 1600-1868--
Fiction. 2. Japan--History--Restoration, 1853-1870--
Fiction. 3. United States Naval Expedition to Japan
(1852-1854)--Fiction. 4. Perry, Matthew Calbraith,
1794-1858. 5. Samurai--Japan--History--19th century.
6. Alternative histories (Fiction) 7. Steampunk
fiction. 8. Historical fiction.   I. Title.
II. Series: Sorensen, Stephanie R. Sakura steam series
novel.

PS3619.O744T67 2016   813'.6
                QBI15-1734

Library of Congress Control Number: 2015917682

ISBN: 978-0-9969323-0-1

Printed in the United States of America

FIRST EDITION

PRONUNCIATION OF
JAPANESE WORDS

Japanese vowels are pronounced as follows:

"a" as in father
"i" as in ink
"u" as in due
"e" as in feather
"o" as in over

Vowels are pronounced separately.
Syllables are given equal stress. The Japanese "r" sound falls
delicately between a very soft "d," an "r" and an "l."
O's and u's with a macron over them (ō) are held slightly longer.

Key names in the text that are pronounced quite differently in
Japanese than they appear from their English spelling include
Lord Date, two syllables pronounced "Dah-tay"
and Lord Abe, pronounced "Ah-bay."

For Aiko

TŌRU

WAYFARER RETURNS

1852 — Spring
Year 5 of the Kaei (嘉永) Era

CHAPTER 1

⊕

HOMECOMING

*"Every traveler has a home of his own,
and he learns to appreciate it the more from his wandering."*
— Charles Dickens

Tōru leaned into his oar, pulling hard, as the open rowboat slipped forward through the calm sea. Silvery light splashed over the four men rowing to shore, lifting their oars in practiced unison. For once the rough sailors were mute, no jokes or boasts ringing out through the night. Tōru glanced back at the sailing ship. She stood, sails furled, her masts black against the full moon hanging low on the horizon. He could see the captain looking down at them, and imagine his cigar a glowing spark even in the bright night.

A dark moonless night would have been safer, true, but Tōru rejoiced to see the land, the familiar twisted trees and craggy rocks of his homeland. A sea lion watched them from a cluster of rocks. Tōru smiled, as though greeting a long lost friend. She waddled forward and leapt into the waves, the splash loud in the stillness. Soon the men were in the rough, leaping out of the boat and dragging the small craft onto the white sand. Tōru leapt out, tugging her to safety onto the beach, his feet wet in the swirling surf. He listened to the achingly familiar call of the night birds.

He gestured to his companions to unload the cargo into a patch of trees and undergrowth. Three traveling trunks, a heavy wooden crate and a few baskets, all he possessed in the world, were soon tucked under the trees.

Tōru bowed deeply to the three men. They clapped him on the back, gruff men awkward at the hushed farewell, but hesitating to leave him. He gestured for silence, his finger to his lips in the American gesture he had learned among them. He bowed again, more deeply this time, bowing into the memory and manner of the boy he had been before his time in America. He remained fixed in this gesture of respect as they pushed off and rowed for their ship. Tōru held the pose long after it was necessary, long after they could no longer see him hidden in the shadows of the trees around him.

He looked once more to the ship and saw the captain, his arm raised in salute. Only then did Tōru straighten and salute the captain. He knew Captain McHargue could not see him, but he saluted as perfectly and crisply as he knew how. A captain ever on the sea is a bad father to his own sons, who find him a brusque stranger on his rare visits home. But such captains can be good fathers to their crews, and to young men like Tōru, who find themselves far from home. Tōru did not expect to see Captain McHargue again. The thought tightened in his chest, for the captain had been good to him, demanding and fair, on the long wintry voyage back to Japan.

Alone under the trees, Tōru fished around in his baskets and found the worn and tattered clothes he had been wearing two years ago when another American trading ship pulled him from stormy waters. He removed the riveted Levis favored by miners digging for gold in California, his blue cotton shirt and sturdy leather boots. He put on his Japanese clothes, rough and battered though they were. Against this day, he had carried the old rags with him everywhere he went for the two long years of his sojourn in America. They were clean and strangely familiar. He tightened his sash and inspected himself as best he could in the dark.

No shoes.

Strange, after two years in leather boots, to find himself barefoot.

No matter. He would find footwear soon enough.

Across the flat sea, Tōru could see his friends climbing aboard their ship and hoisting up the rowboat. Captain McHargue had vanished below. They were too far away for Tōru to hear the grunts of the men as they hoisted anchor, but he could see them battling the weight. He saw the buzz of activity as the sailors unfurled the sails, hoping to catch a breath of wind offshore on the calm evening. He stood watching as the gentlest of breezes bore his companions away, leaving him alone on the beach.

Tōru smiled at the memory of the previous evening as he watched them sail away. His hangover still plagued him a day later. Captain McHargue had declared a rare night of festivity in honor of Tōru, a farewell party for the young man about to leave their company. Opening up his own liquor supply, a singular event in the memory of his men, Captain had encouraged much toasting and singing in honor of their departing charge.

Tōru's English was quite good after two years in America, but as drink slurred their speech and the company grew boisterous, he was certain he missed a phrase here and there from his friends. He knew, though, the Americans were fond of him, and he of them. He had come to understand this strange loud people. Not perfectly, to be sure. But well enough.

They still shocked and amazed him, even until his last day on American soil, when Mrs. Hutchins had grabbed him to her considerable bosom and embraced him tightly. Tears welled from her big round eyes and dripped off the tip of her long red nose as she fussed over him and begged him to stay on with them longer. To be clutched at so, by a respectable woman, and to be wept over so noisily, with much wailing and waving of handkerchiefs, was all so much too much. Even the coarsest peasant in his village would be horrified by such a dramatic display. And yet, he knew the indomitable Mrs. Hutchins to be a good and much respected person among the Americans, wife of the Governor no less. And so he suffered with good grace her exuberant and ample embrace.

He even ventured a small hesitant hug in return. This gesture unleashed a whole new wave of wailing from Mrs. Hutchins.

"See! He is American now, even knows how to give a proper hug! Oh my boy, my poor boy! Stay here with us!"

The strangest thing of all about them was their fervent conviction that everyone on the whole round earth wanted to come to America and be Americans. So proud of their brash young country, they firmly believed anyone who still lived elsewhere either planned to migrate to America immediately and live in loud democratic liberty or had not yet but soon would come to the conclusion they should.

Tōru's kind hosts found incomprehensible his fixed determination to return home.

He had come to understand they considered his land backward and unsophisticated, lacking such marvels as trains and telegraphs and democracy. He tried and failed to explain the subtle poetry and ancient history of his people, the etiquette and protocol of the great courts, the dignity and martial skills of the *samurai*, the grace of even the meanest farmer's wife. The Americans were too busy, in too much of a hurry, settling their vast land, building their railroads, digging for gold, and creating businesses, to listen for more than a sentence or two about matters of poetry or history or the swaying grace of a silk-clad noblewoman or the plucking sweet sound of a *shamisen* in the evening.

So Tōru had fallen silent about Japan and learned much about the Americans.

His small pile of possessions was a treasure trove of knowledge, a small but excellent lending library with a technology bent. Engineering and science books in English, and even a few in German and French. No matter that he could not read any except the English ones. He coveted the knowledge within their covers and trusted that he would be able to extract the foreign learning when needed. Dictionaries of several European languages, maps, a globe. A fine clock, ornately carved and decorated with brass. Designs for all manner of gadgets and machines and ships and contraptions. Several Bowie knives, pistols and a repeating rifle. A copy of the United States Constitution and the Declaration of Independence. Books by Locke, Hume, Smith, Franklin as well as the literary and poetic works of Edgar Allen Poe, Elizabeth Barrett Browning, Nathaniel

Hawthorne, Mary Wollstonecraft Shelley and Herman Melville. Haltingly, he had read them all during his travels, an English dictionary in one hand, English book in the other, his Japanese brain struggling in between.

He carried with him as well an exquisitely illustrated Bible, wrapped in silk bound up within a protective grease cloth inside a leather pouch. He had read no more than a verse here and there when he was taken occasionally to church by one or another of his hosts. This book, heavy and ornate, bound in stamped black leather, provoked in him a certain thudding dread. He found himself reluctant to open its heavy leather binding to touch the delicate gold-leafed pages. As Tōru knew, possessing a Bible in the Shogun's realm was a crime punishable by death, ever since the Christians had been killed and driven underground centuries before by the Shogun's ancestors.

However, illegal or not, he had brought the fearsome Bible with him. Every American home he visited, rich or poor, boasted a Bible and several guns, all prominently displayed. Tōru knew he could not understand this people without understanding their most treasured book and their guns.

The bulkiest and most valuable *omiage* of all was the souvenir he had brought back for his mother. This gift occasioned no small amount of grumbling from the Captain and, it is true, all his officers, for the heavy weight and huge space it commanded on their small vessel. The sturdy wooden crate held a lavish extravagance, bestowed upon him with considerable ceremony by the Governor at Mrs. Hutchins' persistent request: one of the first Singer sewing machines ever made, along with its treadle desk, gently wrapped and padded in yards and yards of the finest New England textiles.

"She can sew you proper men's suits with this. None of this Japanese skirt nonsense for a young man like you!" Mrs. Hutchins had thoughtfully included fashion plates and patterns from the latest magazines, Godey's and Peterson's, with men's styles from London and women's from Paris, so he would be able to help his mother sew clothing in modern style.

Tōru thanked her profusely, but he was as certain of two things as he was of his own name. First, his mother would never be able to puzzle out these patterns, intricate overlays of multiple patterns on single large sheets of fine paper. Second, neither he, nor his mother, nor for that matter any other Japanese would ever voluntarily wear the stiff and binding clothing preferred by the Americans. But he grasped quite well a sewing machine could stitch a *yukatta* or *hakama* as well as a suit coat or ball gown. Technology serves a culture but need not define it.

Mrs. Hutchins had sent one of her maids over to instruct Tōru on the threading, maintenance and use of the noisy contraption. She apologized for teaching him women's work, but, "How else will your mother learn how to use it if you cannot show her?"

Tōru was fascinated by the clicking bite of the sewing needle as it throbbed into the cloth, leaving a perfect seam in its wake as smooth as the neatest hand stitching of the most careful seamstress in all of Japan. He carefully disassembled and reassembled the machine after the maid left, failing at first to get it to work again after his impromptu surgery. He persisted though, until again it sang its clackety clack song as he drove the machine with his foot on the treadle. Satisfied, he sewed seam after aimless seam on bits of scrap cloth begged of Mrs. Hutchins, certain he could show his mother how to use this marvel.

The men on the ship teased Tōru mercilessly over his beloved sewing machine. Why a man needed such a thing was beyond them, when they could repair a sail by hand as well as any seamstress, and their wives and girlfriends kept them in clothes. But he took their jibes in good humor, for he had seen what a simple machine could do and the impact it could have, when good quality clothing could be made quickly and cheaply for ordinary people. He wanted this machine for his mother, and ten thousand copies for his country.

The ship vanished over the horizon on a silver sea reflecting the moon, now high in the clear velvet sky.

Tōru turned from the sea from whence he had come to his homeland.

He found himself facing six armed *samurai*, their swords at his throat. Slowly he extended his arms to show he carried no weapon and meant no harm. He would have bowed, or knelt, but for the blades at his throat. He had hoped the small inlet would be far enough from nearby towns so he could come ashore unobserved. Obviously the watch on the coastline had only been tightened in his absence. Not a good sign, for it meant also the *sakoku* policy of isolation decreed by the Shogun was still in effect. By returning home from a foreign land, he was considered by the Shogun a traitor who had committed an offense punishable by death.

Angry and fierce though the tone was, the sounds of his native tongue, unheard for over two years, were sweet to Tōru's ears.

"*Omae wa dare da?* Who are you? Whose ship is that? Why are you here?"

They forced Tōru to his knees.

He bowed down to the sand and spoke in the rough unhewn Japanese of a fisherman.

"Noble sirs, I am Tōru, of the village Iwamatsu, some days' travel north of here. I was fishing with my father. A terrible storm destroyed our boat and cast us all into the sea. My father gave me a piece of wreckage to cling to as everything sank."

Tōru struggled a moment, the words and flow of his native language catching on his lips after more than two years without a soul to speak with in Japanese. The memory of the storm and his last memory of his father that night rose up before him.

He steadied himself as the men listened intently, their swords never wavering from his throat, nor their gaze from his face.

He chose his next words carefully.

"That night was the last I saw my father. I was picked up by an American ship and taken to America."

He bowed down to the sand again, easing between the blades.

"This night I am returning, to look after my mother. She has no other child to care for her, and no husband to feed her. The Americans brought me home, so I might do my duty by my mother and my people. I beg you, forgive me any crimes I may have committed by landing on your lord's shore, and allow me please to return to my home."

As he looked up into their eyes, he saw they would permit no such thing.

CHAPTER 2

⊕

TRAITOR

"Everyone who does not agree with me is a traitor."
—George III

The *daimyō's* retainers pushed Tōru to his knees before their lord. His hands and feet bound, he fell forward and lay helpless until the *daimyō* nodded for someone to pull him up to his knees. Tōru bowed low and waited for permission to speak. He dared not look up and examine the lord's outer hall, nor count the many men lining its long walls. He could smell the straw of the *tatami* mat pressed against his nose.

"My men say you came on a foreign ship."

Lord Aya indicated the pile of trunks, baskets and the crate brought with Tōru from the shore by his men. "And you bring forbidden foreign weapons and tools with you."

His man held up the rifle and a Bowie knife for the crowded hall of retainers to see. A murmur filled the room.

"You are a foreign spy, a traitor. Tell me why I should not send you to Edo to be executed as the law commands."

Tōru remained silent, his forehead still pressed to the floor.

"Speak!"

"Sir, I am just a poor fisherman, saved from a storm by the Americans." Tōru spoke plainly, a villager's thick accent in his speech. "They brought me back, and gave me gifts."

"Gifts? Or rewards for spying?"

Dozens of retainers growled agreement at this assertion by their lord. Spies were dangerous, to the nation, and to anyone caught harboring them.

"No, sir. Gifts of toys and books." Tōru gestured to a basket. A retainer brought it to him. He pulled out a small doll with a porcelain face, ice-blue eyes and yellow hair. "This belonged to a little American girl, the daughter of a great *daimyō*."

Lord Aya frowned at the doll.

Tōru indicated one of the trunks. One of Lord Aya's men hoisted the heavy trunk up and handed it to him. Tōru looked to the *daimyō* for permission to open it and got a curt nod. He reached inside and pulled out a few leather bound books. He gave one to a man who passed it to his lord for inspection.

"And who can read this? Of what use is a book if no one can read it?"

"Our Dutch scholars, the *rangakusha*, perhaps they could read it for you, and the Shogun."

The *daimyō* snorted, flipped the pages and then tossed the book to the floor. "Do you read, boy?"

"No, sir. No." Tōru held his face perfectly impassive, hiding the deception.

"Then why do you have so many foreign books?"

"Gifts, sir. They are gifts for you and for the Shogun's ministers, so you may learn about the Americans. Some of them are newer than the books our *Rangakusha*, our Dutch studies scholars, possess. They will help our realm become strong."

Lord Aya scoffed. "You, a fisherman, bringing gifts to the Shogun?"

His men laughed.

"I am sorry, sir. I only thought they might be of use."

"The Shogun is not interested in your thoughts, or your books. You have broken the law of isolation. For this, you are a traitor and must die. Take him away, and burn his books before the Shogun's men find them and punish us all."

The *daimyō* turned away to leave the hall. His retainers pushed forward to imprison Tōru and carry away his trunks and crate.

"Sir!" Tōru bowed again. "Before I die, I ask of you one favor."

Lord Aya continued toward the door.

"I am my mother's only son, her only child. She is alone, with no husband to care for her."

The *daimyō* stopped.

"I knew of the Shogun's law, but I returned for her. I am not a traitor. I am no spy. I am just a fisherman who fell into the sea. Every night, I could hear my mother weeping into the wind, all the way to America. She cried for my father. She cried for me, vanished into the sea. I will go with you to Edo, as you command, and the Shogun's men may take my life as the law demands. But first, I beg you, let me say farewell to my mother. She will rest better knowing my bones are here and not drowned beneath the waves."

"A pretty speech for a fisherman!"

Lord Aya grumbled at his chief retainer, Obata, who had arrested Tōru and brought him to Lord Aya's hall.

"You! This is your doing. You have caused me all this trouble, bringing this fool to my door. You should have left him by the sea, or thrown him back in!"

"I'm sorry, my lord." But Obata looked troubled.

Tōru saw the shadow of a slim female figure kneel outside the sliding *shōji* panel, neatly bound ebony hair visible through the partly opened doorway as she leaned forward to bow.

"*O-tō-sama*. Father," the girl began.

"Not now. We are busy."

She began to speak, in a voice soft and liquid, like a murmuring brook, or the sounds of a *koto* played with skillful hands. Tōru had not heard a sound so sweet in all his time overseas. The American women were often loud and somewhat alarming, like Mrs. Hutchins. This voice was gentle, like memory, like dreams.

Tōru leaned forward to see the girl with the soothing voice. She spoke in the most elegant and elevated of language, words no fisherman would use, words used only by noblewomen at court.

"*O-tō-sama*, I lost my own mother the day I was born. All my life I have longed to hear her voice, just once. I humbly ask you to permit this wretched boy to say farewell to his mother. If he is to die, as you justly command, then let him hear his mother's voice just once, as I have wished I might every day of my life. Please, Father." The girl bowed deeply to her father.

The *daimyō* scowled.

"Lock up his foreign belongings. Post a guard. And don't burn the books."

Retainers leapt forward and carried away Tōru's belongings.

He stared after them with concern.

"Where's your village, boy?"

"A few days to the north of here. Near Iwamatsu by the sea."

"We leave at dawn."

CHAPTER 3

HOME

"How does it feel
To be without a home
Like a complete unknown
Like a rolling stone?"
— Bob Dylan

Tōru slept fitfully in the straw and animal smells of the *daimyō's* stable. Strange too was the motionless land after so many nights rocked by the sea. His guards had freed his hands, which was a relief. After locking him into a barred stall, they had even brought him a decent meal of rice, pickled vegetables and salted fish along with a mug of fresh water to wash it down. He ate with a young man's appetite and a returning traveler's nostalgia for familiar fare.

His belongings were piled in another stall across from him, carelessly tossed in, the precious books scattered all around in the filth of the stable. He winced as the men dumped on its side with a sickening thud the crate with the sewing machine so lovingly carried all the way across the sea.

The *saké*-sauced guard posted to watch over Tōru and the foreign contraband promptly fell asleep.

In the grey hour before dawn, Tōru awoke. The guard still slept soundly, slumped to one side and snoring like a dragon through the *saké* fumes he exhaled. Leaning over Tōru's belongings was the girl he had glimpsed the evening before. She was tall, taller than many men, and as lovely as her voice.

His books were now neatly stacked to one side. The girl, or more properly, the young woman, for she was on the threshold of womanhood, was reading a leather-bound notebook.

Tōru started when he saw what she was reading.

She held out the notebook.

"Yours?"

Tōru hesitated. No good reply presented itself.

She held his journal, the record of his two years in America. She held evidence of his close relationships with Americans, his visits to Christian churches, his discussions with military officers. She held a journal written in a forceful, educated hand. She held a record no castaway fisherman could have written or even have read.

Outside the stable, Lord Aya bellowed for his men to hurry up. They were moving out.

The girl looked at him quizzically.

As her father's men entered the stable to get the prisoner, she slipped the journal into her sleeve.

"It is forbidden to possess the Christian book. You should have left it in America, fisherman." She indicated the leather pouch holding the Bible, next to the pile of other books. She spoke to the guards. "Lock everything into his stall. Make sure nothing is touched while we are away."

She reached down and tossed Tōru's boots to him. "You will need these." She grabbed a few of the books from the stack and took them with her as she swept out of the stable.

The guards jerked Tōru to his feet and bound his hands behind him, laughing at his boots hastily shoved onto bare feet. They tied a rope around his waist and tugged him out into the sunshine. Men rushed everywhere, preparing the horses and provisions. Lord Aya surveyed the action from his horse.

The girl stepped into her palanquin. She would not be riding like the men, but would be carried, locked away in her little box, away from the prying eyes of the people they would pass.

"No, daughter. You are not coming with us." The *daimyō* looked down at his daughter's *norimono* palanquin.

She signaled for her bearers to lift her up.

They looked to her father for instruction.

"No!" he bellowed, but his voice bore hints of the frustration of a man who knows he is beaten before the battle even begins.

She signaled once again for her bearers to lift her up. Caught between their implacable mistress and her fierce father, the men looked miserable.

"This is no journey for a woman. We will be gone a week. We have to travel through hostile territory. It is the mud season. There are bandits on the road. We have to move swiftly. Your mother would not approve." Reasons poured out of the *daimyō*, endless reasons, all of them quite reasonable, at louder and louder volume.

His daughter made no answer. She merely motioned for the third time for her bearers to lift her up.

"Toranosuke! I command you, stay here!"

At her nickname, the girl finally popped her head outside the *norimono* in a most unladylike manner. She beamed at her father in joyful triumph, confident now in her victory. "*Hai! O-tō-sama!* I will stay here! For one hour. To make you happy. And then I will follow you, dressed as a man, riding on a horse, wearing your old *hakama*. If I obey you and stay here for that hour, you will force me to face the mud and the bandits alone. Surely it is better for me to travel under your protection. You cannot make me stay here. And I will follow you, Father. You know I will."

"Please, daughter. Just once, just this once, can you not behave like a normal girl? *Hontōni komatta musame de...* This is your mother's fault. She died, and abandoned me all alone with you—you—you wild creature. I should have remarried, gotten you a proper mother to teach you how to behave, how to show proper respect for your poor father."

Tōru nearly laughed at the sight of the crusty old lord reduced to pleading with the girl. She popped her head out of the *norimono* again, smiling with great affection at her father.

"*O-tō-sama*, the day is getting late. Let us go, and take this wicked boy to his mother." She signaled again for her bearers to lift her up. They looked to Lord Aya. He scowled and motioned approval to lift her palanquin and move forward.

"Ah, Toranosuke, what crime did I commit in my last life to be cursed with such a daughter?"

The *norimono* made no answer as it swayed back and forth on its poles resting on the bearers' shoulders.

Lord Aya sighed and motioned the group to move out: himself, a dozen mounted and armed retainers, a couple of servants and horses with provisions, the *norimono* and its bearers. And Tōru, scampering along, dragged by his bound hands, tied behind one of the cook's horses.

Their path wound along the coastline, following the old trade routes between towns. The crashing waves on the ragged shoreline were barely audible under the buzzing hum of insects in the trees and birds overhead. They made good time, with Masuyo's bearers nearly jogging along, as though she and her box weighed nothing, although they had to hold to Tōru's pace. His bare feet inside the boots were soon blistered and raw. By late afternoon, he was limping and staggering badly as he fought to keep up. At a rough patch on the ragged path, he stumbled and fell, unable to catch his balance with his hands tied behind him.

The old *daimyō* waved a halt. His men dismounted and brought out food and drink as they rested under trees. Lord Aya leaned over to his chief retainer Obata.

"Ride on to Lord Tōmatsu's castle. See if he'll give us safe passage and shelter for the night. Tell him we have important matters to discuss."

He stood above Tōru.

"What's wrong with you? Can't walk in your American boots? Show me."

Tōru gingerly tugged off the boots. His feet were bloody and raw, a mess.

"Usually we wear socks inside the boots, but I had none." He stared glumly at his destroyed feet.

"Masuyo! Come and see what you've done. It's one thing that we have to execute him, but there is no need to torture the poor man first. You should have let us just take him to Edo and put him out of his misery."

Masuyo jumped out of her *norimono* in an athletic and most improper way, barely stopping to straighten her kimono before moving swiftly to Tōru's side. Tōru had never met such a woman, in Japan or America, so sure of herself and so strong. She moved and behaved not just like a man, but like a great lord, confident she would be obeyed.

She motioned for the cook to bring one of her baskets. A *daimyō's* daughter, she was not going to touch a fisherman's bloody feet. She supervised closely while the cook washed Tōru's feet, poured *saké* into all the wounds and then bound his feet with soft cloth. Tōru tried not to howl with pain as the alcohol washed over his feet. He almost succeeded.

"*O-tō-sama*, he cannot walk any further on these feet." She turned to Tōru. "Can you ride, boy?"

Lord Aya laughed. "A fisherman, ride? He'll be terrified. Let's just go back and take him to Edo before you damage him further. We have to get him to the Shogun in one piece or it will be our heads too."

Tōru looked at her steadily. "No, my lady. I do not know how to ride, although I have watched it done. I will try if you wish." He flushed, guessing Masuyo saw through him.

"If you want to see your mother in this life, you will learn quickly, boy." Masuyo motioned for one of the cook's old nags to be brought forward.

"Help him up."

Grumbling, a pair of retainers boosted Tōru and his bandaged feet up and onto the horse. He gasped at the pain of their rough grasp. He tried to appear clumsy, but he could sense Masuyo's gaze boring into him and knew she was not fooled. He settled easily onto the horse, and skillfully soothed the mare as she struggled for a moment against her new rider. As much as Tōru pretended awkwardness, he was obviously comfortable on the horse.

The *daimyō* looked at the young man astride the bony old nag. "You are a most unusual fisherman."

Tōru nodded and offered a hesitant smile. "I learned balance in my time on the sea, sir...And you, my lord..." he broke off. He was a prisoner, under guard and sentence of death, with no right to speak freely in front of the *daimyō*.

"Speak! What were you going to say?"

Tōru shrugged, a gesture he had picked up in America, and spoke plainly, without respect for station. "My lord, you are a most unusual *daimyō*. And you have a most unusual daughter."

This provoked a peal of laughter from Masuyo, or Toranosuke, *"Little Tiger,"* as her frustrated father often called her.

The old *daimyō* grunted at him and motioned the troop forward.

"Toranosuke! Back in your box, girl!" Grinning like a wild boy, Masuyo tucked herself back in her palanquin. Tōru could see her reading his journal through the small window in the door.

"And you, ride with me. Tell me about these red-haired Americans."

Tōru pulled up beside the *daimyō* and told the lord the story of his two years in America. He could tell Masuyo was listening as well, for every time her *norimono* fell behind she beat on the roof and barked at her bearers to make them hold pace with her father and Tōru as they spoke.

He told Lord Aya about the terrible storm, how he drifted far from shore for a day and a night alone, clinging to floating wreckage. He described his relief and fear when at last an American trading ship spotted him and turned back for him. How they had hauled him up, weak and exhausted, and nursed him back to strength as they returned to America. How the captain had introduced him to friends in America who cared for him and taught him English.

Tōru admitted he had learned to read, taught by his host's wife who had been a schoolteacher before she married. He told the eagerly listening lord how he had traveled all over the country, from the civilized coast on the East to the frontier lands of the West. He described the crowded bustling cities of the East, the great trading ports of Boston and New York, and the wild open spaces of the West, with mountains vast and endlessly tall, pierced by a treacherous narrow pass here and there. He tried to explain telegraphs and trains, sawmills and sewing machines. He told the *daimyō* of red-haired Irishmen, copper-skinned Indians and ebony black woolly-haired African slaves he had glimpsed in the fields on a visit to the South. He fought for words, both for the rustiness of his tongue in his native language and for the lack of vocabulary to describe his exotic experiences.

As Tōru warmed to his subject, encouraged by the *daimyō's* rapt attention and his awareness of Masuyo listening to every word, he became less careful, drawing sharp questions and keen interest from Lord Aya.

"You visited their War College?"

"Yes, they call it West Point. One of the families I stayed with had a son there training to be an officer. We visited him. I stayed a month and spoke with their lecturers. They are celebrating the fiftieth anniversary of the founding of the college this year, so there were many speeches and festivities."

"They celebrate something so short? Only fifty years?"

"Sir, the whole country is less than a century old. Only last year they were celebrating 75 years since their Revolution against England."

"How can a country so young be sending its traders and sailors all around the world? And defeating the ancient realms like Britain and China?"

"Lord Aya, their country may be young, but their history and ideas go back to civilized people as ancient as China and more ancient than our own land, peoples they call the Greeks and Romans and Egyptians. These Americans are the young sons of ancient lands, bursting with the energy of youth, scions of ancient civilizations planted in a new and untamed fertile land. You must see them to understand. They love big things, loud things, big engines, tall buildings. They are restless and energetic. They--"

"How are they so powerful so fast?" demanded the *daimyō*.

"My time in America was so short, only two years. I'm sure I missed many things. But one thing is clear. They love technology and machines and steam engines. Any task, like sewing, or making a weapon, or building something, the Americans love to build a machine to do the thing. It seems they are all tinkerers and engineers, with the rich men hiring the best engineers to build and invent things."

"What do you mean by this 'engineer'?"

"A man who makes things, invents new machines. Everyone is always dreaming up new ways to do things. For example, instead of horses on a road, they build huge steam engines to pull carts along a special track made of iron. They call them 'trains.' They ship cargo on these trains. Passengers too. Instead of women sewing by hand, they make a machine and the women turn the machine to sew faster."

Tōru began to explain about his beloved sewing machine, how cunning and useful it is.

The *daimyō* waved him off. "No, no, I don't care about toys for women. Tell me about the steam engines. You've seen these trains?"

"Seen them? I rode on them."

Tōru wished he could see Masuyo's face, hidden inside the *norimono*. He could sense her listening to the conversation. He wondered what she thought of him, and of sewing machines and trains. And how he had ridden on a train. He pictured her riding on a train by his side.

"The engineers showed me how they work. They even let me operate the controls. They are amazing machines, these steam engines. So powerful. And dirty. The engineers all have black faces from the smoke pouring out of the engines. The Americans are mad for their railroads and steam engines. Every little town fights to be along the railroads they are building, connecting every major city. They blow giant mountains to pieces and tunnel through them so their trains can get through without going up so high. And canals. They dig endless long straight canals to connect their cities. They fill them with water and make rivers for their barges. They—they like straight lines. The land is invisible to them, just something to build a road or a railroad on, a way to get from here to there as quickly as possible. They do not see the beauty of their tall mountains, only obstacles to be blown up or tunneled through so they can build their roads."

Tōru gestured around them.

They were traveling through particularly scenic countryside, along the top of a narrow ridge, with tidy fields of rice and vegetables terraced down the hillside below in the valley on one side, and the crashing waves of the ocean on the other side. Twisted pines and rustling trees shaded them as they rode. Everywhere was curved and sloping, hidden and intricate.

"I do not know if the Americans can see this land as it is. Some of them would flatten this mountain and fill up the valley so they can build giant square fields and run their railroads."

Lord Aya grunted and shook his head. "I cannot imagine this. How ugly it must be. Straight lines everywhere? Barbaric."

"They are not barbarians, although they are forceful and aggressive. They have complex laws. The people decide who their *daimyōs* are. Their Shogun, their President, they also choose. They have powerful families, and those families are often in the government, but the people must choose them to lead. Leaders are not decided by ancient right of family as here."

The *daimyō* broke in. "If it is not by family, how do they know who is to rule, and who is noble and who is *samurai* and who must till the land and trade?"

"They don't think about it that way. Their leading families are as young as the country or younger. Anyone can do anything they want, farm or start a business or run for office."

Tōru stopped again, stumped by the challenge of explaining in Japanese alien concepts like "democracy" or "voter." He tried again.

"Other than their love for technology and machines, they are shaped by their short history. Their violent history. They are rebels who left the ancient countries. They didn't want to bow down to ancient families. And those younger brothers born into the ancient families of the old countries, they did not want to bow down to an older brother. They escaped. They are the poor, and the younger brothers of the rich and powerful. Rich or poor, they have big dreams, no fear and nothing to lose. They want to make a new world and do things their way. So they invent everything new and fight everything old. And now they want to come here."

Lord Aya considered this.

"Our families, and our ways, are very old."

"Yes."

Dusk had fallen as they rode and spoke. They found themselves at Lord Tōmatsu's gate. His servants ushered them in for the night.

Lady Tōmatsu was known for the feasts offered at the castle on festival days. Even tonight's impromptu meal for the weary unexpected travelers would put many a fine restaurant to shame. Her cooks prepared plate after plate of delicate morsels, from seaweed salads to pickled vegetables, sushi and tempura, savory soups and noodles, pork buns and dumplings. The two lords enjoyed the lavish meal with their retainers, as Masuyo hovered with Lady Tōmatsu supervising the kitchen activities.

"Your father brings you on such a journey?"

Masuyo stayed silent, bowing a nod of assent. She watched as one of Lady Tomatsu's servers readied a tray with the next round of *saké* for the men, who were growing loud and boisterous in the next room. She knew better than to try to explain to such a grand lady what she was doing, muddied and exhilarated from the trip. No valid reason existed, even to avoid death, for a woman of her rank to risk the dangers and dirt of a journey like this.

Lady Tōmatsu was more conservative on such matters than most, as she boasted blood from one of the most ancient and aristocratic of families, a lineage flowing from a lesser branch of a *kuge* family. She was cousin to the Tokugawa clan itself. Her pride was thrice brittle, for she had been married off to a wealthy and vigorous but much lower ranked *daimyō* in Lord Tōmatsu, far from the capital, a nod to the wealth of his clan and the poverty of her own, in spite of its glorious heritage. Masuyo knew her own beloved father was of even more humble rank, though a *daimyō* in name and in truth, than mighty Lord Tōmatsu and his grand wife. Rarely cowed by anyone, Masuyo for once was tongue-tied and quick to behave more like a modest young woman than her usual boyish self.

Lady Tomatsu sniffed ever so slightly. She bowed to Masuyo with exaggerated courtesy.

"Perhaps our honored guest would like to bathe after dinner? The men will be late; you may use the private bath my ladies and I enjoy. Please allow me to lend you something fresh to wear. Your travel clothes are..."

Masuyo cringed. She knew she smelled ever so slightly of the droppings she had slipped on as they searched for Lord Tomatsu's gate in the dark. The hem of her kimono was muddied and ruined. It was one thing to taunt and tease her poor father into letting her run wild. Standing tall in the face of the great lady's chilly judgment was another matter altogether. She bowed her thanks, not daring to speak in her shame at her wild appearance.

Lady Tōmatsu smiled in victory, sending a wave of servants scurrying to prepare a bath and a room for Masuyo. Humiliation of her guest complete, she turned to matters of greater interest.

"The prisoner...your father seems to take a great deal of interest in him. Just a young fisherman...what can he matter? Where is your father taking him?"

The directness of her question took Masuyo by surprise.

Masuyo considered her reply carefully. Instinctively she knew the more people knew about Tōru, the more dangerous for him, and the more certain her father would have to carry out his threat to send him to Edo for execution by the Shogun's government.

"I do not know, my lady. My father does not confide in me."

Lady Tōmatsu eyed her steadily.

"Of course, my dear. The men, they do not wish to trouble us with tedious concerns. Still, I am surprised to see Lord Aya personally escorting a fisherman on such a journey."

"Yes, indeed." With this non-committal reply, Masuyo resolved to flee before Lady Tōmatsu could probe further.

"Forgive me, my lady, but the day has been long..."

"Yes, yes, let us get you off to rest." Lady Tōmatsu motioned for her servants to escort Masuyo to her bath.

Masuyo looked longingly at a plate of pork buns she had hoped to swipe to take out and give to Tōru, but she knew it was impossible. Resigned, she shuffled off to her bath.

She need not have worried.

Even Tōru, tied up again in Lord Tōmatsu's stable with the horses, enjoyed more fine food than he could eat. At last he lay back on the clean straw and rested, satisfied at last, his painful feet forgotten for the moment in the happiness of a full belly. He sat up again when he heard a faint rustle in the straw.

"Masuyo-*sama*! What are you doing here?"

Masuyo, freshly bathed and dressed in one of Lady Tōmatsu's old kimonos, slipped into the stable and motioned for Tōru to speak softly. She slipped him a steaming bowl of red bean soup with *o-mochi* floating in it. She had found the kitchen abandoned except for a young girl tending the fire. Covering her surprise with an imperious tone to match Lady Tōmatsu's, she cowed the girl into giving her the red bean soup and swept out to deliver it to Tōru.

"Why do you pretend to be a fisherman?"

Tōru nearly choked on a *mochi* sticky rice ball at her question. He made a show of choking and sputtering and grabbing for a cup of tea to wash down the offending *mochi*. He bought time, but not enough to come up with a good answer.

Masuyo gazed at him calmly, letting the silence weight her question.

"I-I am a fisherman."

"When my father occasionally takes a boat out onto the sea with the fisherman from his village for sport and to celebrate the bounty of the sea on a clear and lovely day, it is true he fishes. But fishing does not make him a fisherman. You are no fisherman's son, boy."

Tōru bit into another floating *mochi*, stalling. Masuyo's gaze drilled into him, demanding truth. He held his tongue. Longing to tell her the truth, he ventured another lie.

"My father is dead."

"That may be so, but he was no fisherman." Exasperated, she waved his journal at him. "Who taught you to read and write? To write a skilled hand? And don't tell me someone else wrote this journal. We found it in your personal things. It is full of stories about America, stories no one here could make up. Stories like those you have been telling my father all day."

"Your father is an intelligent man." Tōru dropped his attempts to speak like a poor village fisherman. His next sentence was spoken like a minister of the shogun's court, in clear and elegant Japanese with a refined accent and precise vocabulary. "He understands the challenges Japan faces against the foreigners. He knows they will come. He's read the reports by the Dutch learning scholars, the *Rangakusha*. He believes me when I tell him about trains and steamships and factories because he's seen the diagrams and drawings copied by the *Rangakusha*. He knows I tell the truth."

"About some things, 'fisherman.'"

"Who taught you to read? Girls don't..."

"Girls don't generally get to study like a man, no. But Father has no sons, so I got all the dreams he had for sons. What dream did your 'fisherman' father have for you?"

Tōru answered truthfully this time.

"He wanted me to see America. And return to tell him how to defend Japan against her might."

"So you spy after all, boy?" asked Lord Aya. Masuyo and Tōru had not heard her father and Lord Tōmatsu enter the stable. Masuyo flushed at being caught in the stable with the boy, but her father ignored her and focused on Tōru. She could see he was in no mood to jest.

"Sir, you know about America." Tōru spoke forcefully, the fisherman's accent gone. He used respectful language, but in the manner of one lord to another, without the cringing manner of a lesser man. If he was to die, he might as well speak out first. "You know her ambassadors will come again, like Biddle came to Edo six years ago, and Glynn to Nagasaki, three years ago."

"How do you know about Biddle and Glynn? We are forbidden to discuss them except in council! You *are* a spy!"

"I spied on no council, sir. I've never even been to Edo. I learned of their missions from the Americans. Their visits are facts, not secrets, published in every great newspaper. In America, even the common people have heard of China, and the educated and the military officers know of Japan."

Lord Aya interrupted. "I don't care what their common people think. What do their *daimyōs* plan for Japan?"

"They assume their mighty warships will convince us to open our borders to trade, like the British forced the Chinese to open. Refusing to discuss the Americans will not make them vanish like the dew and go away! You know the Americans will return. With guns. And steamships. The government speaks of sending an expedition next year."

Lord Aya and Lord Tōmatsu exchanged a look.

Lord Tōmatsu spoke first. He nodded to one of his men to release Tōru.

"You'd best come in. We have much to discuss."

Tōru rubbed his wrists and ankles where the ropes had scraped his skin raw. He slipped his blistered and bandaged feet into a pair of worn *zori* sandals and followed the lords into the house. Masuyo slipped in behind them, not daring to enter the main hall with the men. Instead she knelt silently on the other side of the thin sliding doors, where she could hear every word through a narrow space between them. She hoped Lady Tōmatsu would not find her there.

"The boy is right."

Lord Aya considered Lord Tōmatsu's statement. He waited for him to continue. Any possible comment could be dangerous; he needed to know where Lord Tōmatsu meant to take the conversation. He knew Lord Tōmatsu somewhat and as neighboring domains long at peace, their houses were traditionally friendly, but Lord Tōmatsu's ultimate loyalties were a mystery.

"He only confirms what the southern lords have been saying for a decade. The Americans are coming, and soon."

Tōru understood what the Lord Tōmatsu left unsaid. The southern lords had long given the Shogun trouble, and all of the Shoguns before him, ever since Tokugawa Iemitsu ordered the realm closed two hundred and fifty years ago under the *sakoku* isolation policy. Never quite rebelling openly, they honored a proud tradition of thwarting the Shogun's orders and obeying them slowly if at all. They bowed to the Shogun's officers in public, grudgingly paid required tributes and hostages and did as they pleased once the *bakufu* officers were gone.

Close by the ancient kingdoms of Korea across the sea, and in the trading paths of the Chinese, British, Dutch and American ships as they patrolled the seas that lay between Japan and the mainland, the southern lords had never quite closed completely to the rest of the world. The Tsushima clan traded with Korea across the straits from Nagasaki.

The Shimazu clan of the Satsuma domain traded with the Ryukyu kingdom, which traded promiscuously with the Chinese and every foreign nation, sending Japanese goods out into the world in a thin but steady trickle. Dutch traders lived penned up on the tiny island of Deshima in the bay off Nagasaki, the only Europeans allowed to trade with Japan at all. A handful of Chinese traders also lurked in the markets of Nagasaki. Much-needed goods were quietly imported, along with news, and a few small fortunes made through hidden exports of Japanese goods and resources.

The *bakufu* government of the Shogun tolerated these exceptions to the isolation policy, but barely. Southern lords made wealthy by trade and armed with foreign weapons were a threat to the Shogun's rule. The *bakufu*'s spies did not care about silks, lacquerware and even silver flowing across the seas, but they were acutely interested in inbound warships and weapons, ideas and movements that might challenge their rule and shatter a peace that had endured for two hundred and fifty years.

Lord Tōmatsu regarded Lord Aya steadily before making his position clear. They both knew the risks.

"We will need to meet them prepared. Our rusty swords will not defeat their guns. We need guns. Big guns. We need ships, these steamships that can speed in any wind."

Lord Aya nodded in agreement, matching Lord Tōmatsu's disclosure with his own statement. "I fear we are too late."

"True enough," agreed Lord Tōmatsu. "We should have been building defenses for a decade."

Tōru looked from one lord to the other, hesitant to interrupt but yearning to speak. He was glad they were listening at last. He ventured a question, knowing the answer but longing to join the conversation. "The Shogun still forbids arming the coastal lords?"

Lord Tōmatsu barked a short, harsh laugh. "The Shogun forbids our cats to grow claws. He knows only how to defend his own council room, filled with councilors who say yes to him and ignore reality. He can no more defend Japan from the foreigners than he can speak Chinese or build one of your trains."

Lord Aya looked troubled. Defying the Shogun rarely ended well. "Tōru, you think the Americans will attack?"

"The Americans? No, not right away, but the British, perhaps, yes, like they did in China with their gunships in her ports. The Americans—they prefer trade to war. They want us to open our ports to their goods and their people. They do not understand our isolation. Their officers speak of Japan as though it is already open, so firmly do they believe we must open to them."

"So they are traders, not warriors?" Lord Aya asked.

"Oh no, sir, they are warriors, and quick to fight."

Tōru had witnessed more than one saloon fight and many a duel in his two years in America. America's young men were as quick to draw their guns as any young *samurai* to draw his sword over a perceived slight to honor. He had also learned the American saying, to "never bring a knife to a gun fight." He knew which weapon Japan was holding.

"They don't understand why we refuse to trade. They believe quite firmly in the benefits of trade and open markets. They see it as a simple matter. They will come to trade, and they will fire their guns if we refuse. Their newspapers beat a drum, shouting they need to show us a thing or two. Their common people may not know the difference between China and Japan, but they are all convinced we must open to American goods and American traders. They are eager to send warships to make the point."

"My lords, there is still time." Tōru continued, his words flowing quickly as his excitement grew. "Lord Aya, in those books I brought back, I have designs to build the latest defenses and weapons, weapons the Americans have not even built yet. I have plans for experimental airships, flying ships they call 'dirigibles,' or drivable airships. I have designs for factories, machines that can churn out mountains of goods for us to sell through the traders protected by the southern lords. We need to create wealth so we can afford weapons. My lords, I know how to do this. Let me—"

Lord Tōmatsu cut him off. "There are many ears, even within these walls. I plan to keep my head safe from both the Shogun's men and the Americans, so be quiet about your ideas."

Lord Aya nodded agreement. "You will ride with us tomorrow? I'm taking the boy to see his mother before we send him to Edo for execution." He looked around, listening for eavesdroppers beyond the paper walls. He knew his daughter listened near the door, but he did not know who might be listening behind other walls.

Lord Tōmatsu nodded, and poured another round of *saké* for the men, including Tōru. "Try this. It's excellent."

Tōru and the lords drank far into the night, with Tōru teaching them American sailor songs in English. The lords sang with gusto, the wretchedness of their English accents surpassed only by the vast quantities of *saké* they consumed. Under the circumstances, enjoying a night of excellent local *saké* was a commendable plan. Developing a better plan, for himself and for Japan, would have to wait until the hangover wore off.

Masuyo slipped away after the men began to sing. She stayed up late into the night, reading Tōru's journal, puzzling over the diagrams in the English books and making notes. She knew well the suffering of the Chinese people as foreigner invaders had taken over Chinese ports and demanded trading privileges. Masuyo knew her father feared the same fate for Japan. Her mind, clear and sober, turned to the making of plans.

CHAPTER 4

⊕

DESOLATION

"They are gone and I am left
and they have taken with them the world."
— Cormac McCarthy, *The Road*

Lord Tōmatsu joined their travel party, bringing along Sugieda, his right-hand man, and a few retainers. For two more days the party traveled north along the winding coast. Lord Aya no longer required that Tōru be bound, but let him ride freely on the cook's horse. Tōru, grown comfortable in their presence, boasted of the fine meal they would enjoy when they arrived at his mother's home.

"It will be simple, my lords, for we are simple folk in my village, but oh so delicious. Fresh fish, vegetables grown by the sea, flavored with herbs, fruit from our small orchard, dumplings so soft and delicate you could serve them in your own castles. My mother is the best cook in our village, maybe the whole realm! You will see."

The lords laughed and promised to test out her cooking for themselves, a most unusual promise for *daimyōs* to make about a meal served by a fisherman's woman, but they too had grown comfortable with the young man, his quick intelligence, rich supply of stories and ready laugh. On the road, as pilgrims and other travelers know, sometimes the rules are relaxed.

Lord Aya found himself watching the young man fondly. For days, no one had mentioned the requirement to send Tōru to the Shogun in Edo for execution. No one watching the group would have thought Tōru a prisoner, but rather imagined him a guide of some kind, leading the lords through his territory.

Masuyo rode along in her *norimono*, carefully ignored by Lord Tōmatsu, who found her presence as unseemly as did his wife. She listened attentively to every word the men uttered. She knew better than to embarrass her father in front of the great lord by attempting to join the conversation, but Tōru noticed she beat on the roof of her *norimono* every time it fell behind to urge her bearers forward so she could hear better.

As they rode along, the two lords discussed the local landscape, noting defensible positions on hills overlooking the sea and arguing over how many great guns might be needed to drive the Americans off. Tōru listened respectfully for a time and then broke in.

"The Americans will not attack our coasts here. They want trade in the great cities, in Edo, in Nagasaki, in Hiroshima. They may want water and coaling stations for their ships here, but they would not waste ammunition brought from so far away on villagers on this empty coast. No, it is Edo we must defend, for our capital is where they will come with their ambassadors and their warships."

Lord Tōmatsu grumbled. "Then let the Shogun defend Edo and old Nabeshima defend Nagasaki. They grab enough taxes, trade and tribute from all of us to buy lots of guns."

Lord Aya nodded. "But the Shogun and his weak-kneed Council won't let us arm with modern weapons. We can't fight them off with rusty blades."

"The Shogun is more afraid of Satsuma than he is of the Americans," continued Lord Tomatsu. "He would rather fall to the Americans than to Shimazu."

A queer look crossed Tōru's face at the mention of Lord Shimazu, *daimyō* of the Satsuma realm. Masuyo beckoned him to her, leaning out of her *norimono* in a perilous and unladylike manner.

She whispered to him, "Fisherman, what counsel would you give the Shogun?"

Her father glared at her, to make her behave in front of Lord Tōmatsu and retreat back into her palanquin. Lord Aya said nothing rather than call more attention to her bad behavior. Masuyo flashed her father a brilliant smile and slipped back inside her *norimono*, beckoning to Tōru to lean in to speak with her.

Lord Tōmatsu held forth on the Shogun's weakness while Masuyo and Tōru whispered a few steps behind.

Tōru whispered, "I would tell the Shogun to unite Japan, to bring together all the *hans*. The Shogun needs Satsuma and all the lords to strengthen themselves and their people if he is to meet the foreigners with strength. If he keeps us weak, we will not be able to stand against them. They will tear us apart, like the British are devouring China."

Masuyo nodded. For all the *sakoku* isolation policy, educated Japanese like her father knew Chinese ports had fallen to the British warships virtually without a fight. The British then demanded ever more trading rights and favorable treatment even as they flooded China with opium, rotting her from within, as their ships bore away mountains of Chinese silver.

Tōru continued, "But if each *han* domain is strong, and stands with the others, together we can fight off the Americans."

"Big words, fisherman." Masuyo held him with a steady gaze, most unlike the demure downward glances of most Japanese young women and well-brought up American women.

Tōru did his best to return her gaze.

"You are not so bold in your journals. Here," she pointed at a page in his forceful script, "you write that they are unbeatable. You marvel at the training they give the common foot soldiers. You admire their officer training, how they use even the common people in their armies and navies. And here," she stabbed at another page, "you describe their factories as endless and huge, filled with hundreds of workers in every one, making guns and trains and stoves. Which is true, fisherman? That the Americans are powerful or that we can beat them?"

"Both, my lady. They are powerful. More powerful than you can imagine. And we can beat them."

Masuyo was ready with her next question, but she had to wait for another day to ask it. Night was falling.

They had arrived at Tōru's village.

Lord Aya pulled up. Tōru rode up to his side as they overlooked the village below, nestled in a semi-circle by a small harbor. "Where is your mother's house?" asked the *daimyō*.

Tōru looked, squinting into the setting sun. He shaded his eyes with his hand, searching for the torchlight where her home would be. He saw nothing. He pointed to where it should be, on the far side of the village, beyond the small docks where a few fishing boats were tied up and up another hill. "Over there. But I don't see a light. May we—."

"Let's go."

They headed down the hill and through the village, riding in a long column of the lords, their retainers, the servants and Masuyo's *norimono* and bearers. Parties with *daimyōs* and *samurai* on horseback were rare in this village. The frightened villagers hid, their few encounters with armed men usually ending badly for them. Even the children playing in the dusty main road scampered away, pulled indoors by whispered commands from hidden mothers. Eyes peered out at them from behind nearly shuttered windows and through half-open doors leading into shadowed interiors.

Tōru looked around in vain for a familiar face, but saw only shadows as everyone slipped away. The village looked more worn and shabby than he remembered, with a few familiar buildings like the old *saké* distillery and the rice shop in disrepair.

At last they climbed back up out of the village. Soon they stood before his mother's home up on the hill.

Tōru dismounted.

No one was there.

One look told them the house had been empty a year or more.

A loose shutter banged loudly against the house as the evening breeze picked up off the sea. The front door was ajar, broken open as though by thieves in search of loot. Weeds, vigorous in the humid warm climate, grew up around the steps. Unkempt and tangled fruit trees surrounded the house. The small garden where his mother had grown a few vegetables and herbs held only weeds and a few scraggly herbs, overgrown and ragged.

The others waited, silent, mounted, while Tōru climbed the steps to the house and pried open the broken door.

Inside the darkness of the unlit dwelling, he found only more emptiness and destruction.

The small mirrored *kyodai* vanity his mother had knelt before as she brushed out her hair in the evenings was overturned and smashed. Broken glass littered the *tatami* mats from the shattered mirror. The drawers were all pulled out and scattered around. A few shards of broken bowls and cups crunched underfoot as he drew open the *shōji* to look at the small room behind where he had slept as a boy. Nothing. Only the evening breeze, blowing strongly now off the sea, poured through the broken window and fluttered the torn paper of the *shōji*.

Tōru stepped across the worn *tatami* mats to the window. He looked out over the sea, silvery under the same rising moon that had guided him ashore just a few days earlier.

A man doesn't cry.

But a man can mourn his mother, alone in a darkened room, for a moment, before going outside to be a man who weeps not.

He heard a small step behind him.

Tōru whirled around.

Masuyo stood there in the shadows, looking nearly as stricken as he felt. For once she said nothing, but only looked up at him.

"We'd best head into the village and see about a meal and shelter for the night. This won't do for the *daimyōs* and you, my lady," he said in a strangled gruff voice.

Little was said. Polite men, even rough warriors, do not show they notice when another man is gripped by grief, even if he is their prisoner. But the effort to overlook Tōru's grief was exhausting for everyone, especially after the long trip. They lapsed into silence as they rode down the hill into the village. Now speckled with lanterns and torches, the village had come alive while they explored the dead and empty house.

They found shelter in the village's only inn, a large and ancient house brought low by neglect and hard times. Separate rooms were provided for Masuyo and each of the lords; the retainers and servants had to double and triple up. Tōru was sent to sleep in the stable, but no one gave the order to bind him. He slumped down in the straw and fell into the deep sleep of the young and weary.

The tavern keeper's wife brought out steaming bowls of noodles with a few thin slices of fish and pickles, while the tavern keeper poured *saké* for each of the guests. The cook was dispatched to rouse Tōru and bring him in to eat.

The lords sat together on the floor at a small low table. Masuyo knelt nearby at another table. The servants shared yet another low table, while Tōru and the retainers clustered together, not quite prisoner and guards, not quite traveling companions, seated on the floor along the long main table in the low-ceilinged dining area.

Tōru ate in silence. The retainers grew boisterous and even ventured a few songs, fueled by *saké*. The men forced themselves to be cheerful rather than embarrass Tōru by focusing on his grief.

A few villagers sat at the other end of the long table. They talked quietly among themselves as they too hoisted cups of *saké* and stole glances at the strangers.

One of them pointed at Tōru. They began to whisper and stare.

Tōru didn't notice them, lost in his thoughts.

Suddenly one of the villagers, wearing his leather blacksmith's apron and filthy *hapi* jacket over equally filthy loose trousers and sooty feet, jumped up from his seat and ran over to Tōru. He bowed low in the exuberant and awkward way of the lowborn. "Himasaki-*sama*! Welcome home, sir!" shouted out the blacksmith as he nearly knocked his head on the tatami mats in front of Tōru.

All eyes turned to Tōru. He stared at the filthy man through the filter of a few flagons of *saké* and a long hard day, unable to place him after two years away.

The blacksmith continued. "It's me, Jiro!" He indicated his blacksmith's outfit. "We thought you were dead! The storm... Where have you been?"

Tōru's head cleared and he recognized Jiro. He motioned with his hand for Jiro to stop bowing. He hissed an urgent whisper, so low the *daimyō's* retainers could not make out the words. "Not here. I'm just Tōru. Not Himasaki. Tōru. Fisherman." He signaled with his chin for Jiro to get off the floor and stop bowing so deeply. The ruckus had caught the attention of the *daimyōs* as well.

Tōru stood, still signaling to Jiro with his eyes to stop making such a fuss. He made himself ask the only question that mattered. "Jiro, friend, do you know where I can find my mother?"

Jiro nodded "no," sobering up from his enthusiastic welcome. "She left in the night, a month after you died. I mean, after we thought you died, in the storm."

The quiet hum of conversation in the wide room dropped to near silence as every ear in the room focused on Jiro's story. "She didn't say where she was going. Just left a few things, dishes, pots, blankets and such, neatly piled up and wrapped, on people's doorsteps, as though to let us know she wasn't coming back. Left my mother her best kimono. She left her home empty, all closed up. We tried to watch over it for her, in case she came back. Some thieves broke in and ransacked whatever was left last year. I'm sorry, sir." At Tōru's urgent look, Jiro amended his respectful language and slipped into more informal speech. "I'm sorry, Tōru. I wish I had better news. You came to see her?"

Tōru nodded, mute.

The *daimyōs* stood, and all their men with them, signaling an end to the evening. As each went off to their respective rooms, Masuyo shot Tōru a questioning glance, and was met only with a "Not now" nod. Tōru went out to the stable, with Jiro trailing after him.

In the stable, Jiro reverted to respectful address. "Sir, Himasaki-*sama*, I am sorry for your loss. We all thought you were dead. Your mother, too. She barely spoke a word after you vanished. Every night she would stand there, up on her hill. Looking out over the ocean, like she was watching for you. Your lord father never came again, either."

Tōru waved him to silence. "Never speak of my father, here or to any of them. They don't know who he is, who I am. I am just Tōru, a fisherman from Iwamatsu, and I have lost my mother, a fisherman's wife. Do not bow to me. Please treat me like you would your younger brother, not—not anyone special. They mustn't know." His voice was urgent, commanding.

Jiro considered this.

His world was a simple one, full of people he must bow to and those he need not bow to but could befriend. Tōru was asking him to overlook a simple pillar of his universe, to neglect to bow to your betters and pretend instead they were as close and familiar as brothers. Jiro struggled to work out the not-bowing part, for Tōru fell into the group to whom Jiro must bow.

The truth was, they *were* close as brothers, and they were good friends. They had grown up and gotten into countless scrapes together as they worked their way through the pranks of small boys in a village. Stealing fruit, swiping *saké*, building forts and fighting battles against hordes of enemy *samurai* only they could see, admiring the prettiest girls in the village. But there had always been a high and unmentioned barrier between the two boys.

Tōru had a mysterious father who would ride into the village every month or so, dressed in traveling clothes, without mark or insignia, but of fine make, riding on a good horse. He would visit Tōru's mother and then take his son away for a day or a week, sometimes even a month at a time. No one in the village knew his name, for he never greeted any of them, but only rode straight to Tōru's mother's home and stayed a night or two before leaving again with Tōru.

When Tōru came back from these trips, he would never explain to Jiro where he had been or what he had done, but he would be full of new facts and skills and information. Like how to read, or the right way to hold their stick swords when fighting imaginary samurai enemies, or how to mount a horse, or who the British and Dutch and Chinese were. Jiro avidly learned the bits about sword fighting and fervently wished he had a horse of his own to practice riding. He didn't care about the differences between the British and the Dutch. Foreigners were all foreigners, and well, foreign and unlikely to enter his world.

Tōru tried to teach Jiro to read, and had even managed to get him to scratch out his name and a few basic characters. But Jiro didn't take to the written word. He always protested his head was too thick to hold all the *kanji* characters and he would rather practice with swords or do something useful like fish or work on his blacksmithing at the forge where he was apprenticed. He was an excellent blacksmith, in fact, and had taken over the forge for the village at a young age when the old blacksmith died suddenly one winter of a bad heart.

As the boys grew up, the villagers accepted Tōru as someone unique, different somehow from the other village boys. Some said he was the son of some great lord, a bastard most likely, hidden away from a wife and a court somewhere. Or he was hidden away in their village to protect him from a curse or unfortunate prophecy, or a vengeful enemy of his house, although personal vendettas were rare these days under the strict peace of the Shogun's iron-fisted rule.

No one had any facts on the matter, of course, and so a web of imagination and speculation hung around Tōru like a whispering cloud. His neighbors proposed many theories, each more absurd and impossible than the last, but no one knew for sure.

His mother kept to herself for the most part, except for the necessities of shopping in town, selling a few vegetables from her garden or selling exquisite hair ornaments she crafted each year for the major festivals. She never came out to dance at the festivals, or to watch the traveling shows visiting town, or to attend parties and weddings. She cared for the sick and birthed the local babies, armed with notable skills in herbs and medicine, but never accepted more than a small gift of sweets in thanks.

She owned a *koto*, and would sometimes play it in the evenings, the delicate melodies wafting down on the village from her tidy cottage on the hillside above. For possessing this rare talent, the villagers whispered she had been a *geisha* in one of the big cities, or a girl from a good family who had fallen into disgrace from an unfortunate lapse in behavior. Some of the more superstitious villagers even supposed she was a magical shapeshifting *kitsune* fox-woman or sea lion woman who had bewitched a lord and held him under an enchantment.

In the usual course of things, the villagers would have ostracized her for any of these reasons. Moral failings and magical beings both were considered exceptionally dangerous to their small and conservative society. However, Tōru's mother was so beautiful, kind and generous to all that none dared mock or treat her badly. Over time, she had treated an illness or injury in every household in the village. Nearly every child younger than Tōru had come into the world with her watching over the laboring mother.

Instead, they treated her with quiet respect. She deflected any questions about her past, her people or Tōru's father with soft questions to her questioner, never answering anything directly. They learned not to ask her anything. They came to accept her as she was, even to treasure proudly her presence among them, still and lovely, an exotic flower that had escaped her garden and wandered off into the wide world and found her way to their muddy coarse village.

And so an unspoken gap lay between Tōru and Jiro and the other village boys, even though they had all fished and swum and fought and wrestled together since birth and wore the same clothes and spoke with the same rough accent. Their parents worked the fields, or owned small businesses, or served as the local chief, or fished. They all knew each other and knew every detail of each other's business, like folk in small towns the world over. The mystery of Tōru's parents remained like a sturdy rock the flowing waters of village life rolled around but could not move or break or wear away in such a few short years. They teased him about his mysterious father, and addressed him with honorifics suitable for a lord, sarcastically and jokingly at first, and more seriously later, as they all grew to manhood.

Tōru had taken it all in stride. Strangely enough, by unspoken agreement among the boys, Tōru had always played the general or *daimyō* in their games, leadership hanging about him like an invisible cloak though he was clothed in the same ragged clothes as the other village boys. By the time Tōru was eighteen, and Jiro twenty, Jiro and the other boys always called him Himasaki-*sama*, after the surname Tōru's mother went by. Few of the village commoners even had surnames, so the mere possession of one, no matter its source or possible taint, made Tōru unique among his friends. Jiro bowed to Tōru as he would to any upper-class personage who wandered into his forge. A joke had become a habit, and habit a reality. Tōru *was* Lord Himasaki to his childhood friends, whatever the reality of his birth or station.

"I'm glad to see you, old friend."

Jiro grinned and mock bowed to his old friend. "Glad you are not dead, sir. Meet any pretty girls in America?"

The next morning, once everyone was mounted and ready to set out on the long journey home, Tōru rode to Lord Aya's side. Lord Aya was deep in conversation with Lord Tōmatsu. Masuyo hovered nearby, listening to the men.

"I'm ready to go to Edo, my lord. None of the villagers know where my mother has gone or if she even lives. I thank you for giving me this chance to say farewell to her. I'm sorry I wasted your time." Tōru bowed, acceptance of his fate and misery mingled in his young face.

The lords exchanged a glance.

Masuyo interrupted the awkward silence, filled with grief and the lords' sympathy for their young prisoner. "*O-tō-sama*, this worthless boy is not worth the trouble of taking him all the way to Edo to execute. Better we keep him, and perhaps put him to work building some of his gadgets. Father, please hide him." She bowed low, capable of maidenly humility and grace when it suited her.

Lord Aya nodded at his daughter. He sighed.

"We won't be sending you to the Shogun, boy. Your story is true, or mostly so. You are a fisherman of this village, known to these people, though the full truth of you no one knows. Lord Tōmatsu and I are willing to neglect to report you to the Shogun's men if you agree to remain quiet about your travels. We must hide your books and diagrams, above all the wretched Christian book, or all three of us will die. We find it cruel to punish an innocent man, and one of such talent and rare and precious knowledge, with death. We see you love our land," Lord Aya gestured at the homely village surrounded by gently green and rolling hills, "as deeply as—as deeply as you loved your mother."

Lords are not accustomed to asking favors of the lesser born. Lord Aya struggled to find the language to ask the young man to cross the line from helpless innocent shipwrecked fisherman, a position from which there might be found mercy for a commoner, even at the Shogun's cruel court, to active defiance of the Shogun's policies, for which the certain end was public and painful execution. He slipped into command, ordering with gruffness what they both knew to be a humble request for help. They all understood the penalty for exposure of their plans. They also understood the stakes for their land.

"Help us fight the Americans, and the other barbarians who snap and circle at our borders. Teach us what we need to do to defend our land. Prepare us for the battle to come."

Tōru dismounted, knelt and bowed low before the two lords.

"I will not fail you. This is what I am meant to do."

As they rode the long way home, Tōru and the lords discussed details of what must be done, arguing priorities and plans. Tōru had spent much time on the voyage home pondering how best to aid his country. He had strong opinions. Lords are lords and unused to being questioned or challenged, and Tōru was out of practice at appropriately subservient behavior after his time with the feisty and independent Americans, each convinced of their right to their opinions and actions no matter their rank or station. The discussions were heated, detailed and frequently loud. The retainers were stunned their lords allowed a young fisherman to speak to them like a peer. Masuyo followed every word from her *norimono* palanquin, beating on the roof in a near constant drumbeat to make her bearers keep pace with the mounted men.

Tōru held firm, for all his youth and inferior status, against all the power and authority of the two *daimyōs*. Over the long journey he convinced them of the need for major innovations in communication, transportation, manufacturing, military training and organization. Any one idea would be a major project. All of them together completely overwhelmed the lords.

Lord Tōmatsu sighed, after grumpily conceding the need for dedicated manufacturing to make weapons.

"I am no merchant, boy, yet you would have me build foundries and factories, and hire whole armies of blacksmiths and seamstresses. Lady Tōmatsu will send me off for execution to the Shogun herself rather than permit such a thing on our land. With our money. Her money, the way she sees it. Worst of all, I'm forced to think about money at all. I'm a warrior, not a merchant."

Lord Aya stared glumly at the ground as they rode.

"The mission is daunting, it is true," he said. "But we have no choice. The foreigners can come any day. If we fail to prepare, the country will fall, like China to the British gunships."

Tōru waited, wise enough to let the lords ripen by themselves into the decisions confronting them. They understood the facts, the urgency and the constraints now. The response required was undeniable once the facts were seen.

"We'll need more men, more money, more skilled labor, more...*daimyōs*, other lords willing to join us. We cannot do it all by ourselves," Lord Tōmatsu stated, knowing recruiting other lords crossed into full-blown treason. He grimaced. "They must become merchants, too, and share our shame."

Tōru spoke up in agreement.

"No sir, we cannot do it by ourselves. We need to win to our plan every *daimyō* we can reach."

Lord Tōmatsu shrugged. "Then we shall get them all. Or die trying." For the first time that day, or even that week, Lord Tōmatsu grinned, like a young man, happy and free, unencumbered by the cares of lordship and middle-aged responsibility. "Come on, Aya. Can you even remember the last good fight you fought?"

Lord Aya nodded "no." He too broke into a grin. "Well, if we are all going to lose our heads to the Shogun, we might as well make sure there are a lot of heads along with us. It's a good fight. A battle worth fighting."

"'Give me liberty or give me death,' the Americans say." Tōru could not help but grin himself. "We fight for our liberty. From the foreigners, and from the Shogun. Let's do this. And let us win."

CHAPTER 5

⊕

MACHINES

*"One machine can do the work of fifty ordinary men.
No machine can do the work of one extraordinary man."*
— Elbert Hubbard

They reached Lord Aya's castle after a week of hard travel on roads made muddy and sodden by the spring rains, stopping only briefly overnight to refresh themselves at Lord Tōmatsu's castle. Lord Tōmatsu accompanied them to Lord Aya's home, over Lady Tōmatsu's strenuous objections, along with a dozen key retainers.

When they arrived at Lord Aya's castle, nestled in the heart of an ancient forest, Masuyo scurried to the kitchen to supervise the staff as they prepared the evening meal for the lords and their men. She couldn't possibly meet Lady Tōmatsu's culinary standards, but she could put up a good effort in honor of their esteemed guest and new ally, Lord Tōmatsu.

Tōru stood uncertainly in the courtyard. When they left, he had been a prisoner, sleeping in the stable. Now he was a treasonous co-conspirator with two *daimyōs*, planning a revolution. Where did co-conspirators sleep?

Lord Aya saw the question in his face and gestured to one of his men. "See that Himasaki gets bedding and a room with the other men. And move his belongings into my personal storage. Post a guard. No one is to touch them."

After the perfectly adequate dinner, served silently to the men by Masuyo's kitchen staff while Masuyo fretted over the quality of the meal back in the kitchen, caring for the first time in her life about the image she might present in the world as mistress of her father's home. The serving trays were cleared away and the lords' men sent off to bed. Lords Aya and Tōmatsu huddled with Tōru over a map of Japan. Lord Aya bellowed for more *saké*.

Instead of sending one of her ladies, Masuyo herself appeared almost instantly, carrying a tray with a *tokkuri* of perfectly warmed *saké* and three small cups. She bowed, ignoring her father's surprise at her entrance, and served the three men their drinks. When she was done, she lingered by the map, examining it in detail.

"Thank you, daughter. You may go now."

"No, *O-tō-sama*. I would like to stay." Masuyo settled into the stubborn pose her father knew so well. Even Tōru recognized it already in their short week together. She turned to Lord Tōmatsu and bowed deeply. "My Lord Tōmatsu, please do not blame my father for my poor behavior."

Masuyo's contradiction of her father's suggestion so startled Lord Tōmatsu he could find nothing to say. Masuyo continued.

"Father, Tōru, Lord Tōmatsu, I would like to help."

"Enough! You may go now," Lord Aya barked at her.

Lord Tōmatsu grinned. He settled back to watch the battle between his new ally and his exceptional daughter unfold.

"No, *O-tō-sama*, I must stay. I have been studying Tōru's books and diagrams, and I know what to do to set up the lab and factory. I am deciphering the engineering books and designs. I can translate them into directions for our staff. You haven't enough men who can read and write. You need my help."

"I'll not listen to one more word of this, especially not in front of Lord Tōmatsu. This is not work for a girl." Her father roared at her again.

Lord Tōmatsu grinned at his new friend's embarrassment.

"She's certainly cut from a different cloth than my wife. Spirited girl you've got there, Aya." Lord Tōmatsu said this as though he did not consider it a bad thing.

"I like this 'engineering,'" Masuyo said, sounding out the English word Tōru had taught them all to explain how the Americans like to design and invent things. "And I am good at engineering, and with languages. I understand I cannot run around the countryside with you men. Even I agree with that, *O-tō-sama*. It would cause too much gossip, and we need to be discreet. But you need someone you can trust to work out the details of the designs, and direct the engineering and manufacture of the weapons while you organize the other lords."

She glanced at Tōru for support. He nodded approval.

Lord Aya turned to his new friend Lord Tōmatsu, his hands outstretched in a gesture half helpless and half pleading. "My daughter is impossible. I have ruined her by over-educating her. Her head's full of strange ideas from Western books she studies through her *rangaku* research. Her mother would never forgive me for what I have allowed her to become. No one can control her, least of all me. But she can help, and I trust her. Do you object to letting her join our team?"

Tōru and Masuyo flashed a smile of victory at each other. Lord Tōmatsu laughed. "Why not a woman engineer? We haven't got any other of these engineers anyway. We need Himasaki organizing everything else. To your health, my lady, and to your designs." He lifted his *saké* cup to toast, along with the others. Masuyo bowed low, victory complete, and slipped from the room.

She had no time for *saké*. She had designs to test and build.

Within a day, Masuyo had put together a preliminary list of the materials, equipment and skills they needed to build modern guns, an experimental dragon dirigible airship and the first pieces of equipment for a telegraph. The list was long. Many items were not available in Japan at all, but must be sourced from Western traders across the straits, quietly, illegally and treasonously.

She presented her list after the servants had cleared away the evening meal. She brought out another round of gently warmed *saké* to the men. Lord Tōmatsu proved quite adaptable for a man of his station and gender, chuckling at first as she presented her list. He marveled aloud that a creature of such beauty could know and speak so confidently of such technical matters. He admired the graceful way she carried herself, causing her to blush at the attention and her father to scowl. Soon, though, he was engrossed in the task and busy arguing over the list with a slip of a girl half his age who should have been, by all laws of custom and nature, pouring tea or practicing her *koto*, not arguing fiercely with him. Her father watched Lord Tōmatsu warily at first, but relaxed as he saw his new ally accepting his daughter's unusual qualities.

"These are all the items we cannot make or buy here in Japan." Masuyo paused to let the others respond to the problem she had raised as she handed out her lengthy list.

Her father turned to Lord Tōmatsu. "How is your relationship with the Shimazus, of Satsuma? Didn't you study with one of Lord Shimazu's nephews?"

"Aye, but long ago. We haven't kept in touch. They are—," he sought the right polite word, "proud. Conscious they are the strongest family in the west. They don't mix much with us lesser folk. And my wife...her family is quite close to the Tokugawa house." He rapped his closed fists together to show Tokugawa and Shimazu in conflict.

Masuyo noticed Tōru had a most peculiar expression on his face at the mention of the Satsuma *daimyō*, Lord Shimazu. She could not ask him about it, for the lords continued their discussion.

"What about Shimazu's top retainers? Can you get to them? The Shimazu trade with the Chinese, the Dutch, the Koreans, even Western traders. If we can get their help, this list is no problem." Lord Aya topped off Lord Tōmatsu's *sake* as he asked.

"It's a delicate matter to ask the Shimazus to smuggle for us. They could turn us in, a cheap way to show loyalty to the Shogun. Besides, we'll insult them if they believe we are treating them like merchants."

"I doubt they would turn us in. No love lost there. The Shogun's men know better than to linger in Satsuma territory long. Satsuma might even agree with the plan."

"Risky to approach them if they don't..."

"We don't have a choice. The Shogun's officers monitor the Dutch traders at Nagasaki too closely. The Shogun looks the other way when the Soh clan of Tsushima trades with Korea and gets repaid with their loyalty and access to the goods. We'd have no luck there, even if the Koreans had what we need. Our list would be in the Shogun's hands within days. And our heads on pikes on Castle Chiyoda the next day."

Lord Tōmatsu stared into his tiny cup of *saké* as he pondered the problem, as though the answer might be floating there. "My wife has a cousin who married a Shimazu, somewhat unwillingly... but I'm not entirely sure I trust my wife. Her clan is proud of their ties to the Tokugawas." He laughed, bitterly, and spoke with sudden and unexpected candor. "I think she'd be happy to turn my head in to the Shogun, and keep my lands and holdings, ruling in our baby son's name until he is of age."

Lord Tōmatsu sighed and made his decision. "Let me try with my classmate from long ago. The more I think on it, the more I believe Satsuma would actually like the plan. And Satsuma would make a powerful ally, both against the Shogun and against the foreigners, if Lord Shimazu is willing."

Problem solved, for the moment.

Masuyo moved briskly to her next topic.

"Here is what we can make here, using Tōru's diagrams and books." She handed them each a lengthy list of manufacturable items. "The big issue is skilled labor. I need weavers, blacksmiths, seamstresses, Babbage calculators—"

"I'm afraid to ask, but what is a 'Babaji calculator'?" interrupted her father.

Tōru jumped in. "An English mathematician has invented a Difference Engine for calculating anything almost instantly. It is a mechanical device that generates calculations we need for making complex parts and planning inventory in our factories. The calculators input the data and push the levers to generate the calculations. In England, they are often young women trained to manage the levers and maintain the machines carefully with their delicate hands. I thought—that is, we could do the same here."

Lord Tōmatsu snorted. "One woman engineer is plenty. Now you want armies of female Babaji calculators running around as well? And why do we need this Babaji Difference Engine anyway? Our land has functioned perfectly well for over a thousand years without any Babaji nonsense. Our merchants can calculate anything needed with a *soroban* abacus—"

"We will need every man, woman and child in both your *han* domains, and a dozen *hans* more, working around the clock if we are to meet the challenge in time. Our battle is against time. To win, we must try new things." Tōru paused to let this sink in. "Women cannot fight or do the heavy work of construction, but we should let them do everything else we can so our men can do what the women cannot. We need the women weaving and sewing day and night to generate goods to trade for the materials we need. And yes, we need an army of Babbage calculators programming the Difference Engines to help us do the calculations so we can work in the most efficient way possible."

Tōru was standing now, and pacing, another of his odd American habits the others found disconcerting. Even Masuyo looked concerned. She wondered if he would wear tracks into her father's *tatami* mats with his incessant pacing. He ran his hands through his short foreign-style hair in agitation.

"And we'll need to work with people you lords don't usually speak with or deal with. In fact, wait here." Tōru ran out of the room, most unceremoniously, after giving an entirely unsuitable command to his superiors. In ordinary circumstances, this would have been unforgivable behavior, but nothing had been normal in Lord Aya's house since Tōru washed up on his shore.

A few moments later, Tōru ran back in, followed by Jiro the blacksmith from his village.

Jiro threw himself on the floor before the lords and bowed deeply. He was filthy and soot covered, still in his blacksmith's apron and work pants, wearing a tattered tunic.

"My lords! My apologies for appearing before you so dirty," he cried out as he knocked his forehead repeatedly on the floor, bowing to the lords.

"My lords, this is Jiro. I've asked him to join us. He can make anything and train anyone. I would like to propose him for head of manufacturing for all our metal items."

Lord Tōmatsu arched a questioning eyebrow at Lord Aya. Lord Aya shrugged and let the young people continue. His daughter jumped into the silence.

Masuyo said, "By my estimates, we need at least ten Jiros working full time to produce the weapons, the dragon ship dirigible, the Difference Engine and the telegraph. Jiro, do you know other blacksmiths we can hire? Other men you trust?"

Jiro hid his surprise at her commanding tone and bowed again before answering. "Yes, my lady, I know the blacksmiths of this area, and who is skilled and who not. You'll have to pay them well and speak with their lords, for they will not want to leave their villages without blacksmiths. But yes, my lady, I can find you a dozen good men."

Masuyo turned to her father, Lord Aya. "O-tō-sama, we need barracks for the workers. When can our people have the buildings up and ready?"

Lord Aya was used to his daughter's commanding tone and too weary to scold her in front of the others. He meekly answered, "I've put them to work on it already. Should have completed buildings by month end. We've framed up your lab, the weavery and gun factory already."

"Excellent. Jiro, ask your blacksmiths to join us at the end of the month. In the meantime, you and I will finalize the plans for the equipment and processes so we are ready for them."

"Yes, my lady." Jiro was startled to hear Masuyo giving commands, to him or anyone else. He looked uncertainly at Tōru, who nodded that he was free to go.

A few days later, Lord Tōmatsu's chief retainer Sugieda galloped into the courtyard and shouted for his lord.

He found Lord Tōmatsu huddled with Masuyo, Tōru and Lord Aya as they surveyed the rising walls of Masuyo's future lab. Masuyo, her face streaked with dust, was wearing a man's *hakama* and a ragged *hapi* jacket. She looked like a young peasant boy wearing a samurai's cast-off *hakama*, a young peasant boy who was used to being obeyed, as she fired off orders to the workman. Lord Tōmatsu, no longer marveling at her, listened thoughtfully as she explained the functions the lab would perform once built.

"What news? Success?" Lord Tōmatsu shouted at Sugieda.

The young man, sweaty and dirty from his hard ride to the furthest southwesternmost tip of Japan and back, leapt off his horse and bowed. When his face rose to meet their gaze, he could not hide his excitement.

"He is with us, my lord. Your classmate has convinced his cousin Lord Shimazu to join with us. Satsuma clan has embraced our cause. The *daimyō* sends a few trusted retainers next week to discuss further plans. He has already distributed requests from our list to a network of trusted merchants, some here and some there, so no one can see the full picture."

"Will he come?" Lord Aya demanded.

"The new *daimyō* cannot join us himself. He is not yet secure in his position after forcing his father to retire last year. And the Shogun's men watch him too carefully. However, he sends you this letter with his advice and counsel. He bids me tell you he supports your plans and will back you with men and resources." The young *samurai* handed over the letter to Lord Tōmatsu, stamped with Lord Shimazu's personal seal.

Sugieda looked past Lord Tōmatsu to Tōru, as disheveled and filthy as Masuyo in peasant's clothes and construction grime and sweat all over his face as he helped her supervise the workers. "Lord Shimazu asked about your fisherman."

"How did he know of our fisherman? You did not mention him— I ordered his presence here be kept secret!"

Lord Tōmatsu's retainer looked abashed. "I did not mean to mention him, sir. My lord Tōmatsu was clear in his orders."

"Indeed I was!" Lord Tōmatsu said. "*Utsuke!* You fool!"

"As I explained about the equipment we needed from abroad, and the Babaji thing and the telegraph, Lord Shimazu became curious and asked why we were interested in such gear. He demanded to know how we had learned of the Western technologies. I - I did not know how to explain. I am sorry. He could see I had no idea what a Babaji or a dirijibi was. He called me a liar and a spy and threatened to behead me or send me to the Shogun. Finally, to calm him, I told him the truth about the wretched shipwrecked fisherman."

Tōru watched Sugieda, rapt.

Masuyo watched Tōru, puzzled. Of course, revealing his presence was unfortunate, given the Shogun's policy of executing such travelers, but what she saw on Tōru's face was not fear of exposure but keen interest or excitement.

"As soon as I told him of the fisherman, and his story of being shipwrecked and rescued by the Americans two years ago, his manner changed. One minute he was threatening to kill me, and then next he had a thousand questions about the fisherman. I tried not to reveal much, but..."

Sugieda looked miserable. He turned to Tōru and bowed his regrets. "He knows your name, your town, your mother's name because of me. I'm sorry."

Lord Aya regarded Tōru and shook his head at the bad news. "Let's hope Lord Shimazu is on our side. Or it's not just your head, boy, but mine as well for harboring you."

Sugieda spoke up again, more cheerfully this time. "My lords, perhaps I read him wrong, but he seemed pleased to hear of our fisherman. In fact, he sends all this to Lord Aya." He tugged out a long slender bundle from under his saddle. He handed over a heavy bag, clinking of coin, and a sealed letter to Lord Aya. He held the long bundle carefully as he watched Lord Aya read the message.

Lord Aya looked up from the letter. "He asks—" He looked incredulously at Tōru as he read, "that I name you a samurai of middle rank. He asks further that I name you as a retainer to myself, and that I use this coin to buy good land for you nearby granting a living of at least 50 *koku* per year."

Tōru stared back at his host and captor, Lord Aya, as amazed as Lord Aya and Lord Tōmatsu themselves at the extravagant gifts and extraordinary requests from Lord Shimazu. He knelt before Lord

Aya. "If it is your will to take me on as retainer, I will serve you well, my lord."

"Stand up, boy! This is ridiculous. You know nothing about being a *samurai*." He spat. "*Fisherman*! Lord Shimazu mocks me." Lord Aya crumbled the message and threw it to the ground.

Sugieda interrupted. "Lord Aya, please forgive me for contradicting you, but I saw Lord Shimazu's face. I did not hear mockery in his voice. There is more." He handed the long slender bundle to Tōru. "Lord Shimazu commanded I give these to you."

Tōru unwrapped the protective leather and cloth around the bundle to reveal a *daishō* pair of beautifully made samurai swords, the long *katana* and short *shōtō*, snug in their sheaths. They were signed by their maker and decorated with the Shimazu crest, a cross within a circle, ornate dragons and sea lions and the inscription "Himasaki Tōru, Wayfarer."

Lord Aya snatched the swords from Tōru. He examined them, holding the *katana* up to the sky and tracing the fine sharpness of the blade with a fingertip. "These are fit for a prince! Do you even know how to hold them, boy?"

He handed them back to Tōru.

He drew his own *katana*. "Let us see what you know."

Tōru looked uncertainly at Lord Aya, no longer jovial but deadly serious and pointing a *katana* at his throat. Tōru stepped back, bowed and swept into an attack position, his *katana* at the ready against Lord Aya's. He held this position, waiting. Lord Aya bowed and then leapt forward with a great blow.

Tōru parried, not the clumsy slash of an untrained fisherman, but an expert swift small block, effortless but solid as stone, sending Lord Aya's blade bouncing back to him. Tōru whirled around and laid a mock blow with the flat of his sword on Lord Aya's arm. Lord Aya glanced down at his arm as though it were in flames. Tōru danced back, holding a guarded but neutral position. "I don't wish to injure you, Lord Aya. You have been so good to me. May we practice rather with bamboo *shinai*, to avoid injury?"

Lord Aya said nothing but pressed his attack again with the naked blade.

Tōru deflected and dodged his blow, then spun around and laid a second mock blow on Lord Aya's shoulder. He danced away.

Lord Aya's good nature dissolved entirely as he attacked for a third time.

Tōru evaded him again, vanishing like smoke where Lord Aya aimed his blow.

Tōru refused to strike any offensive blows against the man who had saved his life and hidden him from the Shogun. However, he also did not allow a single blow to land on himself. He had the strength and speed of wiry youth and the skill of a master swordsman. Long and silently they danced their *katana* together and apart, young Tōru against the skilled but middle-aged Lord Aya, old enough to be his father.

Finally the older man tired and sheathed his *katana*. Panting, he offered a shallow and grudging bow to his young opponent.

Tōru returned the gesture with a deep bow.

"I don't know how a fisherman learned such swordplay in Iwamatsu, but you have been well taught, boy. But how can I take as retainer one whose name I am not sure I know? Whose parents are so...mysterious? Who stands condemned to death by the Shogun's law?"

Lord Tōmatsu nodded agreement. "And yet...Aya, he wins powerful patrons effortlessly. He won us over, did he not, barefoot and shabby though he was? And Lord Shimazu's interest, while unexpected, is welcome. Someone has trained the fisherman masterfully. I will take him into my own household if you do not want him, Aya."

Tōru felt like a prize warhorse being auctioned off as they argued over his fate.

"No, the request came to me, and so I must decide yes or no. He would be too conspicuous in your household. Your wife's ties to the Tokugawas...no, too dangerous. Lord Shimazu knows the boy is safer in my small household, off the beaten track. Curious he would ask such a thing as his price for cooperation."

"Curious indeed," said Lord Tōmatsu, eyeing the young fisherman.

Lord Aya turned back to Tōru.

"It is illegal for a man who is not a *samurai* to wear these *daishō* swords. Obata, my chief retainer, will hold them for you. No point in giving the Shogun a second reason for taking your head. Obata will test your knowledge of the skills and knowledge a *samurai* must have." The older, quiet man constantly at Lord Aya's side nodded curtly at Tōru. Tōru bowed.

"I accept that you will not give me a true name, Himasaki Tōru, whoever you are. I trust your reasons are valid. But do not lie to me or my man about anything else. Not one word. Do not hide a skill. I suspect you read and write. Show Obata how well. He will test you. If he finds you worthy, I will consider Lord Shimazu's request. In the meantime, I will find you the land, so we do not offend your patron, our new ally Satsuma. Perhaps someday you will explain to me why Lord Shimazu takes such an interest in a fisherman."

Tōru bowed deeply. "I understand, my lord. I am loyal to you from this day. Thank you."

The next morning, the two lords and their men gathered in the courtyard.

"Quit skulking around, boy!" Lord Aya barked at Tōru, who had been hovering near the lords preparing to depart. An evening's rest had not improved Lord Aya's mood.

"Sir, one more topic we must discuss..."

Aya turned to Tōmatsu and protested. "You see what I must put up with? My daughter wears *hakama* and runs a research lab and a factory and commands a small army of workers and engineers. Our ally demands that I elevate my prisoner to *samurai* and buy him land, while that very prisoner informs me of additional topics we must discuss. You require me to ride all over creation helping you sell this whole plan..."

Tōmatsu chuckled. "You're the one who rescued him. So all this," he waved at the furious rushing around of everyone in both households as preparations were made and supplies readied, "is your fault, Aya. As much as it pains us both, let's hear the fisherman out. Although I admit I am quite certain we are going to loathe whatever he is about to propose. He has the guilty look he always gets before he wants to talk us into some new American barbarism."

"Whose side are you on?" Lord Aya demanded.

"Mine first. Then yours. Then that of the wild fish you hauled from the sea," he said, pointing at Tōru. "All of us want to keep the Americans off our shores and our heads safe on our shoulders. So out with it, fisherman. What barbaric American trick are we going to learn today?"

Tōru flushed. He was indeed about to spring on them a new American barbarism.

Furthermore, he knew that of all his recent ideas, this was the one they were going to hate the most. The lords Aya and Tōmatsu were not merely *samurai*, but proud *daimyōs*, descendants of great leaders who had fought with honor in battles hundreds of years ago. Even in this peaceful era, where the Shogun's tight control kept everyone from fighting any actual battles against real enemies, still they considered themselves warriors, officers and swordsmen. They adhered to strict codes of honor and prestige among warriors. They were acutely aware of their own special status as *daimyō*, and knew down to the man which of their men descended from the right level of *samurai* to command other *samurai* and how many. All of which meant they were going to hate his new idea.

"We need more men," Tōru began. *Always start from an unarguable premise when you can.*

"Yes, of course. We agreed we would get the other *daimyōs* to commit men to our alliance. We're off, in the mud and rain, to go get them for you." Aya grumbled, pulling his feet out of sticky mud and losing his *geta*.

"No, I mean many more men. Even if all four *daimyōs* you are meeting with agree to join us, all of their *samurai* put together would only be a few thousand. We need more. Tens of thousands, trained and able. In addition to our core army, we need airship captains, train conductors, merchant marines for our trade shipments, and submarine captains, and crews for all of these." Tōru took a breath. He hadn't told them the worst part yet. But they were working out the arithmetic on their own.

Lord Tōmatsu exploded. "You cannot have tens of thousands! Among us all, the six of us would have at most 2,500 *samurai*! Take out the garrisons they each need to protect their own lands and the administrators to run their domains. That leaves only a thousand five hundred or so who can fight. So make your plan with 1,500."

"There is another way." Tōru trailed off. He knew from his reading and visits to West Point other great armies had also faced this moment. He knew how outraged they had been, the French and Prussian and British noble and aristocratic officers who had traditionally commanded. "We can train commoners to fight with the new weapons, in the new airships, and submarines and train cars. They aren't allowed to carry swords, but I can teach them to pilot airships and fire guns."

This time Aya raged. "No. Never. Your swords and Lord Shimazu's strange demands concerning you are going to your head, fisherman. We are not arming commoners. For two hundred and fifty years, the Shogun has kept the peace by entrusting arms only to those worthy of trust. I may not like the *Bakufu* and the Shogun's many errors and weaknesses, but this ancient policy is for the safety of all and the peace of the entire realm. We who are warriors for a thousand years know how to bear this responsibility, and we alone. Do not speak to me of this again."

Tōru persisted. "I've run the calculations—"

"Don't speak to me of calculations. This is honor. This is our sacred trust, for centuries."

Tōru gestured imploringly to his host and mentor. He could not back down, even if it enraged Lord Aya. "We cannot raise a force sufficient to meet and repel the foreigners by next year unless the Shogun joins us and orders everyone to join us. He will not."

"True, the Shogun would rather die than act." Lord Tōmatsu looked unhappy, but he grasped the cold math. The sounds of shouting workmen and the clanging hammers of the carpenters filled a long pause. "We could have commoners serve under *samurai* officers. In the crews. Not the fighting parts, just the crews of the, what do you call them, dirijibi? The flying ships? And the underwater ships." He sniffed distastefully at the idea of going underwater in a small ship crammed with commoners.

"I considered that, sir, but in actual battle, even a ship's cook must be able to use his weapon and help the ship sail and maneuver. We would have to include commoners, many commoners, to fill out all the crews and squads we need. And you would want the most able men in command. Not just those," Tōru hesitated, for he was pushing into unthinkable ground now, "of great birth."

Tōmatsu laughed. "Absurd. Don't worry so much, fisherman. We know how to fight. Trust us to manage this small part of your grand plan. One of my *samurai* is worth fifty of your American barbarians."

Aya roared again. "You would put commoners in command over *samurai*? Are you mad?"

"I would sir, for specialized functions, and for any role they understand best, like the steering of the airships or the tending of the engines. The nobles and the *samurai* are the best officers for direct combat on land," Tōru continued hastily, "as they already understand the discipline and tactics of fighting together. Many of them can read so they can send and receive telegrams and intelligence. But you would want the best commanders in charge, regardless of birth, even in the army. No matter how you organize them, and how brave they are, we simply need more men. Able men. Commoner men."

Tōru paused, letting this sink in. He had a long list of additional arguments, but he knew they would have to understand and agree on their own. For their answer, until and unless they saw his logic for themselves, was that *samurai* were warriors and everyone else was not. So it had always been and always must be.

"Never. We will not discuss this madness further. We are late getting underway. Leave the generalship to us, boy, and go build the factory you promised us." Lord Aya mounted his horse and signaled for Lord Tōmatsu to move out with him, trailing a splendid long line of fully armored retainers in their wake, glorious in their 17th century armor and fine swords.

1852 — Summer

CHAPTER 6

⊕

ALLIANCES

"We cannot live only for ourselves.
A thousand fibers connect us with our fellow men;
and among those fibers, as sympathetic threads,
our actions run as causes, and they come back to us as effects."
— Herman Melville

While the Lords Tōmatsu and Aya galloped around the countryside rallying other western *daimyōs* to their cause, Tōru and Masuyo focused on building their operation, aided, more than anyone had ever expected, by the indefatigable Jiro.

Jiro quickly proved both his worth and his prodigious capacity for drink and song. He was a great favorite among the workmen. Foulmouthed, strong as an ox, surging around from dawn to past dusk directing his army of engineers, blacksmiths and swordsmiths, he never tired nor ceased to sing, shout and tell jokes, except for the moments he took to chug a swig or three of cheap *saké*.

Masuyo, unconventional though she was, was nobly born and gently raised. She had never been around such a man, loud and uncouth and irreverent. Her father's servants always treated her like a fragile china doll.

Jiro was another matter altogether.

He treated Masuyo with exaggerated but sincere respect in his exuberant and unpolished way. Once over his shock at being commanded by a woman, even a woman of rank, he would do anything for her, going far beyond her requests to meet the demands of the goals underneath. Stiff and formal at first, shocked by his irreverent ways and peasant language, Masuyo eventually accepted the jovial blacksmith as a partner. Testing him with an unending series of new demands for equipment and gear, she discovered that Jiro did not know failure, but rose to each new challenge, presenting her each day with new offerings.

Masuyo saw Jiro was practical and hardworking, a near-constant slow infusion of *saké* notwithstanding. Hesitant at first, she began to joke with the wise-cracking blacksmith. Soon Masuyo and Jiro were fast friends, to Tōru's consternation. Within days, she was doing credible imitations of Jiro's hard-bitten peasant accent and telling barbarous stories with his wit and rhythm while hurling low-class slang around like a pirate.

Tōru watched Masuyo's transformation with some alarm. He feared Lord Aya would blame him for inflicting Jiro's unique and exuberant style on her.

Masuyo shrugged off his concerns. "You keep saying it is a new world and we must change to meet it. I like Jiro! He is more intelligent and hardworking than most of the nobles I know. Look what he is able to do! The men all love him. Tōru, he is your secret weapon, more powerful than even your beloved dirigibles and sewing machines!"

"But, my lady! You cannot behave—behave like a blacksmith!" For a revolutionary, Tōru was pretty conservative. The loud aggressive American women had frightened him. Masuyo's transformation he found even more terrifying. His mother had been graceful and feminine, the epitome of traditional femininity and beauty. Masuyo stomping around in men's boots and hakama and swearing in the construction pit with Jiro made Tōru's head spin.

"You sound like my father, fisherman."

To Tōru's astonishment, Masuyo stuck out her tongue at him, a gesture he had never seen in his life, even in America. She laughed and told him, "You ought to be happy I get along with Jiro so well! He works hard for me. Between the two of us, we have found all the workers you are demanding! Jiro is gathering them now."

Jiro was true to his word. Messengers had been sent out to all the blacksmiths he recommended. Bewildered blacksmiths from a dozen

villages were duly fetched and their *daimyōs* compensated for the loss
of their services. Swordmakers, too, he knew and recommended,
believing they could train apprentices to make parts for the first
prototype guns. He recruited skilled carpenters for the constant
building of new warehouses, factories and containers for all the
products being created.

Jiro was in his element, commanding the workmen. He was a
natural leader, unpolished and crude, but universally beloved of his
men. Here the carpenters raised barracks, there the blacksmiths cast
parts. A collection of literate young men, mostly merchants' sons
handpicked by Jiro, became engineers, translating Masuyo's
drawings into detailed specifications for parts: for telegraph systems,
for guns, for trains, for dirigibles and for Babbage Difference
Engines. Each afternoon, as the shadows grew long, the foremen and
engineers gathered in a small school, learning to read and write and
do calculations so they could understand and communicate
engineering diagrams and plans. Other skilled workmen turned
those detailed drawings into pilot parts to make molds for factory
castings.

Mystified at first at the strange summons, the young men eagerly
took to their work, and the solid pay they could send to their families
in a dozen poor villages. Word spread throughout the region of
strange new technologies and an insatiable demand for the services
of any young man, *samurai* or commoner, who could read and liked
to work hard. Lord Aya's quiet, out-of-the-way, country castle boiled
with activity, an anthill disturbed by a stick, as Tōru, Masuyo and
Jiro argued and planned and built all they needed to unite and
defend the country.

Late one overcast gray afternoon, Jiro stepped out of his muddy
boots in the entranceway *genkan* and into the lab, where Masuyo
could usually be found, bent over her plans and diagrams. For once
he was not singing, swearing, swigging *saké* or acting out some
madcap adventure to amuse his workmen.

Rather he was uncharacteristically quiet as he slipped through
the lab, piled high with half-finished projects and experiments, and

made his way to Masuyo's corner. Silently Jiro knelt near her, to be down at her level as she knelt at her low writing table. When she did not greet him, he coughed delicately. She started, and dropped her brush, blotting her page.

"Oh, I am so sorry!" Jiro cried as he attempted to help Masuyo save her page of work.

Masuyo shrugged off his help as she blotted up the mess. "I did not see you! No matter, it wasn't right yet anyway. I'll do it over and get it right."

Jiro paused, working out how to begin.

Masuyo looked at him sidelong, sensing an unasked question hanging in the air.

"Did the new plans explain the brake mechanism to your engineers clearly enough?" Masuyo rarely wasted time on small talk, not with all they had to get done.

"The plans? Oh yes, they were fine. The engineers are building prototypes right now for testing." Jiro hesitated again.

Masuyo turned and faced him full on. "Jiro, is something the matter?"

Jiro twisted and made a face. "Can you, would you, I mean, would it be possible for you to teach me to read?" Jiro's question poured out of him in an urgent whisper, his voice low to avoid Tōru overhearing as he worked in his own corner of the newly built lab.

Masuyo stifled a smile and nodded gravely, knowing what it had cost the swaggering, confident blacksmith to ask for help. "Of course. But I thought you did not wish to learn. Tōru said he tried to teach you when you were boys and you disliked it very much."

"Well, that was then, and now we have so much to do. I can see now how reading can be like fighting. To read and write is as interesting as to swing a blade, and might help us more."

Masuyo nodded. "Certainly. I fight with these dictionaries and diagrams every day. My father will never allow me to go into battle with pistol or *naginata*. But I would defend our shores with every breath in my body, so I fight with my pen and my brain."

Jiro bowed to the young woman, sincere respect in his motion. "Yes, my lady. I thought it...weak and unmanly to write. So I refused to learn. I am no poet, wearing silk and writing *tanka* under a full moon while sipping plum wine from tiny cups." He hung his great head. "But you show me it is brave to fight with the dictionaries. I would not have a—a woman be braver than me. We must defeat the dictionaries if we are to win against the foreigners."

Masuyo laughed. "Yes, we must conquer the dictionaries, and soon. Especially the French ones that frustrate Tōru so! But would you not prefer to learn from Tōru, your friend from so long ago?"

Jiro leaned in, his swagger and good cheer returning. "If you would not mind, I would rather learn from you. Tōru is, well, he is terrible at teaching. He is my friend, my best friend, so please don't tell him I told you this, but he doesn't know how to explain things. Everything comes easily to him, so he doesn't know how to teach a blockhead like me."

Masuyo laughed out loud, her peal of laughter making Tōru look up from his work to see what was going on. She waved Tōru back to work, composed herself and leaned back in to Jiro and whispered, "Of course I will teach you. You are no blockhead, Jiro, but one of the best fighters we have. We should not let Tōru's poor teaching skills get in the way of your learning. Let me find some books for us to practice with."

"And you won't tell Tōru? I don't want him to laugh at me."

Masuyo held back her smile and nodded gravely. "If you wish it so, then it is our secret. But he would not laugh at you, I am certain."

"Thank you. Can we start tomorrow? I'll come early before Tōru arrives."

"Of course." Masuyo smiled at the blacksmith as he arose.

Jiro began to sing one of his favorite foulmouthed drinking songs. She joined in on the chorus, earning the pair of them a glare from Tōru across the crowded lab. Giggling, Masuyo jumped up, grabbed Jiro and steered him over toward Tōru, singing loudly. Masuyo and Jiro stomped and swirled and clapped their hands in a festival dance Jiro had taught her from Iwamatsu as they advanced on Tōru's position in the far corner of their lab.

Tōru sighed. He had been puzzling over the control mechanism design for the dragon dirigibles he wanted to build, a fleet of airships to defend the coasts from American warships. It would be the first military air fleet in the world. He was dazzled by the idea, but thwarted by the reality of actually building one.

The French had built a few prototypes. American newspapers had followed their progress with excitement, breathlessly reporting on the adventures of the dashing airship captains. The pilots from those successful maiden voyages were feted all over Europe.

No one had put airships to practical use yet, though, so his idea to use them as a protective force along the coast was innovative and controversial. His American military friends scoffed at dirigibles as a French fancy flourish with no real military use. "Fat flying targets, tasty as a Christmas goose flying overhead," was how one American officer summed them up. Tōru was unsure what the officer meant by delicious Christian geese, but he grasped the scorn for the idea.

Even if the dirigibles weren't effective as actual weapons, Tōru hoped the airships would at least frighten the foreigners away on their first visit. He wanted to buy time to build more useful defenses. He needed weapons capable of sinking hardened warships, not merely frightening their crews.

One thing at a time.

Tōru pushed his work aside with a string of good solid oaths in English he had learned from the sailors on his return home. The dirigible designs he had brought from America were all in French, which was not nearly as similar to English as he had been led to believe. He lacked a good French dictionary, and ordering one through the Dutch traders at Nagasaki was out of the question. He was forced to crack a smile as his singing, dancing friends approached, though his head hurt with the mind-bending, frustrating work.

He needed a break.

Design work was how he relaxed these days, as a respite from overseeing the constant swarm of activity stirred up by Masuyo and Jiro as they built out the lab and barracks and factories. Usually designing things calmed him, but today, between the heat, the construction noise and the damnable French, design only added to the pressure and stress eating him.

Tōru fantasized sometimes about running away from the whole mad process and actually becoming a fisherman somewhere, maybe up on the far northern coast among the primitive *Emishi* people, where nothing ever happened and no one of note ever came. Single-handedly organizing an industrial and military revolution while evading the Shogun's men was not something he had actually envisioned doing, but here he was.

The future train station was rising from the dust swirling around Lord Aya's castle. All attempts at maintaining secrecy had long since been abandoned. Whenever he remembered how badly they were failing at hiding their activities, Tōru had developed a nervous tic of rubbing the back of his neck where the executioner's blade would fall if the Shogun's men came asking questions. He rubbed his neck as he stood to greet his friends as they twirled to a stamping stop in front of his workspace.

"What's with all the noise? I'm trying to get some work done here."

Jiro and Masuyo exchanged looks and invented a reason for their interruption, one that had the added benefit of being true. Improvising as they went, they began talking over each other in their excitement, a habit they had recently picked up and refined until they spoke as one unit in two bodies.

"Everything is taking too long," began Masuyo.

"We need more wood here, and faster," continued Jiro.

"We're already out of coal and parts for the first shipment of rifles," said Masuyo.

"We're out of everything, and no shipments are due until next week," said Jiro. "Can't get milk unless you feed the cow. Our supply lines have ground to a halt."

"You've got to get the trains built and in place. We'll never meet plan unless we can get the materials here faster," finished Masuyo. She sat down and idly examined Tōru's drawing of the dirigible control mechanism. "You've got it wrong here. This needs to connect here, and here. Not here, as you have it. It will block the motion you need."

Tōru leaned in to see her suggestions. She was right. She usually was, a habit he found annoying. And oddly attractive.

"We don't have the materials or forges to build trains yet. We have to do them later," Tōru insisted.

"There won't be a later unless we get the trains in place. There's simply no way to move enough men and materials fast enough without the trains. We've run the Babaji calculations to prove it."

Tōru sighed. He knew they were right. There were just too many problems, too many projects, too much going on to keep everything straight. But they were right, so what to do?

He began to sketch. "The train tracks will have to be a network, with multiple routes to the traders on the coasts, and between the *daimyōs* who join us. We'll want it as hidden as possible, away from main roads where the Shogun's men might see it. We'll need men we can trust to be the station agents."

"The *saké* brewers in each town would be perfect," said Jiro. "They are nearly always open for business, and we can trade them cheap shipping in exchange for their work as agents for us. Plus I know them all well. I can talk them into joining us, if you'll grant them favorable shipping rates."

Jiro's social skills, prodigious drinking capacity and keen economic sense came in handy when recruiting for the revolution.

"Each *daimyō* who joins us can build the track within his own domain," suggested Masuyo. "Less burden on us. We can connect Lords Aya's and Tōmatsu's domains first, plus a line out to the coast. With those backbone lines in place we can ship wood from Lord Tōmatsu's forests and connect with Satsuma and Lord Shimazu's traders."

"How soon can you have a working locomotive?" asked Tōru.

"We're attempting to cast the bigger parts today," answered Jiro. "I've never cast anything this big before, though, so no promises. If it goes well, we could have a model together by the end of the month."

"All right then, switch over the workers to getting the first train track laid between here and Lord Tōmatsu's domain. Get the locomotive assembled and tested." Tōru gave the command, and turned back to his dirigible design.

Masuyo laid a hand on his shoulder. "Don't worry so much. We'll get it done."

"I hope so." He turned to his work, trying not to show how deeply her touch on his shoulder affected him. Tōru envied Jiro his easy boisterous ways with the young woman. He found himself tongue-tied and red-faced in her presence these days. He urgently wanted to tell Masuyo ideas, ask her opinions, to listen to her soft voice incongruously chant Jiro's favorite drinking songs. Instead, he communicated with Masuyo in short bursts, monosyllables or short sentences, as gruff as a grumpy old man. He was certain she found him a fool. The thought distressed him.

Lord Aya and Lord Tōmatsu and their retinue rode into the courtyard a few days later. They were astonished at all the progress Tōru and his team had made since their departure just a few weeks before. A finished train station and a good start on a train track running west met them as they rode in. Completed barracks, factories and the laboratory peppered the ground littered with stumps where forests had once upon a time sheltered Lord Aya's castle. Pastoral silence was shattered with the clanging roar of engines and machines, falling timber and roaring fires, punctuated by the shouts of workmen. The lords confronted a hellish industrial landscape, bleak destruction invading the island for the first time.

Lord Aya winced at the stripped and barren land all around his once beautiful home. It was ugly. It was brutal. It was a crime against all good taste and a violation of the spirits of the land.

It was necessary.

Lord Aya reminded himself of the urgency of their task and consoled himself. The trees would grow again. In time to shelter his great-grandchildren. Maybe.

True to his word, using his nearly magical ability over all metals, Jiro had managed to cast and assemble the critical parts for the first steam engine, a few early mishaps notwithstanding. An early failure had been turned into a giant planter as tall as a man at Masuyo's direction. It adorned the inner gate area with its alien shape, stuffed full of plants. Another disaster stood by the far side of the gate, similarly adorned with plants. Jiro's crews strained to drag the future engine onto the rough cart that would serve until a finished metal engine wagon could be constructed. Tōru and Jiro wanted to test the engine's strength and ability to pull before building the rest of the cars.

Tōru and Jiro ran to greet the lords, shouting orders to their men to continue their tasks.

"*O-kaeri-nasaimase!* Welcome home, my lords!" said Tōru, chagrined at the damage he had wrought in his host-captor's forest. He hoped the dire danger they were battling would justify to Lord Aya the terrible devastation Tōru had visited upon Lord Aya's country retreat.

"I cannot say I like what you have done with my place," said Lord Aya at last as he took in the destruction. "Was this completely necessary, to destroy a 400-year-old forest park, tended by my family for generations?"

Tōru hung his head. "I am sorry, my lord."

"If you are trying to anger me in order to avoid becoming my retainer, your plan is working, boy. This is unspeakably ugly." Lord Aya sighed. "Tell me what you have accomplished. Aside from sacrificing my forest."

"Come this way and I'll show you." Tōru pointed out the new train station and the first stretch of freshly laid tracks. He walked them through three newly constructed barracks to house soldiers, seamstresses, Babaji girls, blacksmiths and carpenters. He showed the lords the labs, the designs for the fleet of dragon dirigible airships, the model for the first Babbage Difference Engine, and the map of the train and telegraph network he planned.

The *daimyōs* were astounded. Mere weeks ago, they had been arguing over ideas, words, maps and plans. Now the rough seeds of a new economy, a vibrant manufacturing base and a radically transformed military were rising from the soil where the mighty trees had once held sway.

"My lords, may I ask you how your work went, with the other *daimyōs*? Are they with us? Will we connect our trains and telegraph lines?" asked Tōru.

Lord Tōmatsu grinned. "All this is fine work, boy. But for a pair of backward old men, we've done some good work these weeks too. Brains, my lad, not brawn, that's what we bring. Five new *daimyōs* have agreed to join us. They are gathering men and materials now."

Lord Tōmatsu handed Tōru a map, showing their domains. "And to your next question, yes, all the domains connect, so we can run the train and telegraph lines to all of them. They are sending foremen to get your instructions on the sections they will build. Shimazu has sent messengers to each of them to coordinate their import needs as well. Himasaki, this is Saigo-san, one of Lord Shimazu's clerks. He will be coordinating between our efforts and Lord Shimazu's."

A huge young *samurai*, a few years older than Tōru, clad in humble but correct and neatly patched *samurai* attire, stepped forward and bowed to Tōru and Masuyo. "*Yoroshiku onegai itashimasu.* It is an honor to work with you, Himasaki-*dono*." As Saigo rose from his bow, his eyes held Tōru's an extra moment.

Tōru's face was perfectly still. "Himasaki-*dono*, my lord Shimazu sends this gift to you with his best wishes. May he serve you well, and through you Lord Aya, in the days ahead."

A groom led forth a magnificent young stallion, spirited and proud, resisting the lead.

"He is nearly trained, but Lord Shimazu thought you would bond best with him if you finish training him yourself. He is young and can be a companion to you for many years."

Tōru bowed low his thanks. "This gift is too much. Please send my thanks to your lord." He exchanged a look with Saigo, but kept his face impassive.

Masuyo noted the quick exchange and wondered at it.

A second groom carried in his arms an exquisitely finished military saddle and bridle, along with horse blankets and other gear.

Lord Tōmatsu broke in. "The saddle and gear are a gift from me. We were asleep, ignoring the troublesome world around us and hoping it would go away. You came along and forced us all to wake up." Lord Tōmatsu laughed. "And cut down poor Aya's forest. Consider this a bribe to stay away from my forest."

Tōru bowed low in thanks. "I thank you, and humbly accept your generous gift." He turned to Lord Aya. "And I am sorry about your forest."

Lord Aya grimaced, offering up not quite a laugh, but more a bark followed by a resigned sigh. "Not nearly sorry enough. What's done is done. When we get you your land, the first thing I am going to do is to invade and cut down your forest. Anything else we need to discuss tonight? I need *sake* and an *ofuro* bath."

Tōru replied, eager to discuss something other than the rich gifts and strange attention from Lord Shimazu. "We are building the telegraph and the train tracks first. If we set up the telegraph line toward the East, we can get advanced notice of any movements from the Shogun. Then we'll run the line southwest to Satsuma's headquarters, to give real-time communication with the traders. We might get lucky and get advance warning of foreign ships heading up our coast to Edo or Nagasaki as well."

Tōru paused for a moment, expecting arguments, but the lords had simply accepted his decision. Not to mention forgiven him a lost forest. Perhaps they were tired. Tōru pressed on, as long as they were feeling permissive or too worn down to argue.

"Now the Babbage Difference Engine...I wanted to discuss with your lordships the staffing requirements. Jiro had an idea. It's...a bit unconventional." Tōru paused. "He has a friend or two...among... the *geisha* madams." Tōru blushed to mention such a thing, especially in front of Masuyo. "They have offered to have their girls staff the Babaji calculating machines during their off hours."

Tōru had given up on getting his team to pronounce 'Babbage Difference Engines' with a correct English accent. They were Babajis, now and forevermore. "The young women are discreet and intelligent and skilled with fine handwork, and some of them can read. We can hide the Babajis in the *geisha* houses, each with a hidden telegraph line to the central telegraph office at the *saké* breweries in each town. They are downtown, in the entertainment districts of each of our castle towns, and well located centrally to each of our domains. Good places for gentlemen to meet and discuss plans quietly as well."

Lord Tōmatsu laughed. "You are determined to cause me trouble with my wife. I'll need to be inspecting my Babaji and telegraph lines, and she will be raging at me for visiting the *geisha*."

Lord Aya waved a hand wearily. "*Saké* and *ofuro*, now. We can discuss more tomorrow. *Gokuro*. Well done, Tōru."

After the lords went off to sleep off their *saké* and travels, Tōru went out to the stable to brush down his new mount. The gleaming saddle and tack were neatly hung above on the stable wall. He carefully mucked out the stable and filled it with fresh, sweet-smelling straw for bedding. Buckets of feed and water enough for three horses were lovingly placed at the ready. Already the proud animal was calm under his touch. He whispered softly to the horse, pausing now and again to feed him bits of apple, enjoying the scratchy tongue as it whisked over his fingers.

"Excuse me."

Tōru started. He had not seen Saigo enter. He looked around to see if anyone else was there. The stable was empty but for the two young men, the silence broken only by the soft whinnies and rustlings of the *daimyō's* horses.

"Saigo? Takamori, is that really you? You are taller and — and thicker."

Saigo laughed and pounded his firmly muscled solid belly. He was enormous, towering over most men. "I should say, 'Tōru, is that really you?' Except you look exactly as you did, a skinny bean. So you made it back."

The two men embraced.

"They don't know," Tōru began.

"So I guessed. Don't worry. I won't blow your cover. But the lord's daughter..."

"Masuyo-*sama*?"

"She knows, or guesses. She was watching me like a hungry fox eyes a chicken when we were introduced. I tried not to show I know you, but her gaze pierces steel."

"She'll figure it out the soonest, for sure."

"What do they believe?"

"I told what truth I could. That I was lost at sea fishing two years ago and rescued by an American ship. That I returned to seek my mother. Do you know anything of her? We went to Iwamatsu to find her, but she was gone."

"I'm sorry. I was afraid I would have to be the one to tell you. She vanished a month or so after you left. Your father has sought her up and down the coast, but he's had no luck. Even now, he still has a handful of men searching for her. My friend, we have to assume your dear mother has passed. The only thing..."

"Yes?"

"Well, it's a little odd."

"Tell me."

"Remember how we used to tease you about being the son of a shape-shifting sea lion who bewitched your father?"

"You learned it from Jiro. Then you taught everyone in my father's house to mock me, too. I've been waiting a long time to punish you for that. Watch your back, Takamori." Tōru grinned as he said this, but his eyes were serious.

"Well, so here's the thing, you see...there's a sea lion, a she-sea lion, who took up on the coast underneath the windows of your father's castle soon after you left. She sings at night, the nights when the moon is full. The servants who know of you and your father's love for your mother, well, they whisper she has come back to him in her sea lion form. They say her grief over losing you cost her her human form."

Tōru made a face. "And what does my father say of the sea lion singing under his window?"

Takamori bowed gravely. "Lord Shimazu does not discuss sea lions with lowly clerks like me. But I have seen him at the window on a full moon a time or two, when she is singing. His wife has heard the rumors though, and sent hunters after the sea lion."

Tōru looked concerned, in spite of himself. A mother is hard enough to lose; it is doubly painful to lose an idea of her, no matter how odd the reminder. He forced himself to laugh.

"My mother is no sea lion, but I hope Lady Shimazu's hunters do not kill an innocent creature on her account."

"Do not worry, my friend. Lord Shimazu has declared no sea lions are to be killed within his castle town and the immediate areas. His lady wife complains to him about the noise, and declares it frightens her children at night. But he ignores her on this point."

The men laughed together, boyish laughter intruding through their now deep voices. They laughed as they used to when Tōru's father would take him to Shimazu Castle for training in swordsmanship, penmanship, horsemanship, history, geography, poetry and other literary and military arts, with Saigo as his companion and fellow student.

"Here we sit speaking of imaginary sea lions—"

"Oh no, dear Tōru, the sea lion is completely real."

"The completely real sea lion is not my mother."

"Says you."

"I say enough! Say that again and I'll—"

"Tōru, I say your mother is a sea lion, and she sings to your lord father, the mighty Lord Shimazu, mightiest lord in the west, every month under the full moon—

Tōru finally did what he had wanted to do for years, and punched the considerably taller and heavier Takamori hard in the jaw, using an American boxing move he had picked up from some Irish sailors on his journey home. The two began to wrestle and fight, half serious, half joking, until finally they fell back, gasping, into the straw.

"Don't call my mother a sea lion again. Okay?" Tōru said the word "okay" in English.

"What is 'okay'?"

"It means you agree, that things are fine between us. It is sometimes like 'wakarimashita.'"

"Okay. Wakarimashita. Wakatta, yo. I solemnly swear your mother is not a sea lion. Even if she is."

Takamori couldn't help himself as he teased his old friend. Of humble background, *samurai* to be sure, but of the lowest possible rank, he nonetheless had always known his place in the world. A humble, solid, good place it was. This small certainty in a changing world made Saigo Takamori more cheerful by nature than the bastard boy raised by the sea, uncertain of his place in his father's heart, his mother's village, his changing land. Takamori was quick to joke, quick to fight, quick to decide, quick to forgive. His boyhood friend Tōru was more thoughtful, more apt to ponder, slow to smile, slower to act and slow to forgive. Sensing he had pushed Tōru far enough and then some, Takamori let it go at last.

"Okay. *Wakarimashita.* You were going to say something."

"Is my father's support for Lord Aya's and Lord Tōmatsu's plan sincere? Will he commit the men and materials he promised? Defy the Shogun if it comes to that?"

"Yes. He fully supports your plan, Tōru. You are doing everything he trained you to do. He is proud of you, my friend."

Tōru was silent a moment.

Images rose up, all the struggles of the past two and a half years. The day and the night clinging alone to wreckage in the frigid sea, waiting for an American ship his father's men insisted was heading his way, wondering if he would survive the cold and live long enough to see the ship. The months on board ship, unable to communicate until he learned enough English to struggle by. The two years as an alien in a strange place, always eating strange food, hearing odd music and never hearing the sweet flowing sound of his own language. The lonely nights in a dozen different American homes, both humble and grand, as he read dictionaries and histories and diagrams and pored over maps of the world by candlelight, attempting to cram all the knowledge and know-how of the entire Western world into his head. The small humiliations of a thousand social errors in America, forgiven him instantly by his hosts, but painful in the moment. The successful landing on the coast of his homeland, and then his immediate arrest and the impending promise of his execution for returning to Japan from a foreign land.

The loss of his mother, the pain that cut deepest of all.

But his father was proud of him.

That was something.

"My orders are to stay close to Lords Aya and Tōmatsu and to assist you in any way needed. I have access through your father's men to information, trade, fighting men and money. I am not to reveal your identity to your new friends. He has arranged to have you made *samurai*—"

"Lord Aya does not like the idea. He thinks it is an insult to his minor status, to be forced by a great lord to accept a fisherman as a *samurai* of his household. And how is it even possible? *Samurai* are born, not made."

"My great-great-great-grandfather was made *samurai* for saving his lord's life. So I get to be born *samurai*. It happens, every century or so. The lords need good intelligent men around them. So sometimes they graft in some good healthy peasant stock like my ancestors. Technically, you *were* born a *samurai*, but we cannot tell anyone. Anyway, if Lord Aya decides it is so, then *samurai* you shall be. Maybe he'll marry you to Masuyo-*sama* and adopt you as his heir. Then you'll be a *daimyō* someday too, like your father and father-in-law! Maybe you can convince Lord Shimazu to release me from his service so I can come and be your chief retainer. You should not have cut down Lord Aya's forest. You should be thinking of it as your own forest—"

"Enough! I'm not going to be a *daimyō*, marry Masuyo-*sama* or pick you to be my chief retainer! Let's keep our story straight here. I'm a fisherman. I'm a treasonous traitor in danger every second from the Shogun's blade." Tōru rubbed the back of his neck. "I have a train network, telegraph system, five Babajis, sixteen factories, seven kinds of weapons and a dozen dragon dirigibles to build before my American friends show up and blow up our country. So I am kind of busy, and I need your help. Not your marital advice, legends about sea lions or plans for my conquest of the west."

"I said nothing about conquering the west! Although it's not a bad idea. Allied with your father, and future father-in-law we could completely dominate."

"Will you ever stop! Most of all I need a friend. And sleep."

"Sleep, and *saké*. First, *saké*!"

Horse grooming finished, the two young men went back to the castle, renewing their friendship long into the night.

CHAPTER 7

SAMURAI

*"New eras don't come about because of swords;
they're created by the people who wield them."*
— Manga artist Nobuhiro Watsuki

The sky was still dark when Tōru awoke to Obata standing above him.

Lord Aya's chief retainer never said much. Now he said nothing at all. Tōru leapt up and dressed with haste. When Tōru was ready, Obata nodded. He carried Tōru's *daishō* swords, given him by Lord Shimazu of Satsuma. "Let's go."

He led Tōru to the training field. He grunted and pointed at protective practice gear waiting by the field. Tōru put on leather and wooden gear to protect head, arms and chest. A variety of practice swords were on hand as well, from bamboo *shinai*, both the long *daitō* and the shorter *shōtō* used in two-handed *nitō* fighting styles, and dangerous wooden *bokutō* blades. Even without an edge, they were deadly weapons in the right hands.

Obata stood motionless waiting for Tōru at the center practice square.

Tōru stood before him, ready at last. He bowed deeply. Obata returned the bow.

"Onegai shimasu," cried Tōru. He moved to a ready stance.

Obata watched Tōru with snake-steady unblinking eyes.

Tōru, like most young men, found standing still a major trial. He rushed at Obata with an overhead blow. Obata parried easily and swatted Tōru on the arm. Chastened, Tōru held his position this time. Slowly they circled, feinting, occasionally attacking, neither moving out of a defensive ready position. Tōru saw an opening and slashed straight and true, landing a solid blow.

"Well done. Again."

For hours, as the sun rose high in the sky, and the sweat ran down his face, Tōru faced Obata. He thirsted. His arms got so heavy he could barely lift them. Blisters tore open his feet. The older man was impervious to heat, hunger, thirst and exhaustion. On he drove them.

"*Mō ichido.* Again."

"Again."

"*Dame da.* Bad. Again."

"Again."

"*Yosh'.* Good. Again."

Finally, with the sun directly overhead, Obata-san bowed to Tōru and put away his swords.

"Tomorrow, same time."

As Obata left the field, a groom walked up, bringing Tōru his horse and lunch. Tōru thanked him, nuzzled the horse and devoured his meal. He understood. He was to train his horse, nurturing the bond between horse and rider that can make the difference between life and death on the battlefield.

He pretended not to notice Obata watching him from the sidelines. He no longer had to pretend to be unable to ride. Much rested upon proving he could ride and ride well. He worked with the horse, basic paces at first, just to get acquainted. The groom brought out obstacles and training dummies. Tōru shot from the saddle, slashed at straw dummies from the saddle and dodged obstacles. Everything not aching from the morning's workout was soon in pain from the afternoon's exertions. As the sun set, the groom appeared again to return the horse to the stable. Tōru looked around, but Obata had vanished.

Tōru went into the stable to thank his horse.

Masuyo was there, waiting for him. She had brought tea and *onigiri* rice balls for him to eat. He was glad to see her, but too tired to do more than smile as he brushed down his horse.

"Tomorrow he will test you on writing and history," said Masuyo. "I overheard my father telling him what to cover." She handed him an armload of books and scrolls. "You write a good hand. But you'll need to know these histories. Obata is especially fond of the Sengoku Warring States period." She indicated two scrolls. "His family played a key role, although they were eventually defeated. He will ask you not only the history, but also why leaders made the choices they did. Have good answers."

Tōru looked at her helplessly.

"I cannot read all these tonight!"

"You can read some. Sleep when you are dead, fisherman, if you want to be a *samurai* of my father's house."

She left.

Tōru read.

Tōru slept.

Tōru awoke again in the darkness before dawn, shaken awake by a silent Obata.

Swords first, then history.

Again they battled all morning.

At noon, this time Obata indicated they should go into Lord Aya's study, where two small tables awaited them. They ate a silent lunch together at low tables, seated on the *tatami* mats.

"Copy this." Obata unrolled one of the scrolls he'd rescued from the stable, opening it to a famous passage about a final battle before the unification of the country. "Here to here."

Tōru spent a long time grinding his ink.

He had an industrial revolution to run, and he was sitting here grinding ink like Chinese scholars had done for thousands of years. The tutors his father had provided for him as a boy during his visits to Shimazu Castle were adamant about the importance of grinding the ink long and well. He feared Lord Aya might refuse his father's request to make him a *samurai* because he considered Tōru illiterate and unprepared. He knew his captor and host had grown fond of him, but he also knew Lord Aya resented the request from Lord Shimazu. He sought excuses to avoid making him a *samurai*.

So Tōru ground ink, lots of ink.

When he could delay no more, he copied the passage, writing in an elegant hand. He puzzled over a few characters, archaic ones he did not know well. Perfection was the standard, he knew. And he had not written a word except in his journal for two solid years. He did his best.

Obata sat silently reading.

Finally Tōru was done.

Obata examined his work.

Tōru could not read his expression.

Obata asked him questions about the passage. The leaders, the politics, the economics, the whys and wherefores of the period. He asked Tōru what the peasants thought of the leaders. He asked why the leader had chosen to fight a battle he knew he could not win. He asked if Tōru knew the poem the leader had composed on the eve of battle.

Tōru did not know the poem. He did not know what the peasants thought, or the lords, although he answered anyway. He dodged and parried the questions, flying at him as hard and fast as Obata's sword blows had landed on him in the morning. He answered questions until dusk darkened the room.

"*Mō ichido ashita,*" grunted Obata as he turned away.

Tōru bowed to Obata as he vanished into the dusk.

For ten more days, Tōru battled Obata with sword and brush. He was made to compose poems. He was forced to fight blindfolded against three men at once as they thrashed him with wooden training swords. He was made to ride to the far coast and back on his new horse in a single afternoon, a journey usually made in a day. He was asked about economics, marriage customs, the political structure of the Shogunate and how it relates to the Emperor and His court.

His head spun. Blisters opened on his feet and hands and thighs. His muscles ached all the time. His head hurt from reading all night and being bludgeoned with swords and words all day.

Masuyo did what she could, bringing him medicines and bandages and any intelligence she could gather about the next day's examinations. Jiro slipped him *saké* at night, although Tōru was too worn down to enjoy it much. Saigo Takamori brought him textbooks and notes from his own university days. Tōru thanked them, and struggled on.

Finally, on the eleventh day, as the afternoon drew on and the sun burned through the windows of the study, Obata suddenly stopped, mid-sentence in an arcane inquisition into the methods for assaulting high ground on horseback or with ground forces.

"*Ofuro.* You stink. Take a bath. Now."

Tōru bowed his thanks for the unexpected order and went to the baths. Surprisingly, he found a full hot bath drawn and ready. Usually the *ofuro* was only available in the evenings. When he emerged, his swords and ragged clothing were gone. He found instead a formal *hakama* and coat decorated in the crest of House Aya. He dressed and stepped outside.

All the retainers and *samurai* of House Aya were gathered up in rows, with war pennants flying. Tōru hastily smoothed his wet hair and stepped into the bright afternoon sun.

Obata, silent as ever, appeared at his elbow.

Together they walked forward to a dais, erected in the courtyard, upon which sat Lord Aya and several of his top retainers, along with his ally Lord Tōmatsu. They bowed to Lord Aya and his chief retainers.

Obata cleared his throat. He spoke louder and used more words than Tōru had ever heard him speak in all their time together.

"Aya-*sama,* as you requested, I have examined this Himasaki Tōru who was castaway and lived among the barbarian Americans for two years. I tested him in combat with *katana* and *shōtō* swords, with rifle and pistol, on horseback and on foot. I explored his knowledge of history, military tactics, geography and poetry."

Tōru stood ramrod straight as the torrent of words continued.

"His knowledge of history is weak. He is confused about several key domains in the East, but otherwise has a solid grasp of the geography of the Emperor's domain. He is eager to share his knowledge of foreign geographies. He is competent at calculations and mathematics and reads well. He writes a good hand, but cannot compose a poem or a coherent essay. I gave him several opportunities, but he failed them all."

Tōru braced himself for worse.

"He rides well, *this fisherman*, although how and where he learned this ability while fishing I was unable to discover for your lordship." Tōru wasn't sure, because he had never seen Obata smile, but he thought he saw the edge of a smile play at Obata's lips. "He can hit targets with bow and rifle at distances as well as any of your men can achieve, standing or on horseback. This *fisherman* has been trained by a master swordsman in single sword and double-sword styles, and performs superbly at both defensive and offensive *kata*. He is overly fond of foreign military ideas, but demonstrates an excellent grasp of our traditional tactics. He is an adequate archer. More focus and concentration would help him here as in many other endeavors. He is tainted by his foreign ideas and excessively eager to try new things before mastering the old."

"Obata, what is your recommendation?" Lord Aya asked.

Obata bowed low.

"Aya-*sama*, this *fisherman* is among the finest fighters of all your men, well-educated for someone of his youth and skilled in military tactics and strategy. Were it not for his absurd story of washing up on our shores after visiting the Americans, I would swear to you he was a son of a high-ranking *samurai*, provided with an ideal military education from birth. I recommend you claim his talent, strength and skill for your own, make exception to the hereditary laws governing our warriors, and name him a *samurai* of House Aya."

"Then let it be so!" Lord Aya stood.

The gathered men remained silent.

One of his retainers handed Lord Aya Tōru's *daishō* swords.

Obata held out his hands. A servant gave him a bare razor and bowl of soap and water. He signaled to Tōru, who knelt and bent his head before Obata. Obata shaved the top of Tōru's scalp, tying back what hair there remained into a ragged queue in an attempt at the *samurai chonmage* hairstyle.

"He has short American barbarian hair. He will have to grow his hair to be a proper *samurai*."

The men laughed.

"*Dōmo arigatō gozaimashita, Sensei*," Tōru spoke his gratitude to Obata-san. He was certain he saw a small smile as Obata nodded curtly and turned away.

Lord Aya stepped forward with Tōru's swords.

"Take these and wear them well, as a *samurai* of House Aya, Himasaki Tōru, cast up to us from the Western Sea."

Tōru knelt and swore oaths of loyalty to Lord Aya and his house.

He rose in his new garb, wearing his swords legally for the first time as a *samurai*. He turned toward the men. Lord Aya's fighters beat their weapons and banners and roared their approval. Saigo Takamori stood in their ranks, wearing his full armor and crest of House Shimazu, cheering for Tōru. Jiro, sooty and filthy as ever, had slipped away from his forges and mills to witness his friend's ascent. His broad smile was even bigger than usual.

And Masuyo.

Tōru had grown accustomed to her unconventional men's clothing and Jiro-inspired foul-mouthed jokes. He had come to respect her fierce intelligence and spirited defense of her ideas. He knew better than to challenge her on anything she had had more time to think about than he had. He had accepted her as a peer and friend, as he did Saigo Takamori, or his childhood friend Jiro. Their work together had eclipsed the fact of her womanhood and beauty.

He gasped when he saw her, then, standing off to one side. She stood under the shade of a pavilion, surrounded by her ladies. They were a flock of gaudy birds, all in their finest kimonos, trailing the long sleeves only young maidens wear, their hair oiled and piled high, flashing with glittering pins and jewels. Masuyo-*sama* looked like a princess, not the daughter of a minor *daimyō*. She looked like a goddess, flown down from some mist-shrouded mountaintop to witness his ceremony. She looked—she looked at him.

She met his gaze. She inclined her head to him in the smallest of greetings. Her usual widemouthed smile was instead a proper lady's slight curve of red-painted lips on a white-powdered face. Alien, and so beautiful.

Tōru stood, spellbound.

"I'm hungry, lad. Let's go eat." Obata cheerfully grumbled at Tōru and nudged him along.

A generous feast awaited the lords and men in the main hall. The men sang rude songs in Tōru's honor. They made him compose bad poetry and composed their own worse poems. Many bottles of *saké* gave all in the toasts to Tōru, his bad poems and the exploits of all the *samurai* of House Aya back into the shrouded mists of history. They ate and drank too much, long into the night. Finally the newly made *samurai* was carried off and put to bed.

A revolution that needed his attention could wait no more.

1852 — Autumn

CHAPTER 8

PREPARATIONS

"All things are ready, if our mind be so."
— William Shakespeare, *Henry V*

Tōru awoke the next morning at the usual pre-dawn hour for Obata's torment sessions, his head aching. He had done it. He had won Obata's support, enough to overcome Lord Aya's distaste at accepting an unlikely command from Lord Shimazu. Lord Aya had defied all tradition and named him a *samurai*.

He had knelt and sworn loyalty to Lord Aya before all his retainers.

He was no longer a castaway fisherman.

He was Himasaki Tōru, *samurai* of House Aya.

The Shogun would still take his head if he learned of Tōru's return from America.

Sobering thought.

At least this way he would be wearing a pair of swords when the Shogun's men came for him. They would not find a fisherman.

Tōru threw off the covers and dressed quickly in the chilly winter dawn.

He had to get back to work.

He had to be ready before the Shogun's men chased down rumors of a fisherman returned from America with Bibles and guns. Japan had to be ready before American warships steamed up to Edo and began firing huge at the capital. Russian, British, French, Dutch. It didn't matter. He had to be ready to face them all.

Masuyo was waiting for him in the lab, along with Jiro and Takamori. The two men roared another round of congratulations in spite of their own thumping heads. Masuyo was back in her customary unconventional clothing. This morning she wore a pair of black silk pants she had fashioned for herself on his sewing machine, patterned after the blue jeans she had found in his possessions. Tōru found the innovation fascinating but he was not sure if her father knew or approved of snugly fitted black silk pants on his daughter. All he knew is whether she wore a maiden's kimono or strange clothing of her own design, he found it increasingly difficult to breathe around her. Or speak without stammering. This was unfortunate, as they had much to do. He needed to be able to speak calmly with all his teammates.

"Tōru-san, ohayō." Her voice was soft and haunting as she greeted him, even as she slapped a long list into his hand. "Congratulations. We are happy for you, but we've lost weeks while you have been riding around playing warrior with Obata-san. We're falling behind on everything. I've come up with some improvements we need to make. This is a list of items we need. And here—," she handed him a stack of diagrams, "are some ideas Jiro and Takamori and I have been working on."

Her lovely voice went on, but Tōru caught only occasional words as she pointed at this diagram and that one. His head throbbed in its own insistent rhythm. Small sounds scratched the inside of his skull. "New inventions...Better Babajis...sensor devices...night vision eyepieces...automatic rifle...high speed dirigible...engineering school..." He gathered she wanted to build all these things. All he could see and take in to his foggy brain was the soft curve of her jaw and the way it rested atop her delicate neck. A long lock of ebony hair had escaped her messy bun and lay curled over her shoulder just so. He was pondering whether she would be offended if he reached out and tucked the curl back into her hair when he realized she had stopped speaking and was looking up at him expectantly.

He had no clue what she had just asked him.

Desperate, he tossed the question to his friend.

"Takamori, what do you think?"

"She's right. We've got to make the upgrades, even if it sets us back a few weeks. I'll get working on the imports we need. Jiro's already got some of the molds prototyped for testing."

"Let's do it then. Great work, Masuyo-*sama*."

He hoped they hadn't noticed his mental lapse. He hoped he hadn't agreed to anything stupid. He vowed to stay disciplined and focused on their mission. But she was so lovely.

A few weeks later, they had implemented many of Masuyo's inventions.

Tōru was particularly fond of the night vision eyepieces. Wearing them, a team could travel as fast by night as by day, without torches. Her improvements to the Babaji allowed integration with the telegraph system. Calculations could flow to the factories and merchants needing them, allowing just in time delivery of materials on still slender transportation channels.

Train tracks now connected Lord Aya and Lord Tomatsu's domains. Regular shipments chugged back and forth on narrow gauge rails between the domains. Gangs of track-laying workers raced to meet tracks growing from each of the allied domains.

Curious laborers swarmed into towns where the alliance was building factories and laying track, eager to find work. Frightened at first by the strange sights, villagers who would never have considered leaving their ancestral homes were now fighting to be added to the various crews building out new factories and train tracks. Women, too, were clamoring to join the textile and sewing factories, and to work the Babaji computers, although the women from good families refused to enter the *geisha* houses. Soon Babaji and telegraph offices were sprouting on the respectable main streets of alliance towns, full of village women swiftly tapping out messages and tending the great mechanical calculating machines.

The telegraph system now snaked through off-road paths cut through forested valleys to connect Lord Aya and Lord Tōmatsu's domain to the east, toward the road to Edo, as well as all five of the original allies to the west. A separate line ran southwest to Lord Shimazu's stronghold in the far southwestern corner of Japan. Babaji

Difference Engines, safely hidden in *geisha* houses in each of the allied domains and tended by the working girls in their off-hours, cranked away. Information flowed smoothly to a growing network of factories, foundries and merchants, triggering action all bent on a single goal: arming the southwestern coastal domains against the foreign threat.

Tōru nodded with satisfaction as he pored over the reports from yesterday's production. His gun factory was already testing prototypes of Masuyo's automatic pistols and rifles. Train cars were rolling out of a foundry run by a good friend of Jiro's at the rate of one per week. Tōru needed ten or twenty cars per day to move even a tenth of the rising tide of cargo they needed to ship, but it was a good start. Jiro never complained when he thanked him for something and then asked him for ten times more. He just shrugged, made a crude joke and went off to find his crew and figure out how to deliver.

Textiles and lacquerware flowed from their network of factories to Lord Shimazu's traders, who sailed with them to Asian ports where they were converted into silver and gold, yuan and pounds and dollars. The returning ships strained under loads of manufacturing equipment, weapons and parts Jiro and his team couldn't make themselves yet. Takamori worked around the clock with his contacts in Lord Shimazu's far-flung trading network to keep up with Masuyo's ever-growing demands for exotic parts and books to guide her innovations.

Tōru had not forgotten his beloved sewing machine. Under his prodding, Masuyo had disemboweled the precious machine and painstakingly reverse engineered all its delicate parts. Next he had asked Jiro to make him one, using the first as a model. Here he ran into a giant, stubborn, sooty stone wall.

Jiro liked casting giant things. Command him to create huge train engines or mounted cannons or even entire warships and he was in his element. Ask for tiny fine-tolerance parts and the blacksmith edged away making excuses.

After weeks of relentless requests from Tōru, and endless excuses from Jiro, the stalemate was finally broken when Jiro found a watchmaker for Tōru. Tanaka, as the nearsighted clockmaker was called, the only one in all of Japan, made a thin living copying and repairing with hand-cast parts the occasional watches, clocks and mechanical devices smuggled into Japan for *daimyōs* curious enough about the West to risk being caught with Western gadgets. Tōru summoned Tanaka to their lab and gave him the task of figuring out how to manufacture sewing machines at scale, with near perfect precision. Tōru wanted 100 to start, with bigger ambitions to follow.

The sewing machine factory he ordered built in his hometown of Iwamatsu. Tōru longed to go see it himself, but until the train system was in place, he could not be spared from his duties. He managed his impatience by checking on Tanaka's progress each morning before starting his work for the day.

Tōru and Saigo Takamori locked the lab behind them as they left after a long day. Masuyo had declared the evening off, for they were all weary and starting to make stupid errors and grump at each other. She had disappeared into the castle to dine with her father for once, instead of with the three young men as she usually did.

Takamori shouted to Jiro as he walked out of the main gate of Lord Aya's castle.

"Going into town?"

"Yes. The girls are waiting for me!" Jiro grinned broadly. "I promised them I would visit after work."

"Mind if we join you? I'm thirsty. Need a break."

Jiro motioned welcome.

The three young men set off toward town in comradely silence, weariness dampening the conversation though not their moods as they walked. Tōru turned to look back at Lord Aya's castle, now surrounded by dozens of buildings and tracks. He shook his head in awe of all that had been built in so short a time.

"You've done a great job, Jiro. *Gokuro.*"

Jiro smiled with satisfaction. A false humility had never been one of his faults. "We are building something great, for sure. Soon we'll have the dirigibles too."

Tōru laughed, the laughter of exhaustion. "Soon we'll have the dirigibles, too," he repeated numbly, too tired to be excited. He felt overwhelmed with all the next steps that would create. "We'll have to figure out how to fly them. We have no pilots."

Takamori shook his head. "Of course we do. Jiro here can fly them."

Jiro brightened at this fine idea.

While he enjoyed being an engineer and the production chief, the dirigibles had fascinated Jiro ever since he heard of their role in Tōru's plans. Jiro wanted to fight the evil foreigners as much as Takamori or Tōru did, but he knew the *daimyōs* would never let him be a *samurai*, even if an exception in such matters could be made for someone unique like his friend Tōru. Jiro nurtured a secret wish to join the battle against the foreigners from the deck of a dirijibi. In his secret reading and writing sessions with Masuyo, he dutifully worked through the *kanji* characters Masuyo made him memorize each day so he could write in his own language and create plans and diagrams for his workers to use. Afterward, he always asked to see the English diagrams for weapons and French plans for dirigibles.

Since neither Jiro nor Masuyo had any idea how French or English sounded, they made up their own pronunciation. Both were becoming adept at puzzling out the English words and sentences and their meaning, enough to guide their engineering efforts. Jiro found the twenty-six Roman letters a vastly simpler task to learn than the several thousand *kanji* characters a stern but patient Masuyo insisted he needed to learn. Jiro took extra pains to work his way through the French dirigible plans, for it was his job to build the first dirigible. Masuyo joked that he was better at reading French than Japanese, a statement that while not quite true yet, was swiftly nearing truth.

Masuyo had to test his reading skill carefully, for Jiro could often fake his way through by understanding the English and French diagrams even if he had no grasp of the foreign letters. In any case, his reading and writing lessons only fed Jiro's desire to create and master these marvelous flying ships the foreigners had imagined. Jiro jumped on the opening Takamori had given him.

"*Hai*, I could fly them for sure. I've been studying the diagrams, and the foreign newspaper stories about the first flights—"

Tōru scoffed. "What do you mean studying the newspapers? You mean the pictures?"

Jiro reddened. He had not meant to leak news of his secret new skill yet. "Yes, the pictures. And Masuyo explains the articles to me. The principles of flight and navigation are easy. We just have to—"

"He's the only one who can fly them, Tōru," said Takamori, taking Jiro's side. "I know I don't understand how they work, and I am pretty sure you don't either. Just because you heard of them first doesn't mean you understand them better than any of us."

This time it was Tōru's turn to redden as he was forced to admit Takamori was right. "The *daimyōs* would never allow it. He is a commoner. A blacksmith. You've heard them—the officers and leaders have to be *samurai*, and *samurai* of rank!"

"Yes, he is a commoner. He is a commoner like my ancestors were commoners and everyone thought you were until few weeks ago. What of it?" said Takamori.

"The *daimyōs* insist only high ranking *samurai* can command as officers or fly the dirijibi," said Tōru. "I've argued with them for hours. They are giant stones who won't budge."

"Don't argue with a *daimyō*. That is your first mistake. You just make them stubborn if you do that. Do you think I got Lord Shimazu to send me to you by arguing with him? Of course not! I merely made it obvious that I was the only person he could possibly send and then leapt to obey when he commanded me to go!" Takamori grinned.

Jiro followed the conversation closely, wondering how Takamori would make it possible for him to fly the dirigible. The frame of the first prototype was rising just outside the castle gates, each day appearing more like the photos in the foreign newspapers.

"Rather than argue with them, you should invite them to make the first flight with you," said Takamori. "At first they will agree, since it is their place as the leaders. Everyone is very excited about the dirigibles. Set the time and place for the first flight. Jiro should explain that is not a good time because of the wind or something technical that needs testing first. You argue with Jiro and perhaps even scold him for impertinence in front of the *daimyōs*."

"Yes, I am often scolded for impertinence," said Jiro. "I have a talent for it, you know."

"Indeed you do," said Tōru. He saw where Takamori was going. "Then they notice the risks and uncertainties...and they ask me if it is safe. I tell them honestly that we have no idea if it is safe or if it will work, and that we might all crash to a fiery death and therefore perhaps I should test it first myself before we endanger them."

"And I will be impertinent again and tell you in front of them that you don't have a clue how to fly one of these dirijibi!" Jiro finished the plan for them. "Which is also true, by the way. I know how to fly one of these, and you don't."

"You've never flown one either," protested Tōru.

"I have built one. Almost. Soon. How many have you built?" asked Jiro, with his broad grin.

Tōru opened his mouth and closed it again.

"See? Problem solved," said Takamori, as he pounded Tōru on the back. "We have a fine dirijibi pilot, the finest dirijibi pilot in all of Japan, our good man Jiro here. Now let's go get a drink, and meet some girls!"

Back at Lord Aya's castle, Masuyo and her father enjoyed their first private family meal in many weeks, eating together without company or retainers as they used to do before Tōru came and disrupted their peaceful life. Lord Tōmatsu had returned home for a few days, tugged by urgent messages from Lady Tōmatsu about the poor health of their young son. Masuyo and Lord Aya spoke of many things, the small things that families, even great families of noble lineage, discuss when they are alone without visitors, like repairs and local gossip, enjoying each other's company after the long spell of frantic activity.

After a third helping of fish and *tempura*, Lord Aya leaned back with satisfaction. He regarded his daughter as he took a sip of tea. She smiled, pausing in her story of the new cook's difficult personality and how she upset all the other household servants on a daily basis.

"You look happy, *O-tō-sama*. What are you thinking about? It is not our disagreeable cook, I can see that."

"Ah *Toranosuke*. No, I was not thinking about the cook. You've grown into a fine young woman. Your mother would be so proud of you. You are—you are more like her every day, the way you move and speak and think. She was so...alive, so lively, like you."

Masuyo bowed, a little shy suddenly at her father's burst of words. "I am glad you find me so, father. I know I upset you so many times, working on our project. I try very hard not to anger you, but I cannot be a well-behaved lady playing my koto and practicing calligraphy all day when we have so much to do!"

"I know, Little Tiger. You belong in your lab, I see that."

Masuyo looked at her father, her eyes suddenly moist at the supportive words she had not expected to hear from him. More often he was helplessly scolding her.

"I worry about you. How will I find someone to marry you if you are in your lab all the time dressed like a peasant boy chanting drinking songs with Jiro?" Lord Aya sighed. His little daughter, now grown into a lovely young woman, was his world and had been ever since the loss of his wife. He could not bear to make her unhappy by forbidding her the lab and her work.

Masuyo laughed. "Maybe I don't need to marry! I will stay here and take care of you, *O-tō-sama*. That would make me very happy."

"You will want to marry someday," he answered. "It happens, once you are ready, and the wanting takes you by the throat and lets you think of nothing else."

Lord Aya gazed off in the distance at an old memory.

"Not me, father! I am happy here, with you, and my lab, and my friends Takamori and Jiro and Tōru. I don't need a husband."

"Speaking of Tōru, what do you think of him?" asked the old lord, suddenly struck by a series of images he had not put together before. Tōru stammering every time Masuyo entered the great hall. Tōru staring off at his daughter under the pavilion's shade the day he was named *samurai*. Tōru always glancing behind him as he rode or practiced fighting with the other *samurai* to see if Masuyo was watching. Now a new image joined these, even more disturbing.

His lovely daughter blushed as red as the crimson of the kimono she was wearing. "Tōru? Oh, he is fine. A good friend. I admire him. He is very clever, don't you think?" Suddenly she gathered up the used dishes and cups onto a tray and rushed into the kitchen, leaving Lord Aya alone with his newly disturbed thoughts.

The team oversaw their growing network of factories, Babajis, train tracks and telegraphs from their lab. The four friends could usually be found in one corner or the other of the vast lab. The high-ceilinged room, bridged overhead by long wide beams from the mightiest trees in Lord Aya's lost forest, was jammed with tables and desks and workbenches scattered with diagrams, plans, gadgets, devices and prototype equipment in various states of assembly and experimentation.

The mad clutter assaulted the eyes and overwhelmed the brain, even for those who toiled there every day and understood the many projects strewn about. In response, Masuyo had decreed one corner of the otherwise dreary workroom be left as a retreat space for the team, a place where they could rest and think and eat, away from the tumult of the workspace.

Behind sliding *shōji* doors was a serene and near empty room, six *tatami* mats in size, with a low table and a *tokonoma* alcove adorned with a single scroll and an *ikebana* flower arrangement. Masuyo tended to the *ikebana*, refreshing it from day to day. Tōru marveled at her ability to go from engineering track switches and clambering over engine blocks in clumsy muddy boots inspecting Jiro's handiwork to sitting in perfect stillness before the *tokonoma* as she transformed a ragged pile of greenery and flowers into small and exquisite works of ephemeral art.

Late one afternoon, Tōru, Jiro, Masuyo and Takamori ate their lunch in Masuyo's quiet room off the lab. They had spent the morning fine-tuning Tōru's design improvements for his dragon dirigible airships.

Jiro had survived the maiden voyage of their first prototype dirigible, more or less, although he now had a rather dashing scar on his left temple. The dirijibi had only suffered minor damage in the crash as well, and they soon had it back in the air. The burn scars on Jiro's left hand where he had used his bare hand to make an emergency repair to the steam engine were healing nicely as well. Jiro had won the right to be test pilot on all future flights, now that they all realized he was the only one who could actually fly them for now, let alone repair them in mid-air.

Now they argued over strategy for using the wondrous flying machines and defending Japan with their new guns.

"We need guns trained on every harbor where foreign ships might try to make landing. Lots of guns, and bigger guns than what we have now," Takamori insisted. Takamori's master, Lord Shimazu, knew the foreigners better than any leader in Japan, through the contacts made by his vast trading network and his oversight of his vassal state, the Ryukyu Kingdom. Lord Shimazu believed forcible entry by the foreigners was a matter of months away, not years, and only guns would protect Japan.

"We don't have time to build defenses to hold off a real assault this year. We're better off bluffing. We just need a display of enough unexpected capability to frighten the foreigners away. That will buy us time to construct real defenses," countered Tōru.

While they argued, Jiro concentrated on eating vast quantities of fish and noodles, slurping with gusto as he ate. He didn't care what they decided. He liked building both guns and airships. He was happy to crank out both as long as Tanaka took charge of fiddly bits like control mechanisms and firing pins.

"When do Lord Aya and Lord Tōmatsu leave for Edo?" asked Takamori, between bites of excellently seasoned fish over steaming rice. Under the Shogun's decree of *sankin kotai* or alternate attendance, every *daimyō* had to spend alternate years in residence for six months in the capital. Their wives and heirs also had to live in the capital, as hostages under a polite guise of welcome guests. Lord Aya had no wife and no male heir. As a minor *daimyō* in a quiet part of the country, possessed of modest holdings and insignificant capacity to mount a rebellion, the requirement that Masuyo live in Edo to answer for his behavior had long been overlooked.

In Lord Tōmatsu's case, his wife's family's close ties to the Tokugawa clan and service in the *bakufu* allowed Lady Tōmatsu and their infant son to avoid this onerous requirement as well. She stayed in the country with Lord Tōmatsu, in unwilling obedience to her husband's wishes. She would much prefer to be in Edo, enjoying the capital rich with the culture, fashions and political maneuvering her family so enjoyed.

"As soon as they return at the end of the week," Tōru answered.

The two *daimyōs* had become inseparable friends and allies, much to the consternation of Lady Tōmatsu. Lord Tōmatsu refused to tell her why he was traveling so much accompanied by an insignificant *daimyō* of little wealth and less power.

Her attempts to learn more were thwarted by the courteous bland replies of his loyal men. As she wrote to her brother, "He is a changed man, suddenly much involved with matters he refuses to discuss. Armed men come at all hours of the day and night. I fear he will put us at risk. When we come to Edo, you must reason with him, and ensure he does not anger the Shogun. Help me, brother. We both have much to lose if he defies the Shogun." Her messenger rode hard to the east bearing her letter, taking advantage of her husband's absence to depart.

"I will be going as well," announced Masuyo. "The *bakufu* has commanded my father to bring me to Edo this time. It seems we are no longer overlooked and forgotten."

Tōru and Jiro exchanged a look. Tōru had shared with his childhood friend his concern for Masuyo, and his relief that she had not been made a Shogunate hostage thus far.

"When did you learn this?"

"The messenger came yesterday. With Father gone, I received him and thanked him for the Shogun's kind invitation."

They all sat silent, pondering this news.

"Did he give you the impression the Shogun knows of our plans?" asked Tōru. "Or is it mere happenstance, or you coming of age earlier this year?"

Masuyo shrugged. "He said little. I said less."

Saigo Takamori leaned back and stared at the ceiling. "Are we walking into a trap? Or are our plans still secret?"

"Every blacksmith in the country knows you are building trains," offered Jiro. "Every geisha is learning to program your Babajis instead of practicing *shamisen* or their dances. Every bartender can pound out Mōrusu Cōdo for the telegraph. Obviously it is all very secret."

"Seriously, how could the Shogun and the *bakufu* not know?" asked Tōru.

"They know. Count on it." Takamori cleaned his bowl carefully, leaving not a scrap, his large frame constantly in need of more nourishment.

Tōru rubbed the back of his neck. "Then why haven't they come to arrest us?"

"They wait until we go to them. Less trouble for them that way. Plus there must be some who are glad we are working on this. Maybe they are slowing down those who want to arrest us."

Takamori hunted around for more food.

"Everyone talks about our projects. Work for anyone who can walk and talk, enough work to feed their families — you cannot keep that a secret," said Jiro. Jiro's good sense and connections to the common people always grounded their discussions. He never let them get too theoretical. "Think about it. You've got mysterious wires and tracks running every which way, with thundering engines roaring along, scaring the chickens and making the dogs howl. Then you have illicit traders on the coast buzzing with unusual new orders pouring out of the countryside. Even the dogs know we are up to something."

Takamori pondered this. "And among the richer commoners, we've got dozens of bright young sons of merchants learning to be engineers. Yes, the Shogun knows for sure. But look on the bright side. Maybe by the time he comes to arrest us all, we'll be so far along we can't be stopped? Even if we all lose our heads, everyone likes the trains, the telegraph and the Babajis. They will outlive us."

"Pleasant thought," said Tōru, his neck so raw and red he had to stop rubbing it.

"What difference does it make? All we can do is work as fast as we can for as long as we are allowed," said Masuyo.

"Right. Besides, what can they do to us?" asked Takamori.

"Besides kill us, you mean?" asked Jiro. "Or kill you all. They won't bother with me. I'm just a commoner." He gestured with a pork bun and spoke through a full mouth. "It's you fancy *samurai* who get chopped."

"Let them try," bristled Takamori.

"Easy for you to say. Satsuma is as far from the Shogun's reach as is possible," said Tōru. "Lord Shimazu has one of the biggest armies in the country, after the Tokugawa clan. You're right. You are probably fine. It's Lord Aya, Lord Tōmatsu and, well, me, who will get chopped. The Shogun can reach us, and hurt us badly."

On this somber note, and with all the food now vanished into Jiro and Takamori, the friends went back to work, harder and longer than ever. Time weighed on them, for they did not know how long their luck would hold.

Lord Aya and Lord Tōmatsu were now fully dedicated to the cause of waking up Japan to the foreign threat menacing the island realm, come what may. Lord Tōmatsu's greater wealth and family connections allowed them entrée to all of the western and southern *daimyōs*. Lord Aya's passion and superior knowledge about the foreigners from Tōru made him an eloquent advocate for their cause. Together they made an unstoppable team, as long as the Shogun did not get wind of their activities.

Entrusting operations to Tōru and Saigo Takamori, the two *daimyōs* and their representatives, Obata and Sugieda, traveled up and down the western and southern domains seeking support for their plan to re-arm Japan. An additional eight *daimyōs*, greater and lesser, had pledged their support in addition to the original five allies. Others had promised to consider the matter. None had rejected their request outright, or denounced them to the Shogun. Even those who did not formally join them were now quietly building weapons factories based on designs perfected by Tōru and Masuyo, and laying train tracks and casting engines guided by blacksmiths trained by Jiro. Babajis manufactured in Lord Aya's domain were being carefully transported to each realm, along with equipment to build telegraph stations, to tie each domain into the growing network.

Everyone involved faced the same risk—execution for treason. The more *daimyōs* who joined the effort, the greater the punishment for illegal re-armament Lord Aya and Lord Tōmatsu faced.

They had moved beyond the harmless collection of forbidden books and novelties like the clocks and gadgets collected by Lord Shimazu's grandfather Shigehide and other leaders of his generation. Urged on by Lord Tōmatsu and Lord Aya, each new *daimyō* in their clandestine alliance committed to take on the risk of death and quietly defy the Shogun by strengthening coastal defenses within their own domains.

As western lords, they saw the same facts that drove Lord Aya and Lord Tōmatsu—the increased trading activity by foreign ships and the carving up of once mighty China by the foreign powers. Enough books, weapons and other Western technology had been smuggled into Japan that they could see for themselves what they were up against if the foreign powers began to press more forcefully for open borders. Japan may have been declared closed, and ordered so by the Shogun, but its leaders were not ignorant of the outside world. Quite the contrary; they were acutely aware of China's sufferings as the foreign powers dismembered and humiliated her. Many *daimyō* wanted the Shogun to lead and take action to protect Japan from a similar fate.

The Shogun and his squabbling council spent their power keeping themselves in power. They sat atop a quarrelsome pyramid of *daimyōs* obsessed with their own parochial interests. The Shogun's councilors focused their energy on court politics instead of facing the growing and obvious threat from abroad. When a leader no longer protects his people from their greatest threat, he forfeits legitimacy. Lord Aya and Lord Tōmatsu found fertile ground for their plans and ideas as they quietly pointed out the Shogun's failure to meet this most basic test of leadership.

And so, in the west and south, telegraph lines and train tracks tied the co-conspirators together in undeniable and unbreakable bonds, each lord gambling that by the time they were inevitably discovered and condemned, it would be too late for the promised punishment of death. They argued to themselves that their fellow *daimyōs* would see them as loyal heroes, defending the Shogun and the Emperor's realm, rather than traitors, and pressure the Shogun to grant clemency and a change in policy. Either way, they hoped they would together be strong enough for the battle that mattered, the battle against the foreigners.

CHAPTER 9

⊕

DEPARTURE

"A ship is safe in harbor, but that's not what ships are for."
— William G.T. Shedd

At the end of the week, Lords Aya and Tōmatsu arrived as expected, dirty and exhausted from weeks of hard riding gathering more allies and solidifying the waverers. They did not stop to eat or wash, but gathered straightaway with their key retainers and the team, including Masuyo, in Lord Aya's main council hall.

"We ride tomorrow," announced Lord Aya. "We must not seem to hurry, but move at a usual pace and draw no attention. Lady Tōmatsu, their son and our Masuyo travel with us, per the Shogun's command."

He could not hide his concern for his daughter, for them all. "Only a blind man could miss our activities. The Shogun is many things, but blind he is not. We must assume the Council is aware of our plans. Since we have not been arrested, we assume the Council is divided. Their disagreement buys us time, but not much."

"Then let us make our case directly to them! We now have two dozen *daimyōs* who have joined us, who work day and night to re-arm and protect the Shogun's realm. We are aiming our guns outward to the sea, against the foreigners, not east toward the Shogun. Surely the others will flock to our banner us once they understand the facts. They will see we are loyal. Then we would have over a hundred domains preparing to defend the realm against the foreigners," Tōru burst out, forgetting his place.

Lord Aya did not bother to reprimand Tōru, inappropriate though his outburst was, from a junior *samurai* to his lord. Time was short, and matters urgent.

"You are young, and still believe the world to be ruled by wisdom and justice. The world is ruled by the powerful, not the just and not the wise. The Shogun loses power with every gun we build, believing we might turn those guns against him. Our intentions do not matter if he fears us more than he fears the foreigners. And the Tokugawa do fear members of our alliance, especially Lord Shimazu of Satsuma."

"But if the Council is divided, we do not stand alone."

"The Council's division is the only thing keeping our heads on our shoulders this long. Challenging the Shogun in open Council is impossible. Even those who agree with us will not protect us if we threaten to disrupt the Shogun's peace. No, we must go and make our case quietly, outside the Council hall, one by one. Tōru, can your people keep production on track with you gone?"

"Yes, my lord. Jiro knows what we need. The men will follow him."

Lord Aya continued, "I had thought to leave you here, Tōru, to keep you safe. There is no safety anywhere, though, and we will need you to help us convince the other *daimyōs*. Only you have spoken with American military officers and read their newspapers and seen their factories. Any chance of mercy for a poor fisherman is long gone. If we are to make this case, you must risk your neck alongside mine."

"Of course, my lord."

Lord Aya turned to Takamori, Lord Shimazu's man.

"And you, Saigo-*san*. Does your lord recall you to Satsuma or do you travel with us?"

Saigo Takamori bowed low. "My lord asks that I be allowed to travel with you. He suggests I go in guise of one of your men, wearing your *mon*, if it please you, my lord. His men have a way of being followed and watched with particular care by the Shogun's men." The lords laughed, relieving the tension in the room.

"Two and a half centuries since Sekigahara, and the Tokugawa Shogun still does not relax his watch on Satsuma," Lord Tōmatsu chuckled as the men joined in. Ieyasu Tokugawa had defeated the Shimazus of Satsuma and claimed the Shogunate centuries ago, but the *tōzama* outer lords had never grown accustomed to submission. The smile did not linger long on Lord Tōmatsu's face. Serious decisions awaited discussion.

"Please convey our thanks to Lord Shimazu for lending us your assistance." They all knew Satsuma's support for their plan was both powerful and polarizing. Some *daimyōs* looked to his clan for leadership; others expected trouble. Both expectations were usually met. They would have to share news of Satsuma's involvement carefully and strategically. "Obata, assign Saigo and Himasaki to your unit. Keep them out of sight."

Obata bowed to his lord and nodded to the two young men.

"Get some sleep."

The next morning, in the gray misty light of dawn, Tōru and Jiro stood by the train station in Lord Aya's domain, proud and happy. Soot-covered as usual, even though he rarely got to stand before his beloved forge anymore, Jiro barked final orders to his engineers. They would be driving the train while he stayed behind to command the continued manufacturing and transportation operations. Jiro was so capable that no one ever debated whether he could lead and command others as the humblest of commoners. Everyone just did as he ordered.

Tōru and Jiro had disobeyed Lord Aya and gotten no sleep at all. Rather they had worked through the darkness with the engineers and workmen to connect up the longest train they had ever attempted. A first for them, a first for Japan. A dozen cars, for the men, servants, supplies and horses traveling to Edo.

"You're sure you can pull all this with a single engine?" Tōru asked Jiro. He was anxious. The lords were trusting his technology. The train needed to work or his whole plan would lose credibility.

"I told you it will pull and it will. I'm an engineer, not just a blacksmith." Jiro had grown proud of this Western title of engineer, believing it bestowed on him a certain status no blacksmith could ever hope to attain.

Tōru had not discussed his plan to take the train with Lord Aya. The lords were too weary for discussions of logistical details after their long ride yesterday. He hoped they would accept it, for taking the train instead of riding to Lord Tōmatsu's domain would take a few hours instead of several days of hard riding over bad roads. It being easier to seek forgiveness than permission, he had ordered the grooms and workmen to load the horses and baggage onto the train cars. The horses were upset, but not as upset as they were going to be when the train began to move.

Masuyo's *norimono* palanquin and her boxes of clothing were already loaded. She was hovering nearby, managing the loading of the baggage, dressed as a demure woman of rank in flowing kimono under her protective warm *dōchūgi*, since they would be traveling in public before many curious eyes. No black silk jeans for a while. Her dark traveling *dōchūgi* only made her pale skin and black eyes contrast more enchantingly in the silvery morning light.

Tōru tried not to notice her. She made it hard to concentrate. He had much to think about and manage.

Tōru paced, anxious to see the lords' reaction to his plan.

"Where's my horse!" bellowed Lord Aya. His groom was always waiting for him with his mount ready on journey mornings. His groom, who did not approve of trains, and who was adamantly opposed to horses on trains, looked miserable standing horseless in the courtyard.

"Himasaki-*san* ordered me to load him on the train..." stammered the poor groom, bowing deeply.

"Tōru ordered what?"

"Aya-*sama*, I've arranged for us to travel the first leg of the journey by train." Tōru bowed low, hoping humility would soften the blow of his unapproved action. "We can reach Lord Tōmatsu's castle by lunchtime, instead of riding for three days. Everything is ready to go. If you would follow me, I can show you your seat."

Lord Tōmatsu joined them. He too was looking for his horse.

"We cannot ride by train! The horses, all the baggage, the womenfolk," Lord Aya blustered as Tōru knew he would. Tōru knew Lord Aya enjoyed the idea of trains and being the center hub of Japan's first train network in theory. But he was also aware the traditional old lord intensely disliked the noisy, sooty, disruptive reality of trains and missed his forest and its peaceful stillness. He suspected Lord Aya feared the trains but would rather die in battle pierced by a thousand blades than admit the fact.

"I've arranged a private car for your honorable daughter and her ladies, sir. Please allow me to show it to you. This way, if you would, sir." Tōru kept bowing as he led Lord Aya and Lord Tōmatsu to inspect the ladies' car. The outside of the car looked like all the others, black iron and wood with a row of windows on each side.

Once inside the clanging metal outer door, however, the passengers entered a peaceful and elegant haven. In a special extravagance ordered by Tōru, Jiro had supervised a team of highly skilled workman and seamstresses to create a haven for the noblewomen on the loud train. As they stepped up into the train and through a heavy iron and glass door, they were met by a tiny entranceway of polished blond wood, impeccably finished and smooth. Two low rows of open shelves on one side held slippers, new and sized for ladies' small feet. Empty shelves on the other side waited to hold their outdoor footwear.

Tōru slid open the inner door to reveal the narrow interior. All the windows were curtained to protect the ladies from prying eyes, but the bright cheerful fabric let in plenty of light. Polished wooden walls and brass fittings glowed by the light of glass-covered brass lanterns, still lit in the early dawn.

Half the car was filled with soft padded Western seats, covered in fine leather, firmly fastened to the floor. Cunning metal trays were fastened to the back of each seat.

"Please remove your footwear and step inside. I was not sure how the ladies would like to sit, so I made half in the American style, with seats like this." He showed them the seats up front. He demonstrated how the little trays could be unfastened to open down and serve as a tray for the passengers in the seats behind.

"See, they can eat their lunch or enjoy tea on these trays." Tōru spoke quickly, nervous about how the lords would respond. They looked all around, fingering the trays and the soft leather of the seats. They said nothing, but pushed further into the room and stood on the tatami, pulling back curtains to look at the men gathered outside for the departure.

The back half consisted of four *tatami* mats, floor seats and cushions.

"If they find the Western seats uncomfortable, they can sit here in the back, on the *tatami*. I've padded the walls around the edge. Here are handles they can grip for balance as the train goes around curves and slows down or speeds up." Padding, covered in the same soft leather as the seats, about shoulder height for a passenger seated on the floor, protected the walls and provided something for the ladies to lean against as the train swayed and rattled along its tracks. Brass handles for balance, low and at waist height, glowed under the lanterns.

At the back of the car, large sturdy lacquered chests were fastened to the floor. Tōru opened one and gestured for the lords to look inside.

"Here is food prepared by the cooks for the ladies' refreshment. And in this one, *futon* sleeping pads and bedding if we travel by night." Tōru waited for their response.

"Did my daughter put you up to this? Masuyo!" Lord Aya growled, yelling for his daughter, who remained outside supervising the baggage loading.

"No, no, sir! It is a surprise for her and her ladies. I wanted them to be comfortable on their first journey."

Lord Aya grunted and continued his inspection. He tugged at the curtains, pulled the trays down and fastened them back up. He blew out lanterns. He opened the food chest and inspected the *futon* chest. He sat on the *tatami* mats, wiggling his outstretched toes, and then tried out a Western seat up front, leaning back and adjusting the seat to the sleeping position.

The *daimyō* sucked in the air between his teeth, making a low whistling sound. A thoughtful sound, not an angry sound. Tōru decided to view it as a sign of approval.

"Shall I invite the ladies to board, sir?"

"No! My daughter is not going to—"

"*Hai, O-tō-sama?*" Masuyo slipped into the car and looked around. She smiled with delight. "*Nanto utsukushii!* It is so beautiful! Is this how the American ladies ride, in cars like this?" She performed the same inspection her father had, running her long slender fingers along the brass fittings and pulling the curtains open. She peeked in the boxes and tried out a seat.

"*O-tō-sama,* is it not wonderful! Let us go! The Shogun is waiting!"

Lord Aya sighed and turned to Tōru. "You are smarter than you look, boy. Tell the men to load up. We go now."

Tōru bowed deeply. "Immediately, sir. I can show you where you and Lord Tōmatsu will ride, and your men. If we leave within a few minutes, we can be at Lord Tōmatsu's station by noon."

Lord Tōmatsu laughed and caressed a smooth wood panel. "At least you can enjoy a bit of your forest in these walls, Aya. I agree. Let us go by train. If we are to be revolutionaries and defeat the Westerners, we need to ride noisy metal carts pulled by monstrous engines like they do. We'll beat my rider announcing our arrival by a day or two. My wife, ah. She doesn't like surprises. We'll deal with her when we get there. "

The horses were as upset by their ride on the train as Lord Aya's groom feared they would be. Their loud whinnies and anxious shifting about in the stalls Tōru had built for them created a cacophony in the horse cars. Their cries were drowned out only by the warning whistle as the train pulled out of the station and began its trek to Lord Tōmatsu's domain. Terrified themselves, the quaking groom and his assistants rode with their trembling charges, attempting to sooth them.

As the single engine strained against the weight of a dozen fully loaded cars, the train moved slowly at first, chugging out of Lord

Aya's station. His entire household, less those on the train, turned
out to see the sight of their lord riding on the barbarous foreign train.
Fear showed grim in their eyes as their lord boarded the belching
beast. Lord Aya maintained a solemn dignity for his watching people
as he stood in the doorway of the car reserved for the two lords and
their chief retainers. Lord Tōmatsu, ever cheerful, grinned like a
child with a new toy as he moved about the car inspecting each
feature.

Tōru had designed a less luxurious car for the lords. Their car
was still comfortable and tidy, glowing in soft polished wood and
the warm glint of polished brass fixtures. It had no entranceway or
tatami, and the lords and their men did not remove their
footwear as they entered. Their windows had no curtains.
Curious men who opened the windows swiftly slammed them
shut as the smoke from the engine blown back by the wind
poured black soot into the car.

Most of the car was taken up by Western-style benches, firmly
fixed to the floor, padded a bit, but less softly and in a leather more
coarse than the seats made for the ladies. In the back, Tōru
provided a pair of chests, fixed to the floor. One held food, as for
the ladies, and the other held maps and other materials used in
their planning discussions. He had made a large tray, similar to the
trays fixed to the seats, but larger, designed to swing down from the
back wall of the car. When opened down and flat, parallel to the
floor, the tray served as a table to hold a map or other materials the
lords might review as they discussed strategy.

"I need one of these," announced Lord Tōmatsu with
satisfaction as he settled himself into a seat near Lord Aya. "No, I
need ten of these. I shall cover my whole domain with train tracks
and review every one of my villages myself. I'll need plenty of horse
cars, because we need to ride with proper dignity at the other end,
but this way the horses will be fresh when we arrive. Please have
your Himasaki design a nice ladies' car for my wife as well. As soon
as we can build trains openly, we'll get a line built right alongside
the *Tōkaidō* main route to Edo. I can ship her off to visit her brother
in Edo whenever she pleases."

"Ah, yes," Lord Aya murmured politely in reply. His thoughts were elsewhere. He had seen the concern and astonishment on his peoples' faces as he departed. He knew they were not upset merely by the novelty of seeing their lord on a train. He knew, and they knew, that he and his men were heading into danger with every clattering roll of the wheels toward Edo and the Shogun's center of power.

He was troubled that the Shogun had made no move against him, or more likely, Lord Tōmatsu, who was a great enough *daimyō* to draw notice. Neither was near the stature of the great Lord Shimazu of Satsuma, but the Tokugawas had not ruled as Shoguns for two hundred and fifty years by ignoring violations, large or small, of their policies by any *daimyō* in the realm. Rather the Tokugawa Shoguns were famous for punishing the smallest infractions with swift and certain death. He was certain by now the Shogun knew of their frantic activities of the past year. Lord Aya was equally certain the Shogun did not like what he knew. The lack of response troubled him. What was the Shogun planning for them? Why had he allowed them to get as far as they did before sending the summons for their presence and that of Masuyo and Lady Tōmatsu and Lord Tōmatsu's infant son?

And Tōru.

As much as Lord Aya grumbled at the young *samurai*, he had grown fond of him. The brash young man had become in many ways the son he had always longed for.

Like any *daimyō*, Lord Aya needed a male heir, a son, a capable and intelligent son, to carry on and protect his domain after him. His wife's death at Masuyo's birth had cost him that dream. His mother, while she lived, had urged him to remarry, to get sons, but he never found the right woman. All the women in his area of sufficiently high lineage to marry a *daimyō*, even a minor *daimyō* of merely moderate resources, were either fiercely ugly, of unstable mind or unwilling to take on another woman's daughter. The pretty and sane ones young enough to bear children wanted husbands more their own age. Or if they cared not about youth, they wanted a richer, more powerful husband. He was proud of his well-organized and neatly tended small *han* domain, but he could not compete in the noble marriage market as a middle-aged widower with a daughter and a *han* of modest size.

If all these reasons were but flimsy excuses and Lord Aya could in fact win a suitable wife, he had not tried. In truth no one could replace Masuyo's mother in his heart. They had met for the first time days before their great wedding. They had been fortunate, and loved each other deeply for the few brief years they shared before her death. Lord Aya had loved his squalling red-faced daughter with fierce black eyebrows from the moment he first saw her. As she grew into a delightful intelligent girl and then a lovely young woman so much like her mother, he never had the heart to afflict her with a stepmother who might be cruel to another woman's beautiful daughter. So he had no sons, no male heir, a troublesome reality that he mostly ignored but knew he must face someday.

The Japanese were practical about such matters. Families lacking a suitable son routinely adopted strong male heirs into the family to protect a *daimyō's* realm, or in the lower classes, a merchant's business or a farmer's land. For all her rebellious ways—and he had destroyed the black silk pants himself when he glimpsed his daughter wearing them one fine morning—Masuyo was beautiful and well-behaved enough in public to attract a suitable husband. Such a *mukoyōshi* adopted husband-son would be perhaps a second son of another *daimyō* with no realm to inherit but appropriately educated and trained to rule. Such a marriage would cement his ties to another *daimyō* and provide him with the needed heir. The time to find Masuyo this husband was soon approaching, a reality underlined by the Shogun's summons of his precious daughter to the capital as she came of age this past year.

Lord Aya could not help but imagine adopting Tōru as his heir. His mysterious birth and lack of proper lineage were insurmountable barriers, of course. Even a minor *daimyō* is still a *daimyō* and his daughter a *daimyō's* daughter, with certain unyielding expectations about suitable families to marry.

The castaway had shed his fisherman's accent and bearing within weeks of washing up on his shore, adopting an educated accent and rich vocabulary to match his fertile active mind. A proper and well-educated *samurai* Tōru was to all eyes and in all ways except the all-important matter of birth. The old lord admired the young man's energy and intelligence, his loyalty and passion to defend Japan, his curiosity and love for all things new and his respect for tradition. He had noticed Tōru's recent awkwardness around his daughter and felt for the poor boy. She was a *takadai no o-hana*, an unreachable flower in a high place, far above Tōru on the mountain of social station. Naming Tōru a *samurai* was a rare aberration in the normal order of things, an act unheard of for generations. It happened occasionally, when a lord urgently needed the assistance of a lower class man of great warrior abilities. But no ceremony or swords could grant Tōru the fisherman the birth he needed to marry a girl like Masuyo. The old lord knew it even as his thoughts kept returning to the idea.

Lord Shimazu's unusual behavior merited consideration as well. Why would such a mighty *daimyō* take such an interest in a castaway fisherman? One answer was obvious, although impossibly far-fetched—that the boy was his own illegitimate son, born of a lower class woman and hidden away in a remote fishing village. While such a birth was not unheard of for men of his class, such fathers ignored such sons, not educating them, after seeing to the meager living needs of the woman with a farewell gift suited to her station. Someone had lavished a lord's education on Tōru. Obata swore it to be so, and the crusty old retainer only stated what Lord Aya could see with his own eyes as he saw the boy fight, grapple with the foreign books and lead the whole re-armament operation.

But if Tōru was Lord Shimazu's son, or nephew, or even a high retainer's son, why would he educate him but not claim him? He needed an heir just as Aya did, and concubine's sons or retainers' highly capable sons could be claimed in adoption and their status elevated. His wife's family would fight such an adoption, of course, especially as she still was young enough to bear a son for him. However, a lord in need of an heir with a healthy capable adult son from any source would do what he needed to for protection of his domain. Lord Shimazu's delicate noble wife had borne him a frail daughter a year or two ago, and he had adopted a highborn girl left orphaned, but he still had no acknowledged son. Therefore Lord Aya did not believe Tōru could be Lord Shimazu's natural son.

Were Lord Shimazu's strange gifts and requests regarding the orphan boy instead due to his interest in foreign matters? A possibility, to be sure. The Shimazu clan had long been known for two things, beyond their great wealth and power. First, a fierce and bloodthirsty persecution of Christians, feared for their loyalty to a distant and foreign pope. Second, for an unseemly fascination with all things foreign, from gadgets and weapons and books to trade and warships. Geography on the far southwestern coast of Japan and their resulting proximity to the trade routes drove some of this interest. The Shimazu clan was unique in all the clans in Japan in having as a vassal an independent kingdom, the Ryukyu Kingdom. So the canny Lord Shimazu was possibly just collecting Tōru, an illegal and precious returnee from America, as his grandfather Shigehide had collected Western clocks and mechanical devices a half century before.

Lord Aya sighed. It was a mystery and would remain such, for Tōru refused to say a word about his mother after finding her home barren and ruined. He answered no questions about his father except to say he had last seen him on the night of their shipwreck. Lord Aya had quietly sent Obata back to Iwamatsu to learn more of the boy if he could, but old Obata came back no wiser than before about the boy's parentage. Any fantasies about adopting the supremely capable young man, whatever his origins, were just that, fantasies. He did not want to endanger the young man who had become as dear to him as the son he longed for in his dreams. But it was necessary, for he and Lord Tōmatsu needed the boy's testimony about the reality of America to sway the other *daimyōs*, so obstinate and resolutely blind to the rising foreign threat.

Before he knew it, they had arrived at Lord Tōmatsu's domain. The party tumbled out of the train into a pouring rain.

After a short ride to Lord Tōmatsu's gate, slipping through puddles and mud, the servants led the dripping horses away to the stables. The company filed into the grand home. To Lord Tōmatsu's astonishment, fifty men not his own were camped outside the gate, looking miserable in their tents with no fires against the late fall chill. Lord Tōmatsu looked at them curiously, but no officer met him and no challenge growled through the rain, so they passed by the encamped soldiers.

Lady Tōmatsu met them at the *genkan* entryway. With a tightlipped smile she greeted them with deep bows and ushered them inside. Servants helped put away their wet cloaks.

"*Okaeri-nasaimase,*" she said, bowing to the *tatami* mats with perfect courtesy to her husband and Lord Aya as the lords stepped up into the entryway with their men. She did not meet her husband's eyes. "My lords, you have a visitor, Kato-*sama.*"

Kato, a wizened old man in the rich flowing robes of a senior bureaucrat and *samurai* past his fighting prime, bowed low to his host, Lord Tōmatsu. "Lord Abe Masahiro sends his respects, Tōmatsu-*sama*. And this letter, for your eyes only, sir." He handed over a small silk pouch containing the letter. Lady Tōmatsu's eyes never left the small packet as Lord Tōmatsu tucked it away in his sleeve. "Our Lord Shogun is most eager to meet with you and learn more about your...activities here in the West. News of your trains is on every lip in Edo."

"Welcome, Kato-*sama*. Please meet my friend Lord Aya." Bows were made and greetings murmured. "And your master, Abe-*sama*, he is well?" Lord Tōmatsu maintained perfect calm as he ushered the unexpected messenger to a place of honor in his receiving room.

As the lords and their guest settled in, each sitting at individual small tables, Lady Tōmatsu supervised her ladies and servants. Tray after tray of exquisite food was brought to the lords and their men, and to Kato, emissary of Lord Abe.

At a glance from Lord Aya, Obata had hustled Tōru and Takamori out to the stables, where he kept them busy with the grooms unloading the horses, keeping them far from eyes sent all the way from Edo.

"You are so kind to inquire," said Kato, bowing low to his host. "My lord is well, thank you. His days are long, serving our lord Shogun. Word comes from every corner of the realm, of foreign traders, foreign technology, foreign plans. We live in restless times, my friends, when everyone speaks of change and no one agrees what that change should be." He paused to sample the offerings from Lady Tōmatsu's kitchen. "My good Tōmatsu, this is exquisite! The best chefs in Edo could not produce such delicious fare."

Lord Tōmatsu bowed thanks for the compliment. "Please forgive our plain country food. We are so far from the center of things, we cannot offer you the delicacies found in the capital."

Kato took a sip of *saké*, nodding slowly as though considering the merits of Edo cuisine.

A silence had fallen in the full hall, as Lord Aya's and Lord Tōmatsu's men watched the formal dance of diplomatic discussion. The presence of an emissary from the Shogun's Council, a senior aide to *rōjū shuza* Chief Presiding Councilor Abe Masahiro himself, was a unique occurrence in all their memories. Such high-ranking bureaucrats did not travel so far to the west, not in person. Rather the lords of the west were summoned to Edo, the eastern capital.

As they disembarked from the train, no one had missed the sight of Kato's escort of fifty armed men either, settled into their camp outside Lord Tōmatsu's gate. Were their lords to be arrested? Should they defend their lords from this visitor from the Shogun's court? His men were outside, fully armed, while they were inside, without weapons, as is customary within a lord's hall.

"I'm curious about this great iron engine you have constructed. After you have refreshed yourselves from your journey, perhaps you will offer me a tour?" said Kato, breaking the silence. "As you know, my lord Abe is interested in *rangaku* Dutch studies and the technology of the foreign barbarians. He wishes to learn from you how this machinery works. I saw with my own eyes its power, as it drew all the carts full of your lordships, your men, your baggage and your horses. Impressive."

Lord Aya bowed low. "I would be honored to show it to you. Many flaws remain—we are struggling still with the design and our casting methods. But it does work, after a fashion. You have seen its strength." He bowed again and then pressed forward with a bold comment. "It is our humble hope we might assist the Lord Shogun in strengthening the realm through the use of these technologies."

This drew the whistling sharp intake of breath indicating thoughtful consideration from Kato. "Yes, these technologies, they are powerful. The powerful and the new, such things can create fear, you must understand." He paused before continuing, as though debating within himself. "As our time is short, I will speak frankly. Our lord Shogun, Defender of the Realm, is not pleased with the news of your foreign engine. He is most curious...as to how you came by the design. He would inquire of you why your sudden activities have so...consumed you. Much travel, much building, much activity in what was once such a...quiet and peaceful place. These steps...you have taken...without the usual consultations. Most irregular."

Lord Tōmatsu opened his mouth to speak. Kato held up his hand to silence him. Lady Tōmatsu hovered by the door, pretending to supervise servants carrying food and *saké* to the men.

"Say nothing here. Many eyes and ears follow you closely. But listen well. Our Lord Shogun is not pleased. I am here, though, not at his request...but under strict command of my Lord Abe, chief councilor to the Shogun. My lord has sent his own men to escort you safely to Edo and protect you from any...untoward...actions from men loyal to the Shogun. He has many young men in his service, hotheaded young men who might act...hastily...in their desire to please their lord. You will need to meet with the Shogun yourselves and explain your activities. My lord cannot prevent the meeting for you." Kato bowed low. "Nor can he determine its outcome." When he spoke, he raised his voice loud and commanding, an echo of the commander he had been as a young man in Lord Abe's father's service. "At my Lord Abe's command, I will see you safely to Edo." Kato's gaze met and held Lady Tōmatsu's gaze in his own across the hall. She broke eye contact first and fled the room.

Kato leaned in close to Lord Tōmatsu. He whispered, "Sir, your wife has betrayed you and sent word through her brother to the Shogun that you rebel against his rule. You must be watchful at all times, in front of her and any men with you who are loyal to her clan.

My lord Abe is in sympathy with your intentions and goals, for he agrees with you on the imminence of the foreign threat...and the need to improve our technology. But he cannot save you from the Shogun alone. He can protect you for the journey, but once in Edo, you will need to convince the Shogun himself of the purity of your intentions. Or die a traitor's death."

1852 — Winter

CHAPTER 10

TŌKAIDŌ

"There ain't no journey what don't change you some."
— David Mitchell, *Cloud Atlas*

The journey to Edo and the waiting Shogun from Lord Tōmatsu's domain took several weeks. First was a short trip of four days to Kyoto, where the Emperor lived in quiet seclusion. Never appearing outside his shadowy court, the mysterious ruler lived out his days surrounded by nobles of ancient houses in service to the Imperial family for centuries.

The procession had to travel slowly, as there was no train line yet to Kyoto. Lady Tōmatsu and Masuyo and their ladies had to be carried in their *norimono* palanquins by bearers on foot. Their group made an impressive sight, with Lord Aya and Lord Tōmatsu leading the way, accompanied by Kato. Along with the hundreds of *samurai* under their commands, cooks, grooms, bearers and other servants filled out the ranks of the procession.

The lords rode with impressive solemnity, faces impassive, and their men likewise, slowly winding along the narrow country tracks that passed for roads in this less developed part of the country. Such processions were common in Edo and in Kyoto, but as they passed through the countryside on the way to Kyoto, whole towns turned out to watch them pass. Over two hundred armed *samurai* on horseback protected the lords, between Kato's escort and Lord Tōmatsu's men.

Lord Aya had brought just a handful of men to protect Masuyo while the remainder of his men remained at home, guarding his lands in his absence. His retainer Obata led this small guard, and kept Tōru and Takamori hidden from the observant eyes of Kato and his chief commanders.

Once they reached Kyoto, they found their way through the bustling narrow streets full of merchants and travelers to the *ryokan* where they intended to lodge during their time in Kyoto, a planned several days to refresh themselves before the two week journey along the *Tōkaidō* coastal road to Edo. Kato warned them to be cautious and guarded, and never to walk about the streets unarmed or alone. He himself was in a constant state of alertness, watching faces and hands and weapons. Lord Tōmatsu did not seem to notice or care, but Kato's vigilance made Lord Aya uneasy.

The *ryokan*'s proprietor hastened to assist the lords and warriors with stabling their horses in his vast stable. His servants escorted the *samurai* to the barracks-like rooms where they would be staying while the lords and ladies stayed at the *ryokan* proper. He bowed nearly to the ground in his eagerness to please the prosperous and well-armed group.

Once the women were safely settled and the lords seen to their rooms, Obata and Sugieda led Tōru, Takamori and a dozen of Lord Tōmatsu's and Lord Aya's men to the market to purchase supplies for their journey.

"It would be safer if you went in the morning, with a larger group," said Kato, when he saw them assemble to leave.

"We still have an hour of light, and the streets are full. No one will bother a dozen armed men." Sugieda bowed to Kato. "Do not worry, my lord. We will be watchful."

Tōru had visited most of the major cities of America, but never Kyoto, the ancient capital of his own people. Merchants called welcome "*O-koshi-yasu!*" Near Gion, the red-light district they passed on the way to the market, lower ranked *geiko* and their servants running errands tottered by on their tall *okobo*, swaying in a manner the group of young *samurai* found most appealing.

"Stay alert!" Obata growled a warning and steered the young men away from the area they found so tempting. Tōru, less distracted by the *geiko* than the others, still found his eyes darting not from alleyway to doorway watching for enemies but from shop to shrine to temple as each new shiny attraction presented itself. Every corner boasted its own Shinto shrine or Buddhist temple, surrounded by merchants selling fine lacquerware, pottery, *omiage*, silks, tea, and every other imaginable good.

Maintaining proper military awareness seemed unnecessary under the assault of riotous color, rich scents, sing-song calls of the merchants, the distant pounding of drums and bells at the thousands of temples and shrines. Tōru relaxed and let himself take it all in, for how could there be danger in such a crowded and festive place? Just as he was pointing out to Takamori the border of the imperial park, a blow shattered the festive excursion.

Aoki, one of Lord Aya's men who had been walking alongside Tōru to his left, suddenly crumpled and fell to the ground. Tōru had barely noted Aoki's fall before a black clad and masked man was suddenly in his face, dagger flashing. Instinctively he ducked. He whirled away and drew his own katana with a smooth unbroken gesture, as he shouted, "Attackers!" to his companions.

Takamori was struggling with another fighter to his right, dagger on dagger in a close-in grip. Obata and Sugieda shouted commands to their men as a wave of warriors burst out of an alleyway in the dimming light and fell upon the group. The other men formed up in a loose circle, backing each other up as the black wave washed over them.

Tōru took down his own attacker with two swift blows, messy awkward blows, not elegant strikes like his sessions with Obata, but workmanlike slashes sufficient to leave the man motionless and bleeding on the dusty ground. He leapt to shield Takamori from a second fighter bearing down on his friend from behind. Their own opponents down, Tōru and Takamori joined their companions in loose formation, methodically taking down attackers one by one.

No solo heroics, no glorious one-on-five battles, just precise and powerful brutal bloody blows focused on the skillful dancing enemies whirling around them, darting forward to pierce and wound and then slipping back to attack again.

Tōru and Takamori teamed up, grunting warnings to each other as they protected their fellows and bore down on the dark devils one at a time, leaving them bleeding in the dirt.

The group formed a knot around Aoki, their fallen companion. Yamagata fell too, when he foolishly turned his back to the alley as he circled an enemy. A masked enemy burst out of the dim alley and slashed his neck, stopping him mid-step as he crumpled and fell to meet Aoki. He was the last to fall, though, as Obata, Sugieda, Tōru and Takamori and the other men gradually overwhelmed and defeated their attackers.

It was hard, sweaty work.

Tōru's arms grew weary as the companions fought for endless long minutes against men as skilled as themselves but twice their number. Finally it was over. They could stop to breathe, gasping huge gulps of air as they stood, gathered around their fallen companion, hyper-alert now, watching for another wave of attackers from the street or the alleyway. What had seemed moments before to be an endless fight was now but a moment that had flickered like the flash of a rifle in the night.

It was dark now, or as dark as it gets in a bustling city, where every merchant hangs out his lantern. Obata sliced the black garment on the breast of one of the fallen enemies to reveal the *mon* crest beneath. The three hollyhock leaves of the Tokugawa clan gleamed up at him in the flickering light of a nearby merchant's lantern. He spat. "The Shogun's men. Or someone wants us to believe so. Or are they arrogant enough to reveal themselves deliberately this way?" He motioned to the squad to get Aoki and Yamagata before police and other authorities arrived, and led them back the way they had come, bearing their wounded and fallen with them swiftly in the dusk.

At the *ryokan* inn, Masuyo and Lady Tōmatsu and their ladies were ushered inside to the women's wing by the bowing wife of the proprietor. Masuyo's room was next door to Lady Tōmatsu's room. As serving girls knelt to slide open the doors for the two noblewomen and their ladies carried in their traveling trunks, Masuyo bowed to the older woman.

"I trust your journey was comfortable, Lady Tōmatsu?" she inquired politely. They had no opportunity to speak together much along the road, traveling as they did in their individual *norimonos*, shielded from the prying eyes of the townspeople they passed along the way. The regal noblewoman still intimidated the young girl. Masuyo had made up her mind to overcome her fears and connect, if she could, with Lady Tōmatsu.

"Ah yes, indeed, thank you. And you found the journey not tiring?" Lady Tōmatsu's reply, while perfectly correct and courteous, was delivered with a stiff smile under cold eyes. Masuyo would rather die than complain, but riding in the *norimono* was a jarring, hot, cramped torture she had endured for four days. But then, so had Lady Tōmatsu. Masuyo wished she could ride out in the open fresh air like the men, but knew her father would never permit such a scandalous action. Her joy at being able to stretch her limbs at last found its way into her reply.

"Oh no, I found it quite exciting! I've not traveled beyond my father's domain before, so to see Kyoto at last, where His Highness our Emperor and His court live, and to enjoy all the towns along the way...I cannot be tired, for there is so much to see!" Masuyo's nervousness and youth made her run on with awkward enthusiasm. She slowed to silence, embarrassed at her outburst and bowed deeply to the other woman. Lady Tōmatsu inclined her head the slightest bit, as her ladies carried her boxes into her room.

"So you've not been to Edo, then. Poor child, to have no experience in the capital. It's a shame your father has not seen to your education more suitably. Letting you run about like this—"

Masuyo flushed at the insult, and involuntarily looked down at her best traveling kimono, which had been fashionable when her mother wore it a generation ago. She could not summon a suitable reply but bowed to hide the anger in her eyes.

The grand dame continued her faux sympathy.

"I suppose it is not your father's fault. I'm certain he wants the best for you. Men simply do not grasp the details we women must master to present ourselves properly. I would be happy to introduce you to some kimono makers and jewelers of quality when we reach Edo. My husband informs me we have no time to shop here in Kyoto. Such a shame. The southern textiles are the finest in all Japan. But do not fret. We can work on your attire properly once we reach Edo."

"I would be much obliged," managed Masuyo, knowing the invitation was not intended to be accepted. She vowed to herself she would rather be kidnapped by foreign pirates and taken to America than be taken on a humiliating shopping trip with the snake-like Lady Tōmatsu.

To Masuyo's surprise, the older woman waved off her servants, who had arranged her room for her during the brief conversation with Masuyo. "Very well, thank you. To your rooms, and the baths, now, with all of you. I'll join you later after I rest." Lady Tōmatsu continued, "Masuyo-*sama*, perhaps your ladies would like to join mine?" Masuyo nodded to her ladies that they too could go.

"Come, have some tea with me," commanded Lady Tōmatsu, indicating Masuyo should join her in her room. Masuyo dutifully bowed and took her seat at the low table in Lady Tōmatsu's spare but elegant room. Lady Tōmatsu poured steaming green *ocha* into Masuyo's cup, and then her own. She placed tiny artfully decorated sweets on a small wooden plate. "Please, help yourself."

Masuyo bowed thanks and picked up her tea cup, hiding her eyes as she bent to take a tiny sip of the steaming fragrant *ocha*. She was thrown off-balance by the attention from this woman who had so repeatedly made clear her scorn for Masuyo herself, and for her father. Tomboy, inventor and budding scientist though Masuyo was, she was also a woman of good breeding and education, exquisitely attuned to social cues appropriate to her birth and class. She was anxious not to embarrass her beloved father with social disgrace by offending the higher-ranking lady. *What did Lady Tōmatsu want?* The answer was not long in coming.

"I hear your father has elevated the fisherman to be a *samurai*." Lady Tōmatsu paused to unwrap a delicately paper-wrapped tiny sweet. She popped it whole into her mouth, rudely eating before her guest as though Masuyo were a lowly servant. Masuyo said nothing as she frantically considered and rejected possible replies. She sensed danger for Tōru with her whole body.

"How awkward it must be! Forced into the company of a man of such low birth. Your father should not embarrass his house or shame you this way." Protests rose up in Masuyo. She knew how intelligent and educated and resourceful Tōru was. She knew her father was proud of Tōru, even though he himself had protested Lord Shimazu's request to elevate him.

"Himasaki...he is a skilled swordsman," she stammered by way of defense. A *samurai* was, after all, a soldier at the end of the day, and Tōru was undeniably good with his weapons. She instinctively knew discussing his other talents, and his experience with the Americans, was not safe for Tōru. On her guard, Masuyo resolved to reveal nothing harmful to her father or dear Tōru.

"Swordsman! Anyone can flash a blade around. A *samurai* is more than his swords. Your father ought to know better, a man of his background." Lady Tōmatsu sniffed. Energized by her little speech, she unwrapped a second sweet, impolitely gluttonous, as her guest had yet to touch a first sweet. She waved one at Masuyo. "There, child, have one, please."

Masuyo bowed thanks and slowly reached for a sweet, unwrapping it with undue care, stalling for time. As she pulled back each delicate corner of the fine paper wrapping, she pondered how to reply. She could not contradict the older higher-ranking woman. Lies would be punished. Information about Tōru would be shared with the wrong ears. What to say? How to respond? Insipid courtesy provided a way out, as it often does. She struck her blow.

"How exciting to see the capital! I am sure Lord Tōmatsu maintains a beautiful estate in Edo. Are you looking forward to being there?" For all its girlish breathlessness, it was a masterful series of strokes. She had offered her opponent an opportunity to be condescending about Masuyo's lesser experience outside her hometown that Lady Tōmatsu could hardly resist. She had made a compliment that must be countered with a humble denial of any beauty in her husband's estate even by the higher-ranking woman. And she had asked a question demanding a polite and affirmative reply, for no loyal subject of the Shogun could deny any joy at visiting the capital. Lady Tōmatsu would have to fight through three thickets of conversational bracken just to return to her line of inquiry about Tōru. Anything could happen in the meantime to save Masuyo from further grilling.

The older woman glared at Masuyo in frustration before brandishing a thin steely smile. She relentlessly marched through the defenses Masuyo had thrown up, an implacable foe.

"It is a great pleasure to arrive in the capital in time to arrange one's affairs before the New Year's celebrations are upon us. So much to prepare! You have not seen the capital during New Year's, have you? At my father's home—," Lady Tōmatsu's long-winded discussion of the fine excellence of the celebration in her childhood home was interrupted by a furious shout below. Both women rose in alarm and left the room to look over the hallway balcony to the entry hall below.

Tōru, Takamori and a handful of Lord Aya's and Lord Tōmatsu's men staggered into the hall, several of them bleeding visibly, some being carried by their companions on their backs. Tōru helped one of Lord Aya's men to a seat on the floor.

"Bring hot water and bandages. Hurry!" shouted Tōru to the *ryokan* proprietor's wife, who was bustling about near the door.

She ran off to get help.

"Himasaki! What happened?" cried Masuyo from above.

Obata answered for him. "The Shogun's men attacked us, near the Imperial Park. Aoki and Yamagata were killed." Only then did Masuyo notice the two men laid out straight and still, their eyelids smoothed closed and their hands crossed on their chests, across bloody garments. Blood seeped into the worn wood of the entryway.

Obata gestured to Tōru. "Lord Aya and Lord Tōmatsu. Bring them quickly."

Tōru bowed and whirled around to leave. He shot a miserable glance up to Masuyo, who glided down the stairs to the entryway below, graceful yet swift in her slim kimono. By this time, the proprietor's wife and her serving girls had returned with hot water and poultices and bandages for the wounded men. Masuyo quickly knelt and began assessing the surviving men's wounds, tending to the most severely wounded. Her soft but firm commands soon had the *ryokan's* serving girls cleaning the men's wounds and binding them up. She looked around for Lady Tōmatsu, but the grand lady had vanished up above. *Too bloody*, supposed Masuyo. Maintaining one's distance from lower ranked human beings is too difficult when they are desperate and torn bloody with suffering and pain.

Masuyo looked around and stood up.

All the wounded men were now bound up and resting, drinking tea or sipping hot soup brought by the serving girls. One by one, as they were able, they left to go to their barracks, supported as necessary by their fellows. Masuyo and Obata together draped borrowed sheets of soft cloth over the two dead *samurai*.

Obata motioned for four of their fellows to carry the two stiffening bodies to a quiet back room, where they would be prepared for return to their families. Once the fallen *samurai* had been taken away, only Masuyo, Takamori and Obata remained. Ever the responsible commander, he looked at Masuyo.

"Lady Tōmatsu, she is here, she is safe?"

"Yes, Obata-*san*. She was with me just now."

"Good. Keep her close. We must leave here soon."

Lord Aya and Lord Tōmatsu stormed through the entrance, Kato by their side and Tōru trailing in their wake.

Obata bowed to his lord. "I am sorry. I lost Yamagata and Aoki. The others will heal. Lady Aya and Lady Tōmatsu are safe."

Kato drew in his breath in a long low whistle. "I would not think they would attack so brazenly here in the Imperial City. In daylight! Disturbing the Emperor's peace...Where were you and your men?"

"In the market, sir. Buying provisions for the journey. They came at us from all sides. No warning. Were it not for Himasaki and Saigo, they would have done worse." In his pride at their defense of the group, Obata had forgotten to hide their presence from Kato, who seemed not at all surprised. "They defended our wounded like dragons, yielding nothing until we could gather ourselves and get away. I believe we took down a dozen and more of their men, killed or severely wounded."

Lord Aya nodded to Obata and to the two young men. "Prepare to leave at dawn. Tōmatsu, Kato, your men can be ready?" Both nodded grim agreement. "We will buy supplies along the way."

The attack sobered them all. They cut short their stay in Kyoto and set forth at dawn as agreed for Edo, planning to cover the nearly three hundred miles of the *Tōkaidō* coastal road in a fortnight.

Usually the journey along the *Tōkaidō* was a festive affair, a leisurely procession of several weeks with frequent stops to enjoy the sites and sample the food and drink at the way stations along the well-traveled road between the ancient imperial capital and the Shogun's eastern capital Edo. Famous shrines, temples and ancient castles stood at each stop along the way, teeming with the gaudy bright confusion of fellow travelers and pilgrims and merchants selling food, drink and *omiage* souvenirs to the multitudes of travelers passing back and forth between the two capitols.

Even when the group was well-armed, in normal times the *samurai* would be relaxed, knowing no bandits would disturb them, nor rival lords attack them on the Shogun's well-policed road. The lower ranking *samurai* would spend their evenings enjoying the *saké* houses and less expensive *geisha* establishments while their officers pretended not to notice. But these were not normal times, and the sight of the three hollyhock leaves of the Shogun Tokugawa clan's crest on occasional groups of other *samurai* did not ease their anxiety. Rather it increased their vigilance.

At night, the women were ushered into fine *ryokans* with guards posted outside their doors. The men did not stay inside, but rather posted watches and pitched tents outside town as though they were on a military campaign, taking turns to visit the public baths in groups large enough to defend themselves. The officers did not allow drinking or revelry, but ordered the men to rest, the better to arise early each day and cover the needed distance. Supply patrols went in force to the markets, with twice the number ordinarily sent to obtain the needed goods. Half to carry, half to defend.

Kato and the two lords discussed much on their journey. Kato shared what he could about the different Council members and who might be likely to support them and oppose them. He in turn had many questions about the technology and their plans. He never asked about a fisherman, nor did he pry into the reasons for their sudden flurry of activity, contenting himself with understanding what they were doing.

This relieved Lord Aya and troubled him at the same time. Was Kato's reticence about Tōru due to ignorance? Did he simply consider him just another of his men? Lord Aya doubted it. His concern for Tōru's safety continued unabated.

Lord Tōmatsu and Lord Aya volunteered nothing they were not asked, taking care to be precise and careful in their responses to Kato's endless questions. Kato had a genuine and deep interest in the technology, and was fascinated by all they had done. Still, no matter how passionately he inquired of Lord Aya and Lord Tōmatsu about their progress and listened with great intentness, he never abandoned his fierce vigilance, a battle-hardened commander's sixth sense, often spotting potential ambush points and sending his own riders ahead to investigate. At night he posted his own sentries alongside those of Lord Tōmatsu and Lord Aya, explaining more eyes meant more eyes alert.

Their vigilance paid off, and the procession made its way safely into Edo on the evening of the fourteenth day of their journey from Kyoto. Officials of the Shogun saluted Kato at the entry gate to the city, knowing the old bureaucrat well. They checked the procession's documents without interest and did not even ask the ladies to descend from their *norimonos* for personal inspection. It was not difficult for upper class women to enter Edo, only to leave it. Their passage through the gate was swift.

Once in Edo, they made their way through narrow winding streets of the bustling capital to Lord Tōmatsu's home, a spacious wooden structure with elegant spare gardens and ample stables and barracks all hidden behind a discreet high wall.

Lord Aya maintained no residence in Edo, since his need to be there was infrequent. He and his party accepted Lord Tōmatsu's offer of lodging. Lady Tōmatsu had scarcely climbed out of her palanquin before she was readying herself to go visit her brother. Masuyo was relieved to be free of Lady Tōmatsu's supervision.

"I'll leave you now,"said Kato. "You'll be safe within your own walls, guarded by your own men. Do not go out on the streets. Your audience with the Shogun and his Council is in three days."

Lord Tōmatsu bowed his thanks. "We appreciate your protection and your insight, Kato-*sama*."

They had come to trust and appreciate the old man. In spite of Kato's reticence on the matter, they believed Kato and his master, Lord Abe, were sympathetic to their cause.

The constraints on Lord Abe and his man Kato were many and rigid. Lord Abe could not be seen to be thwarting the will of the Shogun, but it was also his duty to bring before the Shogun and the Council opposing views and the necessary information to guide the Shogun's decisions.

Abe rode a fine line, balancing between the powerful Shogun and the Tokugawa clan, the Shogun's enemies, the threatening foreigners and his own opinions about what they should do to meet the threat. He was an adroit political warrior, always maneuvering to get decisions and outcomes to go his way without showing his fingerprints. Abe and Kato could not save them, nor even argue openly for their cause, but they had already proven themselves to be shrewd and helpful allies.

Kato counseled them to meet with several other councilors before their meeting with the Shogun, to test the level of support or opposition to their proposed plan. "Better if the Councilors, especially those of major stature, express support for your plan, or propose it themselves. Better still if they are known to be loyal to the Shogun."

Kato had given them suggestions of Council members known to be both loyal to the Shogun and concerned about the foreign threat. He had sent messengers on ahead. His messengers were awaiting the group at Lord Tōmatsu's gate. They brought word that Kato's introduction had secured Lord Tōmatsu and Lord Aya audiences with a half dozen potentially sympathetic councilors before the meeting with the Shogun.

Kato bowed in return to Lord Tōmatsu and Lord Aya. "My lord Abe respects you for all you have done. I know he wishes you well in your conversations. He will need to be...circumspect...in his public comments, understand. He awaits you tomorrow."

Lord Aya and Lord Tōmatsu bowed their thanks, as did their chief retainers clustered nearby, as Kato and his men saddled up and rode out under the darkening sky.

Later that evening, Tōru went out to see to his horse. As he fed the great stallion slices of apple, he whispered farewell, in case they did not return from Lord Abe's home and the meeting with the Shogun. A sudden crash startled him, as Masuyo's palanquin, stored for the night in an empty stall suddenly flipped over and landed at his feet. A straw-covered Masuyo followed, trying to set it right. A long slim bundle as tall as a man was fastened to the underside of the palanquin.

Masuyo glared at Tōru. "Why are you here?"

She stomped over to her palanquin and tugged at the leather-wrapped pole. The fastenings held. The pole would not come free for her. She struggled with it some more, as Tōru approached.

"What is that?" Tōru gently pushed her aside, and untied the fastenings with a quick small tug. "Oh, Masuyo-*sama*, you didn't..." The daimyō's daughter had broken the Shogun's law and smuggled her *naginata* pole blade into Edo.

Masuyo glared at Tōru, her guilty expression making her look quite fierce.

"What exactly are you planning on doing with that?" asked Tōru. "You cannot take on the Shogun's forces all by yourself. You are fortunate we were not examined more closely at the gate."

Gently he tugged it away from her and unwrapped the weapon, examining its shining blade under the flickering lanterns of the stable. The *naginata* was of beautiful make and venerable age, an inherited gift from an earlier time when the women of aristocratic houses trained to defend the keep and their virtue should their men and the outer walls fall.

"It is a fine blade. You have practiced with it?"

Masuyo nodded, embarrassed at getting caught. "It was my mother's. Father allowed me to train with it for these past ten years. I am...quite good with it. I thought I might have need of it here."

Tōru handed it back to her and helped her wrap it up again. "We can hide it in my horse's stall, see, up here above?"

He climbed up and tucked it up into the rough bamboo and thatch construction of the ceiling. "Can you reach it down from there if I am not here to help you?"

Masuyo climbed up a little way on the stall's wall and was able to tug at one end.

"I think so. Don't tell Father. He will only worry."

"Of course I won't tell him. Don't worry so much. You won't need that here. Lord Tōmatsu's men will keep you safe during our stay. I will explain everything to the Shogun and the Council and we will be made heroes, just in time to defend the realm from the foreigners. You will see." Tōru made his voice hearty and his tone confident, wanting to comfort her. Wanting to comfort himself.

"You don't know that."

Masuyo stuck out her chin in that stubborn pose she took so often, a pose that had become dear to Tōru.

"You don't know that I won't," said Tōru. "Let's go back inside. We've a long day tomorrow no matter what. And then I'll come back and you can show me how good you are with that thing."

CHAPTER 11

EDO

"Different roads sometimes lead to the same castle."
— George R.R. Martin, *A Game of Thrones*

The men summoned to Lord Abe's home arose early the next morning, along with the fishmongers shouting their fresh wares at the Tsukiji wharf. They rode silently through the streets to Lord Abe's stately home in the center of the city. They did not travel in force, to avoid attracting attention, but each had his hand on the hilt of his *katana*.

Tōru and Takamori rode first, the two lords behind, with Obata and Lord Tōmatsu's chief bannerman Sugieda bringing up the rear. The ambush in Kyoto was only two weeks ago, fresh in their minds.

As Kato had suggested, they went to the back of Lord Abe's enormous gardens, at the low gate where servants enter, rather than through the main gate watched by many eyes. Kato was waiting. He greeted them and handed off their horses to waiting grooms.

"*Ohayō gozaimasu.* My lord awaits you at the house. If you would leave your weapons here..." Kato gestured to one of his *samurai* to take and guard the *daishō* swords for the lords and their men. Tōru felt naked without his *daishō* swords at his hip, but no lord in the land countenanced armed visitors in their reception halls.

They followed Kato for several minutes along the path winding through the extensive gardens and groves of Lord Abe's Edo estate hidden in the heart of the city. A few deer watched from a grove. Artfully tended man-made ponds and streams ran through the property, the sound of flowing water masking the traffic clatter on the road outside the estate.

At last they reached the shaded porch of Lord Abe's home, overlooking a *karesansui* miniature rock garden. A gardener was raking the white stones and sand in one corner. Lord Abe rose to greet them as they ascended the few short steps to his porch.

After murmuring polite greetings and introductions, conducted with solemnity by his retainer Kato, Lord Abe gestured to low seats overlooking the Zen garden.

"The winter morning air is chilly, but if you are warm enough from your ride, perhaps you would enjoy sitting out here? I find this view opens my mind when there are difficult matters to discuss."

Lord Abe was young, in his early thirties at most. Tōru wondered how a man so young had risen to be Chief Minister of the Council. Within the circle of those of appropriate birth, surely there were older men to entrust with such responsibility.

They took their seats, the lords on either side of Lord Abe, with Obata and Kato by Lord Aya and Sugieda by Lord Tōmatsu. Tōru and Takamori sat further away, kneeling while the senior men found more comfortable positions. The men accepted *ocha* tea and *okashi* snacks from a serving girl as they murmured thanks and commented on the beauty of the grounds.

Lord Abe and the two *daimyō* from the western part of the country conversed quietly about their journey, the fragrance of the tea, the surprising warmth so late in the year, matters of small consequence. The news of the birth of the Emperor's firstborn son from his favorite concubine had just reached Edo. The child had been born right around the time the party was in Kyoto, or days after they left the imperial city behind. Murmurs of congratulations for the auspicious event were politely offered all around.

Finally a longer pause crept into the stately discussion. Lord Abe turned to Tōru, kneeling respectfully some distance away. "So this is your fisherman?"

Lord Aya bowed deeply, glanced quickly at Tōru and decided. He plunged in. "*Ikanimo.* My men discovered him coming ashore from a foreign ship one evening early last spring."

"You did not execute him and send his head to Edo as our Lord Shogun's *sakoku* policy demands." Abe stated this flatly as a fact, not a question. Tōru was indeed a living fact, a man still in possession of his head. Tōru bowed his head to the floor and held it there, knowing it was not his place to speak, but Lord Aya's.

"And you travel in company with a young but valued retainer of the ever challenging Lord Shimazu. He wears not the Satsuma crest of his master...but your own house *mon*, as though...as though you were attempting to disguise him."

Now Takamori bowed to the floor, another living fact.

"You have burned your forest to the ground to build guns and foreign engine carts capable of travel at high speed on tracks. You have constructed foreign devices called Babajis and Dirijibis no one can explain to me. Your illegal Satsuma traders in Naha Harbor are famous throughout Asia for their strange and extensive demands for foreign technology and materials. Need I go on?" Lord Abe's eyes held Lord Aya's, who bowed his head to the floor in wordless assent.

Lord Tōmatsu cleared his throat and made to speak.

Lord Abe held up a single hand to hush him. Young though he was, he carried himself as the powerful lord he was and demanded respect from all. "I will deal with you later, Lord Tōmatsu. Lord Aya, it is you who first disobeyed our Shogun's commands, harboring a treasonous fugitive returnee. You broke our laws on armaments. You recruited Lord Tōmatsu, loyal subject of the Shogun, married to the Shogun's own cousin, to join you in your crimes. You have built without any consultation foreign monstrosities so new and terrible that we do not even have laws to forbid them. Tell me why I should not take your head, and the fisherman's head," he reached behind him and unsheathed his *katana* with a smooth snick, laying it before him, "and bear them to my Lord Shogun, leader and protector of us all?"

A long silence prevailed.

The three accused kept their foreheads firmly fixed to the floor.

"Speak! Hold nothing back," commanded Lord Abe. "Speak now, or be silent forever."

Lord Aya slowly raised his head and pushed up from the floor, rising about halfway, so he leaned forward in a supplicant position as he spoke. "My Lord Abe-*sama*, all is as you say. I failed to execute the fisherman. Many acts followed from my decision. I humbly take responsibility for this failure and offer you my life in return."

Lord Abe grimaced. "While I appreciate the convenience of you delivering me your head here yourself today, know that if I wanted your head and his," gesturing to Tōru, "in a box, I would already have them. Answer the question: why were you willing to defy our laws and risk your head, even bringing it here personally to me, when you know the penalty for violating for our isolation policy? This I must know before I accept the offer of your head, and that of your new-made *samurai*."

Lord Aya bowed to the ground once more and then sat up fully straight, shoulders back and head high. "Then, Abe-*sama*, I will answer, aided by Himasaki Tōru, now that you know who he is.'

"Ah, but I don't know who he is. We've not been able to discover the name of his father. Do you know?"

"It is a mystery to us as well. He was raised in a small fishing village some days from my home, in Iwamatsu. We found many witnesses to attest to the fact that his mother raised him there alone. But no one was certain of his father."

Lord Abe stared down Tōru. "Well, boy? Who is your father?"

Tōru bowed yet again, straightened and gave his only answer. "I last saw him the night my fishing boat sank."

"His name, boy. His people."

"I humbly beg your pardon, Lord Abe, but I cannot tell you."

Lord Abe turned to Lord Aya. "Command him to tell us!"

Lord Aya bowed deeply. "I am sorry, my lord, but even threats of death have not made him speak a word of his father. I can command, but he will not obey either of us. Especially now that his life is already forfeit."

Lord Abe sighed.

"Then tell us, boy, how and why you came back."

Tōru paused, held Lord Aya's gaze a moment, and then spoke, his voice strengthening as he went on. "After the American ship rescued me when my boat sank, I spent two years living among them. I visited their War College at West Point and spoke with their military officers. I met common laborers and governors, *daimyōs* chosen by their people. I saw their factories. I went inside—inside their Christian churches where I saw them sing and read their book, the forbidden Bible. I rode their trains. I saw them send messages across vast distances instantly. I learned to read their English words, and I read in the newspapers of their plans for China and for Japan. I read of flying ships the French were building, dirigibles," he pronounced it in English, "or dirijibi as my men call it."

"'Your men,'" snorted Lord Abe. "So, fisherman, you have men who follow you?"

"I apologize, my lord. I meant to say the workers and laborers hired by my lord Aya, who have been helping me."

"Now we come to it at last. Helping you do what, exactly?"

Tōru straightened and faced Lord Abe. "I returned to help our people defend themselves from the coming foreign invasion."

A sudden chill breeze made the empty tree branches rustle. The gardener had finished raking the white stones of the garden. His crunching footsteps as he left the garden to put away his tools sounded loud in the abrupt silence torn in the conversation.

Lord Abe called for more tea. The serving girl appeared from nowhere and poured him a fresh cup of steaming *ocha*.

"Well, Aya, you believe him?"

"Yes, my lord."

"Enough to stay your hand and leave him alive in spite of our *sakoku* policy? At the risk of your own execution?"

"Yes, my lord. At the risk of my own life."

"Why?"

"I was going to execute him as the law commands, but he pleaded for a chance to say farewell to his mother. I—I wished to show him this small mercy before his death."

Lord Abe grunted, acknowledging the compassionate act. "My men found she had been gone for a year, no one knowing where."

"Correct, my lord. We did not find her, but on the journey to seek her, Himasaki convinced me of two things. First, we have months, or a year at most, before foreign powers come in force to land on our shores. Probably American, maybe soon enough British. Second, we can repel them and assist our Lord Shogun in protecting the Emperor's realm by using their own technology and weapons against them. I spared his life and brought him to Edo so he might warn the Council. And yes, I built all the foreign things to show it could be done, even by the smallest and most humble of the *daimyōs* in our land."

Lord Aya bowed to emphasize his humility. "For this, I accept whatever punishment our Lord Shogun and the Council may see fit to lay upon me, including my life, but I beg you, please allow us to warn the Council."

Lord Abe stared out at his rock garden for a long while.

No one dared breathe, as they sat as still as his garden rocks awaiting his decision.

At last Lord Abe took a huge breath. He let it out in a long sigh.

"I agree. The Shogun must hear your story from your lips before you die, fisherman. I will deliver you to the Council meeting in a few days. You will remain here until then, so I may keep my promise to deliver you to the Shogun. It is not safe for you without these walls. You have made many enemies since your return, fisherman."

Lord Abe stood and disappeared into his home without further farewell. Armed *samurai* appeared and escorted the six to a row of small but elegantly finished guest bungalows within the gardens.

Lord Abe's men took positions near the bungalows, not quite out of sight. Guards? Protectors? None could say. A plentiful steaming hot breakfast of rice, fish, vegetables and tofu was waiting for the prisoner-guests in each of their rooms. As were their weapons, each neatly wrapped in rich silk and arranged with care in the main room of each bungalow. Each man sat in his room and ate with relish, the impending death sentences notwithstanding. A warrior knows to keep up his strength.

The next morning, Tōru shivered in the morning chill as he dressed in his best *kamishimo* for the Shogun's court, a gift from Lord Aya before their departure from his home, marked with Lord Aya's crest as befits a true *samurai* of a noble house. The waiting was done. He would meet the Shogun, tell his story, give his warning and lose his head.

He was ready for whatever might come.

Three days of enforced quiet and inaction had been surprisingly pleasant, passed in Lord Abe's protected enclave. Until now, Tōru had not let himself give in to the exhaustion of the past eight months of unending effort and stress. In the quiet, he had allowed himself rest for the first time since he was rescued by the American ship over two and a half years ago.

The six men had been allowed to wander the grounds freely, enjoying the small perfect vistas tucked away in corners of the vast gardens. Delectable food of the finest quality and generous quantity was brought to them. Each evening they gathered in a shared bath, artfully hidden among trees and artificial fountains, steam rising from the hot water bubbling up in an elegant large stone-rimmed pool shaded by a tiled roof, open to the outdoors and the views.

Lord Abe's men maintained a polite distance always, allowing them the freedom to speak and plan. If they were prisoners, they were pampered ones.

Lord Tōmatsu in particular had been full of plans and bravado the first day of their confinement. He wanted them to escape, to publish pamphlets, to fight their way out, to rally other *daimyō* to their cause. He was permitted by Lord Abe's men to send messengers, summoning them to meetings.

None came.

After a day or two, even he had fallen into a quiet, almost meditative state, occasionally rousing himself to remind Tōru to speak of this fact or that when he addressed the Shogun's council.

The only plan remaining after they all lapsed into the leaf-rustled near silence was that Tōru would be their main spokesperson. That their actions and plans were widely known was obvious. That someone had allowed them to survive unpunished this long was also clear, although exactly why and whether that happy state would continue was not.

Lord Aya nursed hopes they would be given a reprieve once the threat by the foreigners was fully understood by the council, but steeled himself for worse outcomes. He feared not for himself, but for Masuyo and for Tōru, and Saigo Takamori, all so brave and young and full of life. Masuyo would suffer shame and poverty, alone in the world, if he were executed or ordered to die by his own hand, forfeiting his lands. Tōru had brought an important warning and the Western technology. Takamori, sent by his lord Shimazu, had shown repeatedly he was not there merely out of duty but from a deep passion for protecting and reforming the country to save it from the foreigners. On Tōru rested their hopes. His experience of the foreigners was unique and powerful enough that it might be sufficient to break the logjam that had trapped the country's leadership in a frozen stasis.

The journey to Chiyoda castle, where the Shogun lived and met with his Council, was a matter of minutes once they saddled up and rode forth on the appointed day. They were accompanied by Lord Abe, Kato and several other retainers, departing this time from the main gate in front as befits a procession led by Lord Abe himself.

As though they were tourists visiting the capital, Lord Abe calmly pointed out to his guests the homes of various daimyō as they passed them, on the way to the great outer *Sakurada Mon* gate where they would enter the castle and its outer defensive walls.

Having seen them safely there, Lord Abe's retainers, except Kato, saluted their lord and turned back. The party continued inside the *Sakurada-mon*, an impressively large two-story gate guarded by over sixty *samurai* wearing the Shogunate crest. Tall walls of stone blocks led away on either side from the gate. Inside, they found themselves in a square courtyard, bristling with warriors, from which three smaller gates issued, each overlooked by its own guard tower.

Accompanied as they were by the great Lord Abe, head of the council himself, the officers at each gate treated them with reverence and respect, as they ushered them through first the large outer gate and then one of the smaller gates inside. They were relieved of their weapons, all save Lord Abe and Kato. They handed off their horses as well to waiting grooms who led them off to immense stables with hundreds of horses.

On foot now, the party proceeded through a series of large and small wooden *mon* gates, first heading north, then turning to the west, then south again, protecting each of the inner citadels of the castle complex. At each gate, guards saluted Lord Abe. They were allowed to pass without further questions, as they wound their way through the maze of twisting, turning passages, bridges and moats that defended Chiyoda Castle from invasion.

Finally, a large open plaza opened out before them. They could see clearly for the first time Honmaru Palace, where the Shogun resided and held court. Surrounded by yet another moat and wall, they crossed the bridge into the palace complex, a series of low-lying stately luxurious buildings nestled around the palace keep.

As they entered the *Ou-omote* Great Outer Palace, a young officer led the party through the great rooms where the Shogun or his officials would on occasion hold public audience. They continued through private corridors, lined by private apartments for *bakufu* officials. Finally they were ushered into the *Naka-oku*, the inner receiving rooms, where the Shogun received senior officials and met with his Council.

They stood now outside the receiving hall, waiting to be admitted. Lord Abe was inside already. He had gestured for Kato and the others to remain outside. No one spoke. Long minutes passed as the guards stared impassively ahead.

The five of them waited in perfect silence.

Nothing could be heard of the deliberations within.

Finally the door slid open. A second set of guards motioned them within. Kato entered first, followed by Lord Tōmatsu and Lord Aya, with Tōru and Saigo bringing up the rear. The room was full, to Tōru's surprise. Kato had told them the Elders, the most senior councilors, were only a handful, but the full Council was several dozen, including the function heads of various bureaus. Kato had not been sure, but had supposed their meeting to be with the small core group, the Elders only, perhaps with a few of the more political and military-minded leaders from the broader Council. He had supposed wrong. The full Council and leading daimyōs from all over the country lined the path to the dais where the Shogun sat in front. Anyone who mattered was there.

Kato bowed to the Shogun and Council. He took his place kneeling behind Lord Abe, who sat just below the Shogun. Lord Tōmatsu and Lord Aya knelt and bowed as Lord Abe introduced them. Himasaki and Saigo knelt and bowed, foreheads to the *tatami* as well, until all four were motioned to an empty space up front.

The Shogun, Tokugawa Ieyoshi, was a man of sixty, but looked older and tired. His long high forehead was creased with furrowed lines, worry etched into his pale thin face. He looked impassively down over the gathered lords and bureaucrats, showing no response as the newest arrivals found their seats.

Lord Abe broke the silence.

"This Himasaki is the fisherman who returned from America, against our laws. This Aya is the *daimyō* who captured him, but failed to execute him according to our laws. This Tōmatsu aided and assisted Aya in a massive armament building effort, against our custom and laws for preserving peace in our land. This Saigo is retainer to Lord Shimazu of the Satsuma, whom we note—" he paused and looked around the room, inspecting each face intently regarding the scene as though seeing them for the first time,"—has not responded to our summons and is not here today." The four bowed as the room silently breathed together.

Lord Abe continued.

"Saigo we hold as hostage for his lord's good behavior and timely response to your summons. The others stand condemned to death for their various crimes by our laws and by my independent confirmation of the facts brought by their accusers. This sentence I am charged with carrying out." Lord Abe paused, regarding the room yet again, searching each stony face staring back at him. "My Lord Shogun, Councilors, great leaders of our land, the evidence against them is clear and their punishment necessary. This is my duty and I shall fulfill it, swiftly and without delay."

Tōru's neck itched terribly as he held his fixed pose.

The Shogun nodded for the first time, agreeing with Abe's final statement. Others around the room followed suit, nodding as well, as the faintest of murmurs swept the hushed room.

"However, my lords, as Chief Councilor to our government, it is also my duty to offer advice and counsel. While they must and shall die for their egregious violations of our laws and customs, this Himasaki Tōru in particular has important intelligence to share with us. He has met with the Americans, seen their government, their military, their economy. I would have you hear his testimony before I carry out the sentence. Will you permit this?"

The meticulously choreographed scene played out as planned. The Shogun nodded assent, with one small dip of his high forehead, followed by the Elders.

"Himasaki Tōru, why did you return? Why did you come to Edo?"

Tōru bowed his forehead to the *tatami* and then pushed himself upward to kneel, leaning forward. He gazed up at the Shogun looking down at him with a distant stare. He thought the Shogun looked weary, even perhaps ill. Seeing the dreaded lord at last and finding him looking feeble rather than powerful disconcerted Tōru. His adversary was but a man, a tired old man.

He began to speak, realizing his audience was not the old man on the dais above him but the entire room full of lords. His voice wavered at first, overawed by the great lords and the immense reception hall. Tōru steeled himself and spoke forcefully and passionately by the end.

"My lords, I came back to warn you of the American plans to come to our shores. I violated our laws not from pride or rebellion, but to protect our land from their coming invasion. I returned to bring you the tools and weapons to defeat them and drive them from our shores, so we might revere and protect our great Emperor and his mighty general our Lord Shogun. I came back, because there is no more time for debate. The foreigners are coming, within the year, and we must be ready."

The room burst into loud shouting. Tōru held silent, still holding his humble half-bent bow, resting on his clenched fists. Cries thundered of "How dare he return!" "Spy!" "Traitor!" "Dishonor!" "Fisherman!" "We can defeat anyone."

The Shogun and Lord Abe allowed the uproar to continue for a few moments, until the Shogun nodded at Abe.

Abe stood and motioned for silence.

"Yes, my lords, this is his simple message. The Americans are aggressive, they are coming to our shores and time is short to prepare. I have examined his claims in detail. Reluctantly we have concluded the fisherman is correct about foreign intentions and capabilities. We believe his two years spent among the enemy foreigners make him a valuable source of intelligence. Therefore, I ask you, as leaders of this realm, to allow our military officers time with him. I ask a suspension of his sentence of death for three months, together with his companions, while we ensure we have learned from him and from those who have worked so closely with him for over eight months anything we can use in our future battle with the foreigners. If you will grant me this time, I vow to carry out their sentences immediately afterward, and take responsibility for holding him in the meantime. As for Tōmatsu and Aya, we hold their families. I would send them back to their domains to arrange their affairs and then return, upon their oath of honor, at the end of that period. Contingent upon their timely return, their lands and titles will pass to their families and heirs after sentence is carried out. My lords, how shall we proceed?"

The uproar broke out again. This time Lord Abe and the Shogun sat back and allowed the gathered *daimyōs* and councilors to argue and debate, to whisper and shout. The prisoners knelt as the noise swirled about them, listening as their fates were discussed as though they were not even in the great hall. Finally the tumult in the great hall quieted down and Lord Abe stood, gesturing to an elderly soldier near the front of the room.

"General, what do you suggest?" The elderly general stood, aided by nearby companions.

"My officers wish to learn of the Western technologies from the wretched criminal. We support waiting three months before execution." He bowed and was helped back down by his colleagues.

Lord Abe skillfully wove his way around the room, calling out this *daimyō* and that bureaucrat, this officer and that elder statesman, asking their advice. Nearly all gave him the answer he sought—delay—and those who did not faced a low growl from the gathered room as they put forth their contrarian views. After each lord who mattered, either because of raw power or ceremonial importance, had been thus consulted, Lord Abe turned again to the Shogun, who had remained silent and immobile throughout.

"My Lord, it is the humble request of this assembled Council and other leaders who have come to consult with us that we delay for three months the execution of the three treasonous and craven criminals while we learn from them and document fully both their crimes and their knowledge. Will you grant us this time?"

The Shogun narrowed his eyes at his wily Chief Councilor.

Even Shoguns can be outfoxed by a determined opponent. Today he had lost the battle. Instead of presiding with all due gravity over the just execution of rebels and traitors and ensuring that all the realm knew of his swift and sure enforcement of the *sakoku* policy, lest any of the rebellious *tōzama* lords get any ideas about training their shiny new Western guns on Edo, the Shogun was forced into granting the stay. He had no choice but to agree. But he would not be manipulated again, nor allow Abe the opportunity to pressure him thus again in open full Council.

The Shogun grunted assent.

As the prisoners were led from the room, and the business of the meeting concluded, Lord Abe watched the slim young fisherman, wondering not for the first time who his father was. He knew the victory he had just won over the Shogun had come at a steep cost, a price that would be exacted from him in the future. He hoped the bet he had just made on young Himasaki and his companions would be worth the price he had just paid. He prayed to the old *kami* gods and the blessed Buddha he had bought them enough time to prepare the realm for the coming war.

CHAPTER 12

⊕

LOYALTY

"If by my life or death I can protect you, I will."
— J.R.R. Tolkien, *The Fellowship of the Ring*

Masuyo and Lady Tōmatsu were spending their fourth day together in the capital as they had the first, second and third.

Shopping.

Or more precisely, as wealthy Lady Tōmatsu understood the term, commanding purveyors of the finest kimonos, hairpieces, footwear and other ladies' wear to visit her home and display their offerings. Since the good lady herself already possessed countless luxurious and elegant kimonos, both new and heirloom, and enough fans and hairpins and obis to adorn all the noble women in both the Imperial and Shogunate courts, she devoted her considerable skills in this area to adorning Masuyo.

Masuyo, for her part, pleaded to be left alone and not be given anything, a plea she repeated with a certain honest vehemence that went beyond the polite demands of *enryo* restraint. Desperate not to burden her father with frivolous bills or an obligation to respond to generosity he could not reciprocate with his lesser resources, Masuyo begged Lady Tōmatsu not to give her anything.

But the older woman shrugged off her concerns. "You owe me nothing. Allow me to enjoy making you into the elegant young woman you are meant to be, as I have no daughter of my own, and you have no mother. This is play, and as my guest you must play with me." And so Masuyo submitted, and reluctantly allowed Lady Tōmatsu free rein. Merchants brought fabrics of light colors and bold designs, suitable for a young woman of rank, the finest silks, heavy and light, crafted by firms that long served the courts of both the Shogun and the Emperor. Others brought in armloads of elegant wools and cottons to lay at Lady Tōmatsu's feet, secretly imported and sold privately into the highest ranking homes in the land by a network of traders with clandestine ties to the illegal traders to the west.

By the fourth day, Masuyo possessed a wardrobe in the making rivaling those possessed by any Imperial princess or wife of the highest-ranking *daimyōs* in the land. The wealthy women of Japan were not flamboyant and showy, that propensity being left more to the working women of the stage and the *ukiyo* Floating World pleasure districts. But within the bounds of propriety and dignity guiding the respectable woman's attire, Masuyo's new wardrobe was a treasure trove of luxury. The task of creating it once all the fabrics had been chosen was farmed out to dozens of seamstresses and craftsmen throughout the most exclusive shops and workrooms in the huge city. No detail was overlooked, from the creation of the delicate under kimonos and footwear, to unique and beautiful hairpins and fans to match each outfit intended for outdoor wear.

Lady Tōmatsu bestowed upon Masuyo as well an heirloom kimono, of simpler but elegant make in a discreet charcoal gray silk, passed down from her own family. She unwrapped it from its stiff paper and soft silk wrapping, and presented it with some formality to Masuyo, refusing all protests from the girl.

"You will need this when you are older, on occasions when your goal is to be present and correct but invisible, and not the butterfly catching every eye. My grandmother wore this, and my mother, and I have myself, upon occasion. Please take it, with my best wishes, and may it serve you in those critical times. I have no daughter and shall have none in the future, so please allow me to pass this on to someone who can use and appreciate it."

Bowing deeply, helpless against the grand lady's will, Masuyo humbly thanked her for the lavish gift, and the flood of new items coming her way. After four days in the formidable woman's company, she no longer found herself quite so overawed. Her fear of Lady Tōmatsu's sharp tongue and chilly air had softened to a certain wariness mingled with appreciation. She had come to like and admire certain aspects of her hostess. Lady Tōmatsu had a dry sense of humor, and a self-deprecating wit. She liked to eat, and to eat well. She loved literature, and shared with Masuyo as well volumes from her own library of poetry and classical tales. She was a sharp negotiator with the army of merchants she had commanded to descend upon her home. Lady Tōmatsu may not have cared a whit about spending vast sums, but she found great pleasure in ensuring those sums were well spent.

Masuyo could not believe it at first, but she came to trust the older woman's sincerity in wanting to dress her. She saw Lady Tōmatsu's actions came not from a desire to put her down but from a genuine pleasure in the creativity of the task and a joy in seeing Masuyo at her most lovely. Against her will, by the third or fourth day, Masuyo was enjoying the parade of beautiful silks and seeing herself made as graceful as a court painting.

Lady Tōmatsu had not asked her again about the fisherman, nor interrogated her about Lord Aya's activities. Masuyo instinctively understood the furious shopping activity was a defense against the concern both women felt for their men. Masuyo had begun to wonder if she had misinterpreted Lady Tōmatsu's cool behavior toward Lord Tōmatsu and his guests. Was it just how the highest level of ancient families behaved in public, with perhaps more warmth and affection in private moments?

Masuyo saw the occasional look of worry cross Lady Tōmatsu's face in unguarded moments between fittings and animated discussions of the charms and defects of various *obi* sashes. The sight softened her heart toward Lady Tōmatsu. She realized the grand lady did in fact fear for her husband and the father of her only child, a child born so late in life and therefore doubly precious.

For her part, Masuyo was frantic with worry about her father. And about Tōru. A messenger had come the first day from Lord Abe's home, letting the women know the party would be staying at Lord Abe's "to prepare for the meeting with the Shogun and

Council." Left unclear was whether this stay was voluntary or not. The absence of any messages from Lady Tōmatsu's husband and Masuyo's father left them uneasy. It was unlike either of them to be out of touch, when a messenger could bring word in under ten minutes. Masuyo did not allow her mind to rest upon Tōru. If his face rose unbidden in her mind, she whispered "fisherman" to herself, to make him vanish. She realized this had become a near-constant habit for her. She too said nothing of her fears.

Upon their arrival, Lady Tōmatsu had rushed to her brother's home, only a few minutes away from her own, sharing with him her concern about her husband's and Lord Aya's activities. Her brother had swiftly sent her back to her husband's home, commanding her to urge him to renounce his defiance of the Shogun or lose his life. She would have made the case, but had not laid eyes on him since he departed for Lord Abe's compound their first morning in Edo. She knew he was meeting with the Shogun today, as did Masuyo.

As the day dragged on, with both women carefully avoiding the topic, a silence entered the space between them. After four days of intense effort, neither woman could have endured more shopping, even the indefatigable Lady Tōmatsu. Everything Masuyo could possibly use, let alone need, had been ordered, and more.

After the last merchant had carried the final bolt of fabric away, and left them alone together again, the silence grew. Even the ever proper Lady Tōmatsu, skilled hostess though she was, found no words, frivolous or serious. They sat in silence, Masuyo reading one of Lady Tōmatsu's books of poetry and Lady Tōmatsu listlessly pouring tea she failed to drink. She poured yet another cup of strong green tea for Masuyo, and broke the silence at last. "When you have children of your own, you will understand."

"Pardon me, but understand what, Tōmatsu-*sama*?"

"Why I must do what I must do."

Masuyo stared at her, not comprehending.

"Your father and my husband will be condemned to die today, for their activities with the fisherman." Lady Tōmatsu spat out the word "fisherman" with distaste.

Masuyo stiffened, bracing against the charge against her friend and the penalty for her father.

"To die." Masuyo repeated the word, trying to fathom its meaning for her, for her father, for her life.

"Yes, child, to die. My brother has heard this from court officials. And Lord Abe will be the one to carry out the sentence. He holds them now, so he can carry out this duty."

Masuyo could not move, nor breath, nor speak. Of course she had feared this possibility, but to hear it matter-of-factly spelled out like this made it suddenly real. Not her precious father. Not...Tōru.

Lady Tōmatsu did not look for a response from Masuyo.

"To save my son, I must take him with me to my brother's home and swear fealty to the Shogun. I must reject all my husband has done. My brother has word that my son's inheritance can be spared this way." Lady Tōmatsu stared straight ahead, her gaze falling on a worn patch of *tatami* by the doorway.

"You are leaving Lord Tōmatsu?"

"I am saving his son. This is his wish. His life for his son's freedom and inheritance."

And yours, thought Masuyo.

"How can you leave him?"

"I am not leaving him. I am making my personal allegiances clear. My husband will be dead, perhaps by nightfall, maybe even now. But if he dies honorably and I swear loyalty to the Shogun as guardian of my son, our child will be allowed to grow to manhood and inherit his father's land and role."

"*Wakarimashita*. I understand." Masuyo did not understand, but could think of nothing she could possibly say.

"You, too, should come with me. Bow to the Shogun and denounce your father's actions. Your reputation will be stained by your father's actions, but you can still make a good marriage and carry on your father's line, if you swear loyalty to the Shogun and denounce your father. The Shogun himself will find you a husband of quality, loyal to the Shogunate, with your father's lands as your marriage portion. With time and loyal behavior, you can find your way back into respectability."

The fisherman's face rose in Masuyo's mind again, as Lady Tōmatsu calmly discussed the good marriage she could make, presumably with some stuffy *daimyō's* second son in need of a domain to rule. This husband Lady Tōmatsu envisioned for her would not be well traveled, and personally familiar with customs in New York and Boston. He would not be insatiably curious about the causes of prosperity and how those causes might be harnessed for the good of the common people. He would not speak English, let alone the damnable French. He would not know how to operate a sewing machine, or design a dirigible or send a message on a telegraph. He would not have loyal commoner friends like Jiro the blacksmith. He would not know how to make her laugh.

Her dear father's face rose up as well, impatiently bellowing "*Toranosuke!*" at her over some grievous breach of feminine propriety she had willfully committed, secure in the knowledge he was secretly proud of her intelligence, her skills and her defiance. She held her voice as steady as she could, as anger simmered in her.

"You would have me denounce my father." She uttered it as a flat statement, not a question.

"Yes, for his clearly treasonous actions."

"You would have me denounce my father for risking his life to save an innocent commoner. You would have me denounce him for spending everything he has to defend the Emperor's realm, for knowingly risking his life to bring a warning to the Shogun's court. My father is the most loyal subject in the entire realm, giving everything he has to warn our Shogun and defend our land. You would have me denounce this noble behavior for an *inheritance?*" Masuyo's voice shook as she spat the words out.

Lady Tōmatsu looked at Masuyo now, directly in the face, her own eyes damp and her expression troubled.

"Child—"

"I am not a child."

"Masuyo-*san*, your father may already be dead, alongside my husband. Our world is cruel to a woman alone, without husband or father to protect her. Your father would not want you to suffer over his actions. He would want to see you safe, as my husband wants to see our son safe. It would be your father's wish that you do this."

"I will never denounce my father. I admire what he has done!"

"Do not utter those words again. The walls have ears. You are young, and do not understand. Honor your father's memory by doing what you must. Live, carry on his line and his memory, and raise a fine son to protect his domain."

"I do not need safety. I do not need any inheritance that requires that I denounce my father. I would rather die than—"

"Well, you may get your wish." Lady Tōmatsu stood and gathered her belongings to depart. "I cannot save my husband. I can save my son. I can try to save you. No matter how I feel about any of this, my son is my duty now. I offer you a path to save yourself and your father's legacy, but if you are too foolish to take it, there is nothing else I can do." She swept out of the room, calling for her servants to prepare to take her to her brother's home.

Alone in Lord Tōmatsu's home after Lady Tōmatsu had gone, in a mad swirl of boxes and furious activity, Masuyo considered her options. Lady Tōmatsu had left instructions with the servants that Lady Aya was to be treated as an honored guest for as long as she would like to stay in Lord Tōmatsu's home. She had begged Masuyo one last time to come with her and do what was necessary.

Masuyo could not, she would not, denounce her father. She could not hold the thought in her head long enough to consider it. He was her beloved father, and she admired all he had done. If he was to die for it, then so would she. But...she was young and her heart beat strongly in her chest, thudding the rhythm of life at her. She knew how a woman of her rank should die, when so required. The binding of her legs, to avoid immodesty when she falls. The swift strong stab to the throat, deep and hard, to ensure the task complete, the suffering short. She stared into the dying embers of the fire, imagining this hard blow. But she was not ready, not yet able to take that final step.

Lady Tōmatsu was certain her father was dead, or would be soon, by his own hand at Lord Abe's command. She could wait at least to find out, to see his dear face one last time before she acted.

But then a new thought gripped her. *What if he were not dead? What if the Shogun had shown mercy, had listened to her father's warning?* She could not break his heart with her death if he still lived. So with some relief, as her young heart beat strongly in her chest, she resolved to live until she knew for certain her father's fate as determined by the Shogun in court today.

Yet a worse thought came to her. Lady Tōmatsu had not needed to explain what Masuyo already understood about being a hostage of the Shogun. She would die in her father's place if he did not submit to his own death. *What if the Shogun had not killed her father, but compelled him to do some awful thing by threatening her father with her fate?* This new thought horrified Masuyo even more than the awful thought of her father's death or her own.

She could not be used this way, against her beloved father. She had to escape, to find a way to release her father from fear of harming her so he could freely do whatever he needed to save the country without worry for her.

As she turned her thoughts to planning her escape, a messenger came from Lord Abe's compound. His face was sweaty and sad, uncomfortable at the news he bore. After a deep bow and greetings, he gave her his message.

"Lord Tōmatsu and your own father, Lord Aya, have been condemned to death by will of the Shogun's Council."

"You say they are—"

"No, no, Lady Aya, not yet. They have been given three months to set their affairs in order. And then the...the...Shogun's command will be carried out."

Three months! Three months is an eternity! Lord Abe is a friend after all. Surely this is a signal to her to escape, to free her father from his death by removing herself as a hostage piece from the board. She had time to figure this out. She would escape and save her father.

She remained calm, her face still. She could not look happy, for he had just delivered news of a death sentence. Her joy at the news of a mere death sentence and three months reprieve in place of a death was so great she could not face him, for he would see her joy. She turned her face away, as though overcome with sorrow. Politely he waited until she had composed herself.

"Please take this dread news to Lady Tōmatsu. She is calling at her brother's home. She will want to know as soon as possible."

The young messenger bowed and departed, leaving Masuyo alone in the dimly lit room. She did not call the servants to light the room, but sat there in darkness, plotting her escape.

1853 — Spring
Year 6 of the Kaei (嘉永) Era

CHAPTER 13

$\oplus$

ESCAPE

"Well, Captain, time to get out of Dodge."
— *Solo* (movie, 1996,
director Norberto Barba,
screenwriter David L. Corley)

Two and a half months had flown by for the prisoners Saigo
Takamori and Himasaki Tōru. They passed more slowly for Masuyo,
who lived alone in Lord Tōmatsu's home except for servants
watching her with pitying eyes. Even old Obata was gone, assisting
her father in arranging his affairs before his execution. She had sent
her ladies home to their families in her father's domain, for they need
not share her fate, nor did she have the energy to appear gay and
carefree in front of them. Girlish games held no appeal. Masuyo felt
no appetite, only a cold hard knot of fear for Tōru and for her father
and for the cheerful young giant Takamori.

Each day she practiced with her *naginata* in the hidden back
courtyard of Lord Tōmatsu's spacious compound, slashing and
stabbing for hours at enemies only she could see. There was no
telegraph at Lord Tōmatsu's Edo home, but she practiced her
Mōrusu Cōdo each day in case she ever needed to send or receive a
message after her escape, tapping out poems in the dot dash
code on the low table where she huddled alone in the
evenings. The servants whispered, but she would not speak to
them, but only practiced with her *naginata* and read from the
English books she had brought with her from the countryside.

The time passed much faster for Tōru and Takamori. As reluctantly commanded by the Shogun, the two young men were thoroughly debriefed. Lord Abe did not waste a moment of their imprisonment. Gaining them three months had cost him dearly, and he would see value from his political investment.

He unleashed the full force of the ministries under his influence and dispatched his bureaucrats out to every corner of Japan to gather up military officers serving the *daimyōs* both great and lesser from dozens of domains. He drew in leading merchants and skilled craftsmen, blacksmiths and the like, all amazed to receive a summons from the Chief Minister of the Shogun's Council. He invited them to spend as much time as they liked as his pampered guests in hidden bungalows scattered about his vast property. From dawn until dusk, these representatives from the many *hans* questioned Tōru about his time in America. Lord Abe hired scribes and artists to make copies of sketches Tōru and Takamori made of the technologies they had built from Western models. More scribes copied the Western books Tōru had brought back.

Each afternoon, Tōru shared with the military officers and merchants everything he had learned about the American military, economy and political systems. At first, the two groups were insulted by being forced to spend time with each other, the rich merchants because the *samurai* officers were often so swaggering in their manners, and the officers because merchants, all merchants, were beneath them and unworthy of their notice. But as the months passed, Tōru was glad to see them working together and forming bonds, as the merchants spotted opportunities to earn profit making weapons for the military and the officers saw the potential of the new technologies Tōru outlined for them.

Takamori captured notes from these lectures. A small army of scribes camped in Lord Abe's compound copied these notes. These were bound up and printed as "*Observations of Barbarian America by the Treasonous Returnee Himasaki Tōru.*" The slim volume became an underground best seller throughout Edo and the entire realm, avidly devoured by every literate young *samurai* who dreamed of glory fighting against the barbarian Americans and every merchant who dreamed of profit from selling to them.

Lord Abe personally made sure every *daimyō* in the realm also sent artisans and blacksmiths and their brightest young *samurai* to sit each day in what Takamori and Himasaki called "engineering school," for that is precisely what it was. For seventy-five long days, as ordered by Lord Abe, for five hours each morning they taught the bright young men and the artisans and blacksmiths everything they had learned about building telegraphs, trains, dirigibles, Babaji difference engines and Western modern guns.

Tōru wished he had Jiro by his side explaining how to actually construct these devices, but he did his best in the face of withering questions from the small cluster of belligerent but engaged blacksmiths who sat, filthy and foulmouthed, in the back of the classroom behind the young *samurai* clerks.

Lord Abe had sacrificed a corner of his elegant gardens to build a workshop where Takamori and Tōru demonstrate how they had designed and built each item, noting pitfalls and failures along with their advice on the best way to create each device. The intense young Lord Abe would sometimes appear, silently like a spirit, at the back of the workshop watching as Tōru and Takamori lectured to their charges. Occasionally he would ask them to explain some concepts in greater depth. "Without the *sakoku* isolation policy, we could teach this in every *han* in the country. Someday, we will open our country." Tōru and Takamori were amazed at these statements in favor of opening the country, for if there existed any unquestioned law in all the land, it was the law of isolation.

Lord Abe seemed to long for this unthinkable change.

Tōru was certain the Shogun was unaware of the vast and urgent scope of his "debriefing." Lord Abe occasionally summoned Tōru to his home to meet with a creaky old general or a doddering bureaucrat from some ministry or other. These visitors asked naive questions about the Americans, which he dutifully and respectfully answered. These were the interviews the tired old Shogun was hearing about, Tōru guessed, not the others.

Tōru was grateful, though, that Lord Abe had won him the time to share, at national scale, all the knowledge Lord Aya and Lord Tōmatsu had been working so hard to share among their allies earlier in the year. Lord Abe, by imprisoning him, had given Tōru and Saigo Takamori the means to take their message to the entire realm, under the direct order of the Shogun.

Lord Abe commanded Tōru and Takamori to pass on every bit of knowledge and practice they had to the representatives of the other *daimyōs*. "You will die in ninety days by my hand, as is commanded by our laws, but if you truly are loyal to our Emperor, our Shogun and our people, you will not die without sharing every bit of knowledge you possess that may serve to defend our realm. If you are warriors for our land, this is your duty."

Tōru and Takamori had bowed and promised to do so. Their mission and their duty to help their homeland inspired them. Furthermore, to a young man, ninety days is an eternity. With young men's blind optimism, they were glad of the opportunity to inspire and teach others, as they had hoped to do. They even clung to the slender faith that somehow their executions might be averted, if their ideas served to aid Japan in the looming confrontation with the Americans. Even if they were to die, it would be only after they had done everything in their power to defend and protect Japan. Was dying not the lot of warriors and *samurai* anyway, when required to fulfill their missions?

Tōru did not spend much time worrying about his own death, even as the scheduled day grew closer and closer, a mere three weeks away now. He was too busy. In still moments, though, Masuyo's face rose again and again in the quiet of his heart.

He had not seen her since the day they left Lord Tōmatsu's compound to visit with Lord Abe before their appearance before the Council. As close as they had become in the happy days building the first devices in Lord Aya's domain, he could not contact her, near though she was, just minutes away. She was his lord's daughter, and he a convicted traitor, personally sentenced to die by the Shogun. Her situation was already precarious. He could not further endanger her by making any sort of contact that might taint her reputation. He knew she was safe from any immediate harm at Lord Tōmatsu's comfortable Edo home, well protected by her father's retainers and Lord Tōmatsu's men.

Lord Aya and Lord Tōmatsu had returned, as ordered, to their *hans* in the west to put their affairs in order before their executions, accompanied everywhere by *bakufu* guards. Tōru knew Masuyo's fate as the Shogun's hostage, effectively under house arrest except for chaperoned market visits, if her father continued his rebellion. While Tōru hoped Lord Aya was somehow clandestinely continuing to prepare for the foreign invasion under the watchful eyes of the Shogunate escort sent with him to his home, he was torn, fearing Lord Aya's success might lead to harm for Masuyo.

Tōru was saying farewell to the afternoon's clutch of military officers asking him arcane details about American military strategy. He turned around to see not only the silent Lord Abe but also a subdued Masuyo standing at the back of his classroom.

She was dressed simply and elegantly in a rich silk kimono of drab but luxurious color, a dark charcoal gray, nearly black in the twilight. Her hair was up, twisted in the severe bun favored by Lady Tōmatsu, and her face painted in a stern visage of white skin and black brow and red lips. Her dress and bearing made her look older, even regal, nothing like the laughing girl of his memory and imagination who had lifted his heart whenever he allowed his thoughts to dwell on her during the past two and a half months of his imprisonment and brief but frantic career as an impromptu military tactics and engineering professor. She looked drawn and weary, as though being a hostage in even the most comfortable of surroundings had drained her of her natural life and vivacity.

Lord Abe nodded to Tōru. "We have a guest for supper this evening," he said, indicating Masuyo, who made a small formal bow to Tōru and Takamori. "You will join me." He turned. They followed in his wake, winding through the dim park, lit by occasional torches and lanterns.

When they reached Lord Abe's home, they joined him in a spare and spacious hall. Places were set for nine at low lacquered individual tray tables. Kato was there, as was a young *samurai* wearing the Satsuma *mon* crest of a cross within a circle. Saigo nodded a greeting to the Satsuma *samurai*, who returned the nod. Obata of House Aya and Sugieda of House Tōmatsu were there as well, to Tōru's surprise. He would have expected them to be at their lords' sides back in their domains, arranging their affairs.

A girl a few years younger than Masuyo was playing a *koto* in a corner of the room, sitting before a gold-painted screen of pink and white *sakura* branches laden with blossoms. She set aside her instrument and rose to greet the group, bowing as she did.

"Allow me to present my daughter, Chie. It is irregular, highly irregular, to enjoy the company of a lady at a war council." Lord Abe bowed to Masuyo, who returned the gesture, "and so I have asked my daughter to join us, so Lady Aya might be more comfortable amongst all these men. Please forgive my daughter her wretched *koto* playing and my imposition of my family upon our business this evening. We live, it would seem, in highly unusual times, and must adapt to the demands of our times."

The men bowed greetings to the elegant young women, surprised at their presence, rare as it was for women and family members to join such a supper. Lord Abe indicated the women should sit on either side of him, his daughter to his left. The men took their seats as well, as serving women began bringing tray after tray of the finest *kaiseki ryori* to the gathered guests, of refined flavors and arrangements more Kyoto than Edo. The women sipped *o-cha* and tiny glasses of *umeshu* plum wine.

The men, hesitating at first in the presence of the great Lord Abe and amazed at the novelty of drinking with high born women, enjoyed a diverse selection of *sakés*, gathered with interest and care by Lord Abe himself. Lord Abe had them try one *saké* after another, pointing out the rich body of an unadulterated *junmai saké*, and the light and delicate complex fragrance and flavor of a *ginjo shu saké*.

Somewhere hidden in the reaches of the sprawling home, a skilled flute player played, now haunting soft melodies, now fast-paced dances, adding an undertone of gaiety to the evening. What began as a stiff encounter, shadowed by the impending and never-mentioned executions, soon evolved into a merry gathering. Even the somber and earnest young Lord Abe joined in jests and stories.

Fueled by the generous selection of exquisite *sakés* and the presence of the noble ladies, the men, still gentlemen, still courteous, but cheerful and expansive, toasted their beautiful lady fellow guests and remarked upon this delightful alteration from custom. The ladies blushed, and looked to Lord Abe for guidance on how to respond. Servants carried away the dessert trays, their burdens of sweetened fruits and intricately molded *omochi* barely touched after all the bounty that had come before.

Lord Abe signaled a turn in the conversation to serious matters.

"Enough. Make Lady Aya welcome. As her father's heir, she needs to hear what must be said tonight and participate in our decisions." The men straightened and sat forward to hear what Lord Abe would share next. "Himasaki, Saigo, you have done good work these last months. Every *daimyō* now has men who have mastered the basics of what you have learned. They can take your knowledge back to their *hans*. When you are resting in your graves, know that you have together done more to strengthen and prepare our country than all the hundreds of bureaucrats I have working for me at the Ministry. I thank you for your contribution."

Tōru and Takamori bowed their thanks at the compliment. They shifted uneasily at the ghoulish mention of their graves alongside the clearing of the dessert bowls.

"The Shogun has commanded a meeting with Saigo and Himasaki tomorrow morning. He wishes to confirm some aspects of your debriefing directly himself from reports he has heard second hand from his officers," continued Lord Abe. "He also commands the presence of Lady Aya. I will send Kato and my men along to protect you on the way."

Tōru and Takamori bowed assent to this request.

Masuyo nodded her understanding. She was a hostage of no use to the Shogun unless he had her in his grasp. She understood she might not return from Chiyoda Castle tomorrow. She held herself stiffly immobile lest she shiver and show her fear.

"Obata, Sugieda, Asano. You bear tidings from your lords. Please share them."

Obata bowed and began. "My Lord Aya is ready to make his return to Edo, as he promised to do, that his sentence be carried out in twenty days as commanded by the Shogun. He asks that his lands and domain pass to you, Lord Abe, in trust for his daughter, Lady Aya, to be returned to her upon her making a suitable marriage. He humbly asks you, Lord Abe, to stand in position of father for her after his death. As her guardian, he begs you to find her an appropriate husband, and carry out all necessary ceremony in his name to adopt the young man into House Aya that his daughter may be protected and his House continue."

"I understand, and will watch over Lady Aya as over my own Chie." Lord Abe held Masuyo's eyes in his own gaze.

She saw, most unexpectedly, a father's gaze in the eyes of the powerful young minister. Masuyo felt strangely reassured, even as everyone calmly discussed her father's impending execution. She broke the gaze and looked down at her hands folded in her lap, fearful of errant tears welling up and breaking her barely held composure. When she had gathered herself, she peeked over and saw Chie looking at her, most warmly, although the two girls had never before met. She managed a small nod, returned with a friendly smile by Chie, and turned back to the conversation, staring directly at each speaker as though listening, although the effort to hold herself together consumed all her attention.

Sugieda broke into the pause in the conversation. "My Lord Tōmatsu is also ready to return. His infant son will inherit his land and title, as decreed by the Shogun, held in guardianship by his wife and her brother, the Shogun's official."

Lord Abe nodded his understanding.

Asano, the representative send by Lord Shimazu of Satsuma, now spoke. "My Lord Shimazu will not be coming to Edo." He paused to let them all absorb that fact, a fact that meant the death of Saigo Takamori in his lord's stead for Lord Shimazu's failure to return. Saigo sat expressionless, his large frame a still mountain.

"Does Lord Shimazu have other counsel for us?" asked Abe.

Tōru watched him carefully. Ever since the day he had been condemned to death and learned in nearly the same instant of a three month stay on his execution, he had known even the smallest events were carefully scripted by the wily young politician. Surely Lord Abe had known these reports before asking the questions in front of the group, which meant he already knew the answer Asano was about to give. Curiosity held Tōru rigid with anticipation.

"He does, Lord Abe. Shall we ask him directly?"

At this, Lord Abe permitted himself a small, private smile, as though at a joke only he heard. "Why not? Chie."

Chie flashed a wide grin, putting Tōru in mind of Masuyo-*sama* wild and free in her laboratory. She rose to her feet gracefully but a touch too quickly for a powerful lord's noble daughter, unable to contain her excitement. From behind the golden screen where she had tucked her *koto*, Chie drew out a gleaming telegraph device, all wood and wire and brass.

Tōru would not have guessed Lord Abe was such a technophile, nor such a rebel. Lord Abe must have ordered the telegraph line built, all the way along the *Tōkaidō* to Kyoto and beyond, the moment Kato returned with his report nearly three months ago.

Chie tugged the device forward, uncoiling the wire as she brought it to the center of the cluster of small tables. She knelt beside it, arranging giant brass earphones over her delicate ears and elaborate hairstyle. She placed her finger on the sending switch.

"*O-tō-sama*, what message shall I send?"

Tōru looked at her in wonderment. This strange evening was getting odder yet.

Lord Abe asked Asano, "He is standing by for us?"

"Yes, my lord. We communicated additional details before the meal. He will be there."

"Then ask him to tell us his plan." Lord Abe now grinned openly. He looked at Masuyo and smiled gently. "Do not fret, child. We have other plans for your father."

Masuyo drew in a quick breath and held it, lest she burst into tears in front of everyone. She bowed her head and stared at her hands until she could face the room again.

All watched as Chie confidently tapped out the Morse code, turning transliterated Japanese syllables into short and long beeps.

A silence filled the room as the last beep faded away. Someone had silenced the flute player, leaving the only sound a soft blend of quiet breathing and a faint rustling of trees in the park outside the thin walls. They waited. They waited some more.

Then, like a miracle, the device leapt to life, scratching out the signals on paper, but also into Chie's giant earphones. She began to recite the message, translating directly from the sounded dots and dashes, a sign of a good mind and much practice.

"Rescue...team...standing   by.   Ready...tomorrow...dawn.   In contact...Aya...Tōmatsu?   Can...Lady...Aya...ride?   Fisherman...is... well?   Over." Chie leaned back, proud, and checked her verbal message against the scratched marks. She had done it correctly.

The room burst into laughter and questions.

Lord Abe held out his hands for order. He smiled. "How do you expect me to run a country without proper communications channels? I cannot do it openly yet or involve my useless officials, or the Shogun would have my head too. Furthermore, I cannot have my daughter visiting a *geisha* house or a distillery." He glared at Obata, as though scolding him for Lord Aya's lapses in selecting initial sites for telegraph offices, "so I had a line secretly installed directly here. Chie hid in the storage closet of your classroom and watched your lectures on the telegraph. She tells me she has mastered this Mōrusu Cōdo." He indulgently allowed himself a proud smile at Chie. She covered her mouth with her hand to hide her smile of delight at his praise.

"Tell Lord Shimazu that yes, we are in contact with Lords Aya and Tōmatsu. And tell him the fisherman is fine." Chie began tapping away, and getting a wave of answering beeps in return.

"Lady Aya, I hesitate to ask a lady of your gentle upbringing, but...would you be willing...to disguise yourself as a man? Can you... can you...ride a horse...like a man?" Abe was embarrassed at the question, the unthinkable image, but they all knew a palanquin could not keep up in a fast-paced escape. They also knew that if they moved into open defiance of the scheduled executions, and Lord Aya failed to report as promised, Masuyo would die in his stead, female or no, as his sole heir. Rude soldiers would cut off her head in a public square. No discreet suicide in a private room, watched only by a respectful representative of the Shogun. As the daughter of a convicted traitor, her punishment and death would be public and shameful, a harsh but necessary lesson to one and all.

"Do not tell my lord father, Lord Abe, but yes, I ride well, like a man. I have brought with me suitable clothes, for a male servant. With armor hidden underneath. Forgive me, my lord, but I have been planning my own escape, if it would save my father from returning to save me." Her eyes were bright. She understood lands and position were forfeit, but she would see her father alive again.

Lord Abe laughed. "I should have known. Aya's daughter is a rebel, too. Child, if we pursue this plan, you and your father will lose everything. You will be poorer than the poorest peasant, and hunted from one end of this land to the other, for the rest of your lives, until and unless the Shogun somehow realizes the value of your father's contribution. Do not doubt this. I can save his life this way, but not his lands, nor your claim, if your father does not return in twenty days. Your father is willing to die to see you safe and well provided for after him. As your guardian, since earlier this evening, charged by your lord father with your well-being, I will not pursue this plan unless we have your consent."

Masuyo's carefully cultivated composure finally crumbled. Tears slipped from her eyes. "Save my father, Lord Abe!" She bowed to the *tatami* and wept, marring her fine white painted cheeks. Chie leapt to her side, and gently lifted Masuyo up, cradling the openly sobbing girl. Tōru did not move, but he longed to cradle her in his arms himself and reassure her. He had never seen her falter or break for even an instant. Her outburst tore at him. He turned away, to save her embarrassment at her loss of composure.

"There, there. My father will save him, you'll see. Won't you, *O-tō-sama?*" asked Chie.

"Yes, child. We will save Lord Aya and Lord Tōmatsu, and Saigo Takamori here. And the wretched fisherman who created all this trouble. Chie, let Lord Shimazu know all members of the party ride and will be in appropriate gear."

Far into the night the telegraph beeped and buzzed between Lord Shimazu's Kagoshima Castle and Lord Abe's compound in Edo, minutes from the Shogun's Chiyoda Castle. Plans were made, scrapped, argued over and finally settled. Lord Shimazu's men in disguise would brazenly "kidnap" the prisoners on their way back from the meeting with the Shogun at Chiyoda. Pre-arranged, pre-wounded "witnesses" would send Lord Abe's men and the Shogun's men in the wrong direction, west to the *Tōkaidō*. The party would ride for their lives in the opposite direction to a sheltered patch of forest north of Edo where a dragon dirigible awaited them.

Tōru thought it a fine plan. A worthy plan. He also recalled the words of a Prussian officer, Helmuth von Moltke, whom he had met while visiting West Point. Moltke commented, over excellent whiskey and cigars in the officers' lounge one evening, that "no battle plan ever survived contact with the enemy."

What could possibly go wrong?

CHAPTER 14

FLIGHT

*"To a brave man, good and bad luck
are like his right and left hand.
He uses both."*
— St. Catherine of Siena

Obata and Sugieda left Lord Abe's compound before dawn to return to their lords. Led by Kato and surrounded by a handpicked escort of Lord Abe's men, Tōru, Takamori, Asano and Masuyo rode out of Lord Abe's majestic main gate, plodding forward through a busy narrow street with measured pace on Lord Abe's horses. The streets were crowded with early morning merchants and servants running errands. They had not gone far when a low whistle rang out and Lord Abe's men to either side of Tōru fell without even a moan from their mounts, arrows shot through their necks.

Masuyo's palanquin lurched and fell as her bearers collapsed, clutching arrows to their unarmored chests. Masuyo leapt out as it tottered and crashed. She dashed forward, tiny in the crowd of the busy market street. She yanked her naked and unwrapped *naginata* free from where she had hidden it fastened beneath her palanquin. Masuyo grabbed the bridle of a horse left riderless by one of Lord Abe's men and swung herself up.

Masuyo kicked the horse forward, shouting at Tōru. "Himasaki! Attackers!" Her kimono flew open over her legs, flapping around her, revealing peasant trousers and small leather boots beneath. She leaned down low and kicked her horse forward clutching her *naginata* as she pressed forward through the crowd, smashing aside black-clad attackers who attempted to grab her horse's bridle with her *naginata*.

Tōru shouted a warning to Kato and Saigo and kicked his borrowed horse forward, looking for their assailants. He could see no one, but two more of Lord Abe's men fell as suddenly and silently as the first pair, arrows shot through their necks. Then another pair fell in swift unison, this time from either side of Saigo Takamori. A servant girl shrieked as one of the men fell silently at her feet, knocking her market basket from her hands.

Saigo was at Tōru's side now, his *katana* drawn and ready, looking everywhere, seeking their hidden assailants. Asano raced after Masuyo, *katana* out, and moved protectively to her side. They could not gallop through the crowded streets. They pressed forward through the mass of people, looking for their attackers.

Kato shouted for his remaining men to protect Masuyo and sent one to return for reinforcements from Lord Abe's compound. The crowd parted for their horses, slowly, not nearly fast enough to allow them to escape the trap. They were helplessly exposed to archers positioned on the roofs and windows above them.

"We are betrayed. Forget Chiyoda," barked Kato at them as he wheeled his horse around, looking for their assailants. "Ride north, hard, and get to your dirijibi."

Kato said no more, but fell from his horse as well, pierced at neck and breast with arrows. Lord Abe's men were all down now, shot through with multiple arrows. One stared up from the ground, an arrow through his eye.

Tōru froze, shocked at the fall of the man who had protected him and their party since they left Lord Aya's domain months ago, the dour old retainer to Lord Abe who said little and saw much. Kato was too distant and highly ranked to be considered a friend, but he had become a reassuring figure during the tumultuous past several months.

Saigo grabbed his friend's bridle and dragged him forward as assailants in black poured out of a dark alleyway, *katanas* raised.

"Go! Go now! We cannot help them!" shouted Saigo.

Tōru, Takamori, Masuyo and Lord Shimazu's emissary Asano pushed forward, shouting to the crowd to let them through. Asano and Saigo slashed down with their *katanas* as more men in black came at them with daggers and *katanas*.

Trapped in the middle, Tōru spurred his horse forward, clearing a path for them through the crowd. They reached a broader street where they could move more swiftly. Masuyo clung low to her horse, making herself into the smallest possible target, her *naginata* held close to her side. They raced ahead.

"Should we go to meet Lord Shimazu's men?" shouted Tōru.

Takamori bent low to his horse, urging it forward. "Too late, no need. They were our diversion. Someone else has given us one."

Asano agreed. "Get to the dirijibi. We can send a message there. Go!"

"Let's go!" shouted Masuyo, her voice high and sharp above the morning crowd.

Asano pointed to a narrow bridge looming up swiftly. It was not meant for horses, but ran above a slender stream winding its way through the busy downtown.

"Keep going!" shouted Tōru. He thundered over the slender bridge, followed by the others as pedestrians threw themselves out of the way. Now they were on a wide thoroughfare. They could see the imposing gates of Chiyoda Castle in the distance to their left. On they urged their horses, as fast as the faithful beasts could go.

Up ahead was a checkpoint, where they would be asked for their passage permits in order to leave the city. They had no such permits. Three lethargic soldiers lounged by the gate.

"Ride through them!" shouted Asano. The four riders thundered through the gate as soldiers leapt out of their way, barely escaping being trampled. Shouts rang out, a few wild arrows shot over their heads, but no pursuit came after them. The soldiers had no horses, to the great good fortune of the fleeing riders.

Asano led them. He and Kato had planned the escape, and he had scouted and practiced the route, choosing the weakest points in the Shogunate guard.

"It's three hours hard ride to the dirigible," Asano shouted as they galloped hard, pushing their horses to the limit. They were out of the city center by now. The wide thoroughfare had given way to an unpaved track, rutted by the wheels of peasant wagons bringing food to the great city.

Asano slowed them to a walk, to give the horses a chance to rest. "My lord Shimazu's men were to have left fresh horses up ahead." He looked troubled. They were to have attended the meeting at the Shogun's Chiyoda Castle, and on their return been "kidnapped" by a strong protective force of Lord Shimazu's men in disguise, sufficient to get them safely out of the city. But that plan had been arranged for several hours from now. To avoid arousing suspicion, the relief horses were hidden in several friendly stables, to be brought to the exchange place just in time.

"Is it safe to go there?" asked Tōru. If their escape plans were known, a new clutch of foes would be waiting for them at the stable.

"I'll go scout."

"*Sore wa mazui.* No good. You are the only one who knows the way to the dirigible with Kato gone."

Asano considered this. Tōru was right.

"We can get there on these horses, just slower."

"And we are ahead of schedule now."

Saigo coughed out a bitter laugh. "True enough."

Masuyo joined them. "Let us skip the stables and go on to the dirijibi. We've not been followed," she said. She looked behind them once more, checking to see if her assertion was still true.

No pursuers thundered toward them.

Asano nodded. "Lady Aya, you can keep up?"

At this, both Tōru and Takamori burst into laughter, the first light moment of the troubled morning. "Lady Aya will keep up, and run you into the ground if she wishes."

Around the time of her invention of the black silk trousers, Masuyo had pestered Tōru and Takamori into secretly teaching her to ride, an activity she took to effortlessly, swiftly developing both a love for speed and a graceful seat in the saddle.

"Yes, Asano-*san*, I will keep up," said Masuyo, as demurely as though she were letting him know she would have the flowers arranged and the tea served. She grinned, a full broad smile like the ones Tōru had missed, and kicked her horse forward, leaving them behind as her lighter weight gave her horse an edge.

The men roared with laughter and chased after Masuyo. They were fleeing for their lives from powerful enemies, but they were young, and strong, and the sun shone bright above.

They trotted slowly through a narrower, less traveled track under thick foliage from the trees above. Led by Asano, they had gone around the relief horse stable, giving it a wide berth as they entered the village where it stood. They had stopped at a quiet bend of the road to open up Asano's saddlebags to retrieve for Masuyo an old ragged cloak and a tattered straw peasant hat.

She bound her kimono up around her and hid her female hair and form so she would not attract attention. Tattered peasant leggings with a droopy seat allowed her to ride like a man astride her mount. She wore patched worn gloves over her delicate pale hands, protecting them both from spying eyes as well as the strong sun and coarse leather of the reins of her horse.

The three *samurai* rode slightly ahead of her, as though she were their servant, close enough to move back protectively if necessary. She had shown them her small dagger and a short sword retrieved from her own bag, now belted around her *obi* under her cloak.

Asano recognized her *naginata* as a fine and fearsome weapon.

"Does she know how to use—" Asano began.

"I'm right here. You can ask me, Asano-san." Masuyo flashed him a wicked smile. "I am skilled enough."

"She's a fine archer, but yes, she's particularly vicious with her *naginata*," added Tōru. "Her father taught her to defend herself from an early age. As she likes to explain it, he had no son, so she got some odd lessons."

Masuyo shrugged and murmured soothingly to her horse as they plodded forward. She held her long bladed staff at the ready.

Asano nodded and blinked, unsure how to deal with a warrior female, an innovation little known even in progressive Satsuma. He motioned them to a halt for a moment and pulled out a battered map from his bulging saddlebag. "Let's take a break. Get something to eat." He handed around *onigiri* rice balls wrapped in seaweed, and gave Masuyo a bag of feed for the horses. "We are here," he said, "and this road leads on to this path. Follow along here until it curves up and around that hill and then—"

"Wait, where are you going?" asked Tōru.

"I want to scout ahead and see if we can travel the main road north. Our planned path takes us a much longer route through small villages and country lanes, to keep us away from prying eyes, but it will add hours to our journey at this slow pace. We'll be arriving several hours later than scheduled, even with our unfortunate early start."

"I'd rather stay together, and stick to the back roads," said Tōru.

Takamori nodded agreement with Tōru.

Masuyo let the men argue as she quietly moved among the horses. She fed the panting, thirsty horses and caressed their long noses, as the "servant" of the group.

Asano nodded. They had planned on taking the back roads to avoid attracting attention. And speed would not help them against overwhelming force, which they were more likely to meet on the main road, as well as bandits. "It's a tough call, either way. I agree, we stick to the back roads, but will your man Jiro know to wait?"

"When Kato-*sama* doesn't—doesn't return to Lord Abe's, surely they will investigate, and contact Jiro over the telegraph."

"Hmmm," said Asano. "Someone knew down to the minute when we would be heading to Chiyoda Castle. They knew Abe's men. As accurate as those arrows were, they could not have missed us unless orders had been given to take us alive. They picked off our escort and left us free."

"What are you saying?" Saigo demanded.

"The Shogun and his men knew when our meeting with him was, obviously. He requested it. So did he send them, to do away with us privately, out of sight, and the meeting he requested was all just a ruse to get us away from Lord Abe's protection?"

"He could have just killed us in Chiyoda if he wanted us dead. Use a dozen of his fifty thousand soldiers to squash us." said Tōru.

"No," Asano said. "He cannot kill you openly in Chiyoda. Himasaki-*dono*, you are now famous. And your little book, *Observations of Barbarian America by the Treasonous Returnee Himasaki Tōru*, is an underground bestseller, thanks to Saigo's careful note-taking, with scribes all over the country making illegal copies. The Shogun has banned it, but he cannot suppress it. Lord Abe was brilliant to have you "debrief" representatives from every *daimyō* in the country. Most have returned to their lords and made your case to them, for uniting to re-arm against the foreigners and opening the country for trade with other nations as equals. The Shogun knows there will be opposition raised to your execution in three weeks, as well as that of Lord Aya and Lord Tōmatsu. He is in a *go* match with Lord Abe, and Lord Abe has him nearly surrounded."

"Hey, what about me?" said Saigo Takamori. "I'm due for my final haircut as well!"

"Nobody cares about you," laughed Asano to his friend and fellow soldier of House Shimazu. "Except that yes, they do care. You are treasonous returnee Himasaki Tōru's fellow inventor and faithful companion. You are a hero to many as well."

"Not to mention a famous co-author," said Takamori.

"Seriously, the Shogun knows he cannot kill you openly, not without risking the ire of many of the great *daimyōs*. The *daimyōs* don't like to see any of their number stripped of land and title, so there is a wave of sympathy out there for Lord Aya and Lord Tōmatsu. Think about it. He cannot kill you in Chiyoda Castle, and he probably cannot execute you as scheduled in three weeks. So he wants to get rid of you quietly, out of sight, but Lord Abe has protected you like a mother bear her cubs."

"Then why were we spared, when his men took down our escort from Lord Abe's men?" asked Tōru.

"That's what bothers me. It's no mystery the Shogun's men knew we would be out on the street then. Not killing us when they assuredly had the chance is the odd part. I've been wondering..."

"Wondering what?" asked Tōru.

"If the Shogun's men have tapped our telegraph line somehow, and know our full plan. His people were in your briefing sessions as well. They would want—"

"The dirigible," answered all three.

"And then kill us at their leisure once they have it," finished Masuyo quietly.

Saigo looked around, the peaceful wood around them suddenly more threatening and still. He whispered, "So you think they are following us to get to it?"

"Worse. I think they are racing us to get to it. We were not careful on the telegraph last night, assuming we were the only ones using it. A clever pair of ears could guess more or less where we are meeting the dirijibi. That's why—"

"Main road. Let's go," said Tōru. They saddled up. The horses, rested and fed, picked up their pace as they left the village and headed for the main road.

When they reached the highway, Asano motioned for a halt.

"If we get separated, continue north as fast as you can. Split up if we're attacked—our best hope is reaching the dirijibi before they do. If we stop to fight, we've already lost. You'll see it, up the hill behind Aomori village. Jiro was to land it in time to meet us, hiding further north until then. Follow the sign from the main road to Aomori. We're about an hour from there, pushing a fast trot."

"Let's go," said Tōru.

They raced north as the sun rose above them and beat down on them, warm even on the winter day. Masuyo was a good rider, but unused to the hard riding and the jarring gait they were taking to stretch the horses. She was hot, too, and tightly swaddled in *kimono* and *obi*, all wadded up around her under her filthy peasant cloak. But she would die before admitting discomfort. She urged her horse on, knowing her only safety lay in speed.

Tōru kept pace by her side, admiring her grit and her devotion to her father, to take such risks. The two Satsuma *samurai* held pace at the rear, arguing tactics should they be attacked.

The horses were tiring, even at a moderate trot. They had been pressed hard on the galloping escape from the city center. Though the pace was more comfortable now, it was no walk. They would not have another hard gallop in them if the party were attacked.

The winter sun was sinking toward the horizon, no longer overhead. With the planned horse exchanges, they would have reached the dirigible by now. Tōru worried about his friend Jiro, now exposed in the open, waiting for them. They were close, but were the Shogun's men closer? They were not far now, perhaps twenty minutes from the village by Asano's calculation, but that was an eternity if the Shogun's forces were already there.

"If Jiro is attacked before we get there, is there a plan?" asked Tōru, suddenly struck by this new concern.

Asano grunted, bitten by the same worry. He replied in his usual deadpan way, "We had counted on surprise and our plans being hidden. We have no backup plan. A possibly costly error."

Masuyo pointed to the sky. "Look!"

And there it was, Jiro's dirigible, sailing majestically across the afternoon sky, floating gently toward them from the north. Soon they could see Jiro waving frantically at them, as his crew lowered the airship slowly, slowly down to the ground as it floated toward them. Now they could see riders racing south toward them, specks on the horizon line of the flat plain, but nearby and closing fast.

"That can't be good," said Takamori, indicating the riders.

The dragon dirigible was close enough for Tōru to inspect his dream for the first time, now made real by the magic of Jiro and his mighty team of engineers and craftsmen.

Masuyo had demanded they paint the underside with the image of a dragon, with a dragon's head prow in front. "We must frighten the foreigners. We show our confidence and our power by taking time with the symbols. They will return to their country talking of nothing but our dragon airships, and their leaders will be afraid."

Tōru had grudgingly agreed to the additional time and expense. He was glad he had, for it was an awe-inspiring sight. He could see Jiro now, bellowing orders to his pilot and engineers, the roar of the engines audible above the clatter of their horses' hooves as they raced toward the dirigible. The enemy horsemen were close now. A dozen armed men, maybe more, raced toward them at full gallop.

Jiro threw rope ladders over the side. He was shouting and pointing at the horsemen to the north. Tōru and the others could not understand him over the roar of the engines and the panting of their horses. They urged their horses on, demanding one last sprint.

A pair of rope ladders dragged along the ground a few hundred feet away as they closed the distance.

The enemy riders were nearly upon them.

Masuyo, lightest of them, reached the ladders first. She leapt off her exhausted horse, grabbed her saddlebag and threw it over her shoulder, her *naginata* strapped to her back, and climbed up the swaying ladder, kicking her kimono open with each step so she could find her footing. Tōru tightened his gear and saddlebag on himself and then grabbed Masuyo's ladder, holding it as firmly as he could for her as the airship bucked and tugged above them.

Jiro had thrown down an anchor.

The airship fought the anchor, longing to soar back up into the sky. Takamori was halfway up his ladder, as Asano freed the horses from rein and saddle so they could return home unencumbered.

Tōru looked up.

Jiro's men were hauling Masuyo over the gunwale to safety. They had Takamori safe as well.

Tōru climbed, as did Asano, for the horsemen were upon them.

Jiro was shouting, pointing urgently at something, but Tōru couldn't hear. Just in time he saw the men at the anchor raise a blade and slice down, severing the line to the anchor. He grabbed on with all his remaining strength, twisting his arms into and around the ladder as the airship bucked up suddenly, yearning for the sky, and they sailed up, up, up to the vast blue emptiness, trailing Tōru and Asano in their wake as their ladders swung free behind the airship like the trailing tentacles of some great sea creature.

The enemy horsemen circled in frustration below, their prey soaring up into the sky out of reach.

CHAPTER 15

⊕

OUTLAW

"When a man is denied the right to live the life he believes in,
he has no choice but to become an outlaw."
— Nelson Mandela

Jiro's crewmen pulled Tōru and Asano to safety.

Jiro grinned, bowing to one and all as he welcomed them aboard his ship. The former blacksmith looked positively elegant, if alien, in a long coat of his own design, styled upon military officer coats he found in Tōru's newspapers from America. He sported lovingly polished high leather boots of fine black leather. Glowing goggles of green glass and shining brass hung around his neck from a leather strap. He finished his ensemble with a large and ostentatious hat, also designed around Western models and topped with an absurdly enormous feather. He was fully captain of his airship, and wore his new authority like an old and comfortable cloak.

"You made it, you skinny son-of-a-seal!" Gone was the awkward deference to Tōru, replaced by the childhood friend grown to manhood and natural leadership.

"You are a welcome sight indeed, old friend." Tōru returned Jiro's embrace, wincing as Jiro crushed a wound on his ribs he had taken in the fight that morning. "May we board your ship, Captain?"

Jiro grinned. "Let me give you the tour." And so he did, showing them the cunningly crafted passenger cabin, able to hold 20 fully armed men comfortably seated and, in the adjacent stable, up to a dozen horses. Everywhere was gleaming polished wood and brass.

The crew quarters boasted a sleeping area, where half the crew could rest at a time, a small fully outfitted kitchen and the belching engine room. Finally he brought them to the command deck, where Jiro and his officers ruled over their engines and the skies.

Tōru examined each detail of the ornate control system for flying the great ship. Jiro grinned, watching him note every device and instrument, each one carefully labeled with its name and purpose, to aid the crews in training.

Tōru looked up at Jiro. "You can read these?"

"Of course. A captain must know everything about his ship."

Tōru shook his head. "The ship is a marvel, but you reading is a hundred times a marvel more."

Jiro grinned with pride and nodded silent thanks to Masuyo. She returned his nod with a secret smile. Jiro's sufferings with the *kanji* had been worth the prize.

Tōru could hardly believe he stood on the deck of his own airship. Or more accurately, Jiro's airship, to judge by the confident command of the man and the quick leap to obey from each of his men. It would take a battle indeed to pry Jiro from his proud position behind the ship's wheel, steering his airship. From an idea, a couple of newspaper articles, a diagram and a drawing annotated in the damnable French, Tōru was now standing on a functioning airship, flying above his homeland, soaring over neatly tended rice fields terraced up the gentle hills and valleys, free for the moment from the threat of imminent execution. Lost in the wonder of the moment, he forgot his manners for a moment, then waved over Jiro.

"Introductions! Captain, may I present Asano-*san*, retainer to Lord Shimazu of Satsuma? Asano-*san*, Captain Jiro of the airship...?"

"*Hakudo-Maru.* Since you taught us how to build airships, I thought it a good name for the first—"

Tōru laughed. "Well, I am no celestial being, but it's a good name. Long may she soar."

Asano bowed polite greetings. "*Yoroshiku.*"

Jiro returned the greeting with an elaborate doff of his spectacular headgear and added, "Welcome aboard. I've seen your messages on the telegraph. It's an honor to have you with us, sir."

Asano murmured a courteous *"katajikenai"* before continuing his thoughtful inspection of the marvelous dirigible.

"You are taking us north?" asked Asano, noting the sun sinking in the west.

"Hai. You are hunted men. And lady," added Jiro, including Masuyo. "They will seek you in the west. We have new allies in the north who will hide you. Next stop, Asaka, in Mutsu, in the far north. You will be a fisherman again, Himasaki-*sama.*"

"Indeed. Maybe we will meet the *Emishi* people. I've always wanted to—my mother told me stories of their great archery feats."

Jiro nodded, "Perhaps. They don't raid down to Japanese territory much anymore. The important thing is you will be far from the Shogun's men and nowhere near where they search for you. They worry me more than some hairy *Emishi.*"

Jiro's cook beckoned them to the crew's main room, where a simple but delicious hot meal of rice, dried fish and pickled vegetables awaited them, served alongside excellent *saké*. The cook hovered nearby, proud to have such famous diners at his table, constantly refilling their bowls with rice and roasted fish. They were hungry after their long ride and the excitement of the day.

Jiro filled them in on what he knew. He had a temporary telegraph set up at the planned meeting spot in Aomori. When Lord Abe's few surviving men made it back to his compound, Jiro had received word of the attack and knew they were fleeing, ahead of schedule and without protection from Lord Shimazu's men.

"We had to gamble. Would you come the back way as planned or speed up the main road? We figured the telegraph had listening ears, or you wouldn't have been attacked. We worried there would be ambushes waiting for you at the horse exchanges."

Asano nodded. "We feared so as well."

"So we had to imagine what you would do, with no fresh horses and no escort. The long way made no sense, if surprise was gone. And when the Shogun's men showed up at my anchor hurling flaming arrows at me—"

"We were afraid you would be attacked, that they wanted the airship," broke in Tōru.

"And so they did. I cut my anchor line, headed south to look for you. Had to hope you chose speed over secrecy, because I couldn't have seen you under the tree cover on the long route anyway. By the way, we just cut the line to my only spare anchor. Next time, someone has to jump down and tie us to a good-sized tree."

"We appreciate your sacrifice, Captain Jiro," Tōru bowed gravely to his childhood friend. "We'll get you a new anchor."

"We don't have to lose them if we can hoist them up gently. You just have to work on getting us attacked less often."

Tōru laughed at his friend's protective sense of ownership over the airship. Jiro grinned and poured his friends another round, and another, and another. Even Masuyo sipped a tiny *saké* cup, glad of the warmth curling through her chest after the day's hard ride.

The sun dipped over the horizon and darkness wrapped its embrace over the land. It was cold up so high, so they bundled up in spare crew coats Jiro handed out. They sailed east until they reached the coast, and then turned north. Jiro's navigator stood at the ship's wheel, holding a northern course by the *Hokkyokusei* North Star and the coastline, dark against the glistening moonlight paths traced across the sea. The stars seemed measurably closer, glowing in the absolute black of the sky. Occasionally they passed over the scattered dim lights of a fishing village along the coast.

"It will take us all night to reach Asaka. You are safe now. Why not rest, and we'll catch you up in the morning on all that's been happening while you were away?" asked Jiro.

As much as he wanted to know everything, a bone-tired weariness tugged at Tōru. He nodded assent.

"Lady Aya, we've prepared a place for you." Jiro led her to a tiny cabin, private and neat, furnished in polished wood and sweet-smelling fresh *tatami* mats. A luxurious clean *o-futon* mattress and coverlets lay waiting.

"Oh no, I couldn't!" She tried to decline, recognizing this must be Jiro's personal cabin.

"My lady, I insist. Please."

Masuyo saw the caring warmth in Jiro's eyes and gave in, knowing she would never convince him otherwise. "Just this once. This is the

Captain's cabin and must be reserved for him." She bowed her thanks, slipped into the tiny room and fell asleep at once in the soft bedding.

The others bedded down in the crew quarters, smelly from their ride, but glad of the rest, lulled by the quiet hum of the engines and the wind past their cabin.

Tomorrow they could plan their next steps.

Tōru awoke to the shouts of Jiro's crew as they lowered the airship down into a small clearing and tied off anchor lines to several trees. This far north, the air was cold, and a thin layer of early winter snow lay upon the branches of the trees and the ground below. Tōru could see the top of the ship was still visible above the treetops, the huge rigid airframe glowing dully in the early morning light like an alien whale beached on the hillside.

Jiro had assured him last night they were on safe territory, but the paranoia of the hunted man still held Tōru in its grasp. Just because you cannot see them does not mean they are not stalking you. He wished for a more sheltered spot, but figured Jiro had done the best he could. Dirigibles were not designed to hide.

Masuyo greeted him, dressed in her odd peasant trousers, boots and a hapi coat strapped around her slim frame with a ragged belt. Her hair was wound up and tucked under a small cap. She could pass for an unusually slender and attractive peasant youth, he thought. He was glad to see her smiling like her old self, a wicked gleam back in her eye.

Breakfast was already laid out, with rice, dried fish and vegetables. The rescued four were stiff from their ride, but happy to be free. Jiro bustled up, waving a map.

"*Minna-sama, ohayō gozaimasu.* Good morning all! Glad you are up at last! We've got much to do!" He indicated on the map where he had hidden the ship. They were a short hike, maybe fifteen minutes, to the village and the coast. They were a morning's flight to Aoba castle, in the great northern city of Sendai, where the Date family had ruled with an iron fist and considerable family drama throughout the Tokugawa period.

"Aren't we too exposed here?" asked Tōru, still concerned about the ship's visibility.

"The Date clan have joined your Lord Aya and Lord Tōmatsu and Lord Shimazu in their efforts to defend the country against the foreigners. You are safe here in the north. Lord Date Yoshitaka-*sama* has personally ordered the borders of his realm defended against any who would ride north to take you. Even the Shogun will think twice about provoking Lord Date. Relax and enjoy some breakfast! You all stink, so first order of business is a bath, in the village. Sorry we have no *ofuro* aboard—the water is too heavy to carry when we are flying at nearly full capacity like this."

"Does Lord Abe know where we are?" asked Masuyo. If Lord Abe knew, then her father knew.

"I dispatched a rider to the village, to send a message at the distillery. We are certain they are monitoring our line, given what happened to you. We sent a false message, claiming to be heading west with you, as the Shogun's men would expect. Lord Date knows you are on your way, and Lord Abe knows where we are actually headed. He'll know it's false. We cannot communicate correct details until we get the code key to him, but he'll know we have you. We're back to old-fashioned riders for messages. Never thought the Shogun's people would catch on to the technology so quickly."

Tōru laughed. "Well, it's a good thing, actually. We'll need to communicate throughout all the domains if the foreigners come. Glad they listened so carefully to our lessons, Takamori!"

As they hiked to the village, shuffling through the layer of fresh fallen snow, Jiro caught them up on his progress over the past three months. "This is only the first of the dirijibi. As you can see, it works! We are building ten more, throughout the domains, thanks to your lectures. Lord Date in Sendai is building two. One to fight the Americans here, one to fight them in America."

"Fight them? What are you saying?" asked Tōru, alarmed.

"One of his ancestors was a shipbuilder. He ordered his retainer Hasakira Tsunenaga to sail ships all the way to Rome and the Americas a couple of centuries ago. Lord Date wishes to revive his ancestor's exploratory spirit. He is most anxious to speak with you directly, as he wonders if the dirijibi can make it to America's shores. He—he contemplates attacking the Americans first rather than waiting for them to come here as you say they will."

"Oh no! No, no, no. First, these ships are not strong enough for the journey, at least not these designs. But we don't want to attack America, just get her to leave us alone!" cried Tōru.

"The Date clan is known for being ambitious and aggressive," said Asano thoughtfully in his dry way. "I would have thought two hundred and fifty years of peace would have calmed them down a bit, but I see not."

"Good thing Date is our ally and not our enemy," added Saigo.

"I'm an airship pilot, not a diplomat," said Jiro, promoting himself from his previously coveted position of "engineer." "All the politics and history is above me. But yes, Saigo-*sama*, Lord Date frightens even his friends and retainers. He frightens me, too."

Tōru grimaced. He was glad his ideas were taking root, but realized events were rapidly escalating out of his control, with unforeseen consequences. *What other hotheads had new and dangerous plans? Had he accidentally kindled a revolution? A war with America?* He only wanted to warn the Shogun, to strengthen his homeland and create opportunity for her people, not start wars. He rubbed his neck, afraid to follow the chain of thought too far.

He turned to simpler matters.

"How are we doing on trains and tracks?" asked Tōru. If armies had to be rushed from the inland to the coasts to defend against a foreign invasion, he saw the trains as important as a good supply of guns and ammunition.

"Tracks, great," said Jiro. "We don't have to build in secret anymore. The Shogun himself sees their benefit to his rule. Or at least Lord Abe so claims in the Shogun's name. He commanded all the *daimyō* to connect their *hans* to the line he has ordered built alongside the *Tōkaidō* roadway between Kyoto and Edo. He's going to make the *daimyō* visit Edo more frequently on his *sankin kotai* exchange policy. Regular meetings. The lords hate it, mostly, but they want trains too, so they are building as fast as they can. Lord Date is building a line south to Edo as well, the Tōhoku Line. By summer, we should have lines stretching from here in the far north to the Satsuma lands in the southwest."

"That's tracks. What about engines?" asked Tōru.

Jiro made a face. "You are not a good engineer, sir, or at least not a good engineering *sensei* teacher. The students in your engineering school have all failed in their first attempts to cast the engines. I blame you, sir."

Tōru laughed, "Sorry. I needed you to explain those bits."

"Indeed you did, sir."

"To be fair, you failed the first two times too!" said Tōru to the former blacksmith and former engineer, recalling the giant cast iron flower displays now adorning Lord Aya's courtyard.

"I did, sir. *Shinpai wa irimasen,* no worry. They will figure it out just as we did. You did do a great job of inspiring them. They are determined to build trains, so trains they will build. Eventually."

"Let's hope so," said Takamori. They reached the village. After a glorious scrub and steaming bath at the public *ofuro*, they gathered at the distillery. A bored young bartender served them an indifferent meal. Tōru did not miss the gilded house arrest of Lord Abe's generous hospitality, but he had grown accustomed to fine food. It was a shock to eat overcooked fish in a sauce that smelled ever so slightly off, over dry stale rice. He had forgotten the poor food of ordinary people during his months of luxury in Lord Aya's service and as Lord Abe's guest.

The clatter of the telegraph receiving a message broke into their conversation halfway through the meal. The languid bartender roused himself and rushed to the exotic device. Lacking Chie's skill, he had to read the dots and dashes off the page.

He ran over to Jiro the second he had sounded out the message.

"Aya Tōmatsu arrive nightfall. Over."

Masuyo could not hide her relief. She was even happier when Jiro casually asked, "Shall we go get them?"

Soon they were back on the airship, loaded with supplies and freshly clean crew and passengers. Lords Aya and Tōmatsu were on their way, along with a host of other sympathetic *daimyō*, to Aoba Castle in Sendai. Now that all the hostages were free, they could turn their attention to the next phase in their struggle against the Shogun and their plans to organize a defense of the nation against the foreigners. The sooner they picked up the lords, the sooner the war council could begin.

Finding them took an hour, but a dozen *daimyōs* and retainers in procession are hardly easy to hide from the air, even when they wish to stay hidden. The *daimyos'* party was black against the new-fallen snow. Jiro set down his airship directly in their path, causing several of the lords' horses to rear up in panic. As his crew tied down anchor lines to nearby trees, calming the bucking ship, Tōru, Takamori and Asano shimmied swiftly down the ropes and ladders cast over the sides. Masuyo watched from above.

Tōru saw Lord Aya and ran to kneel before him. He bowed.

"Sir, good to see you. I have your daughter safe with us, above."

Lord Aya drew him up, maintaining his dignity for the moment and hiding his own delight at seeing the young man again. "*Gokurō.* Well done." He looked up at the enormous dirigible swaying gently above them. "You actually get people to ride around in that barbaric thing?" he asked, a twinkle in his eye.

"Yes, sir. In fact—"

"*Wakatta, wakatta.* I get it. You are here to put me in that monstrosity, just like you did with your train. I know how you operate, Himasaki, don't think I don't. And you've left my wild daughter up there to make me eager to do it."

Lord Aya grinned at the young *samurai* and bellowed up to his daughter. "*Toranosuke! Sore wa dame da,* running around dressed like a savage! What would your poor mother say?"

Even as he scolded and blustered, Lord Aya raced up the ladder to greet his laughing and crying daughter, tangling his feet in his wide *hakama* skirts as he climbed the ladder. Jiro's crewmen hauled the old lord unceremoniously over the edge, there being no more elegant way to get him aboard until they had the ship lower and the gangplank extended from the hold below so the horses could board.

The other lords with Lord Tōmatsu, more mindful of their dignity, waited patiently until they could walk aboard, murmuring praise and wonder at the mighty ship. Their horses resisted entering the airship's hold, but their masters urged the frightened creatures to step aboard until they were safely stabled below. It was difficult to tell who was more panicked, the horses or the lords.

Jiro whispered to Tōru, "Ready to go, sir. All are aboard."

Tōru sang out, "Brace yourselves, gentlemen. Take us up, Captain Jiro. Next stop, Aoba Castle!"

The ship lifted off, gently this time, in the crisp still late afternoon air, above the glistening snowy fields and forests of the northlands. The *Hakudo Maru* settled into her voyage to the heart of the north, bearing with her some of the bravest and boldest of Japan's rebel leaders.

CHAPTER 16

⊕

REVOLUTION

"Those who make peaceful revolution impossible,
make violent revolution inevitable."
— John Fitzgerald Kennedy

Jiro and his crew landed the *Hakudo Maru* in a clearing below the castle by the banks of the Hirose River, across from the thriving city of Sendai. Leaving behind the crew to guard the ship, the passengers set out for Aoba Castle.

The city by the river was green and elegant, barely touched with traces of early winter snow, living up to her well-known nickname of *Mori no Miyako*, the City of Trees. Lord Date, lords of the title both present and past, loved trees and had ordered thousands planted over the decades. *Mori no Miyako* indeed, the city was lushly adorned by these now mature plantings.

The castle rose above them on a plateau overlooking the city, protected by deep forest to the west and cliffs to the south and east. Though the first *daimyō* of Sendai and Aoba, Date Masamune, had planned to build more defensive structures to protect the castle, he had never gotten around to the task.

No matter, for men had never taken Aoba Castle, although fire and earthquake had done what they could in the two and a half centuries since the Date clan made the castle their base. The ancient keep was protected by two factors more important than mere walls: the natural defenses of cliffs and forest and the fearsome reputation of the Date lords for long memories and terrible vengeance.

No one messed with House Date.

As the party climbed the long, stoutly guarded road to the castle's main gate, higher and higher in the cool morning light, Tōru pondered what they should do next. His thoughts had been so focused on survival during their flight that he'd had no time to consider what to do with his sudden freedom.

He smiled to see the telegraph line climbing the hill alongside the road, and the spur of train tracks growing from Sendai to the south, as ant-like workers swarmed over the growing edge of the track. Jiro was correct. His lessons in the workshop during his imprisonment at Lord Abe's compound were having a rapid and profound impact across many *hans*, from the original allies in the west, to new supporters here in the north like Lord Date.

Proud as he was to see his ideas and the foreign technologies he had brought home taking root, Tōru was uneasy. He feared events were spiraling out of control, not that he had ever harbored any illusions he controlled anything. In a land where each man knows his rank and position to the finest, most subtle degree, he knew no fisherman's son, nor even a great *daimyō's* unacknowledged illegitimate son, could rise to a leadership role.

He felt responsible, though, for he had brought home the Western technology and fought to share it. If his actions led to dangerous instability, then the suffering of the people would be on his head. True, he had come home from America without much of a plan beyond "make Japan strong by teaching Western technology to anyone who will listen." He hoped her leaders would use the technology to strengthen Japan.

He had little interest in the cross-currents of politics roiling under the surface, between *bakufu* loyalists determined to keep the Tokugawa Shoguns in power no matter the cost and the *tōzama* outer lords, like Lord Shimazu in the west and Lord Date in the north, who favored anything the Shogun disliked. He had learned much about those politics, though, from Kato and Lord Abe during his months of house arrest on Lord Abe's compound. The Tokugawas had excluded the conquered *tōzama* lords from the rule of the country for two hundred and fifty years. This slight hardened into long-nursed resentment, slumbering coals that events could blow into bright flame with surprisingly little provocation. The Shoguns mistrusted the *tōzama* lords, and not without cause.

Such quarrels seemed to Tōru so petty and small next to the greater problems he saw, both with the foreigners and with his homeland's poverty and stagnation. He had returned from simple patriotism, wanting to be proud of his homeland and make her strong enough to stay independent of the foreigners, even the ones he admired, like his American friends. But over the past year, he had become aware of a deeper need in his homeland, a gaping wretchedness that had nothing to do with the foreigners.

He had grown up in a small fishing village, with the great wealth and power of his father reflected only in his excellent education. Though he knew his father's world, he never felt part of it, only a visitor by his father's insistence, tolerated with barely disguised hostility and scorn by his father's wife and his senior retainers.

Tōru's day-to-day outlook on life was built around his life as a rural commoner in a poor and neglected fishing village. Life for Jiro and his other childhood playmates was hard, and their parents' life was hard, and their grandparents' life had been hard, on back as far as anyone could remember. Nothing had notably changed for the better for centuries, although at least the terrible clan wars of the past had been banished by the Tokugawas' iron-fisted rule. Tōru's childhood village friends saw no hope of growth or advancement, only grinding toil from a hard birth to an early death.

Tōru had noticed on his brief return to Iwamatsu that the shabby village of his childhood memories had grown shabbier and more worn, the people ragged and too slender by far. He had now passed through dozens of similarly forgotten villages on his recent travels. He had seen the coarse ugly form poverty takes in the big cities. Tōru pondered how to use the technology he had brought back not just to defend his homeland, but also to build a new and better life for the common people, the ragged villagers he now rode by in the guise of a *samurai* well mounted on a fine horse.

His thoughts dwelt for a moment on Jiro's off-hand remark yesterday that Lord Date wanted to attack America with his dirigible.

The others laughed it off as a joke, but Tōru shivered at the thought. Lord Date could not comprehend what he was proposing. No one could comprehend the scale and scope of the vast American continent without seeing it personally. No one could understand the ambitions and pride of a young aggressive people still building their nation and how swiftly they would respond.

Tōru had learned in his brief time at the capital that what made sense and what leaders decreed were often two entirely different things. An ambitious lord like Date probably *was* a danger to peace and stability in the realm, and beyond her borders, and therefore a threat to the Shogun, as Lord Abe had patiently explained. Worse yet, rather than solving problems at home, Lord Date was proposing creating new wars. If Lord Date was making a joke, it was a bad one.

Tōru's idealistic assumption that the quarrelsome *daimyōs* would unite against the foreign threat had been proven wrong. Instead he seemed to be uniting the *tōzama* lords against their traditional foes, the Shogun and his supporters. Both sides saw the common threat, but worried more about fighting each other than uniting to meet the foreign threat.

He had thrown in his lot with the *tōzama* lords accidentally the moment he landed on Lord Abe's shores, or perhaps back at the moment of his birth as a son, if an unacknowledged one, of Lord Shimazu of the Satsuma clan. But he had no interest in fighting the Shogun. He only wanted to unite the *hans* to defend against the foreigners. He wanted to open the country to trade, as a powerful nation equal to all the great nations, by showing the foreigners Japan's strength. He did not want his homeland to fall to foreigners as once-great China had.

His other hopes were also collapsing, hopes the *daimyōs* and *bakufu* would use his technologies to build wealth, make a dignified peace with the foreigners from a position of strength and bring prosperity to the common people. His telegraphs and dirigibles and trains seemed to be inspiring the great lords to think instead of war with each other, with the Shogun and with the foreigners. No one was discussing how to create prosperity for the commoners and a strong defensive position for Japan so she could remain independent of foreign rule.

The gates opened as they approached.

Tōru shivered as he passed within.

He was entering the stronghold of an ally, not that of the cruel Shogun who had decreed his death. Even so, the ancient gates and high walls whispered warning. The Date clan reputation for vengeance and aggression was well earned. Interactions with such a clan should be undertaken only with great caution.

Grooms led away their horses. A pair of young guards took their weapons respectfully and stored them away.

Soon they were seated in Lord Date's reception hall.

The greatest of the visiting lords sat close to Lord Date and the *tokonoma* while the humble retainers like Tōru knelt respectfully further away. They were in a wide, broad beamed room full of light from opened *shōji* doors on one side, overlooking a spectacular view of Sendai and the Horose river below.

The rustling of branches from many great trees filled the room.

The waiting men sat in expectant silence.

Lord Date Yoshitake greeted the assembly and thanked them for coming. He was a vital man in his 40s, not tall but fit and athletic, with a nervous energy that reached all the way across the room to Tōru, kneeling by the doorway. Unusually, Lord Date did not speak from a seated position, but prowled back and forth near the front of the room, like a leopard stalking prey. He spoke for a moment about the need to work together. He thanked them for the honor of so many great lords visiting his humble castle. He did not sound as arrogant and proud as his reputation had made him out to be.

Rather Tōru saw in Date a quick intelligence and a strong will.

Tōru's thoughts drifted for the moment, thinking of Masuyo, who had remained on the *Hakudo Maru* with Jiro and the commoners. She'd been upset to be left behind, but had not argued the point. The small freedoms she had carved out for herself this past year existed only in the margins, in hidden places, where her father's indulgence and affection allowed her to pursue her unconventional interests. Outside Lord Aya's halls, the rules and conventions of society were too strong to defy. So Masuyo stayed behind, no doubt plotting new improvements for the airship with Jiro and designing an airship uniform for herself, something that did not involve either an action-limiting *kimono* or a peasant's poor rags.

Takamori hissed, "Himasaki!" under his breath.

Tōru blinked out of his daze to discover every face turned his way. "He wants your plan," whispered Takamori.

Lord Date had beckoned him forward.

Tōru moved to the front of the room, his thoughts spinning. *What plan?* When he arrived at the front, after bowing to Lord Date, he turned to face the assembly.

They looked expectantly at him, like older, grayer versions of the young *samurai* and blacksmiths he had been teaching for the past two and a half months. He bowed to the group. His face flushed with embarrassment, realizing he had nothing to say to the great assembly, suddenly glad Masuyo was not here to see his humiliation.

An awkward silence ensued, broken only when Lord Date said, "Please share with us your plan."

Tōru stalled by thanking them all for assembling, and risking their lives on the experimental *Hakudo Maru*. A small burst of laughter at this encouraged him. "We are embarked upon a great experiment," he proclaimed, rather grandly he thought. "We are asking ourselves 'what is the next step?' Lord Date has honored me with his request that I share with you my plan. I am too lowly a poor fisherman to even propose a plan among all these great leaders."

A murmur filled the room. They all knew his story, *Observations of Barbarian America* being well dissected among these men. "But if I were not a poor fisherman, this is the plan I would propose."

Tōru took a deep breath.

Suddenly he did have a plan. An obvious plan, perhaps, and certainly a crazy ambitious plan. It was the plan of his heart, a vision for pursuing the aims disturbing his thoughts this morning, of peacefully uniting the country for defense and of bringing prosperity to the common people.

"We are here to defend our homeland. We will do this, thanks to all of you, to your hard work and bravery in coming here, your commitment of your resources to building defenses in each of your domains. All this is excellent. By summer we will have a thousand gun batteries defending our borders. But it is not enough to defend a coastline. We must strengthen our people. Not just the mighty, gathered here in this room, but each of the villagers under your care." Tōru stopped for a moment as a murmur rose up in the room. He imagined what they were thinking, surprise at his mention of poor commoners during a discussion of great military matters.

"We can drive the foreigners away once, with our dirijibi and our gun batteries. They will not expect such resistance from us, and will withdraw to consider the matter, like Biddle and Glynn before them." He heard growls at the mention of the other two Americans who had attempted to challenge Japan's *sakoku* isolation policy. "They will return, I promise you this. They will return in force, and lay siege to our homeland. A long siege."

Tōru remembered his arguments with Lord Aya about allowing commoners to fight and command other men, even their social superiors, and how Lord Aya had pronounced his ideas ridiculous and refused to discuss the matter further. He knew they must involve not just the *samurai* but also the nine out of every ten Japanese who was a commoner. Tōru pushed on.

"To win a long siege, or better, to avoid one altogether because the foreigners do not believe they can conquer us, we need a strong economy. You cannot arm and feed your soldiers without more resources. Every village needs to turn its attention not to subsistence and survival but to building strength. Food, better food, for our soldiers and workers. Clothing and armor. Weapons and airships. Schools to train engineers." Tōru had their attention. They were mystified at his focus on their villages and food production, expecting rather a plan for dirigibles and gun batteries.

"You, my lords, are powerful. Many of you are wealthy. You have committed your wealth, your fighting men and your courage to the defense of our homeland. This is good. This is a first step. But all your wealth and all your courage will not be enough to stand against all the world if the foreigners come at us in force, united against us."

A rumbling growl arose as the lords resisted Tōru's words.

"You need the lowly as well as the great made strong and educated and committed to strengthening our country. You've met Captain Jiro, of the *Hakudo Maru*."

They nodded. Jiro had been a great favorite during the drinking last night, challenging them to consume vast quantities of *saké* and regaling the lords with humorous stories of his first failed attempts at flight and later his successful escape from the Shogun's men.

"Captain Jiro was a ragged blacksmith in a poor village a year ago, illiterate and knowing nothing beyond the borders of his village. Today he reads. He leads a skilled crew. He navigates from one end of our Emperor's realm to the other. He personally designed, engineered and built the *Hakudo Maru*, working from the sketchiest of plans. Imagine a thousand of our common people, ten thousand, one hundred thousand, similarly skilled and educated and contributing to our nation like Captain Jiro instead of living in rags, hungry and cold, in our villages. Can you see the strength of our homeland if we raise up ten thousand Captain Jiros to fight by our side?" Tōru paused, fearing the grumbling of the lords, but was met instead with quiet attention from the room of men.

"You have asked me for a plan. I give you instead this vision, of ten thousand Captain Jiros. We must lead not just your soldiers, but your farmers and merchants to join this mission. We must educate not just your own sons, but also the sons of the village headmen. We must feed not just your fighters, but also your factory workers and merchants and servants. We must make every village a castle of prosperity and education, defending Japan with foodstuffs and textiles and weapons. We must show the world, through the wealth of our commoners, that we are not a nation to be trifled with, not a nation to be exploited and subjugated like great and fallen China. We must show the foreigners our Japanese ways are superior to theirs, that even the lowliest among us is blessed with education and prosperity. We must remake our land to bring prosperity to every village and unleash the full power of all our people."

Tōru bowed and returned to his seat, spent. He could have gone on, for he had many ideas on how to accomplish this, but his throat suddenly clamped shut, dry and choked. *How dare he address the lords this way?* Surely he would be thrown from the room, stripped of his newly claimed *samurai* status and sent back to the Shogun to die.

A heavy silence filled the room.

Tōru could hear his heart pounding. He feared others could hear it as well, so loudly did it thud in his chest.

Lord Date stood. He began to laugh, a low chuckle that began in his throat and spread down to his belly as it rumbled forth louder and louder. The room stayed silent at this unexpected response. No one could find anything funny in Tōru's earnest speech. Though most people expected the unexpected from Lord Date, his laughter was unexpected even so.

"You warned me, Aya-*dono*, you warned me this fisherman had unusual ideas. I see the truth in your words. You brought a wild revolutionary into our midst to stir up trouble."

Lord Aya bowed to his host, not daring to look at Tōru.

"The fisherman is right. We must enrich our country while we strengthen our military. *Fuguo qiangbing*, as our Chinese scholar friends would put it, or *fukoku kyōhei*, in our own tongue. It is an ancient idea. It is a good idea."

Such was Lord Date's prestige in this group that heads began to nod in agreement.

Tōru breathed again.

"I have been mocked for my habit of planting trees. Why would I need more trees, people ask, when the forests around me stretch forever?" He paced to the open doorway, overlooking the tree-filled city and the surrounding deep forest, and waved his arm to indicate the sweep of tall pines below. "Those over there, the tallest, were planted by my grandfather. These here by my father. Those in the city are by my order."

He paused, still gazing at his trees. "Trees remind us of the past, as my grandfather's tall trees trace the decades between us. Planting a tree forces us to consider the future. Trees are resources, they are wealth. Like wealth, they only grow over time and slowly. I plant trees because planting trees teaches one to look far into the future, and plan for a day one will not see personally. A seed must be planted and nurtured patiently for many decades for the full bounty of the mature tree to come forth. Our people will only be wealthy if we in this room act now to plant the seeds of their wealth, as young Himasaki says, in their education and in their roles in our society. He asks us not only to war against the foreigners, but to make revolution against ourselves, to reach out our hands to help our commoners grow in strength."

Lord Date turned and looked at Tōru.

"You propose dangerous ideas, Himasaki. You ask us to strengthen the weak and to transform the many. To plant and nurture the seeds of our own overthrow. You would change our world, and diminish our place in it. Do you understand this?"

Tōru nodded. He did not think of himself as a revolutionary. He only wanted to ease the suffering of the common people, his friends, his neighbors. He had not considered what the rise of the commoners meant for their rulers. He only saw that they needed to rise, like Jiro needed to rise to the level of his formidable talents.

Lord Date paced down the room, looking at each lord in turn.

"Do you all understand this? Do you see what the fisherman is truly asking us to do, to overthrow ourselves, not today, but in a generation? To rise up and make revolution upon ourselves?"

Tōru could see the implications dawning on the other lords in the room. Once they understood the idea, they did not like it.

"I see why the Shogun wants this fisherman dead. I had asked myself, 'why bother killing a fisherman?' but now I understand. The Shogun is right. If we allow him to live, and share his ideas, then both we and the Shogun are overthrown. The fight is not between the rebellious *tōzama* like myself and the Shogun. No, we are the same. The real battle here is between the fisherman's ideas and the old ways, ways that made us powerful and impoverished our people. The fisherman must die, so we *daimyōs* can live on another generation as we have, ruling our lands as we see fit."

Tōru did not dare reach up to rub the back of his neck in such august company, but the urge to do so was nearly overwhelming.

Lord Aya looked miserable, his prisoner turned protege in mortal peril once again.

"And yet," Lord Date whirled around, his *hakama* swinging around his legs at the sudden violence of the movement, "the fisherman is right!"

Lord Date slammed the side of his fist against the wall. "He speaks the truth! If we do not plant these seeds today, of prosperous and educated commoners, we will perish within a generation, fallen to the foreign barbarians and our own stagnation."

This time, the murmurs sweeping the room were not whispers and sighs but the growling roar of an angered crowd, not a single voice distinct in the buzz, but an inarticulate rumble. Lord Date held up his hands, demanding silence.

A hush fell across the assembly.

Lord Date turned to Tōru and bowed.

Tōru sat frozen, fearing the next bellow from Lord Date. *Was he to live? To die?* Nothing could have prepared him for Lord Date's next statement.

"House Date will raise up ten thousand Captain Jiros, as our fisherman suggests. Who is with me? What say you?"

Lord Aya understood the challenge.

He climbed to his feet, his old limbs stiff from the long meeting. "We are a small *han*, but we will seek out and nurture five hundred Captain Jiros. We already have one!"

The other *daimyōs* laughed. The mood in the room shifted, became light, joyous.

Lord Tōmatsu stood.

"House Tōmatsu will bring ten thousand." The other lords began to stand and shout out their pledges to join the revolution. Soon the whole room was standing and shouting out "Ten thousand Captain Jiros! To our fisherman, *banzai, banzai, banzai!*"

CHAPTER 17

DEFIANCE

"Ransack the history of revolutions,
and it will be found that every fall of a regime
has been presaged by a defiance which went unpunished.
It is as true today as it was ten thousand years ago
that a Power from which the magic virtue has gone out, falls."
— Bertrand de Jouvenel, *On Power*

No one ever records the tedium of revolution.

The historians record the battles at the barricades, the names of the martyrs for the cause, the documents soaring with uplifting language. But no revolution has ever been launched without hours, many hours, of tedious bickering over strategy, tactics and immediate plans. And finances.

Tōru's revolution was no different.

After the roars of approval for his "Ten Thousand Captain Jiros" speech, followed by a fine dinner, the lords settled down the next day for the hard work of the strategizing and planning. They had a vision— ten thousand Captain Jiros — and a slogan — *fukoku kyōhei* or "Enrich our country while strengthening our military." But details, millions of details, had to be worked out.

Doing so took weeks. Lists had to be made, of resources held and resources needed. And lists of the domains loyal to the *fukoku kyōhei* revolution, those that would remain neutral or pick a side that looked to be winning, and those that would fight to the death to maintain the Shogun's power. Messengers had to be dispatched on horseback, the old-fashioned way, to the allied *hans*, carrying key codes, for their telegraph surely did have listening ears. Engineers were sent to assist where Tōru's poor instruction had failed to convey enough technical detail in his workshops for the building of engines and telegraphs and factories.

Spies were sent out throughout the land to observe the Shogun's forces and track their locations and directions. Coded intelligence flowed over the growing network of telegraph lines snaking across the entire country. Informants within the Shogun's household were sought.

A rumor had taken hold in the pleasure district of Yoshiwara in Edo that Tokugawa Ieyoshi, the sixty-year-old Shogun, was ill and failing, even near death, according to some. His bureaucrats and household servants were, of course, long forbidden under ancient laws to frequent the *geisha* houses and *kabuki* theaters of the *ukiyo* pleasure district, a ban they honored mostly in the extraordinary care they took in their disguises as peasants and merchants on their visits there. The brothels and restaurants and *geisha* houses known to be frequented by the Shogun's men were abuzz with nothing else but the Shogun's failing health and his lack of suitable heirs.

The Shogun's 29-year-old son Tokugawa Iesada was considered by all to be a weak man, physically and mentally, not competent to rule, especially at a time of such turmoil. This was also a topic of much conversation in the gossipy pleasure district.

In any case, whether due to the Shogun's illness or a watch-and-wait policy decision or a stalemate among the leaders of the Council, little action was observed. No new defenses were built, no armies raised, no plans promulgated from the Shogun's court. No pursuit was launched for the missing four young people who had left the Shogun's troops circling in frustration below the *Hakudo Maru*. From the Shogun's court came only silence, a silence that rang loud against the hum of furious building activity throughout the countryside controlled by the rebel *daimyō*.

The rebel lords were effectively taxing themselves to provide the resources for this huge burst of building. Creative minds were put on the task of figuring out how to involve the wealthier peasants and merchants and craftsmen, many of whom had more actual liquid wealth than the impoverished *samurai* and their *daimyō* lords, to fund companies to create what was needed and employ the many workers needed to fulfill all the demands of defense and building prosperity. Savvy merchants invented shared ownership schemes and set up financial mechanisms to funnel cash from cash-rich but labor-poor domains to those with rich labor pools but no capital to invest in building trains and telegraphs and factories. New tracks crawled across the land, new telegraph wires sprang from tall poles. New factories rose from ravaged plains of ugly tree stumps, belching black smoke as steam engines powered the factories.

Jiro's fleet of ten dirigibles was now a fleet of ten dirigibles built, with crews in training, and fifty more being assembled in hangars across the land. As the fleet grew, Jiro promoted himself from Captain to Admiral, with the consent and approval of the lords. These were unusual times, and even the conservative old *daimyōs* recognized a brave blacksmith with several hundred hours of flight experience and the ability to fix the complex engines and steering mechanisms was better suited to managing these airships than a *samurai* skilled with a sword but no knowledge of flight.

Crews for the future dirigibles practiced with wooden mockups, training against the day their ships would soar out of the workshops. Hangars sprouted up throughout the realms loyal to the revolution. Dirigibles were status symbols. Any *daimyō* of any size and resources at all wanted one. And the lesser lords were not being left behind either. Lord Aya teamed up with with five other lesser *daimyōs* to build one together, the *Toranosuke Maru*. Naming privileges had gone to him although his investment was in fact the smallest, in recognition of his early contribution to the cause.

Along with Asano, Takamori and Tōru, Masuyo trained as well, until each was ready to captain and pilot a dirijibi airship.

The lords fortified the borders of the *fukoku kyōhei* loyalists against assault by the Shogun's forces. They drew up and signed pacts of mutual defense. They were now officially traitors, defying the Shogun, and committed to defiance through military means if pressed. They expected attacks from *bakufu* forces any day now.

Edo's passivity surprised everyone. A band of treason stretched from the far west, Lord Shimazu's Satsuma domain, on up the western coast of Japan all the way to the far north, where they were gathered in Lord Date's northern holdings.

The east and south were Shogunate *fudai* inner lord strongholds, but the front was being newly defined with each passing day. Each week, more allies flocked to their banner, as a new *daimyō* sent emissaries or arrived personally to join their discussions. At a certain point, they ceased to think of themselves as treasonous traitors and began to regard themselves simply as one side in a civil war, a cold civil war in which blood had not yet been shed nor banners raised in open defiance, but sides surely were being chosen and loyalties declared.

The day of execution for Lord Aya, Lord Tōmatsu and Tōru approached. Failure to appear would be an act of open defiance of the Shogun's decree, with their families subject to punishment and their landholdings to seizure by the Shogunate.

Two days before the day scheduled for the executions, Masuyo approached Lord Tōmatsu. She quietly attended all the meetings, never speaking, but slipping words of advice and insight to Tōru, Takamori and Lord Aya during the breaks. The other men tolerated her presence, understanding her to be an important leader's daughter who had bravely escaped the Shogun and invented many of the new technologies. Out of respect for Lord Aya, they made exception for her unconventional participation in their war councils and in the dirigible pilot training.

"Tōmatsu-*sama*, may I have a word with you?"

"Of course." He was fond of Masuyo and enjoyed seeing her.

"Lady Tōmatsu, she is well?" asked the girl, knowing there had been no communication from Lady Tōmatsu since she had left. She did not wish to pain her father's friend, but in the weeks since her own escape, her thoughts kept turning to her final conversation with Lady Tōmatsu.

Lord Tōmatsu looked at her sadly.

"There is no Lady Tōmatsu."

"Are you sure, my lord?"

"She's gone. I cannot reach her. My son is lost to me as well."

"That is why we must rescue her. And your son. And bring them here to safety."

"She left of her own free will. No. It is impossible."

Masuyo could hear the bitterness and hurt in Lord Tōmatsu's voice. And anger, the bitter anger of hurt pride. He had often joked about his difficult wife and her grand airs, but always with a kind of pride and affection, the kind of pride and affection that is rooted in love. Masuyo was embarrassed to press on, but given the life and death stakes, she persisted. She had seen Lady Tōmatsu's anguish over her difficult choice. She held out her hands, palms up, in a gesture both of vulnerability and pleading, speaking for Lady Tōmatsu as she had come to understood her.

"A woman has few choices and only hard ones in our world. I was with her the day you were condemned to death. She believed herself to have no husband and a helpless fatherless baby to protect. She did what she had to do to protect your son, as she believed you would have wished." Masuyo could hardly bring herself to utter the next words, matters of such privacy and delicacy, so boldly to the powerful older man. "My lord, she was loyal in the only way she knew how to be, acting to save your son. Now that you are free, can you not forgive her? And save her?"

Lord Tōmatsu stared at Masuyo a long time and then slowly nodded. He did not chastise her for speaking out of turn. Masuyo waited long for his reply.

"Yes, I want my wife by my side."

And so the council approved Masuyo's plan to fly her ship, the *Toranosuke Maru*, to Edo to rescue Lady Tōmatsu and her son, although the bold mission risked provoking the Shogun into turning the cold war into a hot war.

Once the decision had been reached by the rebel Council, Tōru pulled Masuyo aside outside the reception hall.

"What are you doing? This is no job for a woman!"

Masuyo pulled her arm away and glared at Tōru. "Of all people, I had hoped you would support me on this. Even my old father gave me his blessing. And the council its approval!"

"It's a great idea. I'm glad we're doing it for Lord Tōmatsu, of course. But it's dangerous. You'll be flying above thousands of *bakufu* troops. Let Jiro, Takamori, Asano and I deal with this."

"Oh, so I'm part of the team until everything gets real. Then the men need to take over."

"That's not what I meant!"

"I know exactly what you meant. I'm leading the mission precisely because I am a woman. Any man goes and there will be a fight for sure. With a woman we have a chance of avoiding a fight."

Tōru made a face, his disagreement clear.

"With me, a mere lowly woman," she said, with exaggerated sarcasm, "I might get a moment of confusion and uncertainty. Lady Tōmatsu's brother's warriors will hesitate to fire on me."

"You can't know that."

"It's our best shot. Lady Tōmatsu trusts me. She will come with me, quickly."

"You could be killed."

"So might we all. Step aside, fisherman. I need to prep my ship."

Masuyo pushed past Tōru, leaving him stunned and silent in the passageway. They had never quarreled in all the long and stressful months, although they had argued over tactics and plans with energy and passion. He had thought his faith in her and her trust in him had been strong, unbreakable. He only wanted to protect her and keep her safe.

But now everything felt broken between them. She would be flying south soon, possibly to her death. There was nothing he could do to protect her, or stop her. And there was nothing he could do to repair what he had damaged between them.

The next morning, the *Toranosuke Maru* took off for Edo to fetch the Lady Tōmatsu and Lord Tōmatsu's son. Lord Tōmatsu's retainer Sugieda and several of Lord Tōmatsu's men went along in case of fighting, joined by Masuyo, Jiro, Asano and Takamori. However, the plan was not to fight. The mission rested upon Masuyo's slender shoulders and an elegantly simple plan.

Tōru knew better than to try to join them and board her ship with the others. He watched hidden in the trees as the mission team prepared to depart. He whispered a prayer of protection to the Buddha in all his emanations, the local *kami* and the Christian God, too, for good measure, asking them all to watch over Masuyo.

Lord Aya waved farewell to his daughter, his eyes glistening as he smiled and waved to his daughter as the *Toranosuke Maru* soared up into the sparkling bright morning sky, the conservative old lord braver and more supportive than Tōru had been.

The journey south took all day, the dirigible skimming over fields and villages, startling the commoners below at the strange sight of a flying ship.

Under cover of night, Jiro landed the *Toranosuke Maru* in a grove on the grounds of Lady Tōmatsu's brother's home. Alone, without escort, dressed in her newly designed airship pilot uniform of trousers, tall boots and a stylish greatcoat, Masuyo approached the grand home from the gardens. She called out for Lady Tōmatsu.

Throwing the household into an uproar with her unexpected appearance, unusual attire and the great dragon dirigible floating serenely above, Masuyo waited until Lady Tōmatsu appeared.

Servants flocked to the garden, their mouths agape.

"Lord Tōmatsu has sent me with a message. He wishes you and your son to join him in exile. You must come now, this moment, and leave all behind. Please, join me, join us, join your husband and help us build the new Japan."

Lady Tōmatsu stared at Masuyo, her habitual composure shattered. She clasped her hands together tightly.

Masuyo could see they trembled even so.

"You are safe? And my husband — he wishes to have me with him?"

"Yes, my lady. But you must hurry. We must leave now, this moment. Leave all behind. Where is your son?"

Already the dirigible had drawn notice, floating boldly above the compound clearly visible above the trees of the garden. They could hear the pounding of soldiers at the main gate.

Lady Tōmatsu looked at Masuyo, her brother and the servants.

"Bring me my son!"

A nurse ran and returned moments later with a squalling red-faced toddler, howling at the commotion.

Lady Tōmatsu bowed to her brother and thanked him for his hospitality. "Please forgive me for any inconvenience I have caused you." He gaped open-mouthed at her and at Masuyo, resplendent in her new airship uniform, glittering with gold braid.

She turned to Masuyo, her son balanced on her hip.

"Let's go."

As the soldiers poured into the house, searching for the rebels, the *Toranosuke Maru* rose up into the moonless sky, black against a million stars, with Lady Tōmatsu, her son and Masuyo clinging to the ropes supporting a large basket dangling below the dirigible.

Jiro cast down a special bag fastened firmly to a stout rope, to bring up the shrieking babe. Lady Tōmatsu hesitated and then bound her son tight into the bag. Tenderly Jiro's rough men pulled the precious parcel up and lifted the screaming child over the edge. Once the toddler was safe, Jiro sent down another rope and a rope ladder. Masuyo bound the rope around Lady Tōmatsu, over her elegant *obi*, and tied it into a kind of harness.

She tested her knots.

Sturdy and strong.

Lady Tōmatsu looked terrified, clinging to the ropes of the swaying basket as they rose ever higher into the sky above the twinkling lights of the capital. Masuyo pretended not to notice Lady Tōmatsu's discomfort and fear.

Masuyo gestured with her hands to demonstrate the hand over hand climbing motion needed for ascending the rope ladder.

"You next," said Masuyo. "I've done it before. Just hold tight and place your foot solidly before you reach for the next hold. Give me your sandals. I'll bring them up for you. It will be easier to climb in just your *tabi*." She put Lady Tōmatsu's sandals into her small knapsack and fastened it. She tugged once more on Lady Tōmatsu's safety harness. "See? This won't let you fall. Now climb, quickly."

Lady Tōmatsu climbed, a sight no one who knew her socially would believe, even if they saw her with their own eyes. She moved slowly, cautiously, awkwardly, her habitual perfect grace mangled by the extraordinary task set for her. She struggled with her kimono until she figured out how to kick the silk folds out of her way before placing each step. The wind from their speed tugged at her, dismantling her carefully done hair, until it streamed free like a long ebony banner floating on the wind. Finally she reached the top.

Jiro's men pulled her to safety in another tremendous shock to her dignity, to be so manhandled by men of vastly inferior rank, tugging her over the rim of the airship. Masuyo was certain the grand dame would rather have died than be subjected to such treatment, but it was necessary. Lady Tōmatsu would survive to live with her eternal embarrassment. And with her precious son.

Jiro gestured to Masuyo and shouted for her to climb.

Masuyo didn't bother with a safety harness but tied the rope ladder to the side of the swaying basket to give it a little stability. As she climbed, she pretended to more confidence than she felt. The first time she climbed a swaying rope ladder she had been fleeing for her life from horsemen with arrows and guns, which focused her mind on getting up fast. This time, she was tempted to enjoy the view, but the sight of the ground flying by below made her dizzy when she tried. *Better climb and climb fast.* Climbing was easier for her in boots and trousers than it had been for poor Lady Tōmatsu tangled up in her *kimono*.

Soon Jiro's crewmen were tugging her over the edge to safety.

Masuyo turned to Jiro.

"Captain, next stop, Chiyoda Castle. Can you hover us in place without landing?"

Jiro scoffed. "Can a fish swim? Can Jiro design anything?"

"To Chiyoda, Jiro. Now, please." Masuyo shook her head fondly at the exuberant Jiro.

Once over the heart of the Chiyoda castle compound, Masuyo gave the next command. Jiro and Takamori watched with pride as she led with calm authority. It was her idea after all, and she was the commanding officer on this particular mission.

"Lights!" Crewmen lighted fifty small lanterns affixed to the sides of the ship. They were no longer hiding. Each lantern alone was puny, casting a dim yellow glow. Together, they collectively made a great light, illuminating the ship and the dragon image beneath. An extra dozen lights ringed the great dragon's head prow.

Like a glowing oval ring of fire, the dirigible floated in the sky.

"Sound the horns!"

With great enthusiasm, crewmembers blasted the ship's foghorn and a handful of other horns of various types assembled for the purpose. They generated a horrendous cacophony, as though demons unleashed from hell were howling their excitement.

"Drums!"

A professional *taiko* player recruited from Sendai beat upon his giant drum, which was fastened firmly to the deck.

Masuyo peered over the rim to check her work.

As she had hoped, hundreds of soldiers, perhaps thousands, streamed out of buildings, torches in hand, waving and shouting up at the airship. The first arrows pierced the sky nearby, falling harmlessly back to the ground.

"I think we have their attention." She smiled with satisfaction. "Bombs away!"

Her crew threw overboard not bombs, but thousands of fluttering strips of paper, filled with a handful of messages, each labeled "A Message to Our Honored Leader Shogun." *Fukoku kyōhei. Unite against the foreign barbarians. Educate our people. Work with us to build our country. One nation under one Shogun and one Emperor. United we stand, divided we fall. We come in peace to build prosperity together. Time is short, we must act now, together. Join us and together we will overcome all obstacles.*

The arrows were coming closer now.

Masuyo nodded to Jiro to take them up. As he shouted the command, she indicated that the crewmembers throwing the paper slips overboard should keep doing so. As the airship steamed up and back to the north and safety, it left in its wake on the streets of Edo and the towns above a long trail of fluttering papers, the first wave of many to follow, intended to reach the hearts of the people and win them to the side of the emergent revolution.

Back at Aoba Castle, Lord and Lady Tōmatsu's reunion was as chilly and formal as any Masuyo had ever witnessed. She found them difficult to understand, for her own dear father was always affectionate and loving with her, even as he tried in vain to get her to behave in public when others were about.

The *daimyō* and his wife bowed to each other stiffly. They inquired after each other's health. They pronounced themselves most pleased to see the other in such fine health.

Lady Tōmatsu handed her husband their shrieking son, a spitting ball of squirmy toddler.

"Your son is safe, thanks to Lady Aya."

"*Yokatta.* That's good." Lord Tōmatsu turned to Masuyo, still in her glorious uniform. "*Hontōni arigatō.* Your hard work and courage is much appreciated, Lady Aya."

Masuyo murmured, "*Dō itashimashite.*"

She turned away to give them privacy.

Lord Tōmatsu pulled his son to his chest and tilted his head to bury his face in his son's black hair. Masuyo saw the tears brimming in his eyes. She slipped away to join her friends while the reunited family retired to their quarters in Lord Date's castle.

Tōru, Jiro, Takamori, Masuyo and Asano gathered in the kitchen of the great castle. The air was still sullied and sere between Tōru and Masuyo, but the others did their best not to notice. Masuyo refused to give Tōru a moment alone to apologize.

They were all hungry after the excitement of the rescue. They were eager to spend some time together without all the formality required when the great lords were in council. The revolution was theirs, their ideas and their energy, but in a world of strict hierarchy, their elders would be deciding strategy, not them. Painful as it was for them to watch the ponderous discussions creep forward, their junior status forced patience upon them.

"Do you think they'll let you stay dressed like that?" asked the irrepressible Jiro. He had given Masuyo the last scraps of his carefully hoarded golden braid to decorate her uniform and obtained for her the smallest boots in all of Japan to fit her tiny feet. He nodded with a certain proprietary pride in her outfit. "You were magnificent, up there shouting commands."

Masuyo smiled demurely. "It was important for the mission that I be appropriately dressed and able to move freely. On mission, yes, I believe so."

She had in fact won a major battle. No one now questioned her sartorial choices, or her right to command missions, even her father. The other lords now simply referred to her as *Toranosuke-sama*, which was fine with Masuyo even if they meant it as an ironic joke. She had found some protected middle space of neither male nor female nature where she was free to act in spite of her gender.

She still held to silence in the meetings, for even the other young people, Tōru and Takamori and Asano, never spoke either unless specifically called upon by the great lords. Jiro, as a commoner, was never even invited to the meetings, although many plans revolved around his dirigible fleet. Some changes were still impossible. But some changes were real, and growing stronger every day.

When summaries of the day's discussions or new ideas were handed out for review and comment, Masuyo's clear intelligent mind had touched and refined them, a fact most of the lords knew. And *daimyōs* whose engineers were stuck on an engineering problem now made frequent polite approach to her father, asking if "Admiral Jiro and Toranosuke-*sama* had any ideas—" Lord Aya had finally resorted to handing out little cards with a map showing where Jiro and Masuyo might be found in Castle Aoba, for consultations with the engineers.

Tōru smiled, chastened by her outburst at him and relieved she had returned safely. He was glad to see her unleashed to her old self even here in this strange and unfamiliar environment.

"We have to go back soon."

They knew Tōru meant to Edo, to Chiyoda Castle. "The lords are almost ready. To go back in force and give the Shogun our ultimatum. Representation on the council for the excluded *tōzama* lords. Pardons for Lord Aya and Lord Tōmatsu, and restoration of their lands and titles. Pardons for you and me as well, Takamori! We got our own line in the document."

Takamori laughed, his large frame shaking with mirth. "We'll burn that bridge when we get to it. For tonight, no work talk. We'll have to save the realm soon enough. For tonight, to old friends and new. *Kanpai!*" He raised his cup of *saké* in toast, joined by Tōru, Jiro, Asano and Masuyo, sipping her plum wine.

"Kanpai!"

They were gathered there together still a few hours later in the early hours of dawn when the telegraph line in the closet clattered to life. Jiro and Masuyo were quickest to decode the message, sent from Lord Shimazu, in the new encoded language.

An American admiral, leading a fleet of warships, was docked in Hong Kong for supplies and fuel. Lord Shimazu's traders said the crew boasted they were heading to Japan next, to force her to open to American trade.

1853 — Summer

CHAPTER 18

PERRY

"The supreme art of war
is to subdue the enemy without fighting."
— Sun Tzu

Satsuma's traders were correct.

The Americans were here at last.

Commodore Matthew Calbraith Perry took another month to gather supplies in Hong Kong and then moved on to the Ryukyu Kingdom, vassal state to Lord Shimazu and the Satsuma *han*. The telegraph lines crackled with the news of each new advance.

On May 26, four American ships sailed or steamed into Naha Harbor in the Ryukyu Kingdom. This in itself was not unusual. American ships were already there, often, refueling and gathering supplies for the long journey back to the United States.

Naha Harbor had long served as a fueling and supplies station to many foreign ships on their way to China. The *sakoku* policy was not strictly enforced in the not-quite-Japan and not-entirely-not-Japan Ryukyu Kingdom, in an elegant bit of unspoken agreement between the Shogun and the Satsuma lords. This non-arrangement was quietly managed by Lord Abe, who saw the benefits to Japan of some inconspicuous trade with foreign powers. Foreign traders exchanged their wares for Japan's thin trickle of exports. Technically illegal, this trade's existence was carefully ignored by the *bakufu* Shogunate as long the Satsuma lords did not flaunt it.

As Lord Shimazu's spies reported, these ships were the steamship *Mississippi*, the two sloops-of-war *Plymouth* and *Saratoga*, and the sidewheel steamship *Susquehanna* that served as Commodore Perry's flagship.

The Prince Regent of the Ryukyu kingdom went aboard the flagship to greet the Commodore. Some days later the Commodore and a handful of senior officers paid a return call on the Prince Regent at his palace. Impressions of the American commander swiftly made their way to Lord Shimazu and the rest of the rebel *daimyos*, and, the rebels hoped, the listening ears of the Shogun.

For more than a month, the crewmen of the four American ships worked to resupply their ships, to repair and maintain them and to train and drill on land and sea. They sent survey missions around the coasts near the harbor, mapping each coastal curve and plumbing the depths of the sea. Perry's crew boasted of their mission in merchant stalls they visited, intelligence that crackled along the telegraph network from Satsuma to all the allied revolutionary domains, and the listening ears of the Shogun's men as well. These messages were sent unencoded, to maximize their impact on the Shogun and his allies.

The long-feared threat was finally here.

The Americans had come. With two sailing ships and two steam-powered ships, puffing black smoke against the pristine sky of the Naha harbor. They intended to challenge the Shogun's *sakoku* isolation policy directly by acting on Commodore Glynn's threat a few years ago "to sail straight to Edo" if his demands were not met.

Tōru and the rebel *daimyō* made good use of the time the Americans spent resupplying and surveying the Ryukyu Kingdom. Gun batteries lined the western and southwest coasts of Japan, wherever the rebel lords ruled. *Samurai* skilled with *katana* and *daikyu* bows drilled with the new repeating rifles modeled on the one Tōru had brought back, now rolling off the assembly lines of a hundred small gun factories throughout the rebel *hans*. New dirigibles took flight nearly every day, guided by their brave and inexperienced crews. Bartenders throughout the land learned to hear the telegraph's long and short beeps as words.

When the Lords Aya and Tōmatsu failed to appear for their executions, the Shogun finally stirred himself to action. The rumors in the *ukiyo* pleasure district carried the whisper that he had arisen from his sickbed and stumbled into a Council meeting, shouting red-faced that the traitors must be punished. Lord Abe's attempts to calm him only enraged the failing Shogun more. He commanded his top generals to capture the two lords and carry out their executions. He overruled Lord Abe who, according to the gossip, had counseled patience and a focus on building up defenses against the impending American visit.

While the telegraph carried news in minute detail of every action the Americans took in the Ryukyu Kingdom, the Shogun did nothing to fortify borders. Instead he sent his forces to attack Lord Aya's and Lord Tōmatsu's lands.

For the first time in Japan's long history, the Shogun's army reached a battlefield by train. The soldiers rode the train day and night from Edo, through Kyoto and then north to Lord Tōmatsu's domain, making the three week journey in a matter of days.

The cold civil war inched closer to bursting into a hot war. Allied rebel lords matched the Shogun's move and sent impressive numbers of men to fortify the borders of Lord Tōmatsu's land closest to the Shogun's forces.

They outnumbered the Shogun's force by at least two to one and held the higher ground. The fleet of dirigibles, now twenty strong, flown by fledgling crews, hung low on the horizon behind the rebels' forces, with Jiro's *Hakudo Maru* holding the center and Masuyo's *Toranosuke Maru* commanding the right flank.

The Shogun's men pointed and murmured with awe as the dirigible lines soared into position. The two armies faced each other across a wide plain, with mounted *samurai* and commoner pikemen arrayed in the thousands. War banners fluttered in the stiff breeze, darkly beautiful like a thousand poisoned flowers.

Not since the battle of Sekigahara two and a half centuries ago had such large hostile armies faced each other on Japanese soil.

A messenger from the Shogun's side picked his way across the rocky plain until he reached the halfway point to the rebel commanders. Shouting to be heard across the distance, he proclaimed, "In the name of the Shogun, defender of the realm, I command that you surrender the traitors Aya and Tōmatsu, that they may be lawfully punished for their crimes against the Shogun's leadership and the peace of the realm."

Lord Aya and Lord Tōmatsu mounted and rode unaccompanied to the messenger in the center of the field, their *daishō* swords belted to their sides.

The Shogun's general and a handful of his honor guards rode out to meet the two rebel lords.

"You see we are here," said Lord Aya.

The general grunted and motioned for his guards to take them into custody. Lord Tōmatsu held up his hand to stop their action.

The young guards fell back.

"We are not here to surrender. Instead, we invite you to join us in protecting the realm," said Lord Tōmatsu.

The Shogun's general stared at him in disbelief. No one had defied the Shogun's command in two hundred and fifty years and lived to tell about it.

"Enough. Let's go." He motioned once more for his guards to arrest the two *daimyōs*.

"I would not do that if I were you," said Lord Aya mildly.

He pointed above them to the sky, where the *Hakudo Maru*, the *Toranosuke Maru* and the *Yakaze Maru* had moved into position directly above them. Archers and riflemen pointed deadly weapons at them from the ships above. Heavier guns bristled from portholes in the lower part of the airships' frames.

"You gave your word of honor you would return. How can you stand here shameless and refuse? Return with me and regain your good name and your honor."

"We sacrifice our honor to save our nation. Tell the Shogun we defend our honor and his by defending the realm against the Americans who sail here even now. We will not shed your blood willingly, but his men may not pass this border until he joins us against the foreigners. The lives of your men are as precious to us as our own, for we will need every soldier of the Emperor to fight off the foreign barbarians." Lord Aya watched the general's face for a response to his mention of the shadowy and hidden Emperor.

In theory, though not in fact, the Shoguns ruled Japan in the Emperor's name and in His service. The rebels had taken to reminding each other of this neglected nuance as they grew more comfortable in their rebellion against the Shogun's rule.

If the Shogun would not defend the people of Japan against the foreign threat, then the rebel lords must, in the name of the Emperor he supposedly served.

The general glanced at the guns and bows trained on him from above and motioned his bodyguard to retreat. He wheeled his own horse around and scowled at them.

"The Shogun will not forget this."

"Nor shall we. We invite you to join us. The American fleet is in the Ryukyu Kingdom even now. You know this. Think on it well, General. In our domains, our coastlines are well defended, and we will keep our people safe. But we know this American, this Perry, is not interested in Satsuma or Ise or Nagasaki or Sendai. Tell the Shogun the American goes to Edo. He is bringing a letter from the American Shogun. He will want a reply. Join us, so we may together reply from a position of unity and strength, whether our reply be written in black ink or spilled blood."

"The Shogun will defend the realm if this American comes."

"With guns from the last century? With fishing boats against steamships? With swords and arrows and pikes against guns? No, the Shogun will fail. Our people will fall to the Americans as the great Chinese nation fell to the British. We must unite. Make use of the technology the fisherman brought back for us. Please," Lord Aya dismounted and bowed deeply to the Shogun's general, "please, for the sake of our people, join us."

Lord Aya's humility halted any response from the general. He stared down at the rebel *daimyō*, still holding a deep bow before him, and then kicked his horse to turn and ride back to his lines. Shouted orders and horns sounded up and down the Shogun's lines.

The Shogun's men turned and retreated the way they had come, east to Edo.

Lord Tōmatsu and Lord Aya watched them go.

"Do you think they'll be back?" asked Lord Aya.

"The Shogun will execute that general and send another with a larger force."

"We'll have to be ready."

"For the Americans, yes," grunted Lord Tōmatsu.

"We must return to Edo. Before the Americans get there. Before we are forced to waste time fighting the Shogun's next general."

And so the *fukoku kyōhei daimyōs* went to Edo.

Together. In force. Under strict discipline. Traveling together, the banners of a dozen *daimyōs* here, two dozen there. They were too many for the limited number of trains to carry on the slender lines now stretching across the country, so they rode and marched, streaming from the north and west toward Edo.

They came armed with modern guns, coordinated with telegraphed orders, some in code, some transmitted openly that the Shogun might know they came. Jiro's growing fleet of dirigibles was sent in squads to protect each procession of *daimyō* lords leading their *samurai* and their servants, floating in precise formations above the marching men.

As the soldiers approached each gate on the *Tōkaidō* and gates of entry into the guarded heart of Edo, Shogunate guards swarmed them demanding their permits of passage. Soldiers not pledged to the *bakufu* were not permitted inside the capital, other than a handful of personal honor guards for each *daimyō*, according to his rank. Politely, respectfully, without arrogance and without threats of violence, the rebel leaders announced they had no permits to enter but that they would pass the gates nonetheless. They showed the Shogun's guards their repeating rifles and their *katanas*.

They pointed to the dirigibles above, bristling with crewmen holding rifles, with the heavier cannon extending out of their portholes on the lower hulls of the airships.

"There is our permit."

The defending *bakufu* soldiers glanced uneasily above.

"We do not wish to harm you," stated each *daimyō* calmly. "The Americans are coming and we are here to protect the capital."

"We know nothing of Americans. You cannot pass without a permit."

"We need no permit. We have come to defend the realm. Join us."

The rebels then stood quietly, impassively, sometimes for hours in the hot summer sun, in groups of fifty, one hundred, several hundred, a thousand. They waited patiently until the frightened guards opened the gates before them without further challenge. Some processions waited by the gates through the night, to find the post abandoned by dawn, allowing them to enter. They left a handful of their own men to police the gates and welcome the next rebel *daimyō* procession.

A few Shogunate guards made brave charges against the overwhelming odds, but were gingerly captured alive and disarmed by rebel soldiers determined not to shed Japanese blood. Soon the *Tōkaidō* was clogged with former *bakufu* guards heading west, leaving behind their Tokugawa uniforms and escaping the reach of the Shogun's wrath and punishment for their failure to keep the rebels out. A handful accepted the invitation to join the insurgents.

The rebel lords braced for a counterattack from the tens of thousands of troops in Chiyoda Castle, but whether due to the Shogun's illness or Lord Abe's calming influence, the Shogun's main forces stayed inside their barracks in the Chiyoda compound.

More rebel troops landed in the city's center by air, on troop transport dirigibles, bypassing the Shogun's gates altogether. A fleet of dirigibles that grew in number each week hovered above the Edo compounds of the great *daimyō* lords.

Returning dirigibles lifted the wives and children and servants of the lords to safety, carrying them over the Shogun's checkpoints, navigating by the *Tōkaidō* to the west, and the newly christened *Tōhokudō* to the north, back to their homes in the countryside, where they were safe and protected by trusted retainers.

Entire forests were leveled in weeks to provide fuel for the airships, coal being scarce without open trade. Day and night without ceasing, the growing fleet of airships ferried troops and supplies into the capital and carried vulnerable families away.

The common people watched the airships overhead with dread. What were these ships in the sky? Why were these armies in the city? Where had the Shogun and his troops gone? Who were the barbarian Americans and why were they coming? Soon a trickle of frightened commoners flowed west and north along the *Tōkaidō* and the *Tōhokudō*, returning to a countryside they found safer than living in a city full of soldiers. Their ragged bundles of possessions strapped to their backs, or carried on poles, they trudged home to their ancestral lands, dodging yet more processions of soldiers traveling east and south to the capital.

Along the coastline, converging on Edo Bay, swarmed another of Tōru and Jiro's inventions, a fleet of steam-powered underwater ships, tiny vessels, only big enough for crews of four brave men. These could pass invisibly beneath the waves and then rise to attack, firing a single big gun. They were prone to capsize and sink, and the guns occasionally backfired, with fatal results for their courageous test crews. But Tōru and Jiro were certain it would take only a few of these to sink even the largest American warship.

It took weeks to gather them all, weeks in which daily reports were transmitted to all the lords of the Americans' progress in re-supplying their ships. Satsuma men disguised as dockhands loitering on the harbor docks in Naha Harbor made careful counts of the American crews and analyzed the capabilities of their ships. Never was a fleet more carefully observed in all the history of ships.

As they gathered in Edo, each *daimyō* went to his own compound, the home where he had always stayed when in attendance at the Shogun's court, calmly and in good order, as though coming to the capital for the normal *sankin kotai* rotation. However, this time their families were safely back in strongholds on their own domains, rescued and sent to safety by dirigible, like Lady Tōmatsu's now famous escape. Their homes in Edo overflowed with soldiers, both *samurai* and commoner, braced and ready to defend the capital. The shouts of squads drilling day and night competed with the cries of merchants calling their wares and priests chanting prayers in the cacophony that was the daily hum of the huge city.

Edo was an enormous city, one of the largest in the world, had its citizens only known it, teeming with every class of person, each engaged in pursuing his or her own goals, whatever those might be. Never in all of its history as the Shogun's capital had so many armed men peacefully walked its streets, wearing the crests of hundreds of different *han*.

Quietly but resolutely and in numbers too great to ignore, the rebel *daimyō* defied the laws that had kept the peace for two and a half centuries and entered the Shogun's city at the head of their own armies, turning *daimyō* households into swarming barracks and defended castles.

The commoners, the farmers, merchants, distillers, geisha, craftsmen and priests and monks who decided to stay in Edo, went about their daily pursuits for the most part as they always had, enjoying the boost in business. They wondered at the sight of so many *samurai* and the strangeness of uniformed commoner soldiers bearing guns within the city, but no word came down from Chiyoda Castle. Other than a few at the gates, no *bakufu* soldier challenged the entry of the Hundred Armies.

Word of the Americans' imminent arrival had not generally reached the ears of the commoners, although whispers flickered ear to ear in the *ukiyo* Floating World of the pleasure districts as the summer heat grew and all waited for the cooling summer rains.

The commoners may have been blissfully unaware, but the great lords and high-ranking bureaucrats of the *bakufu* were not. Within the halls of the *daimyō* compounds, and the walls of Chiyoda Castle, the tension grew as they waited.

They waited for Perry. They waited for the Shogun to strike against the rebels. They waited for the sickly Shogun to die and the succession battle to begin. They waited for the summer rains.

CHAPTER 19

⊕

KUROFUNE BLACK SHIPS

"Awoken from sleep
of a peaceful quiet world
by Jokisen tea;
with only four cups of it
one can't sleep even at night"
* * * * *

"The steam-powered ships
break the halcyon slumber
of the Pacific;
a mere four boats are enough
to make us lose sleep at night"
— Alternate readings of
an anonymous *kyoka* pun poem
about Perry's ships
as translated by Julian Cope

The summer rains were late that year and did not come, but Perry did. On July 8, late in the afternoon, two black-hulled sailing ships towed by black-smoke-belching steamships dropped anchor in Uraga Harbor at the entrance to Edo Bay. Perry's flagship, the steamship frigate *Susquehanna*, had the *Saratoga* in tow, while the steamship *Mississippi* had the *Plymouth* in tow.

As they entered the harbor, Commodore Perry ordered the firing of several shells, as notice of his arrival and salute to those on shore.

Fisherman near the shore ran to town, shouting of dragons belching black smoke.

They leapt into their boats for a closer look. Soon a crowd gathered at the shore, pointing and exclaiming over the novel sight.

As soon as the foreign ships anchored, a flotilla of Japanese fishing vessels swarmed around them. The telegraph wires burned up with the news, sharing it with the connected *hans*. The Americans had come at last, on four black ships that could move straight into the wind without the use of sails.

Local magistrates shouted warnings to the invaders and attempted to board the *Susquehanna*. They were easily repelled. A second wave of a dozen Japanese small boats surrounded the flagship. This time, Nakajima Saburosuke, a local police magistrate, and his interpreter, Dutch-speaker Hori Tatsunosuke, came alongside the *Susquehanna*. They were allowed to remain there when Nakajima claimed to be the governor of Uraga.

Commodore Perry gave orders that a senior official of the Emperor be summoned to receive from him a letter from the American President. Through a tortuous chain of interpreters, Japanese to Dutch to English and back again, most of it badly translated, the imperious American, who remained hidden in his stateroom throughout the exchange, the better to preserve his dignity and power, communicated with the "governor."

"We are here to deliver a letter from our President to your Emperor," Lieutenant Contee shouted down to the "governor." "You must summon a high ranking official to receive our letter."

"I am the most senior person here," replied Nakajima.

"Then receive this letter."

"Oh no, for that will be my death, by the Shogun's order. You are in violation of our laws and must leave immediately. This is the command of our Emperor and the law of our land for centuries."

"We will not leave until we deliver this letter."

"You may sail to Nagasaki and deliver your letter to the Dutch there."

"To force us to sail back to Nagasaki would be a grave insult to our President, possibly even a cause of war between our peoples."

"If you wish, I will send a messenger to Edo notifying the Emperor of your request. It is a two-day journey each way."

"We will wait three days. On the fourth day, we will sail north to Edo and deliver the letter to the Emperor ourselves."

For the next several days, the American ships explored the harbor, heading as far up as ten miles along the coast toward Edo. They sent smaller cutters out to sound the depths of the bay and perfect their crude maps. They were accompanied by hundreds of small fishing vessels, some filled with soldiers, others with curious villagers who simply wanted to see the foreigners and their ships.

Tōru's underwater ships swarmed the black ships as well, returning each hour to shore to transmit their discoveries to the command center in Lord Tōmatsu's spacious compound. They were careful never to surface in sight of the Americans, although they frightened fishermen when docking to disgorge their crews.

The moon being nearly full, it was deemed imprudent to send a dirigible crew to investigate from the air. The rebel leaders agreed to hold back knowledge of the airships from the invaders while they waited to see what the Americans would do.

On land, panic gripped the people as they learned of the foreign ships for the first time. The price of rice skyrocketed. Virtually no fish was delivered to the coastal markets along Edo Bay, as all the available boats were engaged in examining the great foreign ships.

A command came down from the Shogun's court to ignore the ships and not discuss them, on pain of death. Such a command was useless, for no one was speaking of anything but the black ships. Even without the telegraph, the news arrived in Edo nearly instantly, carried there by frightened bearers who had run even faster than usual on their stiff-legged gait with their noble passengers. Rumors swept Uraga and Edo with outrageous stories, claiming the Americans had come to burn Edo to the ground and capture and kill the Emperor or the Shogun or both.

The Emperor did not hear the news for days. Cloistered in his hidden court in Kyoto, he had no telegraph, and no one from the Shogunate court thought to notify him through other channels.

The foreigners were obviously confused about who the Emperor and Shogun were, but their confusion did not remove the need for the Shogun to respond. Lieutenant Contee had made it clear to Magistrate Nakajima that the President's letter would be delivered, by force if necessary, to officials in the capital if their request for a meeting was not met.

Lord Abe, in the Shogun's name, summoned the Council upon the sighting of the black ships off the shores of Uraga. He invited also the rebellious *tōzama* lords, most of whom were already in Edo, promising them on his own honor safe passage through Chiyoda Castle and the streets of Edo.

The greatest of the *tōzama* lords sent emissaries in their stead rather than trust the Shogun to honor Lord Abe's pledge, but many attended in person, trusting in their numbers and the gravity of the situation to protect them.

Once they were all gathered in the great reception hall, crushed together and spilling out into the hallway, the Shogun presided over the Council. Lord Abe deftly guided the meeting, carefully asking the Shogun for permission to move through the discussion at each step, but even his skills could not hide the obvious.

The once fearsome Shogun was dying. He was too enfeebled to lead or make the decisions facing them. The response to the Americans would fall upon young Lord Abe's shoulders, together with all the blame for whatever came to pass.

Lord Abe gave a formal report to the assembly on what was known about the Americans. He shared intelligence rooted in the work of Satsuma's spies and the observations being made by the flotilla of boats surrounding the four foreign ships.

"They violated our laws when they entered the bay," he said, in summary, "But—"

He was interrupted by shouts from the assembly. "Drive them out!" "Destroy them!"

Lord Abe waited for silence. The Shogun was too weak to gesture, but sat stone-faced at the front of the room glaring balefully at his Chief Councilor.

Lord Abe continued when the shouting died down.

"Although they violate our laws, they do not act with violence, but merely request the privilege of delivering a letter from their leader." He paused, expecting outbursts, but this time the silence held. "I share your desire to enforce our laws and maintain our dignity, but we have no navy to drive them away. We must, I believe, accept this letter peacefully for now and take war to them later."

This led to more shouting. "We drove away Glynn and Biddle. We can drive these away as well."

Lord Abe sighed. "Our spies report this Commodore Perry is different, that he has orders to deliver the letter by force if necessary. Where the earlier commanders were courteous men, this Perry longs for an excuse to fight. The others were ordered not to create problems, and so retreated. Perry will not retreat, but will attack Edo if provoked."

Tōru's heart pounded within his chest. He knew, and the rebel lords knew, that they did have the power to drive the Americans away, at least for the moment. He waited for his superiors to rise, the great rebel lords, but none did. Lord Aya and Lord Tōmatsu were not in attendance, as the Shogun had not rescinded their execution orders. Nor were Lord Date nor Lord Shimazu, who did not trust the Shogunate enough to put their heads in danger. While trusted men represented them at the council, those retainers would not speak for their lords on such an important and sensitive topic.

Tōru knew what Lord Abe wanted. He wanted the rebel leaders to step forward with their technology and their defenses to give him the backbone and means to stand up to the foreigners.

Tōru remembered the conversations with Lord Abe he and Takamori had had during the months of his debriefing. He recalled how the Chief Councilor had often hinted that he favored a policy of opening the country to trade, if it could be accomplished with dignity, not under the shadow of a warship's guns like the Chinese agreements had been. Tōru also understood the Chief Councilor could never be the one to mention first such an unthinkable possibility, no matter how much he might favor the idea.

Tōru dared not speak. He was still under sentence of death, relying on Lord Abe's slender promise of safety during this meeting. He was no lord, just a newly minted *samurai* known as "the fisherman" throughout the land, suspected of being an American spy by more than one lord, and not just those *daimyō* allied to the Shogun. None of the great lords were present to protect him or speak up for him.

The Council devolved into chaos, as the sullen and silent Shogun looked on, barely able to hold himself erect.

The young Lord Abe repeatedly called for order. In the hubbub, Tōru found himself rising to his feet and standing, from his humble position near the door. He hadn't even intended to rise but there he was, standing, as all eyes turned to him. He saw the faintest twitch of a smile flicker across Lord Abe's stern face.

"Himasaki! Fisherman!" Lord Abe called out to him, silencing the room. "You have come for your execution?"

The room full of lords and bureaucrats laughed, a moment of levity lost on Tōru, who had trusted Lord Abe's promise of safe passage after all he had done to help them escape. For a moment he thought the usually earnest young lord was serious. He wondered if he should attempt to run out the door and make his way to safety through fifty thousand *bakufu* soldiers. That, he knew, was suicide. But so was voicing what he wanted to say to the assembly.

"No, Lord Abe. I am relying on your oath promising safe passage for this meeting...but if I might have permission to speak?"

Lord Abe nodded his permission, forgetting to pass the request through the feeble Shogun, an omission that earned him a glare from Tokugawa.

"We should accept the letter, for it comes to us peacefully enough, and a confident nation can take part in such conversations with other leaders."

The room murmured. Against or in support, Tōru could not tell. Or out of shock at a junior person, the traitorous fisherman, speaking up in such a meeting.

"But we should make clear to the Americans we accept their letter out of courtesy and not weakness."

The murmur was clearly supportive.

"Those of us," here Tōru struggled to find the right words, for it would not be polite to mention in the Shogun's presence the cold civil war now seething under the surface throughout the land, or the rebellion of hundreds of *daimyōs* against time-honored decrees by the Shogunate, or the presence of tens of thousands of troops from the Hundred Armies inside the capital walls. Finally he settled on the slogan they had rallied around to identify the lords who could help. "Those of us who pursue the path of *fukoku kyōhei* believe we can and should open the country to trade and relations with other great powers."

The murmurs turned hostile again. Tokugawa Ieyoshi himself roused and straightened, glowering down at Tōru with new energy, channeling the fearsome Shogun he had been of old.

"We believe we can do so from a position of strength. We lack a navy, true. But we do have an air force and a considerable number of fighters...here...in the capital." This earned him yet another glare from the Shogun. Lord Abe shot a glance at the Shogun, concern on his face. Tens of thousands of troops illegally stationed within Edo's walls against all custom and law was not a topic for polite conversation nor public announcement in the Shogun's own reception hall, even if everyone knew it to be true.

Tōru thought it quite difficult to navigate political matters when no one was allowed to state the obvious or the true. No wonder the country's leaders had stumbled for so long.

"I cannot speak for the lords, but I believe they would place their dirigibles and underwater ships and their soldiers under command of the Emperor's Shogun," Tōru bowed deeply to the glowering Shogun at the front of the reception hall as he defiantly asserted the Emperor's nominal superiority over the Shogun, "to send a message of our strength, unity and resolve to the Americans. Let us accept this letter. Then we shall peacefully but firmly drive the Americans from our harbor. Aided by the great lords, prevent them from approaching our Shogun's capital. Let them return more respectfully next time. I humbly suggest that the aid of these lords be requested to defend our capital and our Emperor's dignity."

Tōru sat down, as the murmur rose to a roar.

Lord Abe nodded approval, even as he shouted for order. The Shogun shrank, barely able to sit upright, his eyes gazing vacantly on the *tatami* in front of him. The fight faded from his eyes as he stifled a gasp of pain. Asano, Sugieda, Obata and other emissaries for the great lords met Tōru's eyes and nodded approval as well.

The Chief Councilor held his hands out for order, finally calming the roar in the reception hall. "Asano-*san*, does Lord Shimazu support this?"

"Yes, my lord."

"Sugieda-*san*, your lord as well?"

"Lord Tōmatsu agrees. Open negotiations while defending with firmness. He will commit troops, dirigibles and underwater ships to the fight and drive these invaders from our shores. Let us teach these barbarians some manners."

This met with cheers.

Lord Abe questioned each of the lords or their emissaries.

Most agreed to accept the letter. The rebel lords or their chief retainers in their names all offered men and ships for the expulsion of the foreign barbarians. When all the assembly had been thus queried, Lord Abe turned to the Shogun and bowed deeply.

"Lord Tokugawa, it is the consensus of your council and the great lords that we should in peace and courtesy accept this letter from the American President and then drive the foreigners from our waters with the help of..." he hesitated, struggling like Tōru to find words to describe the great lords who were even now in bold defiance of Shogunate law without enraging the Shogun or insulting the *tōzama* lords. Lord Abe finally settled on "*daimyōs* who have prepared defenses for your realm."

The dying Shogun looked up at his Chief Councilor and shut his eyes, as though to shut out the sight of his defeat as the defense of the realm was turned over to his political enemies.

Lord Tokugawa waved his hand weakly and nodded assent.

Lord Abe accepted the Shogun's grudging approval. He swung into action, assembling a committee to write a response, officials to receive the letter, and generals to organize the defense of the capital.

With one final command, he placed Tōru on the team to receive the letter from the Americans. "Do not reveal your understanding of their speech or your knowledge of America. Be our eyes and ears in the room, and learn of this Perry so we can better understand how to fight him. We'll execute you after we've driven away your barbarian friends."

Tōru did not appreciate the Chief Councilor's attempt at developing a sense of humor.

The agreed-upon day for the formal reception of the American President's letter arrived, July 14.

In a frenzied burst of building, workers had hastily erected a great reception hall near the shore at Uraga. A wharf had been built into the water to allow the American cutters to come ashore without beaching their boats. At a few minutes before ten in the morning, small cutters from each of the four American ships filled with officers, two marine bands, an honor guard and finally the much-discussed but never seen Commodore Perry himself.

Each cutter was shadowed by Tōru's underwater ships, prepared to take them out if so commanded. As the boats came ashore and unloaded several hundred Americans, they formed ranks to welcome their Commodore.

As he boarded his own cutter, the flagship's guns sounded a 13-gun salute to the Commodore, the charges echoing from the hills to the black ships and back. As the American leader set foot on Japanese soil, the bands' half dozen drums sounded a long and martial roll to welcome him to shore. The American officers and honor guards lined up in perfect rows to greet their leader as the band struck up a martial tune.

Behind them on the shore, six thousand of the Shogun's men and the men of the Hundred Armies stood in equally perfect rows, all fully armored and bearing their *daishō* swords. Archers held tall bows and pikemen fierce spears. War banners fluttered above them in the stiff morning breeze. Another thousand men from the Hundred Armies stood in formation to one side, their repeating rifles and a few pieces of heavier artillery, prominently placed, clearly visible to the American officers.

A corps of American marines led the parade to the reception hall a few hundred steps from the shore. One of the bands followed them, along with a group of sailors. Next came two ships boys bearing the President's letter and the Commodore's credentials in special fine wooden boxes. Finally came Commodore Perry himself, flanked by two African stewards who served as his bodyguards, their ebony skin swallowing the mid-morning light as they marched impassively behind their Commodore.

Two ancient brass cannons flanked the door to the reception hall. Commodore Perry and a handful of his officers stepped inside and took a moment to adjust their eyes to the dim light within, a pair of braziers offering the only source of light.

Inside two elderly men in silk court robes sat on stools, flanked by a dozen kneeling retainers. Tōru was one of kneeling retainers, placed next to the main interpreter, who served to translate Japanese into Dutch. Tōru wore the livery of the Shogun's house, a necessary subterfuge he found most strange.

As the Americans entered, the two elderly men rose and bowed deeply in greeting. The translator announced them as princes, since Commodore Perry had demanded high-ranking officials receive his letter. The Japanese knew them to be merely the Governor of Uraga and his fellow Governor of Edo. Important men, but no princes, nor even high-ranking officials in the Shogun's *bakufu*. Higher ranking officials had all refused the task rather than take on the filthy shame and disgrace of meeting with the Americans.

A kneeling retainer ushered Commodore Perry to a red upholstered armchair while his officers stood at attention behind.

A long silence fell over the room until one of the Japanese interpreters, speaking Dutch, introduced the parties to each other. The American interpreter translated the Dutch into English for the Commodore. Silence fell over the assembly again.

The Japanese interpreter asked, "Is your Commodore ready to deliver the letter?"

Commodore Perry beckoned to the two boys bearing the rosewood boxes bound in solid gold locks and hinges.

They scurried forward, holding aloft the boxes for the inspection by the two Japanese "princes."

The African stewards stepped forward to unlatch the boxes and display for the Japanese representatives the two letters. One gave the Commodore Perry's impressive and lengthy credentials, most of which were rendered incomprehensible by the translation chain.

The other, more important, was the letter from President Fillmore to the Emperor.

This was easier for the translators, with its flowery talk of friendship between the two nations and the benefits for both of free trade. A polite request, not a demand, for kind treatment of shipwrecked American sailors was also included, along with requests for access to coaling and supply stations and the exchange of envoys to negotiate a trade treaty. Buried amidst the ornate and courteous language was a request to consider changing Japan's ancient laws forbidding trade. The President signed off with a cheery "your good friend."

While the words were clear enough, though bent and mangled through the tortuous translation, the assembled Japanese were profoundly confused by the juxtaposition of the friendly message with the martial and aggressive manner of the messenger. If he was ambassador for such a would-be friend, why did he fire off his ships' guns with such enthusiasm? Why disembark for a friendly meeting with hundreds of armed men? Why did he so aggressively and disrespectfully violate their laws by refusing to deliver the letter to Nagasaki as every other foreign power had long agreed to do?

In return, the Japanese interpreter presented to the American interpreter a lacquered box containing an "imperial receipt" acknowledging receipt of the American letters and promising to deliver them to the "Emperor." The receipt stated the letters had been received under duress in violation of the ancient laws of Japan demanding that all foreign interaction take place only in Nagasaki through the Dutch. The receipt further explained that an exception had been made in honor of the American president.

This language the Council had argued over for hours. Factions determined to kill the Americans outright faced off against those who saw this as an opportunity to throw open the country to trade and those who feared any opposition at all would lead to war and the destruction of Edo. All these competing views were distilled down, harmonized and written into the slim imperial receipt.

The translator droned on with the reading of this peculiar document, concluding finally with, "As this is not a place wherein to negotiate with foreigners, so neither can conferences nor entertainments be held. Therefore, as your letter has been received, you can depart."

Perry bristled visibly at the implied command in the message once it had wound its way through the thicket of Japanese to Dutch to English translation. He had clearly heard the voice of the "kill them now" faction involved in the writing of the receipt. Determined to have the last word, he replied, with yet another barely veiled threat.

"I will be leaving in a few days. As I am sure you have much to discuss within your Government, I will return with the remainder of my fleet next spring for your Government's answer."

The officials present could not hide their shock at the mention of Perry's return with a larger fleet.

Perry beckoned again to one of his African stewards, who produced two white flags on short poles that an American officer had carried into the reception hall. He directed his steward to hand them to the Japanese translator.

"Allow me to explain the use of these flags. In our country, if two parties enter into combat, and one party has no chance of winning, the losing party can hoist these white flags and the other party will cease to fire upon them and accept their honorable surrender."

The Japanese translator stared at Perry in dismay.

Tōru understood Perry's words perfectly, and the gesture as well. He was insulting and threatening his hosts, all in a simple "peaceful" gesture.

The Japanese translator struggled to explain the white flags, not because the meaning was unclear, but because the words were so shameful. Not only was the concept of surrender alien, but the clear and unmistakeable threat implied in the presumption the Japanese would have need of such white flags was distasteful on his lips.

Tōru, who had liked and admired his American hosts during his two years in America, clenched his teeth to hold in the rage rising in his gut as he watched the smiling American Commodore calmly threaten his people. Tōru's heart abandoned his hopes for peace and joined those who would tear the foreigners to pieces rather than hold back to avoid provoking them. He breathed slowly and deeply, trying to calm the anger nearly blinding him. The Governor of Uraga barely restrained the tears glistening in his eyes as he grasped the message grinding its way through the interpreters.

After the Japanese translator stammered through an explanation of Perry's white flags, to thinly disguised rage on the faces of all who understood, he stood and turned to the Americans, repeating his earlier phrase from the imperial receipt.

"As the letter has been received, you can depart."

The Americans stood, marched in order to their cutters and boarded their black ships, serenaded all the while by their bands.

The two Japanese "princes" bowed farewell, much more shallowly than they had at first greeting. The Japanese, maintaining perfect order, waited until the Americans had all boarded their ships before relaxing their military posture.

Tōru stood with other officers on the beach watching the Americans board their ships. He noted grimly the American Commodore had succeeded where he, Tōru, had not.

No matter whether a man wore the *mon* of House Shimazu or House Tokugawa, they were all united in their hatred of the arrogant commodore and his veiled threats. *Tōzama* and *fudai* lords, the rebellious outer lords and the loyal closely allied Shogunate lords, they stood as one in their desire to defy the Americans and defend the realm.

The lords who had attended the ceremony joined Tōru in the reception hall. As commanded by Lord Abe, Tōru translated for them, more smoothly this time, the documents the Commodore had delivered. The telegraph carried his translation instantly to Lord Abe and the Shogun in Edo, where other lords waited in attendance in the Shogun's reception hall.

The American president's letter was friendly and courteous enough. The trouble arose from the side letters written by Perry himself, and from the despicable white surrender flags.

The Governor of Uraga listened as Tōru explained the various documents. He had spent the most time in actual contact with the Americans during the past week, often in a small boat shouting up to the tireless Lieutenant Contee through his interpreter.

"Which of these is true, Himasaki? The friendliness of the President, or the hostility of the Commodore?"

Tōru paused before replying. A wrong answer would have major consequences. "Both are true, my lord. The American President seeks trade, and has used respectful and friendly language. I believe his intent to be friendly. This Commodore, however..." Tōru paused to calm himself. "He is a military man. He sees the world divided into enemies and allies. We are not yet allies, and so he chooses to see us as enemies and treat us disrespectfully as such. The American President would not declare war on us, but this man seeks war. Worse, he seeks to provoke us into giving him an excuse for war, so he may defend himself to his President. The white flags...My lords, I cannot know for sure, but I do not believe those were sent by the President. Their...threat...comes from this man Perry alone."

The Governor spoke. "The American President sits far away on the other side of the world and this Perry with his black ships is right here. This is our problem."

A messenger burst into the reception hall.

"The Americans are heading north. To Edo. They have broken their word and are moving to attack the capital!"

CHAPTER 20

⊕

KAMIKAZE

"Do nothing which is of no use."
— Miyamoto Musashi

"Time for Operation Kamikaze," said Tōru.

The lords in attendance nodded agreement. They paused for a moment in the dim light of the reception hall, where the American letters were still lying in their opened rosewood boxes. Lord Abe's orders were clear. *Do not provoke the Americans. Be courteous to the Americans. Give them no cause for war. But do not, under any circumstances, allow them near Edo. Whatever the cost.*

The telegraph operator had transmitted the news of the black ships heading north along the coast toward Edo. Scout ships were heading out from their positions along the coast to cover the American ships and ascertain whether they were merely surveying and mapping or heading north with more aggressive plans in mind. Both were forbidden, but the response might be different.

Replies were already streaming in over the telegraph. Tōru's heart was heavy. He genuinely hoped for peace between his people and the Americans he had come to admire and respect during his sojourn in America. He had dreamed of Japan's energies and resources harnessed to lift up her people, not to fight a war against a powerful and relentless foe. He believed in the innate friendliness of the American people and the possibility of fruitful interactions with them. He longed to end the *sakoku* policy and not merely because it would render null his death sentence for violating it.

But Perry's demeanor had so insulted all who witnessed the exchange that there could be no peace for now, not with Perry as the messenger. Ambassadors could be sent later, to smooth things over, if the fine line between showing strength and shedding blood could be straddled and bloodshed avoided.

If.

The Shogun's generals were in nominal command of the day's operation, and they stood at the head of their troops and the vastly more numerous troops of the Hundred Armies. Soldiers stood in bristling rows along the wharves and beaches around Edo. Political differences had vanished, for the moment, as soldiers from every *han* in the realm prepared to defend the capital against the American commodore and his black ships. Today at least they were not Shogun's men or rebel men, but Japanese men, for the first time in their long history as a realm of many independent *hans*, loosely bound together by the Shogun's policies and regulations and firmly united by their rage against the foreign foe.

The Shogun's top general was in the reception hall, having played the part of retainer like Tōru, as he had wanted to examine the American warrior with his own eyes. He turned to Tōru.

"So, fisherman, yes. Unleash the *kamikaze* Divine Winds."

Tōru nodded. The time for revealing the dragon dirigibles had come. The dirigible fleet, now 46 airships strong, had stayed hidden out of sight during the reception ceremony. Their captains and crews were eager to join the fight. The airships and their fighters had been built and trained by the rebel lords. The Shogun had been forced to entrust the first line of defense of the realm to his political enemies. But politics did not matter up in the sky. Not today. The airship captains too were Japanese.

The general spoke to the telegraph operator. "Give the order. Position them between Edo and the fleet. No firing guns or dropping bombs except on my command." He turned back to Tōru. "And your underwater ships?"

"They are standing by. Don't reveal them unless absolutely necessary. They are the best way to sink the American ships if it comes to that, but..."

"That will trigger war, a war we cannot yet win. *Wakarimashita*."

The general turned and picked up the despised pair of white flags. Slowly, deliberately, delicately for a hardened man of war and action, as though he were a host formally preparing tea for a most noble guest, he wrapped the flags around their poles and bound them with silk ties.

He presented them to Tōru with an exaggerated bow.

"When you find the right moment, shove these down his smokestack."

Tōru stood on the shore, waiting for Takamori to pick him up in the *Kagoshima Maru*. Masuyo had already flown overhead, captaining the *Toranosuke Maru*. Admiral Jiro as well, at the helm of the *Hakudo Maru*, leading the front of the emerging V formation. The sight was awe-inspiring, as nearly four dozen airships streamed toward the bay from all directions, converging on the airspace above the black ships. Each hull was painted with terrifying creatures. Every prow bore the face of a dragon or hideous demon.

Tōru could spot inexperience in some of the newer pilots as their ships wobbled a bit on their flight paths. The formations were not as tight as they should be. He winced as a pair barely avoided a mid-air collision. *They only need to intimidate the Americans, not actually battle them* he reminded himself, hoping it was true.

Tōru found it strange that the very place he had feared and avoided since his return from America, the Shogun's teeming capital, was now the city he would joyfully give his life for if he could save her. In Edo, he had been sentenced to death and imprisoned for months, and forced to escape, pursued by the Shogun's men.

Over three long years had passed since his adventure began.

He had traveled far, to Boston and New York and Washington, an exile in an alien land, treated with curiosity and friendliness but never with true acceptance. In America, a keen loneliness had struck him, a loneliness that had not faded when he returned home to his village to find it empty of all who mattered to him. He had thought he had no home any longer, that he was an exile and wayfarer forever, condemned to wander alone. However, at this moment, he knew his home was no longer a small fishing village but a whole nation ruled from a great city, a city he would save.

The rope ladder dropped near Tōru, pulling him out of his revery as he watched the magnificent airships stream overhead. He grabbed the rope ladder and climbed. The tail of the ladder scudded along the tops of the waves as the *Kagoshima Maru* headed out over the bay. Exhilaration filled Tōru as he sped just above the waves, rising as he and the airship climbed into the fresh sea air.

Up here, soaring above the waves with a magnificent view of Japan's green hills and her tidy towns and villages scattered along the coast, with the capital coming into view, a fierce love rose up in Tōru for all of it. The commoners tending their fields and their shops and their workshops and dancing in their festivals and praying to their local *kami* and to Lord Buddha. The *samurai* lined up under banners of the Hundred Armies and the Shogunate, side by side as one army. The soft full waving heads of rice in the terraced fields, heavy now with the summer crop. The mysterious Emperor and his newborn son hidden away in Kyoto, descended in an unbroken line directly from the sun goddess herself, a magnificent lineage his friends in America scoffed at, even as he forgave them for failing to understand the wonder of such a thing. The compassion of Lord Aya, the gruff cheerful courage of Lord Tōmatsu, the fierce insight of Lord Date, the crafty wisdom of young Lord Abe, all these were precious treasures to Tōru. Even the feeble Shogun who had condemned him to die—he too was Tōru's and part of it all, his Shogun, keeper of the realm's peace. And Jiro and Takamori and Asano, all fighting by his side. Masuyo too, the *takadai no o-hana* he could never reach, but only treasure in his heart, floating above him captaining her ship. Even the yearning for his missing mother and his noble father, so far away and distant, even that longing faded into the fierce love burning in him at that moment for all of Japan and every soul in her.

All of it was his and he was home at last.

He clambered over the edge of Takamori's ship, the *Kagoshima Maru*, which served as the Satsuma flagship for Satsuma's nascent fleet of five airships. He leapt onto the deck and greeted Takamori.

The two friends spoke little, for nothing needed be said. This was it. All their work of the last year and more had prepared them for this day. They were ready to defend their homeland.

Tōru wished that Jiro and Masuyo could have taken time and figured out ship-to-ship communications without wires. Among the books in his collection was one on theories of electro-magnetism, but there had not been time to sort out anything in the lab. In the meantime, the captains had worked out a cumbersome system of flag signaling, ship-to-ship and shore-to-ship. In the heat of the battle, though, maintaining communications would be difficult. They were on their own. The politicians and the generals had no way to reach them. Only their fleet stood between Edo and the vile Commodore with his *kurofune* black ships of evil mien.

The airship captains knew the stakes.

No matter how angry they were at the Commodore's arrogance — and each one was filled with a cold implacable rage, once the story of the white flags passed to every ear—they understood their first priority was to drive the American ships from Japanese waters without bloodshed or sinking the ships.

As the Shogun's general had told them in their final briefing, "We are communicating with the American President, not his swaggering ill-bred servant. Our message is our strength and our demand for respect for our ancient laws, not our anger. Ignore his monkey slave, and conduct yourselves as ambassadors for our Emperor and Shogun. And drive his ships from our shores."

Each captain was acutely aware that mistakes—too much aggression, too much passivity, too little strength, unclear messages— could lead to disaster for their homeland.

Takamori's crew maneuvered the *Kagoshima Maru* into her position in the formation while he and Tōru conferred at the prow. The wind was gusty and strong today, blowing against them as they fought their way north, but the engines shuddered and persevered, driving the fleet up the coast to converge above the black ships. Soon they were pacing them, flying in an ever more even and perfect formation high above the American fleet. The two friends peered through their spyglasses, Tanaka the watchmaker's latest contribution to the cause, at the black ships steaming north.

Evil pitch-black smoke billowed from the American ships' smokestacks against the otherwise pristine sky, the sailing ships in tow, as they headed toward Edo and a million vulnerable Edoites.

Tōru could see the Americans pointing up at the airships and peering back at them through their own spyglasses. He saw officers shout commands, and sailors and soldiers jump to haul out shot and aim cannons. He laughed as he saw the crew attempt to point the cannons directly upward and fail. They were fastened in place, able to aim high but land their shot on land or ships on their same level, not to aim into the sky. He stopped laughing when he saw soldiers aim their rifles toward them. Takamori saw it too, and shouted to his men to take them up, up, up, out of range, and for the flag signal officer to get the message to Admiral Jiro's ship.

His message crossed another, coming from Admiral Jiro.

"All ships. Overtake them. Defensive formation between Edo and the black ships."

Takamori and his crew pushed the *Kagoshima Maru* to the limits of her superb engineering. The other airship captains did likewise as they received the order. Never before, even in a drill, had the engines worked so hard, fighting such a strong wind. They shuddered and throbbed and complained, but they held, and drove the giant propulsion devices. The airships churned forward swiftly now, leaving behind the black ships. A few shots were fired from the *kurofune*, but all fell harmlessly in the sea.

The airships reached their defensive positions. They aimed their guns toward the black ships steaming toward them. The winds were strong. The engines fought hard just to hold position, but hold they did. Tōru was pleased to see even the inexperienced pilots nudging their way into near perfect formation. Looking good matters, both in war and love. *We win if we drive them away without battle. We win if we frighten them enough.*

Tōru and Takamori watched the ships. The other captains did the same, as did the commanders on shore, peering at them through spyglasses, watching to see what the pugnacious American would do. His mighty steamships were under double strain, with both the heavy wind against them and the burden of towing the sailing ships. Tōru noted with satisfaction that the sailing ships would be nearly useless in a battle with the wind so strong against them.

Perry was no longer pretending to survey the coast and sound the water's depths. His guns were trained on the shore and his marines were in battle dress and armed, lined up along the gunwales of his ships. He steamed full speed toward Edo. He was less than an hour away from reaching bombardment range of the great city.

No one feared that he could take the city or even damage her much. Perry had at most 1,600 men, including his cooks and ships boys, on all four of his ships. Though his guns did have a marvelous and unmatched long range, and heavier caliber shot than anything the rebel lords had yet developed, whatever damage he could inflict on Edo before Tōru's underwater ships sank him was limited. Great Edo could be wounded but not killed by the crude American.

No, the danger was not to Edo herself but to the vision of a prosperous and free Japan. If Perry managed to provoke hostilities, he would succeed at creating a terrible war between both sides, dragging in the friendly Americans and forcing Japan to arm herself instead of building prosperity. The enemy was not the Americans, but Perry himself. Tōru had to find a way to send a message to the American President through the unwilling messenger of Perry.

"Saigo!" Tōru shouted to his friend Takamori, who was across the deck speaking with his pilot. "Can you get me directly above the *Susquehanna?*"

Takamori didn't bother to remind him that doing so would defy their orders. "Sure, but what do you want to do that for? Don't you see his guns?"

"Perry's trying to force us to fire on him. He'll go so close to Edo that we'll have to. He'll neglect to mention to his President that he sailed up to Edo with his guns hanging out. He wants to lose a ship or three, leaving him with one to escape and tell the American people we attacked him, unprovoked, so he can throw us into war. We need to show his thousand men, a thousand witnesses, that we can blow him out of the water effortlessly but choose not to do so. We must send a message that will reach his President, through the mouths of his men. 'Don't mess with Yamato.'"

"And you are going to do that exactly how?"

"I'm going to tell him. And you, and the *Hakudo Maru*, the *Yakaze Maru* and the *Toranosuke Maru* are going to show him. Message to shore—we need a dozen fishing boats we can blow up, to meet us here below the fleet. But you have to drop me on to the *Susquehanna* so I can explain the nuance to him."

Takamori now took the time to explain that Tōru's idea was entirely against orders. "We're not supposed to do any diplomacy or negotiations. You were there—the whole roomful of lords, ours, the Shogun's, all were dead set against any negotiating. Just accept the letter and begone, that's our stance. You don't get to go against all that. Even your father will be against you."

Tōru stiffened at the mention of his father.

All this time there had still been no direct message from Lord Shimazu, who knew by now in a thousand ways that Tōru had returned. He trusted his father's judgment and final order when last Tōru saw him, as he left Tōru on a piece of wreckage in the path of the American trading ship so many years ago, that their relationship must remain secret beyond Satsuma's borders. His father's support had touched Tōru through his many unusual gestures. His request to Lord Aya to make Tōru a *samurai*. The fine horse. The exquisite *daishō* swords. The land grant. Saigo Takamori by his side.

Still, it stung.

"Fair enough, but what do you think?"

Takamori folded his strong arms across his massive chest and pondered the matter. "You are right. Let's do it. What can they do, kill us? Technically we are already condemned to death." He grinned and shouted orders to his pilot and flag messenger.

Within minutes a dozen fishing boats were heading out from the shore to cluster on the sea below the dirigibles. The boats were filled with *samurai* wearing the Shogun's crest, not empty to be used as targets as Tōru had intended.

"They sent soldiers," Takamori pointed out to Tōru. The message had not been clear. The courageous men below thought they were being sent out to attempt to board the black ships.

Tōru sighed. "Get them up here. Leave a couple on each boat to maneuver into position, and then pull them off."

The captains had to send down nimble crewmen on the swaying rope ladders to convince the Shogun's *samurai* on each fishing boat to join them above. They were eager to board and fight the Americans, as pointless an action as that would have been. Only when promised they could board more easily from above did they consent to abandon the fishing vessels.

The better news was that someone had ordered a dozen underwater ships to accompany the fishing boats. They were hidden behind them, on the side away from the black ships. They floated near the surface, so orders could be shouted to their crews. The crewmen tasked with convincing the Shogun's *samurai* to climb the ladders spoke to the crews of the underwater ships directly and arranged for them to fire on the fishing boats upon a signal from above. Or on the American ships. If it came to that.

Asano, Masuyo and Jiro had pulled their ships out of formation and brought them alongside the *Kagoshima*. The V closed ranks behind them, holding formation. Tōru tried shouting, but even so close, the roar of the wind and the engines was too much. They had to spell out the plan with flags, painfully slowly, as the black ships relentlessly pulled closer and closer to the capital.

"Take me in." Takamori nodded and gave the order to his pilot. Leaving behind the main V formation, the *Kagoshima* turned away from Edo and headed straight for the black ships. The *Hakudo Maru*, the *Yakaze Maru* and the *Toranosuke Maru* escorted the *Kagoshima Maru*, trailing a little behind her.

"How are you going to keep them from shooting you?"

"I'll just have to risk it." Tōru tightened the straps on his back, where the hated white flags wrapped around their poles hung like a quiver across his back, still tied with the silk ribbons the general had fastened around them.

Trailed by her escort of the three dirigibles, the small fleet of fishing boats and the hidden underwater boats, the *Kagoshima* approached the *Susquehanna*.

Seeing this, the black ships finally slowed their pace.

Tōru had hoped this would happen. He was pleased to see the *Susquehanna's* engines reversing their direction to glide to a stop. The sailing ships were throwing anchors.

He hoped his other assumption would also hold true, that they would not fire on a lone man climbing down a ladder. Perry might, but Tōru didn't think he would dare in front of his officers. Tōru had liked the American military leaders he met on his travels, mostly men of honor and courage. Most would consider firing on a helpless man dangling on a ladder unsporting and dishonorable.

Tōru turned around once more to look at the capital, safe for the moment behind his fleet of dirigibles and underwater ships. The vast city was a beautiful jewel, spread out for miles along the coast, bustling with a million inhabitants, commoners and lords and warriors alike, all watching and waiting in fear of the *Kurofune*, the Black Ships.

Takamori called the halt. His pilot throttled down the engines to just enough to hold their position.

They were now directly above the *Susquehanna*.

The Americans aimed their rifles skyward, but otherwise held their positions and their fire.

"*Ganbatte, na.* Do your best." Takamori saluted Tōru formally.

"*Itte kuru yo.* I'll be back." Tōru tossed the ladder over the gunwale and checked the straps on the hateful white flags one last time. He saluted Takamori and then climbed over the gunwale and down the ladder to the waiting American flagship.

A pair of officers, who had been among the senior officers who attended the reception ceremony, held the swaying tail of the ladder and assisted Tōru in stepping onto the deck.

A hundred pairs of eyes and a hundred guns were aimed at Tōru as he stood and got his bearings. But for the keening wind and the call of the gulls and the lapping of the sea on the hull, all was silent.

"Get the translators up here, on the double!" shouted an officer.

"That will not be necessary," said Tōru, in clear and nearly unaccented American English, unless the slightest hint of a New England drawl, picked up from the whaling crew that rescued him, counted as an accent. "I am here to speak with Commodore Perry." He ignored the astonishment on the Americans' faces at his perfect English after all the suffering of the morning's translations.

They whispered among themselves as they recognized him from the morning's ceremony.

The Commodore, as was his custom, had scuttled below decks to his stateroom as Tōru came aboard lest his dignity be bruised by encountering anyone ranked lower than a prince.

"I am the highest ranking officer here," said the American. "I can take your message to the Commodore."

"I'm afraid that will be impossible. I need to speak with the Commodore in person." Tōru took the most imperious tone he could manage, and stood erect, fighting the urge to bow, a custom the Americans found servile.

"The Commodore can only meet with—"

"Yes, yes, I know, with princes and high ranking representatives of the Emperor. You may tell your Commodore it will be considered a grave insult to the Emperor and his Shogun if he does not meet with me. Now."

"He will not come out unless—"

"Perhaps...I can convince you...in another way." Tōru turned up to face Takamori, watching him from above the swaying ladder. Tōru motioned thrice with his arms in the pre-arranged signal.

"See those fishing boats?" Tōru indicated a trio floating near the American ship. They were empty now of their *samurai* passengers, who were gathered above on the airship or on a few of the other fishing boats, watching intently.

The American officers nodded.

"If your Commodore does not come up to speak with me, now, it will be considered a grave insult to the Emperor and his Government and the peace loving people of Japan. It would be a terrible shame if a lack of courtesy were to lead to conflict between our peoples." Here Tōru did bow deeply, putting into the gesture all the grace and strength of his people, and sending a signal to the fighters above in the dirigible. He briefly remembered Takamori's protest that any sort of diplomacy or negotiating with the foreigners was strictly forbidden.

Too late.

"I humbly request that the Commodore join us on deck, now, or I will be forced to avenge his insult to my Emperor in this manner upon your fleet." Tōru gestured with a graceful outstretched hand to the three fishing boats, as though he were pointing out a lovely water feature in a garden.

Instantly from the three escort dirigibles fell half a dozen bombs, five of which hit their three targets dead center. Two ships instantly exploded into splinters and sank while the third flamed on one side but continued to float. Tōru thought someone may have packed a few extra explosives into the fishing boats' holds for effect, for the result was far better than anything achieved in tests with just aerial bombs. The third ship then exploded, in a deeply satisfying delayed reaction, as one of the underwater boats surfaced, fired its single heavy gun, and blew the remaining fishing boat from the water before vanishing once more beneath the waves.

Several of the American officers with better vantage points had seen the underwater vessel surface and fire its weapon. With shouts they ran to the side of their ship, attempting to get a better look.

The demonstration had the desired effect on the American officer.

"I'll-I'll get the Commodore for you. May I tell him who you are, sir?"

Tōru smiled and bowed. Graciousness in victory is not servility but good manners.

He drew himself up and said, "You may tell Commodore Perry the eldest son of Lord Shimazu, leader of the Satsuma domain and liege lord of the King of the Ryukyu Kingdoms, is here as special emissary from the His Grace the Emperor Komei, heir to the Chrysanthemum Throne, and his Most High General Shogun Tokugawa Ieyoshi, military leader of the Hundred Armies."

The officer bowed awkwardly, bobbing his head like a duck plucking weeds. "So you are a prince and a high-ranking official."

"We do not think of princes in the same way you do, but yes, I meet regularly with the Shogun in his Council chamber." *Mostly to be condemned to death, but he didn't ask what we meet about.*

"I'll be right back, Your Excellency."

The officer dashed off to fetch the Commodore.

Tōru held his face impassive and cold, resisting the urge to smile at his self-chosen titles. Perry had invented some of his orders and documents as well, figuring his President would never know about such things as his white flags and unscripted explorations around Edo. Tōru figured it would be at least a year before anyone on shore learned he had announced himself as the Emperor's and Shogun's emissary, let alone Lord Shimazu's son. If a touch of exaggeration and theater achieved the goal without bloodshed, so be it.

The Commodore emerged from the hold, fully dressed in spite of the heat in his finest dress uniform, his sword at his side.

Tōru resisted the urge to bow. Not to this arrogant strutter. He held his silence as the Commodore approached.

The Commodore was forced into making the first move. "Commodore Perry, United State Navy. You were in the reception this morning?"

"Yes."

"My officers said you had a message for me?"

"Indeed." He turned to the Commodore and raised his voice so it would carry to all the officers on deck. "This morning we received you and accepted your President's letter with full courtesy out of respect for your President. May he rule forever in excellent health. This we did in spite of your refusal to submit your letter through our usual channels in Nagasaki and in violation of our own sacred laws. We are a peaceful people, but do not mistake our courtesy for weakness or an inability to defend our realm and people. You are well aware of our laws forbidding your entrance into our capital city. Yet here we find you, after our most courteous reception, knowingly violating our laws and turning north to our capital after promising to leave our shores. Over there, yes, you can see our beautiful capital Edo. You have seen it, now go."

"You—you speak English."

"Of course I do. So do most of the officials you met with this morning." Another exaggeration, thought Tōru, but he could see he had the proud Perry off-balance and confused at last. Time to drive it all home. He bowed again, sending the final signal once more to his men above. He continued. "As I was saying, we are a peaceful people and wish to accept your President's friendly message in like manner. We do not wish to harm any one of you, nor damage your magnificent ships. However, do not exhaust our patience. My Emperor and his Shogun sent me here to command you to turn your ships around. Never again approach our capital without their permission."

Commodore Perry opened his mouth to speak, still struck dumb at Tōru's effortless English and commanding tone. Before he could continue, Tōru looked to the six empty fishing boats now clustered in position near the *Susquehanna*. The three dirigibles floated serenely directly above them.

"If you refuse to leave now, and carry this message to your noble President along with our Gracious Emperor's best wishes for his health, we will be forced to do this—" here Tōru made the same graceful gesture as before, this time toward the six doomed fishing boats, "—to your four ships, and to as many hundreds of ships as you might bring to our shores."

At his gesture, fifteen bombs fell on five ships, all with perfect accuracy. Tōru was sure now that someone had put extra explosives into the ships' holds, for the explosions were truly spectacular, sending scraps of flaming wood high into the air, a few shreds even landing on the deck of the *Susquehanna*.

American officers flinched and ducked for cover.

"Ah, it appears they missed one," said Tōru, in the most regretful tone he could muster. He appreciated the little touch of the "missed" target. Whoever dreamed that up deserved special recognition. It deepened the effect admirably. As though on cue, three underwater ships rose up from the sea before the astonished Americans, aimed their heavy guns and blew the small vessel to scraps before vanishing under the waves. By the looks on the American officers' faces, further demonstrations were unnecessary.

The owners of the remaining fishing boats would be grateful.

"As I have delivered my message, I must bid you all farewell. Please give our best to your President. Oh, and I brought these back for you."

Tōru unstrapped the bound up white flags from his back. He looked around, but the smokestacks were far too tall for him to reach. He sighed. He had looked forward to telling the general he had followed his recommendation on the white flags.

He raised his voice to make sure Perry's officers could hear each word as he dropped the flags at Commodore Perry's feet.

The flagpoles clanked loudly on the deck and rolled onto the Commodore's polished black boots.

"We have no need for these. The sons of Yamato never surrender." He bowed again, and climbed the *Kagoshima*'s ladder.

CHAPTER 21

HORIZON

"A wild sea
In the distance over Sado
The Milky Way"
— Matsuo Basho

Perry and his *Kurofune* did as Tōru commanded.

They turned south away from the capital and steamed out of Edo Bay, the sailing ships tugged along behind the smoke-belching pair of steamships. Admiral Jiro and the dirigible captains formed up a new V formation with Jiro's *Hakudo Maru* at point.

The airships kept a stately pace with the fleeing Black Ships, escorting them to the mouth of the bay and beyond, floating above the wide sparkling sea. Dusk was falling and the stars were coming out, bright in a sky demurely lit by the thin light of the new moon.

The airship captains fretted about their fuel supplies as they drew further from shore. Turning in graceful formation at Admiral Jiro's command, the new captains more confident and skilled now, the dragon fleet landed near Uraga on the starlit shore.

Dancing, cheering commoners met the airships as they set down. *Taiko* drums beat the rhythm of the celebration as a hundred bonfires lit the coast. As the captains, the crews and the Shogun's *samurai* spilled out of the airships, crowds met them with song.

Word of their safe arrival had already flown along the telegraph wires to the Shogun and the Chief Councilor in Edo, and through wire and horseback messenger to the cloistered Emperor and his court in Kyoto. Messages of thanks and congratulations from both the Imperial Court and the Shogun flowed back to the Shogun's waiting general in Uraga and the two magistrates who had played the part of "princes" for the morning's receptions. They too waited in the crowd for the airship fleet's captains.

Tōru and Takamori found Jiro, Asano and Masuyo.

The tumult gave them little opportunity to speak, but little needed to be said. They had driven away Perry and his Black Ships. Hoisting the Shogun's banner above them, they were joined by the other jubilant captains. As he saw the general and the magistrates approach, Admiral Jiro called his captains to order, neatly arranged in rows. They saluted the general, who bowed to the captains.

"The Emperor and his Shogun thank you all for your service."

From behind the general, another *daimyō* stepped forward.

His armor and battle helmet glistened in the bonfire light. Tōru knew in an instant the face, the crest and the bearing of the man.

"*O-tō-sama*. Father," he whispered as he dropped to one knee.

Lord Shimazu raised him up and stood for a long moment in silence regarding Tōru with shining eyes.

"You have done well, my son," said the lord in a voice clearly audible to the other officials and to Jiro, Masuyo and his retainers Saigo and Asano. "*Okaeri*. Welcome home."

Tōru stood tall, unable to speak.

The magistrates and the Shogun's general, who also knew well the famed *tōzama* lord, looked at each other in wonderment at the greeting Lord Shimazu made to the fisherman. Lord Shimazu's *son*?

Recovering his composure, Tōru gestured to his friends to step forth. "Let me introduce my friends. Admiral Jiro, of Iwamatsu. Lady Aya, daughter of Lord Aya, the *daimyō* who found me. Your retainers, Captain Asano and Captain Saigo of our new air force. Without them, and our other captains of airships and underwater ships, we would have no victory today."

Lord Shimazu exchanged grave bows with each of them, his manners impeccable as though it were nothing out of the ordinary for him to greet a blacksmith and a woman as fellow soldiers on the field of battle, murmuring congratulations to each.

"The Shogun awaits us. Perhaps after your performance today we can get this death sentence lifted for the two of you, *na?*" Lord Shimazu smiled for the first time, and Tōru and Takamori exchanged grins and laughed. "Lady Aya, will you join us?"

Masuyo blushed and bowed her acceptance, suddenly shy to be in her airship captain uniform in front of the famed *daimyō*.

The refueled *Kagoshima Maru* and the *Hakudo Maru*, carrying the remainder of the airship captains, lifted up into the starry sky and sped toward Edo. Bonfires blazed all along the coast, marking each village and town, a necklace of flaming jewels along the water's edge. They could hear the drums and singing of the people below.

As they approached the great capital, though the hour was now late, they found it too was lit with ten thousand lanterns and thrumming with the beat of drums.

Tōru found Masuyo standing alone at the prow.

She had never looked more beautiful, her hair loosened from its tight bun by the wind. The high collar of her long coat framed her lovely face as she watched the celebrations below them along the coast. She turned and smiled as he approached, the smile of the victorious airship captain, the wicked jesting Masuyo working in her lab, galloping astride her horse, or singing a dirty song with Jiro.

He was suddenly tongue-tied, wanting to reach out and tuck out of the way a long lock of her glossy hair that had escaped its bounds and blown across her face. He looked down, no more the conquering hero but just a boy who loved a girl he could not have. A girl who didn't even want him because he was a traditional fool not wise enough to let her fly as high as she knew how. When he looked up again, her broad grin had vanished. She looked at him, her eyes soft and tender, inviting him to say more.

"I'm sorry. I never should have doubted you."

She didn't reply, but smiled at him again for the first time in days. It was too much. Gripping the gunwale, he broke their gaze and pointed at the blazing bonfires below.

"So bright. So many." He was indeed an idiot. But he couldn't speak of anything...important.

"Yes," she said simply, as they stared down at the lights below together, not speaking, until at last the *Kagoshima* Maru and the *Hakudo Maru* set down in a courtyard within Chiyoda Castle.

The Shogun's general led them in procession through the maze of gates and courtyards and hallways leading to the *Naku-oku*. Lord Shimazu and his honor guard followed close behind, including Saigo and Asano, now wearing the Shimazu *mon* of a cross within a circle once more. After came Tōru and Masuyo, and Admiral Jiro, with the rest of the airship captains and crew bringing up the rear.

The Shogun's *samurai* cheered them as they passed, all doing their best to keep their faces impassive and humble.

As they entered the Shogun's reception hall, Lord Abe helped the ailing Shogun to his feet. As the Shogun struggled to stand, his eyes flickered over Lord Shimazu and widened.

Lord Shimazu bowed silent greetings to his old adversary.

The Shogun Tokugawa Ieyoshi, his title and role slipping from him with each halting breath of his failing body, nodded to his Chief Councilor to speak for him as he trembled with the effort of holding himself erect.

Lord Abe stepped forward and made a long and impressive speech acknowledging the victory and the bravery of those who had made it possible. He signaled to his bureaucrats. One stepped forward with two declarations stamped with the Shogun's seal.

Lord Abe presented the documents to Tōru and Saigo Takamori with great ceremony.

"With the thanks of our great Emperor and his Shogun for your service to His Majesty, your sentences of death are hereby declared null and void."

Tōru and Takamori bowed their thanks and accepted the declarations from Lord Abe.

The general who had accompanied them from Uraga came forward next, trailed by two *samurai* carrying the rosewood boxes and the dreaded letters. He handed them over to Lord Abe who took them in hand as though they held writhing snakes.

"We will discuss these tomorrow. Tonight we celebrate."

When they were finally free to leave behind Chiyoda, the *Kagoshima Maru* and the *Hakudo Maru* took flight once again.

Lord Abe, his duties done for the moment, escorted them to their airships. "May I join you? I would experience these marvelous ships myself."

Once in the air, Lord Abe's delight in flight was unlimited. As he oriented himself, he commanded, "Set us down in my compound, over there. We will rest tonight at my home."

Ever the consummate host, he insisted the entire party, all the airship captains and Lord Shimazu and the rest, stay at his compound for the night. Many of the rebel lords were on hand to greet them. Lord Date, from the north, and Lord Aya and Lord Tōmatsu and many others, brought in by their flagships.

The fleet hovered above Lord Abe's compound, each blazing with a ring of lanterns as though the stars themselves had danced down to gaze on the celebration below. Even though it was near the middle of the night, Lord Abe's servants brought forth dish after delectable dish to feed the heroes. He kept their cups full of the finest *saké* until dawn lightened the eastern sky.

As the toasts and boasts grew quieter, Tōru and Masuyo found a sheltered spot by the *koi* pond behind the great home. They sat together in silence, watching the still surface of the pond and listening to the songs and toasts up in the main house.

Lord Abe approached them, trailed by the lords Aya, Tōmatsu and Shimazu. He stood silently with them for a moment before commenting on the beauty of the *Amanogawa*, the Milky Way, glowing above the horizon. He cleared his throat and coughed delicately. Masuyo and Tōru turned to face him.

"Lord Shimazu has consulted with Lord Aya...about a matter...of some importance. The two lords have asked me...to speak for them...and inquire...into your own thoughts on the matter," said Lord Abe. "That is to say...Lord Aya and Lord Shimazu...being in agreement on the matter...would welcome the adoption of Himasaki as *mukoyōshi* into House Aya. That is, if this proposal meets with your approval."

Tōru turned to Masuyo and saw her answer in her eyes.

Still, a warrior must brave the battle.

"Will you have me, Toranosuke?" he whispered low, so low no one else could hear.

Masuyo leaned toward him. "Yes, fisherman, as long as I can still ride and fly and run our lab."

The couple rose and faced their fathers.

They bowed their acceptance of their fathers' proposal.

They bowed deeper thanks to matchmaker Lord Abe.

Their friends burst out around them, Asano smiling gravely as always, Jiro chanting a rude wedding song, and Takamori tackling Tōru, as the dawn sky lit up a new day.

Ships, black ships, would come from across the sea again.

Together they would be ready.

THE END

AUTHOR'S NOTE

Tōru: Wayfarer Returns is the first book in the Sakura Steam Series, an alternate history of the tumultuous period from the opening of Japan in 1853 to the Meiji Restoration in 1868. This volume covers the year prior to the American Commodore Perry's arrival in Japan and follows the hero and his young allies as they lead Japan through a massively compressed industrial revolution, dramatically altering that pivotal moment in history in their favor.

A few scholars trace the twin tragedies of Hiroshima and Pearl Harbor back to the humiliation suffered by Japan at Perry's hands in 1853. While that may be an extreme view, I have pondered the question of "what would Japan's path—and the world's—have been if the Japanese had possessed the military might and the will to drive Perry away instead of opening under duress as they did?"

The Sakura Steam Series explores this "what if" question.

This may not be a steampunk story at all, a determination I leave to the reader and any steampunk purists determined to defend the borders of true steampunkedness. My alternate history is laced with touches of steampunk, like the dirigible fleet, submarines and Babajis, but carries its steampunk DNA mostly in the story's examination of a traditional society's response to technological change. Unlike traditional steampunk stories that unfold in a world already steampunk, the story of Tōru and his friends begins in the "real" world and together they create a steam-driven alternate universe, with a dramatic impact on the course of history.

Tōru is Prometheus, bringing the fire of Western technology to Japan, but it is Jiro the engineer and Masuyo the inventor who best embody the steampunk joy in inventing, tinkering and making and who best demonstrate in their own individual liberation from traditional constraints the steampunk impulse to "create a better past" as they each take flight at the helms of their own airships.

While my heroes and their dirigibles are fictional, I built my story against a backdrop of the "real" cultural and historical Japan of that period, and wove historical figures into my tale, staying true to their motivations and agendas even as my alternate history warped their actions, history and a few laws of physics.

Tōru, Masuyo, Jiro, Lord Aya and Lord and Lady Tōmatsu are completely fictional. Fictitious characters named for and inspired by real historical people include Commodore Perry, the Shogun and his Chief Councilor, Lord Abe, as well as the rebellious *tōzama* "outer lords" represented by Lord Shimazu of the Satsuma domain in the southwest and Lord Date in the far north. Saigo Takamori is real as well, met here before he steps into the pages of history.

To my knowledge, Lord Shimazu Naraikiri did not have an illegitimate son to send to America, although in later years he did send many young men abroad to study foreign technology. The real Lord Shimazu was famous for his love of learning and his fierce curiosity about the West, building schools of Western learning in his domain and drilling his soldiers in Western military tactics. He also imported the first camera into Japan and ordered the first Western-style ship built for Japan. I like to think he would have sent Tōru to America if Tōru had existed.

The true story of a shipwrecked fisherman named Manjirō inspired my tale of a boy brave enough to return to Japan during the *sakoku* isolation period. Manjiro was taken to America after his 1841 shipwreck, and found his way back to Japan in 1851 where he did play a role in sharing his learning about the West and translating during the negotiations to open Japan to the West. He too was raised to *samurai* status, but in service to the Shogun rather than my fictional and rebellious Lord Aya. Unlike poor Tōru, Manjiro was able to reunite with his mother. Like Tōru, Manjiro argued for a positive image of America, Americans and their leaders' intentions.

One final inspiration I found in today's headlines about income inequality and the end of the American dream of opportunity and upward mobility for ordinary people. Tōru returns to Japan from an America in a time of unlimited possibility and he dreams that dream for Japan, a world where every Jiro and Masuyo can rise to fulfill the measure of their talents and capacities. I wish for a radical Maker Revolution and Tōrus, Masuyos and Jiros of our own to restore that vision of unlimited opportunity to America today.

ACKNOWLEDGMENTS

The word for "thank you" in Japanese can be rendered "the having is hard," expressing the sense that one has incurred a debt for kindnesses received that is nearly impossible to repay. Anyone who has experienced Japanese hospitality understands this great generosity and the deep gratitude that wells up in response. I could never have told this story without the marvelous experience of studying and working in Japan for several years while living in Japanese households. I will never forget the kindness and friendship many Japanese offered to this stranger during my sojourn in Japan.

I thank the Rotary Clubs of Boulder, Colorado and Chiba and Sakura in Japan, who sponsored my first year in Japan, and the seven Japanese host families who watched over their exchange student with such care and affection. I am forever grateful to the students and teachers of Chiba High School, in Chiba, Japan, especially Kitamura Sensei, who patiently explained so much, and Yamamoto Sensei and his kendo club students who shepherded their clumsy American through a black belt in Japanese fencing.

At Brigham Young University, where I earned degrees in Economics and Asian Studies, with minors in physics and Japanese, I especially want to thank Professor Walt Ames, who taught Japanese Culture and Anthropology, and Watabe Sensei, who attempted, somewhat unsuccessfully, to break my habit of speaking like a rather tough male Japanese high school student instead of like a polite young educated woman. I apologize in advance to my physics and economics professors for my exuberant violations of laws of physics and principles of economics in my story.

Naohiro Takita deserves special thanks for so many reasons. He is absolutely correct—it is very difficult to build a train, possibly even more difficult than constructing a dirigible.

I also must thank the National Heritage Mining Museum and their annual Miners Ball here in Leadville, Colorado, for accidentally turning me on to steampunk. I googled "Victorian dress" to find something to wear to the ball, and found myself falling down the steampunk rabbit hole, joining the Maker Revolution and writing a steampunk novel. Things can get out of hand quickly up here at high elevation. I discovered to my shock and amazement that we are accidental steampunks here in Leadville. Who knew?! I am grateful to my neighbors for their tolerance for my attempts to lace our traditional Victorian events with a touch of neo-Victorian futurism and the occasional tea duel.

I am so grateful to Nancy Schloerke, Molly Howe, Francine Sommer, Tim Spong, Craig Wagner, Ken McLeod, the Cloud City Writers and my family for being my first beta readers and sharing their thoughtful and insightful comments with me. Laurel McHargue earns special mention for leading the group and letting me sit by her fire to write. And for so generously sharing her port. Every writer needs a Laurel in her life!

Finally, my gratitude and love go to Tim Stroh, for the love, the laughter, the music, the musicians, the magic beans, the puppy, the freedom to create and the encouragement to write he has given me.

ABOUT THE AUTHOR

Stephanie R. Sorensen is a writer based in the Victorian mining town of Leadville, Colorado, where she lives at 10,000 feet with her husband, five chickens, two bantam English game hens and one Cavalier King Charles Spaniel. She likes her Victorian attire spiced with a little neo-Victorian futurism and the biggest bustle possible.

If you enjoyed this book, please leave a review on your favorite review site. To sign up for news of future books by the author or to contact Stephanie, please visit www.stephaniersorensen.com.

Check with our publisher for other great books at www.palantirpress.com.

CPSIA information can be obtained at www.ICGtesting.com
Printed in the USA
LVOW11*2243100516

487648LV00003B/18/P

9 780996 932301